Karl Ove Knausgaard

My Struggle

BOOK FOUR

Translated from the Norwegian by Don Bartlett

archipelago books

First Archipelago Books Edition, 2015

First published in English by Harvill Secker,
an imprint of The Random House Group Ltd

First published as *Min kamp 4* by Forlaget Oktober in 2010.

Archipelago Books
232 3rd Street #A111
Brooklyn, NY 11215
www.archipelagobooks.org

Library of Congress Cataloging-in-Publication Data
Knausgård, Karl Ove, 1968-
[Min kamp. 4. English]
My struggle : Book 4 / Karl Ove Knausgaard ; translated from the
Norwegian by Don Bartlett. – First Archipelago Books edition.
pages cm
ISBN 978-0-914671-17-6 (alk. paper)
I. Bartlett, Don, translator. II. Title.
PT8951.21.N38M5613 2015b
839.823'74 – dc23   2014049820

Distributed by Penguin Random House
www.randomhouse.com

Cover art: Emil Nolde

The publication of *My Struggle Book Four* was made possible with support from
Lannan Foundation, the New York State Council on the Arts, a state agency,
the Black Mountain Institute, and NORLA (Norwegian Literature Abroad).

PRINTED IN THE UNITED STATES OF AMERICA

My Struggle

Slowly my two suitcases glided around on the carousel in the arrivals hall. They were old, from the end of the 1960s, I had found them among Mom's things in the barn when we were about to move, the day before the removal van came, and I immediately commandeered them, they suited me and my style, the not-quite-contemporary, the not-quite-streamlined, which was what I favored.

I stubbed the cigarette out in the ashtray stand by the wall, lifted the cases off the carousel, and carried them outside.

It was five minutes to seven.

I lit another cigarette. There was no hurry, there was nothing I had to do, no one I had to meet.

The sky was overcast, but the air was still sharp and clear. There was something alpine about the landscape even though the airport I was standing outside was only a few meters above sea level. The few trees I could see were stunted and misshapen. The mountain peaks on the horizon were white with snow.

Just in front of me an airport bus was quickly filling up with people.

Should I catch it?

The money Dad had so reluctantly lent me for the journey would tide me over until I got my first paycheck in a month. On the other hand, I didn't know where the youth hostel was, and wandering blindly around an unfamiliar town with two suitcases and a backpack would not be a good start to my new life.

No, better take a taxi.

Apart from a short walk to a nearby snack bar stand, where I consumed two sausages with mashed potatoes in a cardboard tray, I stayed in the youth hostel room all evening, lying with the duvet over my back and listening to music on my Walkman while writing letters to Hilde, Eirik, and Lars. I started one to Line as well, the girl I had spent all summer with, but set it aside after one page, undressed, and switched off the light, for all the difference that made, it was a light summer night, the orange curtain glowed in the room like an eye.

Usually I would fall asleep at once wherever I was, but that night I lay awake. In just four days I would be starting my first job. In just four days I would be entering a classroom in a small village on the coast of Northern Norway, a place I had never been and knew nothing about, I hadn't even seen any pictures.

Me!

An eighteen-year-old Kristiansander, who had just finished *gymnas*, who had just moved away from home, with no experience of working other than a few evenings and weekends at a parquet flooring factory, a bit of journalism on a local paper, and a month at a psychiatric hospital this summer, I was about to become a teacher at Håfjord School.

No, I couldn't sleep.

What would the pupils think of me?

When I went into the classroom for the first lesson and they were sitting there in their chairs in front of me, what would I say to them?

And the other teachers, what on earth would they make of me?

A door was opened in the corridor, releasing the sound of music and voices. Someone walked along quietly singing. There was a shout: "Hey, shut the door." Afterward all the noise was enclosed again. I rolled over onto my other side. The strangeness of lying in bed under a light sky must have played a part in my not being able to fall asleep. And once the thought was established that it was difficult to sleep, it became impossible.

I got up, pulled on my clothes, sat in the chair by the window, and began to read. *Dead Heat* by Erling Gjelsvik.

All the books I liked were basically about the same topic. *White Niggers* by Ingvar Ambjørnsen, *Beatles* and *Lead* by Lars Saabye Christensen, *Jack* by Alf Lundell, *On the Road* by Jack Kerouac, *Last Exit to Brooklyn* by Hubert Selby, Jr., *Novel with Cocaine* by M. Ageyev, *Colossus* by Finn Alnæs, *Lasso Round the Moon* by Agnar Mykle, *The History of Bestiality* trilogy by Jens Bjørneboe, *Gentlemen* by Klas Östergren, *Icarus* by Axel Jensen, *The Catcher in the Rye* by J. D. Salinger, *Humlehjertene* by Ola Bauer, and *Post Office* by Charles Bukowski. Books about young men who struggled to fit in to society, who wanted more from life than routines, more from life than a family, basically, young men who hated middle-class values and sought freedom. They traveled, they got drunk, they read, and they dreamed about their life's great passion or writing the great novel.

Everything they wanted I wanted too.

The great longing, which was ever present in my breast, was dispelled when I read these books, only to return with renewed vigor the moment I put them down. It had been like that all the way through my latter years at school. I hated all authority, was an opponent of the whole limited society I had grown up in, with its bourgeois values and materialistic view of humanity. I despised what I had learned at gymnas, even about literature; all I needed to know, all true knowledge, the only really essential knowledge, was to be found in the books I read and the music I listened to. I wasn't interested in money or status symbols; I knew that the essential value in life lay elsewhere. I didn't want to study, had no wish to receive an education at a conventional institution like a university, I wanted to travel down through Europe, sleep on beaches, in cheap hotels, or with friends I made on the way. Take odd jobs to survive, wash dishes at hotels, load or unload boats, pick oranges . . . That spring I had bought a book containing lists of every conceivable, and inconceivable, kind of job you could get in various European countries. But all of this was to culminate in a novel. I would spend some time writing in a Spanish village, go to Pamplona and run the bulls, continue on down to Greece and write on one of the islands, and then, after a year or two, return to Norway with a novel in my backpack.

That was the plan. That was why I didn't do my military service when gymnas was over, like so many of my friends had done, nor did I enroll at university, as the rest had done, instead I went to the employment office in Kristiansand and asked for a list of all the teaching opportunities in Northern Norway.

"Hear you're going to be a *teacher*, Karl Ove," people I saw at the end of the summer said.

"No," I answered. "I'm going to be a writer. But I have to have something to live off in the meantime. I'll work up there for a year, put some money aside, and then travel down through Europe."

This was no longer an idea in my head but the reality I was in: tomorrow I would go to the harbor in Tromsø, catch the express boat to Finnsnes and then the bus south to the tiny village of Håfjord, where the school caretaker would be waiting to welcome me.

No, I couldn't sleep.

I took the half bottle of whiskey from my suitcase, got a glass from the bathroom, poured, drew the curtain aside, and took a first shivering sip as I gazed at the strangely light housing estate outside.

When I woke around ten the following morning my nerves were gone. I packed my things, called for a taxi from the pay phone in the reception, stood outside with my suitcases at my feet, and smoked as I waited. This was the first time in my life I had traveled anywhere without having to return. There was no "home" to return to. Mom had sold our house and moved to Førde. Dad lived with his new wife farther north, in Northern Norway. Yngve lived in Bergen. And, as for me, I was on my way to a first flat of my own. There I would have my own job and earn my own money. For the very first time I had control of all the elements in my life.

Oh, how incredibly good it felt!

The taxi came up the hill, I threw the cigarette butt to the ground, crushed it, and put the suitcases in the trunk, which the driver – a plump elderly man with gray hair and a gold necklace – had opened for me.

"The harbor, please," I said, climbing into the back.

"The harbor's a big place," he said, turning to me.

"I'm going to Finnsnes. On the express boat."

"That can be done, no problem."

He set off downhill.

"Are you going to the gymnas there?" he asked.

"No," I said. "I'm going on to Håfjord."

"Oh? Fishing? You don't look much like a fisherman!"

"Actually, I'm going there to teach."

"That's right. A lot of southerners do that. But aren't you pretty young to have a job like that? Don't you have to be eighteen?"

He laughed and looked at me in the mirror.

I gave a short laugh too.

"I left school in the summer. I figure that's better than nothing."

"Yes, I'm sure you're right," he said. "But think of the kids growing up there. Teachers right out of gymnas. New ones every year. No wonder they give up on school after ninth grade and go fishing!"

"Yes, I guess it isn't that surprising," I said. "But it's not my fault."

"No, not at all. And fault? Who's talking about blame! Fishing's a much better life than studying, you know! Much better than hanging around studying until you're thirty."

"You're right. I'm not going to study."

"But you're going to be a teacher!"

He looked at me in the mirror again.

"Yes," I said.

There was silence for a few minutes. Then he took his hand off the gear-shift and pointed.

"Down there, there's your express boat."

He stopped outside the terminal, set my suitcases on the ground, and closed the trunk again. I gave him the money, not knowing what to do about a tip, I had been dreading this the whole journey and solved the problem by saying that he could keep the change.

"Thank you!" he said. "And good luck!"

Bye-bye, fifty kroner.

As he rejoined the road, I stood counting the money I had left. I didn't have much, but I could probably get an advance, surely they would understand that I wouldn't have any money before the job started?

With its one main street, numerous plain concrete buildings, probably hastily erected, and its barren environs girdled by mountain ranges in the distance, Finnsnes, it struck me a few hours later, sitting in a patisserie with a cup of coffee in front of me and waiting for the bus to leave, looked more like a tiny village in Alaska or Canada than Norway. There wasn't much of a center, the town was so small that everything had to be considered the center. The atmosphere was quite different here from in the towns I was used to, because Finnsnes was so much smaller, of course, but also because no effort had been made anywhere to make the place look inviting or homey. Most towns had a front and a back, but here everything looked pretty much the same.

I leafed through the two books I'd bought in the nearby shop. One was called *The New Water* by a writer unfamiliar to me, Roy Jacobsen; the other was *The Mustard Legion* by Morten Jørgensen, who had played in a couple of the bands I had followed a few years ago. Perhaps it hadn't been such a good idea to spend my money on them, but after all I was going to be a writer, I had to read, if only to see how high the bar was set. Could I write like that? This was the question that kept running through my brain as I sat there flipping through the pages.

Then I ambled over to the bus, had a last smoke outside, put my suitcases in the luggage compartment, paid the driver, and asked him to tell me when we were in Håfjord, walked down the aisle and sat on the penultimate seat on the left, which had been my favorite for as long as I could remember.

Across from me sat a lovely fair-haired girl, perhaps one or two years younger than me, she had her satchel on the seat, and I imagined she went to the gymnas in Finnsnes and was on her way home. She had looked at me when I got onto the bus, and now, as the driver shifted into first gear and pulled away from the stop with a jerk, she turned to look at me again. Not lingeringly, no more than a glance, and barely a fleeting one at that, but still it was enough to give me a boner.

I put on my headset and inserted a cassette into the Walkman. The Smiths, *The Queen Is Dead*. So as not to appear intrusive, I concentrated on staring out the window on my side for the first few kilometers and resisted all impulses to look in her direction.

After passing through a built-up area, which began as soon as we left the center and extended for quite a distance, where around half the passengers got off, we came to a long, deserted, straight stretch. Whereas the sky above Finnsnes had been pale, covering the town beneath with its vapid light, here the shade of blue was stronger and deeper, and the sun hanging over the mountains to the southwest – whose low but steep sides obscured a view of the sea that had to be there – caused the red-flecked, in places almost purple, heather, which grew densely on either side of the road, to glow. The trees here were for the most part deformed pines and dwarf birches. On my side the green-clad mountains the valley rose up to meet were gentle, hills almost, while those on the other were steep and wild and alpine, although of no great height.

Not a person, not a house, was to be seen.

But I hadn't come here to meet new people; I had come to find the peace I needed to write.

The thought sent a flash of pleasure through me.

I was on my way, I was on my way.

A couple of hours later, still engrossed in music, I saw a signpost up ahead. From the length of the name I concluded it had to be Håfjord. The road it pointed to led straight into the mountainside. It was not so much a tunnel, more a hole, the walls seemed to have been blasted out, and there was no light in there, either. Water streamed down from the roof of the tunnel in such quantities that the driver had to turn on the windshield wipers. When we emerged on the other side, I gasped. Between two long rugged chains of mountains, perilously steep and treeless, lay a narrow fjord, and beyond it, like a vast blue plain, the sea.

Ohhh.

The road the bus followed hugged the mountainside. To see as much of the landscape as I could I stood up and crossed to the other row of seats. From the corner of my eye I noticed the fair-haired girl turn toward me and smile when she saw me standing there with my face pressed against the window. Below the mountains opposite there was a small island, densely packed with houses on its inner landward side, completely deserted on the outer side, at least that was how it looked from this distance. There were some fishing boats moored inside a harbor with a mole around it. The mountains continued for perhaps a kilometer. Closest to us, the slopes were clad in green, but farther away they were completely bare and gray and fell away with a sheer drop into the sea.

The bus passed through another grotto-like tunnel. At the other end, on a relatively gentle mountain slope, in a shallow bowl, lay the village where I would be spending the next year.

Oh my God.

This was spectacular!

Most of the houses huddled around a road that wound its way through the village like a U. Beneath the road at the bottom was what looked like a factory building in front of a quay, it must have been the fish-processing plant, beyond it there were lots of boats. At the end of the U stood a chapel. Above the road at the top was a line of houses, behind them were dwarf birches, heather, and scrub up to the point where the valley stopped and a large mountain rose on either side.

That was it.

Well, almost: above the point where the top road met the lower one, right by the tunnel, there were two large buildings, which had to be the school.

"Håfjord!" said the bus driver. I stuffed my headset into my pocket and walked up the aisle, he followed me down the steps and opened the door to the luggage compartment, I thanked him, he said no problem without a smile and climbed back up, whereupon the bus turned in the square and reentered the tunnel.

With a suitcase in each hand and a seaman's kitbag on my back, I first looked up, then down the road for the caretaker while drawing the fresh, salty air deep into my lungs.

A door in the house right opposite the bus stop opened. Out came a small man dressed in only a T-shirt and jogging pants. From the direction he was heading, I could see this was my man.

Apart from a little wreath of hair around his ears, he was completely bald. His face was gentle, his features were pronounced, as happens when you are in your fifties, but the eyes behind the glasses were small and piercing, and it struck me as he approached that in a way they didn't quite match the rest.

"Knausgaard?" he said, proffering his hand but without looking me in the eye.

"Yes," I said, and took it. Small and dry and pawlike. "And you must be Korneliussen?"

"That's right," he said with a smile, his arms down by his sides, taking in the view. "What do you think?"

"About Håfjord?" I asked.

"Nice, isn't it?" he said.

"Fantastic," I said.

He turned, looked up and pointed.

"You'll be living there," he said. "So we'll be neighbors. I live just there, you see. Shall we go up and have a look?"

"Yes," I said. "Do you know if my things have arrived?"

He shook his head.

"Not as far as I know," he said.

"They'll be here on Monday then," I said, and set off up the road beside him.

"You'll have my youngest son at school, from what I've heard," he said. "Stig. He's in the fourth grade."

"Do you have many children?" I said.

"Four," he said. "Two live at home. Johannes and Stig. Tone, my daughter, and Ruben live in Tromsø."

I scanned the village as we walked. Some people were standing outside what must have been a shop, where a couple of cars were also parked. And outside a snack bar stand on the top road there were a few people with bikes.

Far out in the fjord a boat was coming in.

Seagulls were screeching down by the harbor.

Otherwise all was still.

"How many people live here actually?" I said.

"Two hundred and fifty or so," he said. "It depends on whether you include the kids going to school."

We stopped in front of a black, 1970s timber house, by the porch.

"Here it is," he said. "Go ahead and step in. The door should be open. But you might as well have the key right away."

I opened the door and went into the front hall, put down my suitcases, and took the key he handed me. It smelled as houses do when they haven't been inhabited for a while. A faint, vaguely outdoor, whiff of damp and mold.

I pushed a half-open door and went into the sitting room. The floor was fitted with an orange wall-to-wall carpet. A dark brown desk, a dark brown coffee table, and a suite upholstered in brown and orange, also dark wood. Two large panoramic windows facing north.

"This is great," I said.

"The kitchen's in there," he said, pointing to a door at the end of the tiny room. He turned. "And the bedroom's in there."

The wallpaper in the kitchen was a familiar '70s pattern: gold, brown, and white. There was a little table under the window. A fridge with a small freezer compartment at the top. A sink set in a short laminate counter. The floor, gray linoleum.

"And, last of all, the bedroom," he said, standing in the doorway while I went in. The carpet on the floor was darker than the one in the sitting room, the wallpaper light, and the room empty except for an enormously wide low bed made of the same wood as the other furniture. Teak or imitation teak.

"Perfect!" I said.

"Do you have any bed linen with you?"

I shook my head. "It's being sent."

"You can borrow some of ours if you like."

"That would be great," I said.

"I'll drop some off then," he said. "And if you have any questions, anything at all, come down and see us. Visitors are welcome here!"

"OK," I said. "Thank you."

From the sitting-room window I watched him walking down toward his house, which was maybe twenty meters down the road from mine.

Mine!

Unbelievable, I had my own place.

I walked around inside, opened a few drawers, and glanced into some cupboards until the caretaker returned carrying a pile of sheets in his arms. After he'd left I started unpacking the little I had brought with me: my clothes, a towel, the typewriter, a few books, and some typing paper. I placed the desk beneath the sitting-room window, put the typewriter on top, moved the standard lamp, arranged the books on the windowsill, as well as a literary magazine, *Vinduet*, which I had bought in Oslo and decided I would subscribe to. Next to them I stacked the fifteen, maybe twenty, cassettes I had brought along, and beside the pile of paper on the table I laid the Walkman and the spare batteries for it.

When my writing alcove was finished I put my clothes in the bedroom wardrobes, shoved the empty cases onto the top shelf, and stood in the center of the room for a while, not sure what to do next.

I felt an urge to call someone and tell them what it was like here, but there was no telephone. Should I go out perhaps and look for a phone booth?

I was hungry too.

What about the snack bar stand? Should I go over there?

There was nothing to do here anyway.

In front of the mirror in the little bathroom that led off the hall I put on my black beret. On the doorstep I stood for a few seconds looking down. In one sweeping gaze you could scan the whole village and everyone who lived in it. There was nowhere to hide. Walking down the road, the surface of which was gravel underneath asphalt, I felt utterly transparent.

Some teenage boys were hanging around outside the snack bar. Their conversation froze as I approached. I walked past without looking at them, went up the steps to the veranda and over to the serving hatch, which shone bright yellow in the wan late-summer evening light that seemed to hang over the landscape. The window was smeared with grease. A boy around the same age as the ones behind me appeared at the hatch. A couple of long black hairs grew from his cheek. His eyes were brown, his hair was black.

"Hamburger with everything, fries, and a Coke," I said. Listened intently to hear if any of the mumbling behind was about me. But it wasn't. I lit a cigarette and paced up and down the veranda while I waited. The boy lowered a landing-net-style receptacle full of thin potato sticks into the boiling fat. Slapped a hamburger down on the hotplate. Apart from the low sizzle of the meat and the by-now excited voices behind me, there was no sound. The houses on the island across the fjord were illuminated. The sky, which hung low there, higher by contrast above the mouth of the fjord, was a bluish gray and rather heavy, though far from dark.

The silence was not oppressive, it was open.

But not to us, I thought for some reason. The silence had always been like this here, long before people existed, and would remain so long after they had disappeared. Lying here in this mountain bowl, with the sea spread out before it.

Where did it end actually? America? Canada?

Yes, that had to be it. Newfoundland.

"Here's your burger," the kid said, placing a Styrofoam tray containing a hamburger, a few strips of lettuce, a quarter of a tomato, and a pile of fries on the shelf outside the serving hatch. I paid, grabbed the tray, and turned to go.

"Are you the new teacher?" asked one of the boys hanging over the handlebars of his bike.

"Yes," I said.

"You're going to have us," he said, spat, and pushed his cap farther up his forehead. "We're in ninth grade. And him, he's in eighth."

"Oh yeah?" I said.

"Yeah," he said. "You're from the south?"

"Yes, from Sørland," I said.

"OK," he said, nodding, as though indicating the audience was over now, and I was free to go.

"What are your names?" I said.

"You'll find out soon enough," he said.

They laughed at that. I gave an unabashed smile but felt stupid as I walked past them. He had outmaneuvered me.

"And what's your name?" he called out after me.

"Mickey," I said. "Mickey Mouse."

"He's a comedian as well!" he shouted.

After I had eaten the hamburger, I got undressed and went to bed. It was still only around nine o'clock, the room was as light as if it were the middle of a gray day, and the silence that was everywhere magnified the sounds of every movement I made, so even though I was tired, it took me a few hours to fall asleep.

I woke in the middle of the night to a door banging somewhere. Immediately afterward I heard footsteps on the floor above. Half awake, I imagined I was sleeping in Dad's office in Tybakken and it was him walking above me. How on earth had I ended up here, I found myself thinking, before I sank back into the darkness. The next time I woke I was in a state of panic.

Where was I?

In the house in Tybakken? The house in Tveit? Yngve's studio? The youth hostel in Tromsø?

I sat up in bed.

The glances I cast around the room didn't find anything to hold them; nothing I saw gave any meaning. It was as though my whole person were sliding down a slippery wall.

Then I remembered.

Håfjord. I was in Håfjord.

In my own flat in Håfjord.

I lay back in bed and mentally retraced my journey here. Then I imagined the village as it was outside the windows, all the people in all the houses whom I didn't know and who didn't know me. Something that could have been expectation, but could also have been fear or insecurity, erupted inside me. I got up and went into the tiny bathroom, showered, and put on a green silky shirt, baggy black cotton trousers, stood in front of the window for a while looking down toward the shop, I would have to go there to buy something for breakfast, but not right now.

There were several vehicles in the parking lot. A little cluster of people was gathered between them. Now and then someone came out the door carrying shopping bags.

Well, might as well dive right in.

I went into the hall and put on my coat, beret, and white basketball shoes, glanced at myself in the mirror, straightened my beret, lit a cigarette, and went out.

The sky was as serene and gray as yesterday. The mountains plunged into the water on the other side of the fjord. There was something brutal about them, I saw that in a flash, they didn't care, anything could happen around them, it meant nothing, it was as though they were somewhere else at the same time as being here.

There were five people gathered outside the shop now. Two were old, at least fifty, the other three looked a few years older than me.

They had seen me from way off, I knew, it was inevitable, it wasn't every day a stranger in a long black coat came down the hill, I imagined.

I raised the cigarette to my mouth and inhaled so deeply that the filter became hot.

Either side of the door hung a white plastic flag advertising the newspaper *Verdens Gang*. The window was full of green and orange paper plates emblazoned with a variety of special offers, written by hand.

I was fifteen meters away from them now.

Should I say hello? A chirpy, easygoing "hi"?

Stop and talk to them?

Say I was the new teacher? Make a little joke about it?

One of them looked at me. I gave a slight nod.

He didn't nod back.

Hadn't he seen it? Had my nod been so slight that it had been perceived as an adjustment of the way I held my head, or a twitch?

Their presence felt like knives in me. A meter away from the door I threw the cigarette to the ground, stopped, and stepped on it.

Could I leave it there? Litter the sidewalk? Or should I pick it up?

No, that would look just a bit *too* pedantic, wouldn't it?

To hell with it, I'll leave it, they're fishermen, I'm sure they toss their cigarette butts away when they've finished with them!

I placed my hand on the door and pushed, took one of the red shopping baskets, and began to move down the aisle between the various shelves. A rotund lady in her midthirties was holding a packet of sausages in her hand and saying something to a girl who must have been her daughter. Thin and gangly, she stood there with a sullen, obstinate expression on her face. On the other side of the woman there was a boy of around ten leaning over a rack, rummaging. I put a whole-wheat loaf in the basket, a packet of Ali coffee, and a box of Earl Grey tea bags. The woman glanced at me, put the sausages in her basket, and continued to the other end of the shop with the boy and girl in tow. I took my time, wandered around looking at all the food items, added a brown goat's cheese from a cabinet, a tin of liver paste, and a tube of mayonnaise. Then I picked up a carton of milk and a packet of margarine and went over to the counter, where the woman was now packing her items into a bag while her daughter stood reading a notice board by the door.

The assistant nodded to me.

"Hello," I said, and started to empty the basket in front of him.

He was short and stocky, his face was broad, his nose curved, and his powerful chin covered with a patch of grizzled bristles.

"Are you the new teacher?" he said as he was entering the prices on the till beside him. Over by the notice board, the girl had turned to look at me.

"Yes," I said. "Arrived yesterday."

The boy was tugging at her arm, she yanked it free and went out the door. The boy followed her, and a moment later so did the mother.

I needed oranges. And apples.

I hurried over to the modest fruit counter, filled a bag with some oranges, grabbed a couple of apples, and went back to the till, where the assistant was ringing up the last item.

"And a pouch of Eventyr tobacco and rolling papers. And *Dagbladet*."

"You're from the south?" he said.

I nodded. "Kristiansand."

An elderly man wearing a cloth cap entered the shop.

"Good morning, Bertil!" he shouted.

"Oh, so it's you!" the assistant said, giving me a wink. I squeezed a smile, paid, put my purchases in a bag, and left. One of the people standing outside nodded, I nodded back, and then I was out of their range.

Up the hill, I gazed at the mountain rising from the end of the village. It was completely green, all the way to the top, and that was perhaps the most surprising feature of the countryside here, I had expected something bleaker, with less color, not this green which seemed to resonate everywhere, drowned out only by the grays and blues of the vast sea.

It was a good feeling going back into my flat. It was the first place I'd ever been able to call mine, and I enjoyed even the most trivial activities, like hanging up my jacket or putting the milk in the fridge. Admittedly, I had lived for a month in a small flat next to Eg Psychiatric Hospital earlier in the summer, that was where Mom had driven me when I moved from the house we had occupied for the past five years, but it wasn't an actual flat, only a room off a corridor with other rooms where in the old days the unmarried nurses had lived, hence its name the Henhouse, in the same way that the job I had there wasn't an actual job either, just a short summer temp job without any real responsibility. Also it was in Kristiansand. For me it was impossible to feel free in Kristiansand, there were too many ties with too many people, real and imagined, for me ever to do what I wanted in that town.

But here! I thought, lifting a slice of bread to my mouth while looking out the window. The reflection of the mountains across the fjord was broken kaleidoscopically by the ripples in the water below. Here no one knew who I was, here there were no ties, no fixed patterns, here I could do as I liked. Hide away for a year and write, create something in secret. Or I could just take it easy and save up some money. It didn't really matter. What mattered was that I was here.

I poured some milk into a glass and drank it in long swigs, placed the glass next to the plate and the knife on the counter, returned the food to the fridge, and went into the sitting room, plugged the typewriter in, put on my headset, turned the volume up full, inserted a sheet of paper into the type-writer, centered it, and typed a 1 at the top. Looked down at the caretaker's house. A pair of green rubber boots stood on the doorstep. A broom with red bristles leaned against the wall. There were some toy cars lying in the mixture of gravel and sand covering the area in front of the door. Between the two houses grew moss, lichen, some grass, and a few slender trees. I tapped my forefinger against the table edge to the rhythm of the music. I wrote one sentence: "Gabriel stood at the top of the hill looking over the construction site with an expression of disapproval on his face."

I smoked a cigarette, brewed a pot of coffee, and looked out across the village and fjord and up at the mountains beyond. I wrote another sentence: "Gordon appeared behind him." Sang along to the chorus. Wrote. "He grinned like a wolf." Pushed back my chair, put my feet on the table, and lit another cigarette.

That was pretty good, wasn't it?

I picked up *The Garden of Eden* by Hemingway and browsed through it to get a feel for the language. I had been given it by Hilde as a graduation present two days before, at the Kristiansand railway station when I was about to leave for Oslo to catch a plane to Tromsø. Lars was there too, and Eirik, who went out with Hilde. Not forgetting Line. She was going to travel with me to Oslo and say good-bye there.

It was only now that I saw there was a dedication on the copyright page. She had written that I meant something special to her.

I lit a cigarette and sat looking out the window while I chewed that over. What could I mean to her?

She saw something in me, I felt that, but I didn't know what she saw. To be friends with her was to be taken care of. But the care that resides in understanding always makes the recipient smaller too. It wasn't a problem, but I was aware of it.

I wasn't worth it. I pretended I was, and the strange thing was that she rose to it, because there was nothing wrong with her intelligence in such matters. Hilde was the only person I knew who read decent books, and the only person I knew who herself wrote. We had been in the same class for two years and at once she caught my attention, she had an ironic, sometimes also rebellious, attitude to what was said in the classroom, which I had never seen in a girl before. She despised the other girls' mania for makeup, the way they always did their best to be proper, their often affected childishness, but not in any aggressive or bitter manner, she wasn't like that, she was kind and caring, she had a fundamentally gentle nature, but there was a sharpness to it too, an unusual stubbornness, which made me look in her direction more and more often. She was pale, she had pale freckles on her cheeks, her hair was a reddish-blond color, she was thin and there was something physically fragile about her, fragile in the sense of the opposite of robust, which in another, less sharp, less independent soul would perhaps evoke a need in those she met to take her under their wing, but there was definitely no need for this, quite the contrary, it was Hilde who took whoever crossed her path under her wing. She often went around in a green military jacket and plain blue jeans, which signaled politically that she was on the left, but culturally she was on the right because what she was against was materialism while what she was for was the mind. In other words, the internal rather than the external. That was why she scorned writers like Solstad and Faldbakken, or Phallusbakken as she called him, and liked Bjørneboe and Kaj Skagen and even André Bjerke.

Hilde had become my closest confidante. Actually she was my best friend. I was in and out of the house where she lived, I got to know her parents, sometimes I stayed the night and had dinner with them. What Hilde and I did, occasionally with Eirik, occasionally on our own, was talk. Sitting cross-legged on the floor of her cellar flat, with a bottle of wine between us, the night pressing against the windows, we talked about books we had read, about political issues that interested us, about what awaited us in life, what we wanted to do and what we could do. She was very serious about life, she was the only acquaintance of my age who was, and she probably saw the same in me, while at the same time she laughed a lot and irony was never far away. There was little I liked better than being there, in their house, with her and Eirik and sometimes Lars; however, there were other things happening in my life which were irreconcilable, and this caused me to have a permanent guilty conscience: if I was out drinking at discos and trying to pick up girls, I felt bad about Hilde and what I stood for when I was with her; if I was at Hilde's place and talked about freedom or beauty or the meaning of everything, I could feel pangs of guilt toward those I went out with, or toward the person I was when I was with them, because the duplicity and hypocrisy that Hilde, Eirik, and I talked so much about was also present in my own heart. Politically, I was way out on the left, bordering on anarchy, I hated conformity and conventionality, and like all the other alternative young people growing up in Kristiansand, including her, I despised Christianity and all the idiots who believed in it and went to meetings with their stupid charismatic priests.

But I didn't despise the Christian girls. No, for some strange reason it was precisely them I fell for. How could I explain that to Hilde? And although I, like her, always tried to see beneath the surface, on the basis of a fundamental yet unstated tenet that what lay beneath was the truth or the reality, and, like her, always sought meaning, even if it were only to be found in an acknowledgment of meaninglessness, it was actually on the glittering and alluring surface that I wanted to live, and the chalice of meaninglessness I wanted to drain – in short I was attracted by all the town's discos and nightspots, where I wanted nothing more than to drink myself senseless and stagger around chasing girls I could fuck, or at least make out with. How could I explain that to Hilde?

I couldn't, and I didn't. Instead I opened a new subdivision in my life. "Booze and hopes of fornication" it was called, and it was right next to "insight and sincerity," separated only by a minor garden-fence-like change of personality.

Line was a Christian. Not ostentatiously so, but she was, and her presence at the railway station, close to me, somehow made me feel ill at ease.

She had curly black hair, pronounced eyebrows, and clear blue eyes. She moved with grace and was independent in that rare way that does not impinge on others. She liked drawing and did it a lot, perhaps she had some talent; after she'd said good-bye to me she was going to study creative arts at a folk high school. I wasn't in love with her, but she was good-looking, I was incredibly fond of her, and occasionally, after we'd shared some white wine, passionate feelings for her could rise inside me anyway. The problem was that she had clear boundaries as to how far she would go. During the weeks we had been together I had asked her twice, begged her, to let me as we lay there, seminaked, kissing in bed at her house or in my room at the Henhouse. But no, it wasn't me she was saving herself for.

"Couldn't I do it from behind then!" I once burst out in my desperation, without really knowing what that involved. Line snuggled up to me with her supple body and smothered me in kisses. Not many seconds later I felt the hated spasm from down below as my underpants filled with semen and I discreetly moved away from her; fired still by a driving passion, she didn't realize that my mood had changed completely from one moment to the next.

On the station platform she stood beside me, hands in her rear pockets and a little backpack on her back. There were six minutes to go before the train was due to leave. People were still getting on board.

"I'm just going to run over to the kiosk," she said, eyeing me. "Need anything?"

I shook my head.

"Oh, maybe a Coke."

She dashed over to the Narvesen kiosk. Hilde looked at me and smiled. Lars's eyes were wandering. Eirik was gazing in the direction of the harbor.

"Now that you're venturing out into the big wide world, I'll give you a piece of advice," he said, turning to me.

"Oh yeah?" I said.

"Think before you act. Make sure you're never caught with your pants down. And you'll survive. If, for example, you want some of your pupils to suck you off, for God's sake do it *behind* the teacher's desk. Not in front. OK?"

"Isn't that a double standard?" I said.

He laughed.

"And if, while you're up north, you've got to slap a girlfriend around, do it so the bruises don't show," Hilde said. "Never the face, however much you might feel like it."

"Do you think I should have two, then? One down here and one up there?"

"Why not?" she said.

"One you hit and one you don't," Eirik said. "Can't get a better balance than that."

"Any more advice?" I said.

"I saw an interview with an old actor on TV once," Lars said. "He was asked whether there was anything he'd learned over the course of a long life that he'd like to pass on to the viewers. He said yes, there was. The shower curtain. Make sure it was inside the bath, not outside. Otherwise when you turned the water on it would go all over the floor."

We laughed. Lars, pleased with himself, looked around.

Behind him, Line came back empty-handed.

"The line was too long," she said. "But I guess they'll have a bar on board."

"They do," I said.

"Shall we go?"

"OK," I said. "Thet was thet, as Fleksnes used to say. No more Kristiansand!"

They hugged me one after another. That was something I had started doing in my junior year: whenever we met we hugged.

Then I slung my kitbag over my shoulder, grabbed my case, and followed Line onto the train. They waved a few times, the train set off, and they strolled down to the parking lot.

It was unbelievable that was only two days ago.

I put down the book and, while rolling another cigarette and taking a swig of lukewarm coffee, read the three sentences I had written.

Down the hill the shop was less busy. I went for an apple from the kitchen and sat down at the typewriter again. In the course of the next hour I wrote three pages. About two boys on a construction site, and it was good as far as

I could judge. Perhaps three more pages and it would be finished. And that wasn't bad, finishing a short story on the first whole day up here. At that rate I could have a collection ready by Christmas!

As I was rinsing the dregs from the coffeepot, I saw a car coming up the road from the shop. It stopped outside the caretaker's house and two men, who looked to be in their midtwenties, got out. Both were well built, one was tall, the other shorter and rounder. I held the pot under the tap until it was full and put it on the burner. The two men were walking up the hill. I stepped to the side so they couldn't see me through the window.

Their footsteps stopped outside the porch.

Were they coming to see me?

One of them said something to the other. The ring of the doorbell pierced the silence of the flat.

I wiped my hands on my thighs, went into the hall, and opened the door.

The shorter of the two stretched out a hand. His face was square, his chin curved and jutting, his mouth small, his eyes alert. He had a black moustache and stubble on his jaw. A heavy gold chain around his neck.

"I'm Remi," he said.

Embarrassed, I shook his hand.

"Karl Ove Knausgaard," I said.

"Frank," the tall one said, reaching out a hand, which was enormous. His face was as round as the other man's was square. Round and fleshy. His lips were thick, the skin was delicate, pink almost. Hair blond and thinning. He looked like an overgrown child. His eyes were kind, also like a child's.

"Can we come in?" the one called Remi said. "We heard you were on your own up here and thought you might like some company. I suppose you don't know anyone in the village yet."

"Oh," I said. "That was kind of you. Do come in!"

I took a step back. *Kind! Do come in!* Where the hell did that come from? Was I fifty?

They stopped in the sitting room and looked around. Remi nodded a few times.

"Harrison lived here last year," he said.

I looked at him.

"The last temporary teacher," he said. "We were here a lot. He was a great guy."

"A good guy," Frank said.

"*No* wasn't in his vocabulary," Remi said.

"He's already deeply missed," Frank said. "Can we sit down?"

"Yes, of course," I said. "Would you like a cup of coffee? I just made some."

"Coffee? Yes, please."

They took off their jackets, laid them across the arm of the sofa, and sat down. Their bodies were like barrels. The upper arms of the one called Frank were as wide as my thighs. Even with my back to them, in front of the counter, I could feel their presence, it filled the whole flat and made me feel weak and girly.

That was kind of you. Would you like a cup of coffee?

For Christ's sake, I didn't have any cups! Only the one I'd brought with me.

I opened the cupboards above the counter. Empty, of course. Then I opened the lower ones. And there, next to the downpipe from the sink, was a glass. I rinsed it, sprinkled some coffee in the pot, banged it on the tabletop a few times, carried it into the sitting room, and looked around for something to put it on.

It had to be *The Garden of Eden*.

"Well?" Remi said. "What do you think, Karl Ove?"

I was uncomfortable at hearing my name used so familiarly by a man I had never seen before and felt my cheeks flush.

"I don't really know," I said.

"We're going to a party tonight," Frank said. "Over'n Gryllefjord. How'd you like to come along?"

"There's a place free in the car, and we know you won't've had time to go to the liquor store, so we've got some booze for you too. What do you say?"

"Not sure," I said.

"What? Would you rather mope around here in this empty room?"

"Let the man make his own mind up!" Frank said.

"Yeah, OK."

"I'd planned to do some work," I said.

"Work? On what" Remi said. But his eyes were already fixed on the type-writer. "Do you write?"

I flushed again.

"A little," I said with a shrug.

"Ah, a writer!" Remi said. "Not bad."

He laughed.

"I've never read a book in my life. Not even when I went to school. I always got out of it. Have you?" he said, looking at Frank.

"Sure, lots. *Cocktail.*"

They both burst into laughter.

"Does that count?" Remi said, looking at me. "You're a writer. Does porn count as literature?"

I gave a strained smile.

"Fiction is fiction, I guess," I said.

There was a silence.

"You're from Kristiansand, I hear," Frank said.

I nodded.

"You have a girl down there?"

I mulled that one over.

"Yes and no," I said.

"Yes and no? That sounds interesting!" Remi said.

"Sounds like something for you," Frank said with a glance at Remi.

"For me? No. I'm more the either-or type."

There was another silence as they took a mouthful of coffee.

"Any children?" Remi said.

"Children?" I said. "Jesus. I'm only eighteen!"

At last, a comment from the heart.

"It's happened before in the history of the world," Remi said.

"And do you two have children?" I said.

"Frank doesn't. But I do. My son's nine. He lives with his mother."

"He's from the 'or' time," Frank said.

They laughed. Then they both looked at me.

"Well, we shouldn't bother him any more on his first day here," Remi said, and got up. Frank got up too. They took their jackets and went into the hall.

"Think about the party tonight," Remi said. "We'll be at Hege's if you change your mind."

"He doesn't know where Hege lives," Frank said.

"You walk up the top road. Then it's the fourth house on the left. You can't miss it. There'll be cars outside."

He held out a hand.

"Hope you'll come. Thanks for the coffee!"

After I'd closed the door behind them, I went into the bedroom and lay down. Stretched out my arms and legs and closed my eyes.

A car came up the hill and stopped outside.

I opened my eyes. More visitors?

No. A door banged somewhere else in the house. It was my neighbors, whoever they were, coming home. After shopping in Finnsnes maybe.

Oh, I was dying to call someone I knew!

I couldn't sleep, which I was also eager to do, to get away from all of this. Instead I went to the bathroom, undressed, and had another shower. It was a way of tricking myself into believing something new was beginning. Not as good as sleeping, it was true, but better than nothing. Then, with wet hair and my shirt sticking to my back, I sat down and went back to writing. I had the two ten-year-olds walking around in the forest. They were scared of meeting foxes and had cap guns in their hands to frighten them away if they showed up. Suddenly they heard a shot. They ran over to where the sound had come from and saw a garbage dump in the middle of the forest. There were two men lying on the ground shooting at rats. That's when something seemed to flash through me, an arc of happiness and energy; now I couldn't write fast enough, the text lagged slightly behind the narrative, it was a wonderful feeling, shiny and glittering.

The men shooting at the rats went on their way, the two boys pulled up two chairs and a table in the forest and sat there reading porn magazines. One of them, the one called Gabriel, stuck his dick in a glass bottle and suddenly felt a terrible stinging pain, he pulled it out and there was a beetle on the end of it. Gordon laughed so much he fell back into the heather. They forgot all about time, then Gabriel realized, but it was too late, his father was furious with him when he got home, punched him in the mouth, which began to bleed, and locked him in the tiny room with the hot-water tank, where he had to stay all night.

When I had finished, it was almost eight, and seven closely written pages lay in a pile beside the typewriter.

So great was my sense of triumph that something inside me screamed out to tell someone. Anyone! Anyone!

But I was all alone.

I turned off the typewriter and buttered some slices of bread, which I ate standing in front of the kitchen window. A figure hurried past on the road under the graying though still blue sky. Two cars emerged from the tunnel, one right after the other. I had to go out. I couldn't stay inside any longer.

Then there was a knock at the door.

I answered it. A woman of around thirty, in a T-shirt and slacks, stood outside. Her face had gentle features, her nose was big though not obtrusively so, her eyes were warm and brown. Her hair was dark blond and tied in a knot at the back.

"Hi!" she said. "I just had to say hello. We're neighbors. I live upstairs. And we're also colleagues. I'm a teacher too. I'm Torill."

She held out her hand. Her fingers were thin, but her grasp was firm.

"Karl Ove," I said.

"Welcome to Håfjord," she said with a smile.

"Thank you."

"You arrived yesterday, I hear?"

"Yes, by bus."

"Yes, well, we'll have to talk another time. I just wanted to say that if there's anything you need just ring the bell. I mean, sugar or coffee or bed linen or whatever it is you're short of. A radio, for example. Do you have one? We've got at least one we don't use."

I nodded.

"I have a Walkman," I said. "But thanks anyway. It was very kind of you to come down!"

Very kind.

She smiled.

"I'll see you later," she said.

"Yes, see you," I said.

I stood in the hall long after she had gone. What was happening actually? Every meeting here was like a dagger to the soul.

No, I had to get out and walk.

I put on a coat, spent a few seconds in front of the mirror in the bathroom straightening my beret, locked the door behind me, and started walking down the hill. Some way down you could the see past the edge of the mountain and out to sea, the razor-sharp horizon against the sky. Two large very white clouds hung motionless, hovering on high. On the other side of the fjord a little fishing boat was chugging back toward the harbor. The fjord was called Fugleøyfjord. Bird Island Fjord. OK, they, the first people who arrived here, must have thought: What shall we call this fjord? Fishfjord? No, that's what we called the last one, didn't we. What about Birdfjord then? Yes! Good idea!

I continued along the road past the fish-processing plant, which was deserted apart from the seagulls huddled on the roof, and on toward the bend that led to the higher part of the village. Beyond the last house the mountain soared straight up. There was no intermediate stage, which I was used to where I had grown up, those diffuse, hard-to-define places, which were neither private property nor open nature. This was real nature, and not the low, gentle Sørland type of nature but wild, harsh, windswept Arctic nature, which confronted you as soon as you opened the door.

Were there a hundred houses here in all?

Way up here, beneath the mountains, by the sea.

I had the feeling I was walking on the edge of the world. That it wasn't possible to go any farther. One more step and I was gone.

But, my God, how fantastic it was to be able to live here.

Now and then I saw movements behind the windows in the houses I passed. The flickering lights of TV sets. All somehow submerged beneath the crash of the waves as they washed up on the shore below, or woven into it, for so even and regular was this roar that it seemed more like a quality of the air, as though the air could not only be colder or warmer but also louder or softer.

In front of me appeared the house where I assumed the woman they had called Hege lived, at any rate there were lots of cars in the drive, music was coming from an open veranda door, and behind the large 1970s-style windows I glimpsed a group of people sitting around a table. It was tempting to go over and knock on the door, they could hardly expect anything of me, after all I didn't know anyone, a certain shyness would only be natural, so it would be OK just to sit there drinking without uttering a word until the alcohol kicked in and loosened everything in me, including my heart, which was now so small and constricted.

While I was thinking this I didn't stop walking, I didn't even slow down because if they saw me standing there wavering and then I set off for home again they would think they knew something about me.

Maybe I was longing for something to make my heart swell, but this wasn't vital, and I was supposed to be doing my writing, I thought as I walked on, and then I was past the house and it was too late.

When I came to a halt by my front door I looked at my watch.

It had taken me fifteen minutes to walk around the whole village.

So it was within these fifteen minutes I was to live my whole life this coming year.

A shudder went through me. I walked into the hall and took off my coat. Even though I knew nothing was going to happen, I locked the door and kept it locked all night.

The next day I didn't go out, I sat writing and staring at the people who appeared and disappeared again on their way downhill. I paced back and forth in the flat pondering more and more what I was going to do when classes started on Tuesday, formulating one introductory sentence after another in my head while also trying to decide what strategy to adopt for dealing with the pupils. The first priority was to establish what their level was. Perhaps test them in all the subjects right from the beginning? And then plan everything after that? Tests? No, that was a bit harsh, a bit too authoritarian, a bit too schoolmarmy.

Some exercises, then, that they could do at home?

No. There was so much time to fill in every lesson that it would be best to give them the exercises at school. I could work on them tomorrow.

I went into the bedroom and lay down on the bed, finished the two books I had bought, and once that was done started on the articles in the literary magazine I had picked up in Oslo, although I didn't understand much. I was familiar with most of the words, but what they described seemed to be constantly beyond my reach, as though they were about an unknown world which the language of the old world was not equipped to approach. But one thing did emerge from these pages with greater force than anything else, and that was the description of a book, *Ulysses*, which in its singularity sounded absolutely fantastic. Before me I saw an enormous tower, glinting with moisture as it were, surrounded by mist and a pallid light from the overcast sun. It was regarded as the major work of modernism, by which I imagined low-slung racing cars, pilots with leather helmets and jackets, zeppelins floating above skyscrapers in glittering but dark metropolises, computers, electronic music. Names such as Hermann Broch, Robert Musil, Arnold Schönberg.

Elements of earlier, long-gone cultures were assimilated into this world, in my mind's eye, such as Broch's *Virgil* and Joyce's *Ulysses*.

At the shop the day before I had forgotten today was Sunday, so I was eating bread with liver paste and mayonnaise when there was another ring at the door. I wiped my mouth with the back of my hand and hurried into the hall.

There were two girls standing outside. I recognized one of them at once. She was the girl sitting across the aisle from me on the bus coming here.

She smiled.

"Hi!" she said. "Do you recognize me?"

"Of course," I said. "You're the girl on the bus."

She laughed.

"And you're the new teacher at Håfjord! I thought you were when I saw you, but I wasn't sure. Then someone at the party last night told me you were."

She stuck out a hand.

"My name's Irene," she said.

"Karl Ove," I said with a smile.

"This is Hilde," she said, nodding in the direction of the other girl, whose hand I then shook. "We're cousins," Irene said. "I dropped in on her today. But actually that was just an excuse to come and say hello to you." She let out a laugh. "No, I was just joking."

"Would you like to come in?" I said.

They looked at each other.

"Love to," Irene said.

She was wearing jeans, a blue denim jacket, and, beneath it, a white lace blouse. She was chubby, her breasts under the blouse were full and her hips broad. Her hair was blond, shoulder-length, her skin pale with some freckles around her nose. Eyes large, blue, and teasing. Standing next to her in the hall, smelling the fragrance of her perfume, which was also full, as she passed me her jacket – there were no hooks in the hall – with a slightly searching look, I got another boner.

"I can take yours too while I'm at it," I said to Hilde, who had nowhere near the same presence as her cousin, and who passed me her jacket with a shy, bashful smile. I hung them over the back of the desk chair and slid a hand into my trouser pocket so that the bulge was not visible. The two girls went somewhat hesitantly into the sitting room.

"My things haven't arrived yet," I said. "They'll be here soon."

"Yes, it is a bit drab in here," Irene said, smiling.

They sat down on the sofa, both with their knees tightly together. I sat on the chair opposite them, with my legs crossed to hide the bulge, which had not become any smaller. She was sitting only a meter away from me.

"How old are you?" she asked.

"Eighteen," I said. "And you?"

"Sixteen," Irene said.

"Seventeen," Hilde said.

"So you just finished gymnas?" Irene said.

I nodded.

"I'm in my junior year," Irene said. "At the gymnas in Finnsnes. It's a boarding school. So I've got a room there. You can come and visit me if you like. No doubt you'll soon be coming to Finnsnes quite a bit."

"Yes, I'd like that," I said.

Our eyes met.

She smiled. I smiled back.

"But I'm really from Hellevika. That's the next village. Across the mountain. It's just a few kilometers away. Do you have a driver's license?"

"No," I said.

"Shame," she said.

There were a few moments of silence. I got up, went for an ashtray and my pouch of tobacco, and rolled a cigarette.

"Can I have one?" she said. "Mine are in my jacket."

I threw the pouch over to her.

"I had to laugh when we were on the bus yesterday," she said as she was making her rollie. "You looked as if you were trying to climb out the window."

They grinned. She licked the gum, folded the paper over with her forefingers against her thumbs, put it in her mouth, and lit up.

"It was so incredibly beautiful," I said. "I had no idea what it would be like up here. Håfjord was just a name to me. In fact, not even that."

"Why did you apply to come up here then?"

I shrugged.

"I was given a list of names by the employment office, and so I chose this one."

Someone crossed the floor above.

We all looked up at the ceiling.

"Have you met Torill yet?" Irene said.

"Yes, briefly," I said. "Do you know her?"

"Of course we do. Everyone knows everyone here. Well, in Hellevika and Håfjord."

"And on Fugleøya," Hilde said.

Silence.

"Would you like a cup of coffee?" I asked them, half getting up from the chair.

Irene shook her head. "No, I think we should be going. What do you think, Hilde?"

"Yes, I think so too," her cousin said.

We got up, I took the jackets from the chair, went closer to Irene than strictly speaking I had to as I handed her the jacket. I was filled with a sense of her hips, covered by her tight jeans, and of her thighs and legs and surprisingly small feet, of her neck and her full breasts, her short nose and blue eyes, at once innocent and sassy, I closed the door behind the girls. The whole visit had lasted ten, maybe fifteen minutes.

I was on my way to the kitchen to put on some coffee when there was another knock at the door.

It was her, alone this time.

"There's a party in Hellevika next weekend," she said. "In fact, that was why I came by, to tell you. Would you feel like coming? It's a good way to meet people from around here."

"Of course," I said. "If I can make it I will."

"If?" she said. "You just have to get in a car. Everyone's going. See you there!"

She winked. Then she turned and walked down the hill to where Hilde was chipping away at the edge of the asphalt with the tip of her shoe.

A little after eight the following morning, I left the flat for the first time in more than a day. The sun that hung above the mountains to the east shone directly on the door, and the air that met my face when I closed it behind me was mild and summery. But only a few meters away, where the country-side lay in shadow behind the mountains, it was colder, and the impression I had of small pools existing in the air, like currents and eddies, rapids and waterfalls, seemed strangely uplifting. Ahead of me, atop a small plateau, was the school, and if I wasn't absolutely dreading going in, I was certainly nervous enough for tiny flashes of apprehension to shoot through me as I approached.

It looked like any other school, a long single-story edifice on one side, connected to a tunnel-like corridor with a larger, newer, and taller block housing a woodwork room, gymnasium, and small swimming pool. Between the two buildings was the playground, which extended behind them to a full-sized soccer field. On a mound above it, standing proudly, was what I guessed was the community center.

Two cars were parked in front of the entrance. A big white jeep and a low black Citroën. The sun gleamed on the row of windows. The door was open. I went into the hall, the yellow linoleum floor was almost white in the sunshine, which fell in long stripes through the glass door panels. I rounded one corner, there were three doors on the right, two on the left, and at the end the hall opened into a large space. A man stopped and looked at me. He had a full beard and a bald patch. Probably in his early thirties.

"Hello!" he said.

"Hello," I said.

"And you are . . . Karl Ove?"

"That's me," I said, stopping in front of him.

"Sture," he said.

We shook hands.

"Karl Ove was a pure guess," he said with a smile. "But you didn't look like a Nils Erik."

"Nils Erik?" I said.

"Yes, we have two teachers from the south this year. You and Nils Erik. The rest of the untrained staff are local people, so I know them."

"Are you local?"

"I certainly am!"

He looked me straight in the eye for a few seconds. I found it unpleasant, what was this, some kind of test, but I didn't want to be the first to look away so I held his gaze.

"You're very young," he said eventually, and looked away toward the door we were standing next to. "But we knew that of course. It'll all be fine! Come on, you have to meet the others."

He stretched out an arm toward the door. I opened it and entered. It was the staff room. A kitchenette, armchairs, and a sofa, a small room full of papers and a photocopier, an adjacent rectangular room with workstations on both sides.

"Hi!" I said.

Six people were sitting around the table. All eyes turned to me.

They nodded and mumbled "hi" in return. From the kitchenette appeared a small but powerful and energetic man with a red beard.

"Karl Ove?" He beamed. After I had nodded and he'd shaken my hand, he addressed the others.

"This is Karl Ove Knausgaard, the young man who has come all the way from Kristiansand to work with us!" And then he said the names of all those seated, which I had forgotten an instant later. They all had a cup of coffee in their hands or on the table in front of them, and everyone, apart from one elderly woman, was young. In their early twenties or so it seemed.

"Take a seat, Karl Ove. Coffee?"

"Please," I said, and squeezed down at the end of the sofa.

For the next few hours the head teacher, who was called Richard and must have been in his late thirties, told us, the two temporary teachers, about the school. We were shown around the rooms, given keys, allocated workstations, and then we went through the timetables and various routines. It was a small school with so few pupils that classes were grouped together for many of the lessons. Torill would be the homeroom teacher for the first and second graders, Hege for the third and fourth, me for the fifth, sixth, and seventh, Sture for the eighth and ninth. Why precisely I had been made a homeroom teacher I had no idea, and it felt a little uncomfortable, not least because the other temp from Sørland, Nils Erik, was considerably older than me, twenty-four, and planning to embark on teacher training after this year. He was serious about it, this was his future, while I had no such plans: becoming a teacher was the last thing I wanted to do in this life. The other temps came from the area, knew the ins and outs, and ought to have been better suited than me to taking responsibility for a class. Presumably the head teacher had based his decision on my application, and that made me uneasy because I had laid it on thick.

The head teacher showed us where the syllabuses were and demonstrated the range of teaching aids we had at our disposal. At one o'clock we were finished, and I walked down to the post office, which was at the other end of the village, arranged a PO box number, sent a few letters, did some food shopping, made dinner at home, lay on my bed listening to music for an hour or so, jotted down some key words regarding the ideas I'd had for my classes, but they looked stupid, too obvious, so I crumpled up the paper and threw it away.

I had everything under control, everything.

Early that evening I went back up to the school. It was a strange feeling to unlock the door of the main building and walk along the corridors. Everything was empty and still, filled with the gray light that seeped in through the windows. All the shelves and cupboards were empty, the classrooms somehow untouched.

In the staff room there was a telephone in a small cubicle, I went in and called Mom, she'd also had her first day at a new school today. She was busy unpacking in the new place she was renting, a terraced house some way outside Førde town center. I told her a bit about what it was like here and how nervous I was about teaching the next day. She said she knew I would manage just fine, and even though her character reference didn't count for a lot – after all she was my mother – it did help.

When I had finished the call, I went into the photocopier room and made ten copies of the short story I had written. The idea was to send it to people I knew the following day. Then I wandered around all the rooms in the school. In the gym I swung open the panel door to the little equipment room, threw a ball out, had a few kicks at the handball goal at the far end. Switched off the light, went into the swimming pool area. The water lay dark and still in the pool. I went up to the woodwork room and on to the natural science room. From the windows you could see across the village lying beneath the mountains, lots of small houses in a variety of colors which appeared to vibrate, and beyond, across the sea, the endless sea, and the sky that rose from it, in the far distance, full of elongated, smoke-like clouds.

Early tomorrow morning the pupils would come, then it was down to business.

I switched the lights off after me, locked the door, and walked down the hill with the large key ring jangling in my hand.

Upon waking the next morning I was so nervous I was on the point of throwing up. A cup of coffee was all I could get down me. I walked up to the school half an hour before the first lesson was due to begin, sat in my place flipping through the books we were going to use. The mood among the other teachers buzzing around between the photocopier, classrooms, kitchenette, and sofa suite was lighthearted and cheery. Outside the window the students were beginning to appear in dribs and drabs, coming up the hill. My chest was frozen with terror. My heart was beating as if it were being strangled. I saw the letters on the page I had opened but couldn't make any sense of them. After a while I stood up and went into the kitchenette to get myself a cup of coffee. When I turned I met the eyes of Nils Erik. He looked relaxed, leaning back against the sofa, his legs wide apart.

"You're free in the first lesson, aren't you?" I said.

He nodded. His cheeks were slightly flushed. His hair was black and he had the same unruly tufts of hair that my old best friend Geir had. His eyes were light blue.

"I'm so damned nervous," I said, sitting down in the chair opposite.

"What are you nervous about?" he said. "You know there are only five or six pupils in each class, don't you?"

"I do," I said. "Nevertheless."

He smiled.

"Shall we trade places? They don't know who's who anyway. I'll be Karl Ove and you're Nils Erik."

"Why not," I said. "But what do we do when we have to swap back?"

"Swap back? Why would we have to?"

"No, you've got a point there," I said, glancing out the window. The pupils were standing around in groups. Some were running around. Scattered between them were also some mothers. The children were smartly dressed.

Of course they were. Some were here for the first time. It was their very first school day.

"So where am I from?" I said.

"Hokksund," he said. "And me?"

"Kristiansand."

"Great!" he said.

I shook my head.

"No, you're wrong there," I said.

He looked at me with a twinkle in his eye.

"You might think so *now*," he said. "But just wait a few years."

"What's happening in a few years?" I said.

Just then the bell rang.

"In a few years you'll think of your hometown as paradise on earth," he said.

What the hell do you know about that? I thought, but said nothing, just got up, took my coffee cup in one hand, the pile of books in the other, and headed for the door.

"Good luck!" he said from behind me.

There were five pupils in the seventh grade. Four girls, one boy. In addition to them, I was also responsible for the three in the fifth and sixth grades. So, in all, eight pupils.

When I stopped in front of the teacher's desk and put my things down, all of them were staring at me. My palms were damp, my heart was thumping, and as I drew breath it was with a tremble.

"Hi," I said. "My name's Karl Ove Knausgaard. I come from Kristiansand and I'm going to be your homeroom teacher this year. I thought we might begin with a little roll call? I've got your names here, but I don't know who's who yet."

While I was talking they exchanged glances; two of the girls giggled. The attention they were paying me was not hostile, I sensed that at once, it was childlike. They were children.

I took out the list of names. Studied it, studied them.

I recognized the girl from the shop. But the one who made the strongest impression on me was a girl with reddish hair and black-rimmed glasses. She was skeptical, I could tell. There was no sharpness from any of the others.

"Andrea?" I said.

"Here," said the girl from the shop. She said it with downcast eyes, but as her voice trailed off she looked up at me.

I smiled to reassure her.

"Vivian?"

The girl beside her giggled. "That's me!" she said.

"Hildegunn?"

"Yes," said the girl with the glasses.

"Kai Roald?"

He was the only boy in the seventh grade. Wearing jeans and a denim jacket, he sat fiddling with a pen.

"Here," he said.

"Live?" I said.

A girl with long hair, a round face, and glasses smiled. "Yup, that's me."

Then there was the boy and the girl from the sixth grade, and the girl from the fifth.

I put down the list and sat on the desk.

"You'll be with me for Norwegian, math, religion, and science. You're all very good, though, aren't you?"

"Not that good," said the redhead with the glasses. "We've always had unqualified teachers from the south who only stay for a year."

I smiled. She didn't.

"What subjects do you like?"

They looked at one another. No one seemed to want to answer.

"How about you, Kai Roald?"

He squirmed. A pink flush spread across his cheeks. "I don't know," he said. "Woodwork maybe. Or gym. Not Norwegian anyway!"

"And you?" I said, motioning to the girl from the shop as I looked down at my list. "Andrea?"

She had crossed her legs under the desk and was leaning forward, drawing something on a sheet of paper.

"I don't have any favorite subjects," she said.

"Do you like them all or dislike them all?" I said.

She peered up at me. A glint appeared in her eyes. "Dislike!" she said.

"Is that the same for all of you?" I said.

"Yes!" they said.

"OK," I said. "But the thing is that we have to be here for all these lessons whether you like them or not. So we may as well make the best of it. Don't you agree?"

No one answered.

"Since I know *nothing* about you, I'm going to spend the first few lessons getting to know you better and find out what we have to work on."

I got up, took a swig of coffee, and wiped my mouth with the back of my hand. In the corner on the other side someone started singing. A clear, high-pitched voice, that had to be Hege, and then some very young children's voices joined in.

They were the first graders!

"So I thought I would simply start by giving you an exercise," I continued. "You have to write a page about yourselves. A presentation."

"Oh no. Do we have to write?" Kai Roald said.

"What's a presentation?" Vivian asked.

I looked at her. There was so little angularity about her chin that her whole face seemed almost square, though not harsh. She had something soft and puppylike about her. Her blue eyes almost disappeared entirely when she smiled, and she smiled a lot, I could already see that.

"It's writing about who you are," I said. "Imagine you have to say who you are to someone who doesn't know you. What's the first thing you would write?"

She shifted her position on the chair and pressed her calflike knees together.

"Maybe that I'm thirteen years old. And in the seventh grade at Håfjord School?"

"Yes, that's good," I said. "And maybe that you're a girl?"

She laughed. "Yes, he'd have to know that," she said.

"OK," I said. "So write a page about yourselves. Or more if you like."

"Are you going to read it out loud?" Hildegunn said.

"No," I said.

"What are we supposed to write on?" Kai Roald said.

I smacked my forehead. "You're right! I haven't given you any books!"

They cracked up, they were children, they thought things like this were funny. I dashed to the staff room, grabbed a pile of exercise books, handed them out, and soon they were all writing while I stood by the window gazing at the mountain peaks across the fjord where they seemed to *writhe* their way upward, so cold and black against the airy light.

When the bell rang at the end of the lesson, I gathered my papers with an exuberant, almost jubilant, feeling in my body. It had gone well, there was nothing to be afraid of. And after twelve years of continuous education, the next moment – opening the door and going into the staff room – was a particular pleasure: I had crossed the line, I was on the other side, an adult and responsible for a class of my own.

I put down my books and papers in front of my spot at the table, poured coffee into a cup, sat down on the sofa, and observed the other teachers. I was backstage, I mused, but what at first was a wonderful thought was immediately replaced by its antithesis, for this was not what I wanted, for Christ's sake, I was a *teacher*, was there anything sadder than that? Backstage, that was bands, women, drinking, tours, fame.

But that was not what I wanted either. This was just a step on the way.

I took a mouthful of coffee and glanced at the door as it opened. It was Nils Erik.

"How did it go?" he said.

"It went well," I said. "Certainly nothing to be afraid of."

Behind him appeared the woman called Hege.

"They're so *lovely*," she said. "Little sweeties!"

"Karl Ove?" came a voice from the kitchenette. I looked across; Sture was standing with a cup in his hand, looking at me.

"You play soccer, don't you?"

"I do," I said. "But I'm not much good. I played in the fifth division two seasons ago."

"We've got a team here," he said. "I'm the coach. We're in the seventh division, so you shouldn't have any difficulty hanging in there, I bet. How about a game?"

"Sure," I said.

"Tor Einar's always up for it. Isn't that right, Tor Einar?" he said, sticking his head into the room with the workstations.

"Are you talking nonsense about me again?" we heard from inside. A second later a man poked his head around the corner.

"Tor Einar used to play in the fourth division as a junior," Sture said. "Sadly though he has no other talents."

"At least I haven't lost my hair," Tor Einar said, coming closer. "So I don't need to grow a beard to retain my masculine dignity, like some people I know."

Tor Einar came from Finnsnes, had pale skin and freckles, bristly reddish hair, and a constant grin playing on his lips. His movements were slow and laborious, in an almost demonstrative way, as if with them he were trying to say here comes someone who does everything at his own pace and is not concerned about anyone else.

"Where do you play then?" he said.

"Midfield," I said. "And you?"

"Midfielder/ball winner," he said with a wink.

"Ah, a terrier," I said. "I was called the elk myself when I used to play. That tells you everything . . ."

He laughed.

"Why the elk?" Hege said.

"My loping gait," I said. "Long, unsteady stride and no change of pace."

"Are there any other animal metaphors on the soccer field?" she said.

"There are, aren't there?" I said, looking at Tor Einar.

"Yes, you've got the striker who's as strong as an ox and rams the ball into the net."

"And then you've got the cat," I said. "Lots of goalkeepers called the cat. And incidentally there's a midfield general too."

"What's that?"

"Someone who always knows where the others are and can deliver pin-point passes at precisely the right moment."

"How unbelievably childish!" Hege said.

"And a sweeper," Tor Einar said.

"And there's often a dynamic duo up front. And then there's the lone wolf, of course."

"You've forgotten the referee," Nils Erik said. "The ref's an asshole."

"And you do this of your own free will," Hege said.

"Not me," Nils Erik said.

"But the two of you do," she said, looking at me.

The bell rang. I got up to collect my books for the next lesson. Sture placed a hand on my shoulder.

"You have my class now, don't you?" he said.

I nodded.

"For English."

"Watch out for a kid called Stian. He might try to nettle you. But don't rise to it and you'll be fine. OK?"

I shrugged.

"Hope so," I said.

"Make sure you always leave him a way out and he's no problem."

"OK," I said.

English was my worst subject, and I was only two years older than the oldest pupils, so while I was walking over to the other building, where the eighth and ninth grades had their classroom, my stomach was churning again.

I put my pile of books down on the raised table. The pupils were scattered across their desks as if they had just been hurled out of a spin dryer. No one paid any attention to me.

"Hello, class!" I said. "My name is Karl Ove Knausgaard, and I'm going to be your English teacher this year. *How do you do?*"

No one said anything. The class consisted of four boys and five girls. A couple of them watched me, the others sat scribbling something, one was knitting. I recognized the boy from the snack bar stand: he was wearing a baseball cap and rocking back and forth on his chair while eyeing me with a smirk on his face. He had to be Stian.

"Well," I said. "Now I would like you to introduce yourselves in English."

"*Snakk norsk!*" Stian said. The boy behind him, a conspicuously tall, thin figure, taller than me, and I was six foot four, guffawed. Some of the girls tittered.

"If you are going to learn a language, then you have to speak it," I said.

One of the girls, dark-haired and white-skinned, with regular, slightly chubby facial features and blue eyes, put up her hand.

"Yes?" I said.

"Isn't your English a bit too bad? I mean, for teaching?"

I could feel my cheeks burning, I stepped forward with a smile to hide my embarrassment.

"Well," I said. "I have to admit that my English isn't exactly perfect. But that isn't the most important thing. The most important is to be understood. And you do understand me?"

"Sort of," she said.

"So," I said. "And what's your name?"

She rolled her eyes. "Camilla."

"Full sentences, please."

"Oh, my name is Camilla. Happy?"

"*Ja*," I said.

"Do you mean yes?" she said.

"Yes," I said, blushing again.

"So, what's your name?" I asked the girl sitting behind Camilla. She raised her head and looked at me.

Ay-yay-yay.

What a beauty!

Gentle blue eyes that narrowed when she smiled. Large mouth. High cheekbones.

"My name is Liv," she said with a chuckle.

"Camilla, Liv. And you?" I said, motioning with my head to Stian.
"*Æ heitte Stian*," he said.
"Well," I said. "What would that be in English?"
"Stian!" he said.
Everyone laughed.

When the bell rang and I left the room, I was absolutely exhausted. So much had to be parried, so much had to be tolerated, so much had to be ignored, so much had to be repressed. The girl called Camilla had yawned and stretched her arms above her head while staring straight at me. She was wearing only a T-shirt, and her breasts, which were large and round, were delineated in unmistakable clarity against the white material. I had an erection, it was impossible to avoid, no matter how hard I tried to concentrate on other matters. How glad I was that I was sitting behind the teacher's desk! And as if that weren't enough, the girl called Liv was as charming as she was beautiful, somehow shy and outgoing at the same time, apart from the vague wildness there was about her – which above all was embodied in her big dark-blond hair and wide selection of jangling bracelets, but also in the contrast between her reserved body language and the sparkle in her eyes – which made it impossible for me not to think about her when she was in the room. Then there was Stian, who kept fidgeting with a penknife while taking every opportunity to taunt me and refused to do anything I told the class to do, and his friend Ivar, who laughed at everything Stian said, a hollow, slightly inane laugh that was always followed by sweeping glances around the room. But his gaze was ingenuous, sometimes even toward me, I could win him over, he had even grinned once or twice at something I had said.

In the staff room I slumped down onto the sofa. The teacher called Vibeke stopped and smiled at me. She was nineteen, had a full body and a round soft face, happy blue eyes, curly, permed blond hair.

"How's it going?" she said.

"It's going fine," I said. "How about you?"

"Fine too," she said. "There's not as much that's new here for me as there is for you, I imagine. I attended this school when I was growing up."

I couldn't think of a response, and she smiled again before going into the workroom. Beside me sat Jane, she was also from the village, in her early twenties, also large: her upper arms were perhaps twice the size of mine. She had a long, straight, almost Roman nose, flat cheeks, thin lips that often sagged at the corners as though she wouldn't touch what she saw before her with a bargepole. Her eyes were grumpy, indeed her whole bearing was grumpy. But a couple of times I had seen her laugh, and then all of her brightened up, the transformation was total, she could hardly stop laughing once she had started, and it was a pleasure to see her struggling to regain her composure.

In addition to all the young temporary teachers, there was an older woman on the staff, Eva, she was in her late forties, but looked older, she taught needlework and home economics, was small, lean, with a pointed face, thin fair hair, and a piercing voice, and at this moment she was sitting in the chair on the other side of the table, knitting. She was skeptical about me, I could see that from the way she looked at and didn't look at me. And with absolute justification, for what was I doing here actually? What did I want from this job?

When I came in after the English lesson, she glanced up at me, and I think she knew what feelings were coursing through me.

Of course that was impossible, but it was what I thought anyway.

During the lunch break I went down to the post office at the other end of the village. The mountainsides were bright green in the sunshine. The sea was deep blue. Something about the light or perhaps the cool draft I felt in the air, somehow *beneath* what the sun heated up, so typical of August, evoked the atmospheres I recognized from when I started school after the holidays: the excitement, the anticipation, the perhaps-something-fantastic-is-going-to-happen-this-year?

On the slope behind the last row of houses there was already a hint of yellow in the green. Of course autumn came earlier here. I nodded to a car driving past. The driver, who looked like a mother, nodded back, and I walked down the graveled incline to the post office, which was housed in the basement of a block of flats. In the hall were the PO boxes, inside was the office with counters, posters on the walls, stands of postcards and envelopes.

The woman behind the counter was probably about fifty. Permed thinning reddish hair, glasses, a delicate gold necklace. A man with a walker stood by the small table under the window scraping a scratch card with a coin.

"Hello," I said to the assistant, and placed the envelopes on the counter. "I just wanted to mail these."

"Yes, of course," she said. "By the way, there's some mail for you already."

"Is there?" I said. "Not bad!"

While she weighed the letters and selected the appropriate stamps, I unlocked my box. It was a letter from Line.

I went in and paid, opened the letter, and started to read while walking up the gravel road.

She wrote that she was in her room and thinking about me. She liked me a lot, she said, we'd had so much fun together, but she had never actually been in love with me, so now, with us living in two different places, she thought the best and most honest thing to do would be to end it. She hoped everything would go well for me in my life, urged me to take writing seriously, as she would with her drawing, and also hoped that I would not be angry with her, for our new lives were starting now, we were far apart, tomorrow she would be traveling to the folk high school, and by now I had probably arrived in the village where I was going to work, and as long as this felt the way it did and she didn't love me, anything else but breaking off the relationship would be a betrayal of herself. But I was a wonderful person, I should know that, that was not the reason, you can't control feelings, they are how they are.

I stuffed the letter in my coat pocket.

I hadn't been in love with Line either, everything she said about me I could have said about her, yet still I felt sad and also a bit angry with her when I read what she had written. I wanted *her* to love *me*! And even though I didn't want to be with her, and was glad it was over, it should have been me who ended it. Now it was her who had the high ground, who said no to me and who would also probably go through life convinced that I had loved her and had been crushed by her letter.

Oh well.

There was great activity down at the fish-processing plant. Several boats had docked, forklift trucks were plying back and forth across the concrete and into what looked like a dark hall. Men in high rubber boots bustled here and there, a group of women wearing open white coats and white caps stood smoking outside the end of the hall, and the air above them was full of flapping, screaming seagulls. I went into the shop and bought some rolls, some mild cheese, a packet of margarine, and a liter of milk, said hello to the assistant, who asked whether I had settled in all right, fine, I said, everything was great.

I didn't have a class in the next slot, so after eating two rolls and putting the rest in the tiny staff room fridge, I sat down at my workstation to plan the next few days' teaching. The temporary teachers had been allocated a mentor, who would come to see us once a week so that we could discuss any problems or difficulties we had in our classes. We were also going on a course next week, in Finnsnes, with all the other temporary teachers in the district. There were a lot of them; the locals who trained as teachers seldom moved back when the training was over. All sorts of measures had been implemented to remedy this, it was a big problem, of course. Where Dad lived now there were huge tax incentives, and that was one of the reasons that he and Unni had moved north. They both worked at a gymnas but actually, for now, only Dad was working because Unni was expecting a child. The last time I saw them, a few weeks ago in the terraced house they had bought in Sørland, which would be waiting for them after they had completed their contract in the north, her belly had been enormous.

That was where I'd gotten the idea to come up here. We had been sitting on the veranda, Dad bare chested, as brown as a nut, with a beer in one hand and a cigarette in the other, me with a crucifix dangling from one ear and wearing sunglasses, when he had asked me what I was going to do in the autumn. His gaze was anywhere else but on me, also when he asked, his voice was tired and apathetic, a touch slurred from all the beers he had drunk since I arrived, and so I answered in a sort of lackadaisical way, although it hurt me. I shrugged and said I definitely wasn't going to study or do military service. Work somewhere, I said. In a hospital or something.

He straightened up and stubbed out his cigarette in the large ashtray on the table between us. The air was heavy with pollen, everywhere there was the buzz of bees and wasps in the air. Why don't you do some teaching, then? he said, and slumped back in the chair, perhaps twenty kilos heavier now than the last time I had seen him. You can get a job in Northern Norway any day of the week, you know. As long as you've been to gymnas they'll welcome you with open arms. Maybe, I said. I'll think about it. You should, he said. If you want another beer, you know where the crate is. OK, why not, I said, and went into the living room, which was pitch black after the bright light outside, and into the kitchen, where Unni was reading the paper. She smiled at me. She was wearing khaki shorts and a baggy gray top. I'm going to have another beer, I said. Why not, she said. It's your summer holiday after all. True, I said. Is there an opener anywhere? Yes, there's one on the table over there, she said. Are you hungry? Not particularly, I said. It's so hot, isn't it. But you're going to stay the night, aren't you? she asked. Yes, I said. So we can eat later, she said. I leaned back and took a long swig. I should be doing some work in the garden, she said. But it's simply too hot. Yes, I said. And my stomach's beginning to get in the way. Yes, I said. I can see. Don't you want to go for a swim in the lake? Sounds like there are lots of people down there today. I shook my head. She smiled, I smiled, and then I went back out to Dad. You got yourself one, I see, he said. Yes, I said, and sat down again. In the old days he would have been working in the garden now. And if not he would have been observing everything going on around him, even if it was only a car stopping and a young man leaning over to a window that was being wound down. But all that had gone. In his eyes was only indifference, apathy.

However, the situation was not so black and white because when I observed him, and his eye caught mine, I could sense *he* was still there, the hardness, the coldness I had grown up with and still feared.

He swayed forward and put the empty bottle on the floor, took another and flipped the top off with the opener on his key ring. He always fetched three or four bottles at once so that he wouldn't have to keep running into the kitchen, as he put it. Lifted it to his lips, glugged down a few mouthfuls. Mm, he said. Sun's nice. Yes, I said. I've got a tan anyway! he said. Yes, I said. Me too. Know what? he said, blowing out his cheeks. We've bought ourselves a solarium up north, you know. Have to in all that darkness. Yes, I said. I saw it when I was up there. Yes, you may have, he said. Took another long swig, put the empty bottle down by the previous one, rolled a cigarette, lit it, opened another bottle. When do you want dinner? he asked. Makes no difference, I said. You two decide. Yeah, I don't get hungry in this weather, he said, snatching the section of the newspaper that lay on the table. I rested my arm on the balustrade and looked down. The grass beneath the veranda was scorched, more yellow and brown than green. The gray road was deserted. This side of it was a dusty gravel area, beyond it some trees, behind them the walls and roofs of houses. They knew no one here, neither in the immediate vicinity nor in town. A small propeller plane flew past high in the blue sky. From the living room I heard Unni's heavy footsteps on the floor. Another head-on collision on the E18, Dad said. A car and an eighteen-wheeler. Oh? I said. Almost all these accidents are disguised suicides, he said. They drive straight into a truck or into a mountainside. No one can possibly know whether it was intentional or not. So they're spared the shame. Do you really believe that? I said. Indeed I do, he said. And it's effective too. A little swing to the side and seconds later they're dead. He lifted the paper to show me. Not much chance of surviving that, is there, he said. The photo showed a car that had been completely crushed. No, I said, and got up, went downstairs and into the toilet. Sat down on the seat. I was slightly drunk. Got up again and splashed some cold water over my face. Flushed the toilet in case anyone noticed such details. When I reappeared on the veranda he had discarded the newspaper and was sitting with his elbow over the balustrade, and I remembered he used to sit like that when he was driving the car in the summer, with his elbow sticking out of the open window. How old was he actually? I wondered and counted. Forty-three this May. Then I thought about his birthdays, how we had always bought him the same green Mennen aftershave and how I had always wondered what he did with it as he had a beard. I smiled. He rose to his feet unsteadily, paused for a second to find his balance. Then he walked into the living room, taking his usual long strides and hitching his shorts up from behind.

The idea he had sown, to work as a teacher in Northern Norway, had grown and grown afterward. In fact, there were only advantages: 1) I would be far away, far from everyone and everything I knew, and totally free. 2) I would be earning my own money doing a respectable job. 3) I would be able to write.

And now here I was, I thought, looking down at the book in front of me again. At the end of the little vestibule just outside the staff room, where our two toilets were, Torill breezed into sight. She smiled but said nothing, bent forward and took out a thin file from her shelf.

"Great being a teacher!" I said.

"Give it time . . . !" she said, flashing me a smile, and was off again. Outside, Nils Erik was crossing the playground with my pupils around him.

Five years ago I had been the same age as them. And in five years I would be the same age as him.

Oh, by then I would have made my debut. By then I would be living in a city somewhere, writing and drinking and living the life. I would have a beautiful lissom girlfriend with dark eyes and big breasts.

I got up and went into the staff room, picked up the coffee Thermos, and shook it. It was empty, I filled the pot with water, poured it into the machine, popped a filter paper into the funnel, measured five spoonfuls, and started the whole shebang, lots of spluttering and gurgling, the slow rise of black liquid in the pot, and the bright red eye.

"All going well so far?" a voice worryingly close to me said. I turned. It was Richard, he was staring at me with those intense eyes of his and a broad smile. What was this? Could he move through the school without making a sound?

"Yes, I believe so," I said. "It's exciting."

"It is," he said. "Being a teacher is a very special, a fine profession. And, not least, a responsible one."

Why did he say that? Did he feel I needed to hear it, that it was a great responsibility, and if so, why? Did I give off an aura of irresponsibility perhaps?

"Mm," I said. "My father's a teacher actually. A bit farther north."

"You don't say!" Richard said. "Is he from Nordland?"

"No. It was the tax incentives that brought him up here."

Richard laughed.

"Would you like a cup?" I said. "It'll be ready any second."

"Pour it in the Thermos, will you, and I'll have some later."

He stole away as soundlessly as he had come. I didn't know which was worse, *pour it in the Thermos* or *will you*. It was patronizing whichever way you looked at it. Because I was only eighteen didn't mean he could treat me like a schoolboy! I was an employee here, no different from him.

Just afterward the bell rang and the teachers came in one by one, some silent, others with chirpy one-liners for everyone. I had put the Thermos on the table and was standing by the window with a full cup in my hand. The pupils were already running around outside. I tried to put names to the faces, but the only one I could remember was Kai Roald, the boy in the seventh grade, perhaps because I had sympathized with him, the reluctance I had sensed in his body occasionally countermanded by an interested, perhaps even an enthusiastic, glint in his eyes. And then Liv, the stunner in the ninth grade, of course. She was standing up against the wall, her hands in her back pockets, wearing a beige anorak, blue jeans, and worn gray sneakers, chewing gum and stroking away some strands of hair that the wind had blown into her face. And Stian, over there, standing legs apart, hands in his pockets, chatting to his beanpole of a friend.

I turned back to the room. Nils Erik smiled at me.

"Where do you live?" he said.

"Down the hill from here," I said. "A basement flat."

"Under me," Torill said.

"Where did you end up?" I said.

"At the top of the village. Also a basement flat."

"Yes, under me!" Sture said.

"So that's how they've organized it," I said. "The trained teachers get the flats with the view and everything while the temps get the cellars?"

"You may as well learn that right from the start," Sture said. "All privileges have to be earned. I slaved away for three years at a teacher-training college. There has to be some sort of payback."

He laughed.

"Shall we carry your bags for you too, then?" I said.

"No, that's too much responsibility for the likes of you. But every Saturday morning you're expected to come and clean for us," he said with a wink.

"I've heard there's a party in Hellevika this weekend," I said. "Anyone here going?"

"You've settled in fast, it looks like," Nils Erik said.

"Who told you about it?" Hege said.

"Heard it through the grapevine," I said. "I was wondering whether to go or not. But it's not much fun going alone."

"You're never alone at a party up here," Sture said. "This is Northern Norway."

"Are you going?" I said.

He shook his head.

"I've got a family to take care of," he said. "But I'll give you some tips. If you want." He laughed.

"I was thinking of going," Jane said.

"Me too," Vibeke said.

"What about you?" I said, looking at Nils Erik.

He shrugged. "Maybe. Is it on Friday or Saturday?"

"Friday, I think," I said.

"Maybe not such a bad idea," he said.

The bell rang.

"We can talk about it later," he said, and got up.

"OK," I said, put my cup down on the counter, grabbed my books from my workstation, went to the classroom, sat on the teacher's desk, and waited for the pupils to arrive.

When I walked down to my flat after school, my boxes were waiting on the porch. They contained everything I owned, which wasn't much: a box of records, another with an old stereo in it, one full of kitchen utensils, and one with the odds and ends that had accumulated in my old room, plus some of Mom's books. It still felt as though I had been given a huge present as I carried them into the sitting room. I assembled the stereo, stacked the records against the wall, flicked through them, selected *My Life in the Bush of Ghosts* by Brian Eno and David Byrne, one of my all-time favorites, and with it resounding through the room I started to organize the other items. Everything I had brought with me from home when we moved – pans, plates, cups, and glasses – I'd had around me ever since I was little and we lived in Tybakken. Brown plates, green glasses, a large pot with only one handle, blackened underneath and some way up the sides. I'd had the photo of John Lennon in my room all the time I was at gymnas and proceeded to hang it on the wall behind the typewriter. I'd had the enormous poster of Liverpool FC, the 1979/80 season, since I was eleven, and it was now given a position on the wall behind the sofa. It was perhaps their best team ever: Kenny Dalglish, Ray Clemence, Alan Hansen, Emlyn Hughes, Graeme Souness, and John Toshack. I'd grown tired of the Paul McCartney poster, so I put it in the bedroom cupboard, rolled up. When everything was in shape, I flicked through the records again imagining I was someone else, someone who had never seen them before, and wondered what they would have made of the collection, or rather of the person who owned this collection, in other words me. There were more than 150 LPs, most from the past two years, when I had been reviewing records for the local paper and spent almost all the money I had on new ones, often the complete back catalog of bands I liked. Every single one of these records embraced an entire little world of its own. All of them expressed quite definite attitudes, sentiments, and moods. But none of the records was an island, there were connections between them which spread outward: Brian Eno, for example, started in Roxy Music, released solo records, produced U2, and worked with Jon Hassell, David Byrne, David Bowie, and Robert Fripp; Robert Fripp played on Bowie's *Scary Monsters*; Bowie produced Lou Reed, who came from Velvet Underground, and Iggy Pop, who came from the Stooges, while David Byrne was in Talking Heads, who on their best record, *Remain in Light*, used the guitarist Adrian Belew, who in turn played on several of Bowie's records and was his favorite live guitarist for years. But the ramifications and connections didn't only exist between the records, they extended right into my own life. The music was linked with almost everything I had done, none of the records came without a memory. Everything that had happened in the past five years rose like steam from a cup when I played a record, not in the form of thoughts or reasoning, but as moods, openings, space. Some general, others specific. If my memories were stacked in a heap on the back of my life's trailer, music was the rope that held them together and kept it, my life, in position.

But this wasn't its most important aspect, which was the music itself. When, for example, I played *Remain in Light*, which I had done regularly since the eighth class and never tired of, and the third track started, "The Great Curve," with its fantastic rolling, multilayered accompaniment, brimful of energy, and the horns joined in, and afterward the voices, it was impossible not to move, impossible, it ignited every part of my body, me, the world's least rhythmic eighteen-year-old, sitting there squirming like a snake, to and fro, and I had to have it louder, I turned it up full blast, and then, already up on my feet, yes, then I had to dance, at that moment, even if I was alone. And, toward the end, on top of all this, like a bloody fighter plane above a tiny dancing village, comes Adrian Belew's overriding guitar, and oh, oh God, I am dancing and happiness fills me to my fingertips and I only wish it could last, that the solo would go on and on, the plane would never land, the sun would never go down, life would never end.

Or *Heaven Up Here* with Echo and the Bunnymen, the diametric opposite of Talking Heads, because here the essence is not rhythm or drive but sounds and moods, this tremendous wailing that springs from them, all longing and beauty and gloom, which swells and subsides in the music, no, which *is* the music. And even though I understand a lot of what he is singing about, even though I have read tons of interviews with him, as is the case with most of the bands whose records I own, this knowledge is obliterated by the music; the music doesn't want to know about it, because in music there is no meaning, there is no explanation, there are no people, only voices, each with its own special distinctive quality, as though this is its essential quality, its essence, unadulterated, no body, no personality, yes, a kind of personality without a person, and on every record there is an infinity of such characteristics, from another world, which you meet whenever you play the music. I never worked out what it was that possessed me when music possessed me, other than that I always wanted it.

Furthermore, it made me someone, of course. Thanks to music I became someone who was at the forefront, someone you had to admire, not as much as you had to admire those who made the music, admittedly, but as a listener I was in the vanguard. Up here in the north probably no one would see that, as hardly anyone in Kristiansand had been aware of it, but there were circles where it was seen and appreciated. And that was where I was heading.

I spent some time arranging my records in such a way that the impression made by each one would be enhanced and perhaps lead to surprising new associations for whoever thumbed through them, then I walked down to the shop and bought some beer and a ready-made frozen meal, pasta carbonara. In addition, I bought a rutabaga, a cauliflower, some apples, some plums, and a bunch of grapes, which I intended to use in the science class with the third and fourth years the following day in a grand illustration of the cosmos, an idea that had occurred to me while skimming through their syllabus the day before.

When I arrived home I put the meal in the microwave and ate it straight from the tray on the kitchen table while drinking a beer and reading *Dagbladet*. Well sated, I lay on my bed for an hour's rest. Images of teachers and pupils and the school interior flickered through my consciousness for a long time before at last I was gone. An hour and a half later I was roused by someone ringing the doorbell. I no longer knew what to expect, all sorts of people rang, so it was with a mixture of sleepiness and nervousness that I hurried to the door.

Three of the girls in my class stood outside. One, Andrea, smiled brazenly and asked if they could come in; the second, Vivian, giggled and blushed; the third, Live, stared shamelessly at me from behind her large, thick glasses.

"Of course," I said. "Come in, all of you!"

They did what other visitors had done, looked around as they stepped into the sitting room. Huddling close to each other, they pushed and shoved and giggled and blushed.

"Come on, take a seat!" I said, nodding in the direction of the sofa.

They did as bidden.

"Well?" I said. "What brings you here?"

"We wanted to see how you were. We were bored," Andrea said.

Was she some kind of leader? She hadn't exactly given that impression at school.

"There's nothing to do here," Vivian said.

"Nothing," Live said.

"No, doesn't seem like there's much," I said. "But I'm afraid there's not a lot going on here either."

"No, it's a hole," Andrea said.

"My flat is a hole?" I said.

She flushed to the roots.

"No, silly. The village!" she said.

"I'm going to move away the second I finish the ninth grade," Vivian said.

"Me too," Live said.

"You always copy what I do," Vivian said.

"Yeah? So?"

"Yeah? So?" Vivian said in a perfect imitation. It even included Live's little tic: two wrinkles of the nose under her glasses, in rapid succession.

"Ooohh!" Live said.

"You can't have a monopoly on leaving the village when you're sixteen," I said, looking at Vivian, who smiled and lowered her eyes.

"You speak so *weirdly*, Karl Ove," Andrea said. "What does *monopoly* mean?"

The use of my name caught me off guard, so much so that, while looking at Andrea, since she was the one who was talking, I reddened and bowed my head.

"Someone who is the only person to do something," I said, looking up.

"Oh, yeees," she said, pretending to keel over with boredom. The other two girls laughed. I smiled.

"I can see that you kids have a lot to learn," I said. "You're lucky that I came up here."

"Not me," Andrea said. "I know all I need to know."

"Except for how to drive a car," Vivian said.

"I can drive a car!" Andrea said.

"Yeah, but you're not *allowed* to drive. That's what I meant."

There was a pause. I smiled at them, obviously failing to conceal a patronizing air because Andrea narrowed her eyes and said: "We're thirteen years old, by the way. We're not little kids, if that was what you were thinking."

I laughed.

"Why should I think that? You're all in the seventh grade, I know that. I can even remember how it felt."

"How what felt?"

"Starting at a new school. It's your first day at the *ungdomsskole* today."

"And don't we know it," Vivian said. "It was even more boring than the sixth grade, I think."

The doorbell rang. The three girls exchanged glances. I got up to open the door.

It was Nils Erik.

"Hello there," he said. "Are you going to offer an old colleague a cup of coffee?"

"Wouldn't you rather have a beer?"

He raised his eyebrows and put on a thoughtful, or perhaps it was a skeptical, look.

"No thanks. I'm going for a drive afterward. Better safe than sorry."

"Anyway, come in," I said.

The three girls stared at him as he stopped in the middle of the sitting room.

"So this is where you hang out in the evenings," he said.

"Haven't they been to your place yet?" I said.

He shook his head. "But some fourth graders came over this afternoon. While I was frying fish cakes."

"We're just so bored," Live said.

The two others sent her an angry glare. Then they got up.

"Well," said Andrea. "We'd better be going."

"Bye," I said. "And feel free to come by another day!"

"Bye!" Vivian said from the hall, before the door was slammed shut.

Nils Erik smiled. Shortly afterward we saw them trudging down the hill toward the shop.

"Poor kids," I said. "They must be pretty desperate if all they have to do in their free time is visit teachers."

"Perhaps to them you're exciting?" Nils Erik said.

"And you're not, I guess?" I said.

"No, I'm not," he snorted. "I was thinking of going for a drive, Karl Ove. Feel like coming?"

"Where to?"

He shrugged.

"Other side of the fjord maybe? Or Hellevika?"

"I wouldn't mind going to Hellevika," I said. "After all, we can see the other side of the fjord from here."

It transpired that Nils Erik was the outdoor type. He had applied for a job up here because of the natural beauty, he said, he had brought a tent and a sleeping bag with him intending to go on hikes every weekend. Did I want to join him?

"Not every weekend," he added with a smile as we drove at a snail's pace alongside the fjord in his yellow car.

"It's not really my thing," I said. "Think I'll give that a miss."

He nodded.

"Thought so," he said. "But what makes a sophisticated city slicker like you move up here?"

"I want to write," I said.

"Write?" he said. "What? Fill out forms? Job applications? Quick reminders to yourself? Letters? Limericks for radio shows? Letters to the editor?"

"I'm working on a collection of short stories," I said.

"Short stories!" he said. "The Formula One of literature!"

"Is that what they call them?" I said.

"No," he said with a laugh. "Not really. I think that's what they call *poems*. The Stunt Poets, you know. One of them said something like that."

I didn't know but said nothing.

"But you can still come with me on walks, can't you? A couple of weekends anyway. There's a fantastic nature reserve only an hour away from here."

"I don't think so. If anything's going to come of my writing I have to work."

"But the nature, man! God's wondrous creation! All the colors! All the plants! That's what you have to write about!"

I laughed in derision.

"I don't believe in nature," I said. "It's a cliché."

"What do you write about then?"

I shrugged. "I've just started. But you can read it if you want."

"Love to!"

"I'll bring it in with me tomorrow."

We returned to the village around eight in the evening. It was as light as day. The sky above the sea was so magnificent that I stood by the porch staring for several minutes before going in. It was empty, there was nothing there, yet it seemed gentle and friendly, as if it wished those who lived beneath it well. Perhaps because the mountains for their part were so hard and barren?

I had some supper, lit a cigarette, and drank tea as I went through the exercise my pupils had done.

My name's Vivian n I'm thirteen years old. I live in a village called Håfjord. I'm happy here. I have a sis called Liv. Dad's a fisherman n mam's a housewife. My best freind is Andrea. We do a lotta things together. School is boring. Sometimes we work at the fish factory. We cut the tungs off cod. With the money I'm gonna buy a stereo.

So Vivian and Liv were sisters!

For some reason this gave me a lift. There was also something about the awkwardness she showed that touched me. Or perhaps it was her openness?

I decided not to correct the words. That would be far too demoralizing, so instead I wrote a little comment in red underneath: *"Well done, Vivian! But remember it's 'and' not 'n,' 'a lot of' not 'lotta,' and 'going to' not 'gonna.'"*

Then I leafed through the next exercise book.

My name is Andrea. I'm a thirteen-year-old girl and I live on the far side of an island in northern norway. I have a brother who is ten and a sister who is five. Dad goes fishing and Mom is at home with Camilla. I like listening to music and watching movies. My favorite is Champ. *And I like hanging around the village with my friends Vivian and Hildegunn and Live. It's a little boring here, but it will be better when we're old enough to go to partys!*

I had thought of Andrea and Vivian as two of a kind – I had barely been able to tell them apart on the two occasions I had seen them – but from their answers I could see there was quite a difference, or was it just that one of them was more used to expressing herself in writing?

I wrote a similar comment in Andrea's book, read the three last ones, which all fell somewhere between the first two, made a comment in each, slipped the pile into my bag, put on "My Bag" by Lloyd Cole, and gazed across the village as the music made the hairs on my arms stand on end. Slowly I began to move to the beat, a shoulder here, a foot there at first, then, after switching off the light so that no one below could see me, I danced away with my eyes closed, and sang from the bottom of my heart.

That night I came in my sleep. A wave of pleasure washed through me, carried me up toward the surface, where I had no desire to go, and I didn't, because just before I reached consciousness and the vague notion of who I was, how happy I was, became a reality, I sank back down into dark, heavy slumber, where I stayed until the alarm clock rang and I opened my eyes to a room full of light and to underpants that were sticky with semen.

At first I had feelings of guilt. God knows what I had been dreaming about. Then, when I remembered where I was and what I was doing, the pressure in the pit of my stomach returned. I got up and went into the bathroom, telling myself there was nothing to be nervous about, the class was small, the pupils children, but it didn't help, it felt as if I had to walk out onto a stage without any lines to deliver. I tried to recapture the wonderful mood I had been in previously, when I had been enjoying marking the presentations and the new sensation the role of teacher gave me, seeing pupils, planning what could be done to help them, but as I stood there, surrounded by steam, drying myself, all of that was gone, for I was not a teacher, I wasn't even an adult, I was just a ridiculous teenager who knew nothing about anything.

"Oh, *hell!*" I shouted. Wiped the condensation from the mirror with the towel and studied my face in the few seconds it took before the glass was covered with moisture again.

I looked damned good, actually.

That was something after all.

I'd had the long hair at the back of my neck cut just before I left. Now my hair stood in a thick, maybe three-centimeter-high carpet across my skull, layered down to my temples and neck. From my left ear hung a cross.

I smiled.

My teeth were white and even. There was a glint in my eyes that I liked to see, until the incredible indignity of the situation, a person smiling and what was tantamount to winking at himself in the mirror made my stomach constrict again.

For Christ's sake.

I put on my *Dream of the Blue Turtles* T-shirt, my black Levi's, a pair of white tube socks, stood in front of the mirror putting on alternately the thin green military jacket and the blue denim jacket, finally choosing the former, tried on the beret, it didn't go, and two minutes later walked bareheaded up to the school with a white Ali coffee bag full of books and materials hanging from my hand.

The third and fourth graders, who had been put together in one class for all their lessons, numbered twelve pupils: five girls and seven boys. It seemed like more, they were always roaming around, running and shouting, and would never sit still. Once they had finally sat down on their chairs, there were legs twisting and turning here, arms twisting and turning there, their minds, like agitated dogs, were forever on the move.

They hadn't had me before, they had only heard about me and seen me from a distance, so when I loomed up in their part of the school all eyes were fixed on me.

I smiled and put my bag down on the teacher's desk.

"What have you got in there?" one of them said. "What's in your bag?"

I looked at him. White puppy-dog skin, brown eyes, extremely short hair.

"What's your name?" I said.

"Reidar," he said.

"Mine's Karl Ove," I said. "And there's one thing you may as well learn right from the start. You have to put up your hand before you say anything."

Reidar put up his hand.

A smart-ass.

"Yes?" I said.

"What have you got in your bag, Karl Ove?"

"It's a secret," I said. "But you'll soon find out. First of all, though, I have to know what your names are."

The boy behind Reidar, a little squirt with fair hair and hard – for his age – pale-blue eyes put up his hand.

"What's your name?" I said.

"Stig," he said. "Are you strict?"

"Strict? No!" I said.

"My mom says you're too young to be a teacher!" he said, looking around for a reaction.

They laughed, all of them.

"I'm older than you anyway!" I said. "So I think everything will be fine."

"Why do you have a cross in your ear?" Reidar said. "Are you a Christian?"

"What did I just say about raising your hand?"

"Whoops!" He laughed and raised his hand.

"No, I'm not a Christian," I said. "I'm an atheist."

"What's that?" Reidar said.

"Your hand? Where is it?"

"Oh."

"An atheist is someone who doesn't believe in God," I said. "But now you have to tell me your names. Let's start at the end there."

One after one they called out their names.

Vibeke
Kenneth
Susanne
Stig
Reidar
Lovisa
Melanie
Steve
Endre
Stein-Inge
Helene
Jo

I connected with some of them at once and would remember them easily from now on – the girl who was so unbelievably pretty and doll-like in everything from her facial features to her body and her dress, the boy with the pudgy face, the little squirt who seemed angry, the boy with the big head and the warm eyes, the loudmouth, the blond-haired girl with pigtails who gave the impression of being so rational and sensible – others were more nebulous and revealed too little for me to get a handle on them.

"So you're the third and fourth graders!" I said. "What's the name of the place where you live?"

"Håfjord, isn't it!" Reidar said.

I said nothing, just looked at them. Then two or three of them realized what I was getting at and raised their hands. I nominated the little doll-like creature.

"Lovisa?" I said.

"Håfjord," she said.

"What's the name of the county Håfjord is in?"

"Troms."

"And the country?"

Now everyone had a hand in the air. I chose the fatty.

"Norway," he said.

"And the continent?"

"Europe," he said.

"Good!" I said, and he smiled.

"But what's the name of the planet we're on? Does anyone know? Yes, Reidar?"

"The world?"

"Yes, it is. But is there another name?"

I turned and wrote the whole address on the board: HÅFJORD, TROMS, NORWAY, EUROPE, EARTH. Turned back to them.

"And where is the earth?"

"In the cosmos," said Stein-Inge.

"Yes," I said. "It's in the solar system, in a galaxy called . . . ?"

On the board I wrote, THE MILKY WAY.

"Have you heard about that?"

"Yes!" several of them shouted.

"For us this galaxy is enormous. But in comparison with the rest of the cosmos it's teeny-weeny."

I observed them.

"What do you think is outside the cosmos then?"

They stared at me with mouths agape.

"Have you ever thought about that? Endre?"

Endre shook his head.

"Is there anything outside?"

"Well, no one knows," I said. "But there can't just be nothing. There has to be something, don't you think?"

"What does it say in the textbooks?" Reidar asked.

"It doesn't say anything," I answered. "As I said, no one knows."

"No one?"

"No."

"Why should we learn that then?" he said.

I smiled.

"You need to learn about where we live. And that is of course the universe.

Well, if we take a broader view of it, the cosmos. What you see above us every night. Or what you don't see because you're little kids and have gone to bed."

"He-ey, we're not little kids!"

"Just joking," I said. "But the stars you can see when it's dark. And the moon and the planets. You have to learn about them."

I turned and wrote THE UNIVERSE on the board.

"OK," I said. "Can anyone in the class name any of the planets in our solar system?"

"The earth!" Reidar said.

Scattered laughter.

"Any more?"

"Pluto!"

"Mars!"

"Good!" I said. When no more suggestions were forthcoming, I drew the whole solar system on the board.

SUN
MERCURY
VENUS
EARTH
MARS
JUPITER
SATURN
URANUS
NEPTUNE
PLUTO

"Here on the board it looks as if they're right next to each other. But there's an incredible distance between the planets. It would take many, many years to travel to Jupiter, for example. I'd like to give you an idea of the distances. So put on your coats and we'll go out onto the soccer field."

"Are we going out? During the lesson?"

"Yes, get moving. Put your coats on and we'll be going."

They jumped up from their seats and converged on the line of coat hooks. I stood waiting by the door with the bag hanging from my hand.

They flocked closely around me as we walked across the field. I felt a bit like a shepherd, so different from these small, eager creatures.

"Good, we'll stop here!" I said, and took a ball from the bag. Placed it on the ground. "This is the sun, OK?"

They looked at me somewhat skeptically.

"Come on. Now let's walk a bit farther!"

We walked for another twenty meters or so before I stopped and placed a plum on the ground.

"This is Mercury, the planet that is closest to the sun. Can you see the sun over there?"

Everyone stared over at the ball, which cast a light shadow over the shale, and nodded.

Next I placed two apples, two oranges, the rutabaga, the cauliflower, and, last of all, right up by the door of the community center, the grape, which was supposed to represent Pluto.

"Do you all understand now how far it is between the planets?" I said. "The tiny sun so far away, and Mercury, which is like a plum, we can't even see it from here. And all this," I said, looking at them as they stared blankly across the soccer field, "is just a teeny, weeny, weeny, weeny bit of the cosmos! Teeny tiny! Isn't it funny that the earth we live on is millions of miles away from the other planets?"

Some of them were thinking so hard you could see the smoke. Others were gazing across the village and the fjord.

"Let's go back in now," I said. "Come on. Run, run, run!"

In the staff room I took out a copy of my short story, stapled the pages together, and passed it to Nils Erik, who was sitting on the sofa reading *Troms Folkeblad*.

"Here's the short story I was telling you about," I said.

"Interesting!" he said.

"When do you think you'll have read it? By tonight?"

"Urgent, is it?" He looked at me and smiled. "I was planning to go to Finnsnes this afternoon actually. Would you like to come, by the way?"

"I'd love to. Good idea."

"Then I can read your short story by tomorrow, and we can have a little seminar afterward?"

Seminar, which to me meant universities and academia, studies, girls, and parties.

"Great," I said, and went to get a cup of coffee.

"What actually were you doing outside with them?" Nils Erik said to my back.

"Nothing special," I said, "I was just trying to help them visualize the cosmos."

When I entered the classroom for the next lesson, three of the girls were standing in a huddle by the window whispering excitedly. My entrance hadn't made the slightest impression on them.

"You can't stand there all day chitchatting!" I said. "The lesson has started! Have you forgotten? You're pupils. You have to obey the rules and do what the teachers tell you!"

They spun round. When they saw that I was smiling, they just continued.

"Hello there!" I said. "Come and sit down!"

Then, with a dilatoriness I would later that day consider exquisite because their movements became so strikingly sophisticated and their ungainliness suddenly transformed into feminine poise, they went to their seats.

"I've read your presentations now," I said, handing out their books. "They were very good. But there are a couple of things we can clear up right away since they apply to all of you."

They opened their books to see what I had written.

"Don't we get grades?" Hildegunn said.

"Not for such a small exercise," I said. "I gave you the assignment mostly so that I could get an impression of you."

Andrea and Vivian compared their comments.

"You've written almost the same thing for both of us!" Vivian said. "Are you that lazy?"

"Lazy?" I said with a smile. "You'll get grades which will show you all where you stand soon enough. I'm not sure that's much to look forward to."

Behind me, the door opened. I turned. It was Richard. He went over and sat down at a table by the wall while motioning me to carry on.

What was this? Was he going to *observe* me?

"The first thing we have to get to talk about is your dialect," I said. "You can't write like you speak. That's *no* good at all. You have to write *jeg*, not *æ*. *Er*, not *e*. *Hvordan* rather than *koss*."

"But that's what we *say*!" Vivian said, and twisted around in her chair to glance at Richard, who sat with his arms crossed and face impassive. "Why do we have to write *jeg* when we say *æ*, huh?"

"And Harrison said we could write like that last year," Hildegunn said.

"He said it was better to write *something* than to write correctly," Live said.

"Last year you were at a school for children," I said. "This year you're in a higher school. Where your language has to be standardized, as it's known. This is how it is up and down the country. We can talk as we like, but when we write, it has to be standard Norwegian. There is nothing to discuss. Unless you want your essays covered in red ink and low grades, you *have* to do this."

"Oh!" Andrea said, looking first at me, then Richard. The others giggled.

I asked them to get out their books and then, when they had all turned to the same page, I asked Hildegunn to start reading. Richard got up, nodded briefly to me, and left the room.

During the break I went to his office and knocked on the door.

He looked up from his desk as I walked in.

"Hi, Karl Ove," he said.

"Hi," I said. "I was just wondering why you came into my lesson."

The gaze he sent me was partly probing, partly curious. Then he smiled and chewed his lower lip, this was a quirk of his, I had realized, his bearded chin jutted forward and made him resemble a goat.

"I just wanted to see how things were going in the class," he said. "I will be doing that now and then. There are quite a few of you who have no training. I need to get an idea of how you are managing. Teaching is not easy, you know."

"I promise to tell you if I have any problems," I said. "You can trust me."

He laughed.

"I know that. That's not the issue. Go and have yourself a break now!"

He looked down at the papers in front of him. That was a rank-pulling number, and for a few seconds I refused to yield to it; however, there was nothing else I could do, I had nothing else to say, and there was nothing unreasonable about what he'd said, so finally I turned and went into the staff room.

There were three letters in my PO box when I went to the post office after school. One from Bassen, who had started university in Stavanger, one from Lars, who had moved in with his girlfriend in Kristiansand, and one from Eirik, who was now studying at the Institute of Technology in Trondheim.

Bassen told me about an incident that had taken place just before he moved. He had gone home with a girl, or rather a woman, because she was twenty-five, and while they were on the job, as he put it, she had suddenly had some kind of fit. He had been scared out of his wits. It was as though she was being convulsed by electric shocks, he wrote, her body was quivering and shaking, he thought it was epilepsy, he withdrew, and stood up.

I was terrified, Karl Ove! I didn't know whether to call for an ambulance or what. What if she died! In fact that's what I thought she was going to do. But then she opened her eyes and pulled me back down and asked me what I was doing. Keep going! she shouted. Can you imagine? She'd just been having an orgasm! That's mature women for you!

Walking along, I laughed as I read his letter, but I also felt a stab of something else, because I had never slept with a girl, I'd never had sex, in other words I was a virgin, and was not only ashamed that for two years I had been lying about the amount of sexual experience I'd had, which Bassen and several others were presumably taken in by, but I was also desperate for it, to sleep with a girl, any girl actually, and to experience what Bassen and my other friends experienced on such a regular basis. Whenever I heard about their adventures, it was as though equal portions of enervation and desire spread through me, equal portions of powerlessness and power, for the longer I went without sleeping with a girl, the more afraid of it I became. I could talk to others about almost any other problem I had, to ease my mind, but I couldn't reveal this, not to anyone, not ever, not under any circumstances, and whenever I thought about it, which was not seldom, it must have been several times an hour, I was overcome by a kind of black gloom, a gloom of hopelessness, sometimes only fleetingly, like a cloud drifting past the sun, sometimes for longer periods, and whatever form the hopelessness took I couldn't surmount it, there was so much doubt and torment associated with it. Could I? *Could I?* If, against all the odds, I succeeded in maneuvering myself into a suitable situation and was in a room alone with a naked girl, would I be able to make love to her? Would I be able to go through with it?

All the secrecy and pretense surrounding this didn't make it any easier for me.

"Do you know what it says on the teat of condoms?" Trond once said, in a break that spring, as he fixed me with his eye. We were standing in a group on the grass outside the school and jabbering away.

It was me he singled out.

Why? Did he suspect that I was lying about the girls, about the sex I'd had?

I blushed.

What should I say? No, and give myself away? Or yes, and then invite the natural follow-up question, what then?

"No, what does it say?" I said.

"Have you got *such* a little prick?" he said.

They laughed.

I laughed too, relieved.

But Espen was staring at me, wasn't he? Kind of knowingly, and semi-reveling in it as a result?

Two days later he drove me home at night. We had been at Gisle's together.

"How many have you actually done it with, Karl Ove?" he said as we drove up the gentle slope by Krageboen, flanked on both sides of the road by crumbling old houses.

"Why?" I said.

"I was just wondering," he said, sending me a glance before returning his eyes to the road ahead. The smile playing on his lips was furtive.

I frowned and pretended to concentrate.

"Um," I said. "Six. No, hang on, *five*."

"Who were they?"

"Is this the Inquisition or what?"

"Noo. But surely you can tell me that much."

"Cecilie, you know, the girl I went out with from Arendal," I said.

Outside, the shop where I had stolen so many pieces of candy drifted past. It had closed down a long time ago. Espen signaled.

"And?" he said.

"And Marianne," I said.

"Did you *fuck* Marianne?" he said. "I didn't know that. Why didn't you say?"

I shrugged. "You've got to keep some things private."

"You devil! Of all the people I know, you're the one I know least about. But that's just two."

The big man with the enormous gut and the ever-open mouth stood by the fence watching us as we went past.

"Quite a family, they are," I said.

"Now, don't you wriggle out of it," Espen said. "There are three left. I'll list mine afterward, if you're interested."

"OK. There was an Icelandic girl working at an ice-cream stall next to mine in the summer. When I was selling cassettes on the street in Arendal. I went back to her place one night."

"Icelandic!" Espen said. "Sounds great."

"Yes, it was as well," I said. "And then there were two one-night stands in town. I don't even know their names."

We drove down the last hill. The deciduous trees were as compact as a wall along the river. At the bottom the countryside opened out and I looked across the field to the small soccer field, where three tiny figures were shooting at a fourth in goal.

"And yours?" I said.

"There's no time for that now. We're here."

"Come on," I said.

He laughed and stopped the car.

"See you tomorrow!" he said.

"You bastard," I said, opened the door, and walked up to the house. As I listened to the sound of his car hammering down the hill and soon disappearing, I reflected that I had given him too much information, it would have been better if I had just said it was none of his business. That is what he would have said.

How come he could do it and I couldn't?

He didn't admire girls as much as I did, that was one thing. Not that he liked them any less than me, far from it, but perhaps he didn't consider them *better* than him, put them on such a high pedestal that you couldn't chat with them or do normal things with them; for him they were on the same level or perhaps he was even higher than them, for if there was one thing he had, it was self-confidence. That meant he didn't care, and when they saw that, he was someone they wanted to conquer. I looked upon them as completely unapproachable creatures, indeed, as angels of a sort, I loved everything about them, from the veins in the skin over their wrists to the curves of their ears, and if I saw a breast under a T-shirt or a naked thigh under a summer dress, it was as though everything in my insides was let loose, as though everything began to swirl around and the immense desire that then arose was as light as light itself, as light as air, and in it there was a notion that everything was possible, not only here but everywhere and not only now but forever. At the same time as all this arose inside me, a consciousness shot up from below, like a waterspout, it was heavy and dark, there was abandon, resignation, impotence, the world closing in on me. There was the awkwardness, the silence, the scared eyes. There were the flushed cheeks and the great unease.

But there were other reasons too. There was something I couldn't do and something I didn't understand. There were secrets and there was darkness, there were shady dealings and there was laughter that jeered at everything. Oh, I sensed it, but I knew nothing about it. Nothing.

I stuffed Bassen's letter in my pocket and hurried up the hill. Nils Erik was supposed to be picking me up in half an hour and before that I had to have something to eat.

A couple of hours later we were driving along the main street of Finnsnes. Coming here from Oslo and Tromsø, I had regarded Finnsnes as a crummy little hole, but now, only five days later, coming from Håfjord it seemed like a large, complex, almost sophisticated place, rich with possibilities.

Nils Erik parked in the supermarket parking lot and then we walked off to find a liquor shop. I bought a bottle of Koskenkorva vodka for the party, four bottles of white wine, and half a bottle of whiskey to take home with me; Nils Erik bought three bottles of red wine, which came as no surprise, he was the red-wine type, not the beer and spirits type. After we had stowed the bottles in the trunk, I took him along to an electrical goods shop that also sold stereos. Mine wasn't good enough, I had thought that for quite a while, and now that I had a steady job I decided to do something about it.

In the shop they had only racks, they weren't the best, but I could buy a decent stereo later, I figured, and looked around for an assistant.

A man was standing behind the counter with his back to us, opening a large cardboard box with a small paper knife. I walked over.

"I need some help," I said.

He turned to face me.

"Just a moment," he said.

I went back to the wall of stereo racks. Waved to Nils Erik, who was flicking through a crate full of records.

"Which one would you buy?" I said.

"None of them," he said. "Racks are shit."

"Agreed," I said. "But this is probably all they've got. And I only want it for while I'm up here."

He looked at me.

"Are you shitting money? Or is Knausgaard a family of shipowners? You never told me!"

"You can get one on an installment plan. Look, three thousand four ninety-nine kroner for that one. That's only a few hundred a month."

The assistant straightened up and looked around for me. A thin man with a bit of a gut, metal-rimmed glasses, and a comb-over.

I pointed to the Hitachi rack.

"I'd like that one," I said. "I can buy it in installments, can't I?"

"As long as you've got a job," he said.

"I'm working as a teacher in Håfjord," I said.

"Sure," he said. "Then you'll have to fill in a few forms, so if you come over to the counter with me . . ."

While I stood writing he went to the storeroom to get the stereo system.

"Is this such a good idea?" Nils Erik said. "In installments you pay almost double in the end. And the monthly payments are painful. Our salary isn't *that* good, either."

I glared at him. "Are you my mom or what?"

"OK, OK, it's your business," he said, and went back to the records.

"Yes, it is."

At that moment the assistant returned from the storeroom with a large cardboard box in his arms. He handed it to me, I held it while he checked the papers and my ID, and when he was satisfied, I carried it to the car and placed it in the back seat.

The last item on the agenda was the supermarket. Each pushing a shopping cart in front of us, we walked around plucking things that weren't available in the village shop from the shelves. My first target was two packs of cigarettes. At the back of the shop, next to the fruit counter, while Nils Erik was over by the pasta, I put the packets in my jacket, one in each pocket, then went on filling the cart with food as normal. I always stole cigarettes when I shopped in supermarkets, and it was completely foolproof, I had never been caught. Stealing was closely related to freedom for me, about not giving a shit, doing what you wanted, not what you were supposed to do. It was a rebellious, nonconformist act while, in a sense, pushing my personality toward one of the places where I wanted it to be. I stole, I was someone who stole.

It always went well, nevertheless I was nervous as I pushed my trolley toward the little island where the cashier sat. But there was nothing unusual about her expression and there were no men discreetly approaching from any direction, so I placed the items on the conveyor belt one by one with my sweaty hands, paid, packed them into a bag, and walked, quickly but not conspicuously so, out of the shop, then I stopped, lit up, and waited for Nils Erik, who arrived at my side a minute later carrying two bulging plastic bags.

The first kilometers were driven in silence. I was still annoyed with him for his moralizing tone in the shop where I had bought the stereo. I hated it when people interfered with what I was doing, regardless of whether it was my mother, my brother, my teacher, or my best friend: I didn't want to hear it. No one had any business telling me what to do.

He cast intermittent glances at me as he drove. The countryside around us had leveled out. Low trees, heather, moss, brooks, shallow, completely black tracts of water, and in the distance, chains of tall, rugged peaks. He had filled the tank just outside Finnsnes, there was still a smell of gasoline in the car, it made me feel slightly nauseous.

He glanced at me again.

"Could you put some music on? There are some cassettes in the glove compartment."

I opened it and transferred the pile of cassettes to my lap.

Sam Cooke. Otis Redding. James Brown. Prince. Marvin Gaye. UB40. Smokey Robinson. Stevie Wonder. Terence Trent D'Arby.

"So you're a soul man," I said.

"Soul and funk."

I inserted the only cassette I'd heard before: Prince, *Parade*. Leaned back in the seat and gazed up at the mountains, which, at the bottom, were covered with a green tangled carpet of bushes and small trees, farther up with moss and heather, also green.

"By the way, why did you steal the cigarettes?" Nils Erik said. "It's got nothing to do with me. You can do what you like as far as I'm concerned. I'm just curious, that's all."

"You saw?" I said.

He nodded.

"You *do* have the money, after all," he said. "It wasn't as if you took them out of sheer deprivation, was it?"

"No," I said.

"What if you'd been caught? How would that have looked? As a teacher, I mean."

"Was I caught?"

"No."

"No? So then it's purely hypothetical," I said.

"We don't have to talk about it," he said.

"I don't mind talking about it," I said. "Talk away."

He gave a short laugh.

The ensuing silence was long but not unpleasant, the road was straight, the mountains were beautiful, the music was good, Nils Erik an outdoor type I didn't much care for.

But then my attitude changed. It was as though I had gone so far in one direction and now I was beginning to return because there was something unresolved here. Nils Erik, he hadn't done anything to me, didn't wish me any harm, he was curious, that was all, and maybe a bit pushy, and out here, where I didn't know anyone, perhaps that wasn't such a bad thing.

I hummed along to "Sometimes It Snows in April."

"Have you heard Prince's latest?" I said. "*Lovesexy.*"

He shook his head. "But if he comes to Norway or Sweden in the summer, I'll go and see him. His concerts are fantastic these days. I talked to someone who had seen him on the *Sign o' the Times* tour. They said it was the best concert they'd ever seen."

"I'd be up for it too," I said. "But it's good, the new one, that is. Not as good as *Sign o' the Times* but . . . As a matter of fact I reviewed it when it came out for *Fædrelandsvennen* and almost made a huge blunder."

I looked at him.

"I'd read in some English music mag that he was illiterate, and I was going to write that, you know. I was on the point of pitching the whole article that way, that Prince couldn't read, but luckily it struck me as a bit odd and I dropped the idea. Afterward I realized it was probably music that he couldn't read. But I don't know. And it's not good, all the vague information you accumulate, the stuff you carry around with you that's not remotely true. If you say anything, it's a little embarrassing, but if you actually write it and it's in the newspaper the day after, that's worse."

"I thought that was what newspapers were all about," Nils Erik said, smiling, his eyes on the road.

"You can say that again," I said.

Farther ahead lay the road to Håfjord, a thin gray line leading to a small black gap in the mountain.

"By the way, I got a long letter from my girlfriend on Tuesday," I said.

"Oh really?" he said.

"Yes. Well, girlfriend may be stretching it. We were together during the summer. Her name was Line . . ."

"*Was*? Did she die this week?"

"For me, yes. That was the point. She broke up with me. Wrote that I was a nice person blah blah blah, but she'd never been in love with me and it was a good time to end it now because I was moving up here."

"So you're free as a bird," Nils Erik said.

"Exactly," I said. "That's what I was about to say."

A car emerged from the tunnel, it was small and black like a dung beetle, but soon it grew in size, it was going at a considerable speed.

The driver raised a hand as he passed, Nils Erik responded, slowed down, and turned into the last short stretch before the village.

"It's strange, isn't it," I said. "Everyone knows who we are while we don't know anyone."

"It's true," he said. "We've ended up in an incredibly intimidating place."

He twisted one of the levers by the steering wheel for full beam and flicked the other up to activate the windshield wipers. Drops of water splashed on the hood, windshield, and roof. The drone of the engine rebounded off the rock face, it surrounded us like a kind of shell, which vanished the moment we exited the tunnel, and the blue fjord spread out before us.

"Are you a free man then?" I said.

"Oh yes," he said. "I'm very free in fact. I haven't had a girlfriend for several years."

Was he gay?

Oh, no, don't say he was one of them?!

He was in fact a bit odd. And those rosy cheeks . . .

"There's not much of a selection up here," he said. "But nor is there much competition. So I figure they cancel each other out."

He laughed.

Not much of a selection. What was that supposed to mean? There weren't many other gays here?

My insides chilled as I stared across the matte blue surface of the sea.

"Torill is a cheery type," he said.

Torill!

False alarm!

I looked at him again. Even though his eyes were on the road some of his attention was on me.

"But she's old," I said.

"Old? Not at all!" he said. "If I had to guess, I would say twenty-eight. Maybe thirty. It's possible. But, first off, she's not old! And, second off, she's sexy. Yes, *very* sexy."

"Well, that hadn't even crossed my mind," I said.

"I'm not eighteen years old, Karl Ove. I'm twenty-four. So twenty-eight isn't old. Or unattainable." He chuckled. "The fact that she may be unattainable *for me* is quite a different matter."

We drove slowly down the narrow road squeezed under the mountainside. The local motorists drove just as fast here as anywhere else, but not Nils Erik, he was the cautious, sensible type, I had begun to realize.

"And you?" he said. "Have you got your eye on anyone?"

I smiled. "In fact, there was a girl on the bus when I was coming here. She's at the gymnas in Finnsnes. Lives in Hellevika."

"Aha!"

"We'll have to see. Other than that I don't know."

"Vibeke's a friendly girl," he said.

"Do you mean fat?"

"No, but you know . . . she's very nice. A bit chubby maybe, but what does that matter? And Hege, she's . . . well, high maintenance, I bet. But attractive. Isn't she?"

"You're game for anything, aren't you?" I said.

"Women are women, that's what I say."

Then the village lay beneath us. Nils Erik pulled up outside my flat, carried in the shopping bags while I took the big cardboard box containing the stereo, then he said good-bye and drove off to his place. I set up the stereo, put on *Sulk* by the Associates, an utterly insane LP that I listened to stretched out on the sofa. After a while I began to write some letters, kept them brief as I had a lot of them to do, what was important right now was not what I wrote but the short story I enclosed with all of them.

In one of the breaks the next day Sture came over to me.

"Can I have a word with you?" he said, scratching his bald head.

"Of course," I said.

"I'd just like to give you a bit of advice," he said. "About the third and fourth graders. I heard you covered the whole cosmos with them yesterday . . ."

"Yes?" I said.

"They're very small, you know. It might not be a bad idea to start at the other end. Make a map of the school here, for example. And then one of the village. And then one of the island. Do you see what I mean? Start with the known and work outward, to Norway, Europe, and the world. And then you can tackle the cosmos. If you're still here, of course!"

He grinned and winked at me so as to appear more of a friend and less of an authority figure. But this was not advice, this was a rebuke. When I met his eyes, my blood was boiling.

"I'll give that some thought," I said, then turned and went.

I was furious while being embarrassed at the same time because I could see he was right. They were so small, probably they hadn't understood a thing, and what had been exciting for me when I was ten was not necessarily exciting for them.

In the staff room I didn't want to talk to anyone, so I sat down at my workstation and pretended I was reading until the bell rang and I could go out to my pupils.

It was strange, I thought, standing by the desk and waiting for them to saunter in, it was strange that I should feel more at home among the pupils than among the teachers in the staff room.

But where were they?

I walked over to the window. There wasn't a soul in the area between the two buildings. Were they on the soccer field perhaps?

I looked up at the clock. It was already five minutes since the bell had rung. Something must have happened, I thought, and walked down the corridor to the door. Sture came striding along from the other end. He opened the door and went out, I followed and saw him break into a run.

There was a fight. Two of the boys had their arms wrapped around each other, one was thrown to the ground, he got back to his feet. Around them stood a cluster of pupils watching. They were completely silent. Behind them lay the village, behind that the mountains and the sea.

I broke into a run too, mostly for appearance's sake because I knew Sture would break this up and I was glad.

The two boys fighting were Stian and Kai Roald. Stian was stronger, it was him who had thrown Kai Roald to the ground, but Kai Roald wouldn't give in and flew at him again.

Both stopped the moment Sture reached them. He grabbed Stian by the back of his jacket and held him at arm's length while he bawled him out. Stian hung his head like a dog. He wouldn't have done that with me, that was for certain.

I came to a halt in front of them.

Kai Roald was looking at the ground. The knees and tops of his jeans were filthy. His eyes were wet with tears.

"What are you doing?" I said. "Are you fighting?"

"Oh, shut up," he said.

I placed my hand on his shoulder. He wrenched himself away.

"Come on, let's go in," I said, then looked at the others in the class. "And the rest of you! What are you doing out here? You haven't even been fighting!"

Kai Roald peered up at me as if he'd been expecting a punishment but now he could see there wasn't going to be one.

"Come on," I said. "Let's go. Kai Roald, you go to the washroom and clean yourself up. You don't look great."

Sture's class was already by the door.

"Any blood?" he asked me.

"No," I said. "Just snot and dirt."

We talked a bit about what had happened; when Kai Roald came back I told him he could fight as much as he wanted as long as he didn't do it on school premises. On weekends you can fight from the moment you get up until you go to bed, and in the afternoons too, but not at school. Can you manage that? I said. He shook his head. It was Stian who started it, he said. OK, I said. You'll have to settle your differences with him when you get home. But not here. If it happens again, I'll have to punish you, do you understand? And it isn't worth that. Wait a few hours and you can do whatever you like. Now, though, I'm afraid we'll have to start the lesson. You have to learn too, all of you. Especially you, I said. You don't know anything!

The four girls sent me a particularly sulky expression.

"Nothing at all!" I said. "So, get out your books."

"And how much do you fuckin' know?" Hildegunn said.

Vivian and Andrea laughed.

I raised a forefinger.

"No swearing! I don't want to hear that in the classroom."

"But everyone swears in Northern Norway," Vivian said.

"The same rule applies to swearing as fighting," I said. "Swear as much as you like at home. But not here. I'm serious. I mean it. All right. You can carry on with the exercises you started last time. Page thirteen onward. If you need any help, I'm here. At the beginning of the next lesson we'll go through any problems that arise. OK?"

I went to the window, leaned against the frame, and crossed my arms. Heard Nils Erik's voice at the other end of the open-plan block, he had English with the fourth grade. I thought of Stian, saw that smart-alecky smile of his in my mind's eye, and saw the girls in the class, their eyes watching his every movement. They admired him, I was fully aware of that. Perhaps they even dreamed about him?

They probably did.

The thought stung. He was just a little shit.

I went to my desk, glanced at Hege, who had taken her pupils over to the little library corner, where they sat on cushions in a circle around her and listened while she read.

She noticed that I was watching, looked across and smiled. I smiled back, sat down at the desk, thumbed through the textbook to see what I could do in the next lesson.

When I looked up again, my eyes met Andrea's. Blood suffused her cheeks. I smiled. She raised her hand and lowered her gaze. I got to my feet and went over to her.

"What do you need help with?" I said.

"This part," she said, pointing. "Did I do it right?"

I leaned forward and went through what she had written. She sat motionless, following my finger as it moved down the page. A faint fragrance redolent of apples emanated from her. It must be the shampoo she used, I thought, and felt a quiver spread through my chest. Her breathing, the hair that fell over her face, her eyes staring through it. All so close.

"We-ell," I said. "It looks right to me."

"Does it?" she said, looking up at me. When our eyes met, I straightened up.

"Yes, it does," I said. "Stick with it!"

No one was in the staff room when I entered after the lesson. It was only when I had sat down that I noticed Torill – she was in the kitchenette buttering a slice of bread.

"Did you have a free period?" I said.

She nodded and took a bite, holding a finger up while she chewed and swallowed.

"Yes," she said. "But I've been busy preparing for my next lessons!"

"Good," I said, reaching over for the newspaper on the table. As I browsed through it I was aware of her movements. The slice of bread that went up to her mouth and down again as she hustled around.

She leaned forward and opened the fridge door. I looked up. She was wearing a pair of black stretch pants. I examined her thighs so clearly outlined in them, and her bottom. It was broad but not too broad; on the contrary, it was curvaceous and so utterly feminine.

The blood began to throb in my member, and I crossed my legs without shifting my gaze. How wonderful it would be to sleep with her and feel her thighs and bottom against my body. Oh Lord. To penetrate her. Oh Lord God. Oh. Her breasts cupped in my hands! Oh, just her skin! Oh, just the smooth insides of her thighs!

I swallowed and studied the ceiling. It would never work. Even in the highly unlikely event that I ended up in bed with her or someone like her, it would never work. I knew that.

She stood up with a carton of milk in her hand. Opened it and started filling a glass as she shot me a brief glance. When our eyes met she smiled.

She had noticed everything.

I blushed and smiled back, feverishly trying to think of something that might divert her attention from the color in my cheeks and what I had just seen and thought.

She threw back her head and finished the milk in one swig. Wiped the white moustache off with the back of her hand and looked at me again.

"Would you like some coffee, Karl Ove? You look like you could use some!"

What did she mean? Why did I look like I needed coffee?

"No, thanks," I said.

But a no drew attention!

"Well, actually, maybe I will," I added quickly. "Yes, please!"

"Milk?"

I shook my head. She poured out two cups and brought them over, passed me one and sat down beside me with a sigh.

"You sighed," I said.

"Did I?" she said. "It's just late in the day. I slept badly last night."

I blew on the black, impenetrable surface with the small, light brown bubbles at the edge and took a sip.

"Do I make a lot of noise?" I said. "The music and all that, I mean."

She shook her head. "I can hear you're there," she said. "But that doesn't matter."

"Sure?"

"Of course I'm sure."

"OK, but tell me if it's too loud."

"Can you hear anything from our flat?" she said.

"Hardly anything. When you walk across the floor, that's all."

"That's just because Georg is away fishing," she said. "I'm a lot quieter when I'm on my own."

"Is he going to be away for long?"

"No, they're back on Saturday actually."

She smiled and her lips were so soft and red and supple against her hard white teeth.

"Oh," I said, and looked up because the door at the end of the room opened and Tor Einar, then Hege and Nils Erik, came in.

"Here they come, in serried ranks," I said.

"Yes, some of us respect lesson times," Nils Erik said. "We know that every minute is important for the pupils' future lives. So we cannot, I repeat, *cannot* finish three minutes before the bell rings. That would be grossly irresponsible. In fact, I would go so far as to say it would be *unforgivable*."

"Yes, regular temps have a heavy cross to bear," I said. "Why didn't you become a homeroom teacher like me? Then you would have had more control over your time, you know."

"It's my ultimate goal to become a head teacher without studying," Nils Erik said. "It's not very common, and it won't be easy, but that's what I've set my heart on." He rubbed his hands and grimaced in a caricature of greed. "Now for a few decent slices of dry bread with a bit of hard goat's cheese!"

Then in came Vibeke, Jane, and Sture. I got up, thinking I should make some room for those who wanted to eat and stood by the window staring out with a cup in my hand.

The sky was gray but not heavy. The girls from my class were standing by the wall on the far side chatting. The eighth and ninth graders were allowed to stay inside if they wanted, and they invariably did, at least the girls. The children in the lower school generally stayed on the other side by the soccer field.

I still hadn't done a break duty.

I turned to the others.

"Who's on playground duty?" I said.

"A wild guess – you," Sture said, leaning against the door frame with one hand pointing in my direction.

I went over to the list on the wall. And yes, it was me.

"Shit, I'd forgotten all about it," I said, and went into the corridor, grabbed my jacket, and put it on as I hurried out.

From the wet-weather shelter a small, plump figure came toward me. This was a boy called Jo. I pretended I hadn't seen him and made for the other side of the playground, where a whole crowd of kids rushed one way, then the other in front of a goal with a heavy gray ball in their midst.

They saw me and stopped the game.

"Do you want to join in?" they said.

"Why not," I said. "For a little while anyway."

"It's you against the rest then!"

"OK," I said.

They gave the ball to the goalkeeper, who kicked it into the melee. There were lots of boys, but their legs were short, so it was relatively easy to get the ball and keep it. Occasionally I knocked some of them flying, they shouted for a free kick, I shouted that they were little weeds, and they were put in again and chased after me. A couple of times I let them have the ball, just to keep them motivated, but in the end I ran toward the goal and shot the ball past the keeper and shouted I had won and the game was over. No, don't go, they shouted, we're going to smash you! Some of the smallest boys grabbed my trousers. I freed myself and had to run a few steps to get away. They were soon engrossed in the game again, and I started to walk over to see to the pupils on the other side.

Jo was standing on his own by the wall with his hat tugged down over his forehead.

"Don't you want to play soccer with the others?" I said as I passed.

He came after me and I had to stop.

"I don't like soccer," he whimpered.

"Just try!" I said.

"No," he said. "Can I come with you instead?"

"Me?" I said. "I'm just walking around."

He took my hand and looked up at me with a smile.

"OK," I said. "If you want."

Didn't he understand how this would look to his classmates, walking around hand in hand with the teacher?

Obviously not.

With the chubby little boy in tow I went toward the other part of the playground, where the pupils in my class had now been joined by the eighth and ninth graders.

"Yesterday I finished my homework and tried the next part," he said, looking up at me again.

"Really?" I said. "That's very good. Did you understand any of it?"

"I think so," he said. "Some of it anyway."

"But if you don't like soccer, what do you like?"

"Drawing," he said. "I love that."

"No outdoor hobbies?"

"I like cycling. With Endre."

"Is he your best friend?"

"Off and on."

I looked down at him. His face was completely expressionless.

So the poor boy had no friends.

His eyes met mine and his face softened into a smile. I rested my hand on his shoulder and crouched down in front of him.

"What about if we go and play soccer?" I said. "You and I can be on the same team."

"But I can't play soccer," he said.

"Get away with you," I said. "Of course you can. All you have to do is run around and kick the ball! I'll help you. Come on, we'll have to hurry if we're going to get a game. The bell will go soon."

"OK," he said, and we jogged over to the goal.

I stopped in front of the boys and raised my arm.

"I'm back," I said. "Jo's on my team. So it's Jo and me against the rest of you. OK?"

"But Jo's so bad!" Reidar shouted.

"You're all bad," I said. "Come on then!"

He really was bad! If I passed the ball to him he could barely kick it. But he was running around now with a smile on his face, and then fortunately the bell rang a couple of minutes later.

"You take the ball, Jo, and put it in the staff room. OK?"

"OK!" he said, and headed off with the ball under his arm. I quickly followed, hoping to catch a brief glimpse of Liv, the girl in the ninth grade, before she went in.

And I did. She was walking beside Camilla as I arrived, and she sent me a stolen glance as she turned into the corridor. I eyed her slim, firm backside, formed to perfection, and a kind of abyss opened inside me.

After the last lesson, I remained in the staff room waiting for the others to go home, partly because I longed to be alone but in a different way from how I was in my flat, and partly because I wanted to use the phone.

Eventually only Richard's car was left in the parking lot. He was in his office but could come into the staff room at any moment, so I sat leafing through an encyclopedia as I waited for him to pack up and go home.

In the past few hours the clouds had slowly darkened, and while I was sitting there the first raindrops began to pitter-patter on the windowpanes. I turned and watched them hitting the asphalt at first without leaving a mark, as though it wasn't really happening, then a few seconds later the dark wetness spread as the heavens opened. It poured down, stripes of rain cut through the air and with such force that I could see the raindrops bouncing off the ground. The water gushed out of the drainpipes from the gutters and down the hill along the side of the building opposite. A hard drumming sound came from the windows and the roof above me.

"Now that's what I call a storm!" Richard said from the door with a smile. He was wearing his green anorak and had a knife on his belt.

"It's no passing shower," I said.

"Are you doing some overtime?" he said, coming in.

"Well," I said. "I was planning to anyhow."

"How has your first week been?"

"It's gone well, I think," I said.

He nodded.

"Next Friday you can talk to Sigrid. The mentor, you know. Wouldn't be a bad idea to write down all the questions and thoughts you have before you meet her. So you can make the best use of the opportunity."

"OK, I'll do that," I said.

He chewed his lower lip and looked like a goat again.

"OK then," he said. "Have a good weekend!"

"You too," I said.

Half a minute later he appeared outside running toward his car with his briefcase over his head.

Keys out, door open, in.

The car lights came on, shivers ran down my spine. The rear lights shone red against the wet black asphalt and the headlights cast two shafts of yellow light against the wall, which seemed to diffuse them as it was lit up.

The pattering rain, the broad Vs of water running down the hill, the overflowing gutters.

Oh, this was the world and I was living in the midst of it.

What should I do? I felt like hammering my fists on the windows, running around the room and yelling, tossing tables and chairs aside, I was full to the brim with energy and life.

"IT'S THE END OF THE WORLD AS WE KNOW IT!" I sang out at the top of my voice in the staff room.

"IT'S THE END OF THE WORLD AS WE KNOW IT!

"AND I FEEL FINE!

"AND I FEEL FINE!"

Once Richard's car was out of sight, I went for a walk around the school building to see whether anyone might still be there. The caretaker, for example, could have been pottering around fixing things. But it was deserted, and after I'd made sure this was the case I went into the little telephone cubicle and dialed Mom's number.

She didn't answer.

Perhaps she'd been working late and had stopped by a supermarket on the way home, if she wasn't eating out.

I called Yngve. He picked up right away.

"Hello?" he said.

"Hi, this is Karl Ove," I said.

"You're in Northern Norway, aren't you?"

"Yes, of course. How are things?"

"Fine. Just got back from lectures. Going to chill first and then I'll be off."

"Where to?"

"Hulen nightclub probably."

"Lucky you."

"You're the one who chose to go to Northern Norway. You could have moved to Bergen, you know."

"Yes, I know."

"How are things up there? Do you have a flat and everything?"

"Yes. It's nice. Started teaching on Tuesday. Actually it's really a lot of fun. I'm going out tonight too. But not to Hulen exactly. It's a local community center."

"Any nice girls up there?"

"Yeees . . . There's one I met on the bus. That might develop into something. Otherwise they've all left home. Seems like they're either schoolgirls or housewives."

"It'll have to be schoolgirls, then, huh?"

"Ha ha."

There was a brief silence.

"Did you get my short story?" I said.

"I did."

"Have you read it?"

"I have but only quickly. I skimmed through it. I was going to write to you about it. Not easy to do that on the phone."

"But you did like it, didn't you? Or you're not sure yet."

"Yes, I did. I liked it well enough. It was nice and lively. But let's talk about it later, as I said, OK?"

OK.

Another silence.

"What about Dad?" I said. "Heard anything from him?"

"Nothing. You?"

"No, nothing. Thinking about calling him now."

"Say hello from me. It'll save me having to call him for a few weeks."

"I will," I said. "I'll write to you in the week."

"That'd be good," he said. "Catch you later!"

"OK," I said, and hung up, went into the staff room, and sat on the sofa with my feet up on the table. Something about the conversation with Yngve had depressed me, but I didn't know what. Perhaps that he was going to Hulen in Bergen with all his friends while I was going to a party in a village in the middle of nowhere and didn't know anyone.

Or was it the *well enough*?

Yes, I did. I liked it well enough, he had said.

Well *enough*?

I had once read a short story by Hemingway, it was about a boy who accompanied his father, who was a doctor, to an Indian reservation – a woman was giving birth, it didn't go so well, as far as I remembered, per-haps the woman had even died – anyway after they had been there they went back home and that was that. All very straightforward. My short story was just as good, I knew that. The context was different, but that was because Hemingway wrote in a different era. I wrote in today's world, and that was why it was as it was.

But what did Yngve really know? How much did he read? Had he even read Hemingway?

I got up and went back into the telephone cubicle, took the slip of paper from my back pocket, and dialed Dad's number. May as well get it over with.

"Yes, hello?" he said. Brusque voice. The conversation was going to be brief, no doubt about that.

"Hi, this is Karl Ove," I said.

"Oh, hi, son," he said.

"I'm all set up here now," I said. "And I've started working."

"That's good," he said. "Are you doing all right?"

"Yes."

"That's good."

"How are things with you?"

"Well, same as always, you know. Unni's at home and I've just got back from work. Now we're going to eat. But it was nice that you called."

"Say hello to Unni!"

"Will do. Bye."

"Bye."

The deluge had eased when I headed down the hill from school to my flat, but it was still raining enough for my hair to be soaked by the time I opened the door. I dried it in the bathroom with a towel, hung up my jacket, put my shoes by the stove, and switched it on, fried some potatoes, some onions, and a sausage, which I chopped up into pieces, ate it all at the sitting-room table as I read yesterday's paper, then went to bed, where I fell asleep within minutes, swathed by the comforting pitter-patter of rain on the window.

I woke to the bell ringing. Outside it had not only stopped raining, as I saw when I got up to open the door, the sky over the village was also blue.

It was Nils Erik.

He was holding his arms to his sides like two brackets, with his knees bent outward, his lips compressed into a zany smile, and his eyes wide and staring.

"Is this where the party is?" he squeaked in an old man's voice.

"Yes, it is," I said. "It's here. Come in."

He didn't move.

"Are there any . . . any . . . any really young girls here?" he said.

"How young?"

"Thirteen?"

"Yep! Come on in! It's freezing!"

I turned my back on him and went in, took a bottle of white wine from the fridge and opened it.

"Do you want some white wine?" I shouted to him.

"My wine should be as red as a young girl's blood!" he wheezed from the hall.

"Nasty," I said. He came into the kitchen with a bottle of red wine in his hand and put it on the counter. I passed him the corkscrew.

He was wearing a blue Poco Loco shirt, a black leather tie, and a pair of red cotton trousers.

The impression he made on people didn't bother him anyway, I thought with a smile. Not caring what others thought about him was an essential part of his personality, it seemed.

"I must say you're colorful tonight," I said.

"You've got to strike while the iron is hot," he said. "And I've heard you have to dress like this if you want to attract women up here."

"Like that? Red and blue?"

"Exactly!"

He put the bottle between his knees and pulled out the cork with a pop.

"Wonderful sound!" he said.

"I'm just going to have a quick shower. Is that all right?" I said.

He nodded.

"Of course. I'll put some music on while you're in there, OK?"

"No problem."

"No one can say that we aren't polite young men," he said with a laugh. I went into the bathroom, undressed at speed, turned on the water and stepped under the shower, hastily washed under my arms and between my legs, looked at my feet, leaned my head back and wet my hair, then I turned the shower off, dried, put some gel in my hair, wrapped the towel around my waist, and went into the sitting room, past Nils Erik, who was on the sofa with studiously closed eyes listening to David Sylvian, and into the bedroom, where I put on clean underpants and socks, a white shirt, and black trousers. I buttoned up my shirt, then put on my shoelace tie and went back to Nils Erik.

"But I was told that's exactly how you *shouldn't* dress!" he said. "If you want them to flock to you. White shirt, shoelace tie with eagle, and black pants."

I tried to come up with a smart retort, but failed.

"Ha ha," I said, filling my glass with white wine and drinking it in one long swig.

The taste was of summer nights, discos bursting at the seams, buckets of ice on the tables, gleaming eyes, tanned bare arms.

I shuddered.

"Not used to drinking?" Nils Erik said.

I sent him a withering glance and refilled my glass.

"Have you heard the new Chris Isaak single?" I said.

He shook his head. I went and put it on.

"It's brilliant," I said.

We sat for a while without speaking.

I rolled a cigarette and lit it.

"Did you have a look at my short story?" I said.

He nodded. I got up and lowered the volume.

"I read it before I left. It's good, Karl Ove."

"Do you really think so?"

"Yes. Lively style. Actually I don't have much more to say than that. I'm not exactly a literary expert or a writer."

"Is there anything you particularly liked?"

He shook his head.

"Nothing really, no. The writing's even and good. Hangs together well."

"OK," I said. "What do you think about the ending in relation to the rest?"

"It was a strong ending."

"That's what I want, you know," I said. "Something completely unexpected, the part about the father."

"It is as well."

He filled his glass. His lips were already red from the wine.

"Have you read Saabye Christensen's *Beatles* by the way?" he said.

"Hell yes," I said. "It's my favorite novel. That was what made me decide to become a writer. That and *White Niggers* by Ambjørnsen."

"Guessed as much," he said.

"Oh? Is it similar?"

"It is."

"Too similar?"

He smiled.

"No, I wouldn't say so. But I can see you were influenced by it."

"What did you think of the blood part? The part that comes in the middle? Where everything changes into the present tense?"

"I don't think I noticed that."

"That was what I was most pleased with, in fact. I describe him seeing Gordon's blood and veins and flesh and sinews. It's pretty intense in the middle there."

Nils Erik nodded and smiled.

Then there was another silence.

"It was much easier to write than I'd thought," I said. "It's the first short story I've ever written. I'd written things in papers and that sort of thing before, but that's different. That was sort of why I came up here. I just wanted to try and write a book. And then I began and well . . . yes, all I had to do was write. It wasn't difficult at all."

"I see," he said. "Are you planning to go into writing as a career?"

"Yes, yes, that's what this is all about for me. I'm planning to write another short story this weekend. Have you read Hemingway, by the way?"

"Oh yes. Part of growing up."

"Sort of like that, yes. Straight to the point. Simple and clear. With weight behind it."

"Yes."

I refilled my glass to the brim and drank it in one go.

"Have you wondered what it would have been like if we had applied for a different school?" I said.

"What do you mean?"

"Well, it's just by chance that it happened to be Håfjord. It could have been anywhere. Then we would have had to adjust to whoever lived *there*, wouldn't we, and life would have been very different from what's going to happen *here*."

"Not to mention the fact that two completely different people would have been listening to wine and drinking Chris Isaak. Or vice versa. The wine would have been listening and Chris Isaak drinking. Well, have you ever heard the like? Or is it: have you ever leard the hike? I'm all inside out! Spoutside up! Upside down!"

Nils Erik laughed.

"*Skål*, Karl Ove, and I'm glad it's you sitting there and not someone else!"

We raised our glasses and said *skål*.

"Although, if it'd been someone else, would I have said the same to him?"

At that moment the doorbell rang.

"That must be Tor Einar," I said, getting up.

He was standing with his back to me and staring down at the village when I opened the door. The gray August light hung between the mountainsides, seemingly of a completely different texture from that which illuminated the sky, for that was blue and gleamed like metal.

"Hi," I said.

Tor Einar turned in a slow, studied manner. Here was a guy who had plenty of time.

"Hi," he said. "May I enter?"

"Step right in."

He did so in the same punctilious way I had associated with his personality from the first moment I saw him. It was as though he had thought through his movements a couple of times before he executed them. All with a smile playing on his lips.

He raised his hand and waved in greeting to Nils Erik.

"What are you two talking about?" he said in broad dialect.

Nils Erik smiled.

"We're talking about fish," he said in his own dialect.

"Fish and fanny," I said in mine.

"Salty fish and fresh fanny or fresh fish and salty fanny?" Tor Einar asked.

"What's the filleting difference, can you tell me that?" I said.

"Yes, now listen here: salty sole and sole salt, they're not the same thing. Nor are fish and fanny. But they're close. Incredibly close."

"Soul salt?" I asked.

"Yes. See, now you're saying it."

He laughed, hitched up the knees of his trousers, and sat down beside Nils Erik.

"Well?" he said. "Have you done a roundup of the week?"

"That's what we were doing," Nils Erik said.

"They seem to be a good bunch," Tor Einar said.

"Are you thinking about the teachers?" I said.

"Yes," he said. "In fact, I already know them all, apart from you two."

"But you're not from here?" Nils Erik said.

"My grandmother lives here. I've been up every summer and Christmas since I was small."

"You've just finished gymnas as well, haven't you?" I said. "In Finnsnes?"

He nodded.

"You don't know someone there called Irene, do you?" I said. "From Hellevika?"

"Irene, sure," he said, brightening up. "Not as well as I'd like, I must admit. How come? Do *you* know her?"

"That would be saying too much," I said. "But I met her on the bus on my way here. She seemed nice."

"Are you meeting her this evening? Is that the plan?"

I shrugged. "She's coming anyway," I said.

Half an hour later we were walking up the hill from the flat. I was drunk in that pure joyful way you can be from white wine, when your thoughts collide with one another like bubbles and what emerges when they burst is pleasure.

We had been at my place, I thought, and this filled me with pleasure.

We were colleagues and on our way to becoming friends, I reflected.

And I had written a damn good short story.

Pleasure, pleasure, pleasure.

And then there was this light, dim down among humans and things human, attended by a kind of finely honed darkness which became diffused in the light though did not possess or control it, only muted or softened it, high up in the sky it was gleamingly clean and clear.

Pleasure.

And there was this silence. The murmur of the sea, our footsteps on the gravel, the occasional noise coming from somewhere, a door being opened or a shout, all embraced by silence, which seemed to rise from the ground, rise from objects and surround us in a way which I didn't formulate as primordial, though I sensed it was, for I thought of the silence in Sørbøvåg on summer mornings when I was a child there, the silence above the fjord beneath the immense Lihesten Mountain, half hidden by mist. The silence of the world. It was here too, as I walked uphill, drunk, with my new friends, and although neither it nor the light we walked in was the main event of the evening it played its part.

Pleasure.

Eighteen years old and on my way to a party.

"That's where she lives," Tor Einar said, pointing to the house I had strolled past one evening a few days ago.

"Big house," Nils Erik said.

"Yes, she lives with someone," Tor Einar said. "His name's Vidar and he's a fisherman."

"What else!" I said, stopping at the door and raising my arm to ring the bell.

"Here everyone just walks in," Tor Einar said. "We're in Northern Norway now!"

I opened the door and went in. From upstairs came the sound of voices and music. Smoke hung in the air above the stairs. We quietly took off our shoes and went up. The floor above was open plan with the kitchen straight ahead, a living room at the back to the left, presumably the bedroom was at the back on the right.

There was a group of perhaps ten people in the living room chatting and laughing, squeezed around a table covered with bottles and glasses, cigarette packets and ashtrays. They were all stocky, many had moustaches, age-wise they ranged between twenty and forty.

"Here come the teachers," one of them said.

"Perhaps we'll be given detention this evening," another said.

Everyone laughed.

"Hi, folks," said Tor Einar.

"Hi," said Nils Erik.

Hege, the only woman there, got up and brought in some chairs from the dining-room table by the window.

"Sit yourselves down, boys," she said. "If you need glasses, you'll find them in the kitchen."

I went in and stood alone staring up at the mountainside behind the house while mixing myself a screwdriver. For a moment I lingered in the doorway observing the people around the table, thinking they looked like trolls sitting there with their variously colored drinks, depending on what they mixed with their vodka – a variety of juices, Sprite, Coke – with their pouches of tobacco from which they made endless rollies and with their moustaches, their dark eyes and the succession of stories, thinking how they came from the four corners of the earth to meet here once a year and act out their exotic natures among their own kind.

However, it was the other way round. They were the rule and I was the exception, the teacher among fishermen. So what was I doing here? Shouldn't I be at home writing rather than here?

It had been a mistake to go into the kitchen alone. Nils Erik and Tor Einar had already been through the introductory rites, they were now comfortably ensconced alongside the fishermen, and I could have done that too, tagged along behind my colleagues and slipped in without being noticed.

I took a swig and went in.

"And here we have the writer!" one of them said. I recognized him at once, he was the fisherman who had dropped by to see me on the first day, Remi.

"Hi, Remi," I said, holding out my hand.

"Have you been on a name-learning course or what?" he said, grasping it. Shook it up and down in a way that had not been done since the 1950s.

"You're the first fisherman I've ever met," I said. "So of course I remember your name."

He laughed. I was pleased I'd had a drink before we left. If I hadn't, I would have stood tongue-tied in front of him.

"The writer?" Hege said.

"Yes, he writes, this guy does. I've seen it with my own eyes!"

"I didn't know that," she said. "Do you have such fancy ideas?"

I sat down and nodded to her while smiling semi-apologetically and taking the tobacco pouch from my shirt pocket.

For the next hour I said nothing. I rolled cigarettes, smoked, drank, smiled when the others smiled, laughed when they laughed. Looked at Nils Erik, who was pretty drunk and seemed to be in on the jokey tone but wasn't, he was different, there was something light and Østlandish about him, always on the outside. Not that they rejected him, because they didn't, it was just that his jokes were of a fundamentally different character, which in this context seemed to expose him. He made puns, they didn't, adopted a variety of roles, made faces and raised and lowered his voice, they didn't. When he burst into laughter it was somehow unrestrained, bordering on the hysterical, it struck me; that too was completely different from them.

Tor Einar was more on their level, he knew the appropriate tone and was on nodding terms with everyone there, although he was not one of them either, I could see; he was not an insider, he was more like an ethnological researcher who knows his stuff well enough to be able to mimic it because he likes it so much, and perhaps that was the nub, he *liked* the tone, whereas for them the tone just came naturally to them. They had never thought about whether they liked it or not.

Tor Einar slapped his thighs when he laughed, which I had only ever seen in films. He would occasionally also rub his hands up and down his thighs when he talked.

The pre-party, as they called it here, excluded discussion. Issues regarding politics, women, music, or football were not on the agenda. What they did was tell stories. One story gave way to the next, laughter billowed across the table, and the tales they came up with, they being the trolls they were, all had their origins in the village and the people who lived there, which despite its modest proportions appeared to be an inexhaustible treasure trove of stories. There was the fisherman in his sixties who had been seasick all his life and who only needed to jump on board his trawler to start feeling ill. There was the gang of fishermen who after a good season had hired the suite at the SAS hotel in Tromsø and spent vertiginous sums of money in the course of a few intense days of abandon there. One man called Frank, with the fleshy face of a child, was said to have burned his way through twenty thousand kroner, and it took me a while to realize that "burned" meant exactly that, he had set fire to it. Then someone had been drunk shitless in an elevator, they said, and again it took me a while to catch on that this had to be interpreted literally: he had been so drunk that he'd shat himself. Judging by the conversation it had indeed happened in the elevator. Frank in particular got so drunk that waking up in his own shit was not an unusual occurrence, from what I could glean. His mother, who was the older teacher at the school, had a hard time, it seemed, because he still lived at home. Hege's stories were different, but no less bizarre, such as the one about the girlfriend who had been terrified before an exam and whom she had taken into the forest and hit on the head with a bat so that she would have a justifiable reason for being absent. I stared at her. Was she pulling our legs? It didn't seem like it. She met my gaze and grinned, and then narrowed her eyes to a slit and frowned, opened them again, smiled and looked away. What did that mean? Was it the equivalent of a wink? Or did it mean that I shouldn't believe everything I heard?

They not only knew one another well, they knew one another inside out.

They had grown up and gone to school together, they worked together, they partied together. They saw one another virtually every day and had done so virtually all their lives. They knew one another's parents and grandparents, many of them were first or second cousins. One might conclude this was boring, indeed intolerably boring in the long run, because nothing new ever entered their lives, everything that happened, happened among the 250 people who lived here and who knew everyone else's most intimate secrets and quirks. But such did not appear to be the case; quite the contrary, they seemed to be having a whale of a time, and if there was anything that marked the atmosphere among them, it was their carefree attitude and their joy.

While sitting there I was formulating what I was going to write in the letters I would send south, such as: "They all had moustaches! It's absolutely true! All of them!" Or: "And the music they listened to, do you know what it was? Bonnie Tyler! And Dr. Hook! How long ago is it since that music was heard anywhere in the world? What is this godforsaken place I have ended up in?" And: "Here the expression 'to drink yourself shitless' means just that. Say no more . . ."

When at last I got up to go to the john, I had drunk just over a third of my bottle of vodka and I knocked against the man sitting next to me, who was holding a glass in his hand and spilled some of the contents.

"So . . . rry," I said, straightening up and stepping across the living-room floor.

"One does the talking and the other does the drinking!" he said behind me and laughed.

He must have been referring to Nils Erik and me.

As soon as I got some speed up my balance was fine.

But where was the bathroom?

I opened a door. It was a bedroom. Hege's bedroom, I presumed, and closed the door as fast as possible. If there was one thing I didn't like, it was seeing other people's bedrooms.

"The bathroom's on the other side," a voice behind me said from the kitchen.

I turned.

A man with brown eyes, thick, collar-length dark hair, and a moustache that hung down on either side of his mouth looked at me. It had to be Vidar, Hege's partner. There was something about the self-assured way he stood there that told me this.

"Thank you," I said.

"No problem," he said. "Just don't piss on the floor, that's all."

"I'll try not to," I said, going into the bathroom. I leaned against the wall while peeing. Smiled to myself. He had looked like a bass player from a 1970s band. Smokie or someone like them. And incredibly muscular.

What was she doing with such a macho?

I flushed the toilet and stood swaying in front of the mirror. Smiled at myself again.

When I emerged from the bathroom, they had decided to leave. They were talking about a bus.

"Do buses run at this hour?" I said.

Remi turned to me. "It's our band bus."

"Is there a band here? Are you in it?"

"Yes, I am. We call ourselves Autopilot. We play at dances in the community centers around here."

I followed him down the stairs. This was getting better and better.

"And what instrument do you play?" I said, putting on my coat in the hall.

"Drums," he said.

I put my arm around his shoulder.

"Me too. Or I did. Two years ago."

"You don't say," he said.

"Yes," I said, retracting my arm, leaning forward and trying to put on a shoe. Bumped into someone. Vidar again.

"Sorry," I said.

"That's fine," he said. "Did you remember your bottle?"

"Oh, no, shit," I said.

"It's this one, isn't it?" he said, holding up a bottle of vodka.

"Yes, that's the one," I said. "Thank you very much! Thanks!"

He smiled but his eyes were cold and impassive. That wasn't my problem though. I put the bottle on the floor and concentrated on my shoes. When they were on, I staggered out under the light night sky, down to the road, where the rest were waiting. The bus was parked in a driveway a hundred meters away. One of them opened the door and got into the driver's seat, we clambered aboard and moved toward the back of the big old vehicle. It was furnished with sofas and tables and a bar, all in plywood, and plush, it seemed. We sat down, the engine started with a growl and it was out with the bottles and off down the road. As we jolted along following the bank of the fjord we had a drink in one hand and a cigarette in the other.

What an adventure.

I sang *Pølsemaker, pølsemaker, hvor har du gjort av deg* – Sausage maker, sausage maker, where have you gone, at the top of my voice while swinging my arms and trying to get the others to join in. The bus had conjured up memories of the old film in which Leif Juster was a bus driver, and Leif Juster had made me think of the film *The Sausage-Maker Who Disappeared*.

An hour or so later the bus pulled up in front of the community center, I jumped out and was swallowed up in the overcrowded room.

When I woke, at first, I couldn't remember a thing.

Everything was a complete blank.

I didn't know who I was or where I was. All I knew was that I had woken up from something.

But the room was familiar, it was the bedroom in my flat.

How had I gotten here?

I sat up and could feel that I was still drunk.

What time was it?

What had happened?

I held my face in my hands. I had to have something to drink. Now. But I was too wiped out to go into the kitchen and slumped back on the bed.

I had been to the pre-party and on a bus. And had sung. Sung!

Oh no, oh no.

And I had put my hand on his shoulder. As if we were pals. But we weren't. I wasn't even a man. Only a stupid Sørlander who couldn't even tie a knot. With arms as thin as drinking straws.

No, now I *had* to have something to drink.

I sat up. My body was as heavy as lead and totally uncooperative, but I forced my feet onto the floor, braced myself mentally, and pushed myself onto my legs.

Oh God.

The yearning for my bed was so strong that I had to mobilize all the will-power I had not to go back. The few paces to the kitchen exhausted me, I had to hang over the counter for a while before I could summon the energy to run the tap, fill a glass, and drink. One more, and one more. And the distance to my bedroom seemed so immense that I stopped halfway and lay down on the sofa instead.

I hadn't done anything stupid, had I?

I'd danced. Yes, I'd danced with all and sundry.

Hadn't there been a woman in her sixties too? Whom I had smiled at and danced with? And pressed myself against?

Yes, there had.

Oh my God. Oh my God.

Oh Christ.

Then it was as though the pressure inside me was ratcheted up, although there was no particular place that hurt, everything was painful, and the pain grew and grew, it was unbearable, and then my stomach muscles went into a spasm. I swallowed, dragged myself to my feet, and tried to hold it back as I stumbled toward the bathroom, the pressure mounting and mounting, that was all that existed, and then I snatched at the toilet seat, flung it up, knelt down, wrapped my arms around the bowl, and spewed a cascade of yellow and green vomit into the water with such force that it splashed back into my face, but it didn't matter, nothing mattered anymore, it was so wonderful to feel the relief, so fantastically wonderful.

I slumped to the floor.

Oh God, how good it was.

But then it came back. The muscles in my stomach writhed like snakes. Oh God. I leaned over the bowl again, caught a glimpse of a pubic hair next to my forearm resting on the porcelain as the cramps tore through my empty stomach, and I opened my mouth and groaned ooooh, oooooooh, oooooooh, and nothing came out.

But then, without warning, a gob of yellow bile was expelled. It slid down the white porcelain, a sliver still hung from my mouth and I wiped it away, and I lay down on the bathroom floor. Was that the last? Was it over now?

Yes.

Suddenly everything was as serene as in church. I lay in a fetal position on the bathroom floor enjoying to the full the calm that had settled over my body.

What had I done with Irene?

Everything inside me tensed up.

Irene.

We had danced.

I had pressed myself against her, hard, rubbed my erect dick against her stomach.

And then?

Anything else?

It was as if this one scene was surrounded by darkness on all sides. I remembered it but nothing of what came before or after.

Anything bad?

I imagined her in a ditch, strangled, with torn clothes.

No, no, what nonsense.

But the image returned. Irene in a ditch, strangled, her clothes torn.

How could the image be so clear? Her blue trousers, with those wonderfully full thighs beneath, a white blouse ripped open, part of a naked breast exposed, her eyes lifeless. The mud in the ditch, between the scattered blades of grass, yellow and green, the insane light, late in the night.

No, no, what nonsense.

How did I get home?

Hadn't I been standing by the bus when the band stopped playing and the parking lot outside the community center was packed with people laughing and screaming?

Yes.

And Irene was there!

We were kissing!

Me with a bottle of booze in one hand, drinking straight from it. She grabbed my lapel, she was the type of girl who grabbed lapels, and then she looked up at me, and then she said . . . ?

What did she say?

Oh hell, no.

Out of nowhere the snakes in my stomach entwined themselves again, and since there was nothing left below they were furious and squeezed so hard that I groaned. OOOOOHH, I went. OOOHHHH. I wrapped my arms around the toilet bowl and hung my head over the hole, but nothing came, I was empty.

CHRIST ALMIGHTY! I shouted. STOP THIS! NOW!

Then came a mouthful of unbelievably thick bile, I spat it out and thought that was it, but it wasn't, my stomach continued to churn, and I tried to alleviate it by hawking, from the bottom of my throat, for if only a little came up surely the vomiting would stop.

OOOHH. OOOHH. OOOHH.

Some phlegm came up.

There. That's the way.

Finished now?

Yes.

Ah.

Oh.

I grabbed the edge of the sink with one hand and pulled myself up. Rinsed my face with cold water and staggered into the sitting room, not too difficult, fine, lay back down on the sofa, thought I should find out what the time was but didn't have the energy, all that counted now was to wait for my body to recover and then the day could begin. After all, I was going to write another short story.

I had experienced blackouts like this, after which I remembered only fragments of what I had done, ever since I first started drinking. That was the summer I finished ninth grade, at the Norway Cup, when I just laughed and laughed, a momentous experience; being drunk took me to places where I was free and did what I wanted while it raised me aloft and rendered everything around me wonderful. Only recalling bits and pieces afterward, isolated scenes brightly illuminated against a wall of darkness from which I emerged and disappeared back into, was the norm. And so it went on. The following spring I went to the carnival with Jan Vidar, Mom had made me up as Bowie's Aladdin Sane, the town was heaving with people wearing curly black wigs, hot pants, and sequins, everywhere there was the throb of samba drums, but the air was cold, people were stiff, there was a huge amount of embarrassment to be overcome all the time, and this was visible in the processions, people were squirming rather than dancing, they wanted to feel emancipated, that was what this was about, they were not, they wanted to be, this was the 1980s, this was the new liberated and forward-looking era in which everything Norwegian was pathetic and everything Mediterranean was alive and free, when the sole TV channel which had informed the Norwegian population for twenty years about what one small circle of educated people in Oslo considered important for them to know was suddenly joined by new, very different TV channels that took a lighter approach, they wanted to entertain, and they wanted to sell, and from then on these two entities fused: entertainment and sales became two sides of the same coin and subsumed everything else, which also became entertainment and sales, from music to politics, literature, news, health, in fact everything. The carnival marked this transition, a nation moving away from the seriousness of the '70s to the levity of the '90s, and this transition was visible in the awkward movements, in the nervous eyes and the wild triumphant looks of those who had overcome this awkwardness and nervousness and were now wiggling their lean bottoms on the backs of the trucks that crawled through Kristiansand's streets on this cold spring morning with a light drizzle in the air. That was how it was in Kristiansand and that was how it was in all the other towns in Norway of any size and any self-respect. Carnival was the rage and would become a tradition, they said, every year these stiff white men and women would affirm their emancipation to the best of their ability on trucks, decked out as Mediterraneans, dancing and laughing to the drums that former school-brass-band musicians played with such a seductive, hypnotic beat.

Even two sixteen-year-olds like Jan Vidar and me understood that this was sad. Of course there was nothing we wanted more than a Mediterranean-style explosion in our day-to-day reality, for there was nothing we yearned for more than inviting breasts and bums, music and loads of fun, and if there was anything we wanted to be, it was dark-skinned, confident men who took these women at will. We were against meanness and all for generosity, we were against constraints and for openness and freedom. Nevertheless we saw these processions and were overcome by sadness on behalf of our town and country because there was an unbelievable lack of pride about all this, indeed it was as if the whole town was making a fool of itself, without realizing. But we did realize and we were sad as we strolled around, each with half a bottle of spirits in an inside pocket, becoming more and more drunk and cursing our town and the idiotic people in it while always keeping an eye open for faces we knew and could perhaps get together with. That is, girls' faces, or in a pinch boys' faces we knew who were with girls' faces we didn't know. Our project was doomed, we were never going to meet girls this way, but we didn't give up as long as there was a glimmer of hope, we strolled on, getting drunker and drunker, more and more depressed. And then, at some point, I disappeared from myself. Not from Jan Vidar, he could see me of course, and when he said something to me he received an answer so he imagined that everything was fine, but it wasn't, I had disappeared, I was empty, I was in the void of my soul, there was no other way for me to describe it.

Who are you when you don't know you exist? Who were you when you didn't remember that you existed? When I woke up in the studio in Elvegaten the following day and knew nothing about anything, it felt as if I had been *let loose* in the town. I could have done anything, because when I was as drunk as I was, there were no longer any limits in me, I did everything that entered my head, and what would not enter a person's head?

I called Jan Vidar. He was in bed asleep, but his father dragged him to the phone.

"What happened?" I said.

"We-ell," he said, keeping me on tenterhooks. "Strictly speaking nothing happened. That's what was such crap."

"I don't remember any of the last part," I said. "Somewhere on the way to Silokaia, that's the last thing I remember."

"Really? Nothing?"

"No."

"Don't you remember standing on the back of a truck and mooning at everyone?"

"Did I do that?"

He laughed.

"No, of course not. No, relax, man. Nothing happened. I mean, yes, something did happen when we were walking home. You bent all the wing mirrors along one street. Someone shouted, "Hey!" at us and so we ran for it. I didn't notice any difference in you. Were you that drunk?"

"Yes, it was the spirits."

"I fall asleep when I get that drunk. Jesus, though, what an awful evening. You won't get me to go to carnival again, that's for sure."

"Do you know what I think?"

"What?"

"When they have the carnival next year we'll be there again. We can't afford not to be. Not much happens in this fucking hole of town after all."

"True."

We hung up and I went to wash the Aladdin Sane lightning off my face.

The next time it happened was on Midsummer Night, also with Jan Vidar. We had dragged ourselves, each carrying a bag of beer, down to a place on the coast, to some sea-smoothed rocks below the forest in Hånes, where we wandered around drinking and freezing in the pouring summer rain, surrounded by Øyvind's many pals and a few people we knew from Hamresanden. Øyvind had chosen this evening of all evenings to break up with his girlfriend, Lene, so she sat crying on a rock, away from the others. I went over to console her, sat beside her, and stroked her back while telling her there were other boys, she would get over it, she was so young and beautiful, and she looked at me with gratitude in her eyes and sniffled, I thought it was a shame we were outdoors and not somewhere indoors, where there were beds, and that it was raining then outside. Suddenly she looked at her jacket and screamed, her shoulder was covered in blood and, as it turned out, her back too. It came from me, I'd cut my hand without noticing and it was bleeding profusely. You moron, she said, and stood up. This jacket's brand new. Do you know how much it cost? Sorry, I said, it wasn't on purpose, I just wanted to cheer you up a little. Go to hell, she said, and headed toward the others, where in the course of the evening she found herself back in favor with Øyvind while I sat drinking alone staring across the gray surface of the water, which the falling rain continued to dot with small, evocative rings until Jan Vidar came over and sat down next to me and we could pursue the years-long conversation we had about which girls were pretty or not and who we most dreamed of sleeping with, all while we slowly but surely got drunker until in the end everything disintegrated and I drifted into a kind of ghost world.

The ghost world: when I was inside, it went straight through me, and when I woke up from it, I couldn't remember much, a face here, a body there, a room, a staircase, a backyard, pale and shimmering, surrounded by an ocean of darkness.

It was nothing less than a horror film. Now and then I would remember the most peculiar details, like a rock at the bottom of a stream or a bottle of olive oil on a kitchen shelf, everyday items in themselves but as symbols of a whole night's mental activity, in fact all that was left of it, it was bizarre. What was it about that rock? What was it about that bottle? The first two times it happened I hadn't been afraid, I registered it simply as a kind of objective fact. Then, when it happened again, there began to be something eerie about it because I was so out of control. No, nothing had happened and probably nothing was going to happen either, but the fact was, I had no control over my actions at all. If I was basically a nice person, that was how I would be then as well, but *was* I? *Actually?*

On the other hand, I was also proud: occasionally getting so drunk that I couldn't remember a thing was cool.

At that time, I was sixteen that summer, there were only three things I wanted. The first was a girlfriend. The second was to sleep with a girl. The third was to get drunk.

Or, if I am being totally honest, there were only two things: sleeping with a girl and getting drunk. I had lots of other interests, I was full of ambition in all sorts of areas: I liked reading, listening to music, playing the guitar, watching films, playing soccer, swimming and snorkeling, traveling abroad, having money and buying myself bits of equipment, but in effect all that was about having a good time, about spending my time in the most agreeable fashion possible, and that was fine, all of it, but when it came to the crunch there were only two things I *really* wanted.

No, when I *actually* came down to it, there was only one.

I wanted to sleep with a girl.

That was the only thing I wanted.

A fire burned inside me, one that never went out. Even when I was asleep, it flared up, a glimpse of a breast in a dream was all I needed, and I came.

Oh no, not again, I thought every time I woke with underpants sticking to my skin and my pubic hair. Mom washed my clothes and at first I always rinsed them thoroughly before putting them in the laundry basket, but there was something suspicious about that too. What are all these sopping wet underpants doing here? she must have thought, and after a while I stopped and put the semen-drenched underpants, which after a few hours became stiff, as if permeated with salt flakes or something, in the basket, and even though she must have noticed, because it happened at least two, often three, times a week, I dismissed the thought of her bemusement as I replaced the laundry basket lid. She never mentioned it, I never mentioned it, and that was how it was with so much, and probably had to be, in the house where she and I lived alone: some things were said, commented on, pored over, and attempts were made to understand them; others were not articulated, not mentioned, and no attempts were made to understand them.

My urges were strong, but they rumbled in the empty rooms of ignorance, where what happened simply happened. Naturally I could have asked Yngve for advice, after all he was four years older and had endlessly more experience. He had done it, I knew that. I hadn't. So why didn't I ask him for advice?

It was unthinkable. It belonged to the realm of the unthinkable. Why, I didn't know, but it did. Besides, what good would advice do? It would be like receiving advice on how to conquer Mount Everest. Yeah, well, you go right there, and then you keep going straight on up, and there you are.

I would have given absolutely anything to sleep with a girl. Any girl actually. Whether it happened with someone I loved, like Hanne, or with a prostitute, made no difference, if it happened as part of a satanic initiation ceremony with goat's blood and hoods, I would have said, yes, I'm up for that. But it wasn't something you were given, it was something you took. Exactly how, I didn't know, and then it became a vicious circle, for not knowing made me unsure of myself, and if there was one thing that disqualified you, one thing they didn't want, it was a lack of self-assurance. That much I had understood. You had to be confident, determined, convincing. But how to get to that position? How in God's name could you do that? How did you go from standing in front of a girl in broad daylight, with all her clothes on, to sleeping with her in the darkness a few hours later? There was a chasm between these two states. When I saw a girl standing in front of me in broad daylight, there was a bottomless chasm between us. If I stepped off the edge I would fall. What else? Because she wouldn't come halfway, she could see I was frightened, she would withdraw, retreat into herself or turn to someone else. But actually, I thought, actually the distance between the two states was very *short*. It was just a question of lifting her T-shirt over her head, unfastening her bra, unbuttoning her trousers, pulling them off – and then she was naked. It would take twenty seconds, maybe thirty.

There was nothing more deceptive in existence. Walking around, knowing that I was approximately thirty seconds away from all I ever wanted, separated only by a chasm, was driving me insane. Quite often I caught myself wishing we were still in the Stone Age, then all I would have needed to do was go out with a club, hit the nearest woman on the head, and drag her home and do whatever I wanted. But it was no good, there were no shortcuts, the thirty seconds were an illusion, as almost everything concerning women was an illusion. Oh, what a mockery that they were accessible to the eye but in no other way. That everywhere you turned there were women and girls. That everywhere you turned there were breasts under blouses, thighs and hips under trousers, beautiful smiling faces, hair blowing in the wind. Pendulous breasts, firm breasts, round breasts, bouncing breasts, white breasts, tanned breasts . . . a naked wrist, a naked elbow, a naked cheek, a naked eye looking around. A naked thigh in shorts or a short summer dress. A naked palm, a naked nose, a naked neck. I saw all this around me constantly, there were girls everywhere, the supply was infinite, a well, no, I was drifting in an *ocean* of women, I saw several hundred of them every day, all with their own individual ways of moving, standing, turning, walking, holding and twisting their heads, blinking, looking – take for example a feature such as their eyes, which expressed their utter uniqueness, everything that lived and breathed was here, was revealed, regardless of whether the gaze was meant for me or not. Oh, those sparkling eyes! Oh, those dark eyes! Oh, that glint of happiness! The alluring darkness! Or, for that matter, the unintelligent, stupid eyes! For in them too there was an appeal, and no small appeal either: the stupid vacant eyes, the open mouth in that perfect beautiful body.

All this was never far from my mind, and all of them were thirty seconds away from the only thing I wanted – but on the other side of a chasm.

I cursed this chasm. I cursed myself. But no matter how frustrating this was, no matter how depressing this became, women shone with undiminished radiance.

Then a chance presented itself.

Some weeks after the dismal Midsummer Night party I traveled with the soccer team to Denmark. The town we were going to was called Nykøbing, on the island of Mors in the Limfjord. We stayed in a kind of hostel, perhaps it was a boarding school, just outside the town, surrounded by large fields bordered by shady old deciduous trees. In the evenings some of us sneaked out, it wasn't allowed, but the town wasn't far away and as long as we didn't miss the training sessions a blind eye was turned, if indeed our absence was noticed at all. We bought cheap wine from the supermarkets, sat outside on the benches drinking, and went to the nearby discotheque. On the second evening I met a Danish girl, and we got together every day for the rest of the time we were there. She was sweet and lively and intense, we sat on the benches and made out, danced in the disco, one night we went for a walk in the park, and on the final evening I thought, now's the time, I wouldn't have another opportunity, it was tonight or never.

On our last night everyone was outdoors; we started with a barbecue on the beach, the group leaders had bought beer, and when that was gone we took a taxi to a big restaurant in a forest not so far from where we were staying. She was coming, she'd said, and she did too, greeted me in the same warm way she usually did, stretching up on her toes, giving me a kiss and grasping my hand. We sat down at a table, I was knocking back the wine to summon up the courage for what I was about to attempt. In the bar I confided my intentions to Jøgge and Bjørn, told them I was going to try to get her into our room and go all the way. They smiled, wished me luck. It was a wonderful evening, outside, the grayish-black clouds hung heavily over the green trees, inside, under the glittering chandeliers, people mingled, they drank and laughed and danced, there was a smell of sweat and perfume, cigarette smoke and alcohol, she sat at our table and talked to Harald, but kept looking in my direction and she lit up when she saw me coming with another bottle of wine in my hand. My stomach ached as I sat down next to her. She leaned forward, we kissed, I was about to pour wine in her glass, she held up a palm, she had to work the following day. She had a sudden idea: did I want to go back to her place? But we're leaving tomorrow, I said. No, she said, no, you're not. You're never going home, you're staying here with me. You can go to school here! Or find a job! What do you say to that? Fine, I said, that's what we'll do.

We laughed and a wave of anguish washed through me: soon we would be in my room, soon she would be standing close to me and whispering, convinced I knew what I was doing.

"Feel like going for a walk?" I said.

She nodded.

"What about the wine?" she said.

"We'll be back," I said, and got up. Put my hand on her shoulder and guided her out of the room. Turned and met the eyes of Jøgge and Bjørn, they gave me a thumbs-up and smiled. Then we were outside.

She looked up at me.

Where are we going?

Into the forest? I said. I took her tiny hand in mine and we set off. I had already kissed her breasts, on a bench I had put my head up her jumper and kissed everything I found, she had laughed and held me tight. This was what I did with girls, lay on top of them, made out with them, and kissed their breasts. Once I had pulled down a girl's panties and poked a finger inside, that was already two years ago now.

A shiver ran through me.

"What is it?" she said, wrapping an arm around me. "Are you cold?"

"A bit maybe," I said. "It's turned colder."

The big heavy clouds that had been drifting in and were now over the forest had cast a pall over the gathering darkness between the tree trunks. A gusty wind had picked up. Above us the top branches swayed.

Blood was pounding through me.

I swallowed.

"Would you like to see where we're staying?" I said.

"Yes, I'd love to."

The moment she said that I had an erection. It pressed hard against my trousers. I swallowed again.

In the dusk the light in the buildings where we were staying was a deep yellow. It hovered around the lamps in halos. I felt sick and my palms were damp with sweat. But I was going to do it.

I stopped and put my arms around her, we kissed, her tongue was smooth and small. My dick was throbbing so much it hurt.

"It's over there," I whispered. "Are you sure you want to go in with me?"

A bewildered flicker appeared in her eyes. But she said nothing apart from yes.

I took her hand again, squeezed it hard, and we walked quickly over the last two hundred meters. Hugged her again outside the unmanned reception area, almost suffocating with desire. Down the corridor to the room I shared with three others. Key out, into the lock with trembling hand, a twist, handle down, door open, and in we went.

"You back already, Karl Ove?" Jøgge said with a laugh.

"Have you brought a visitor with you?" Bjørn said.

"How nice!" Harald said. "Would you like a beer, Lisbeth?"

There was nothing I could say. They were my roommates and had just as much right to be there as me. Nor could I say that they had run back here as a cruel joke, or the cat would have been out of the bag, and although Lisbeth may well have guessed my plans, this was not the sort of thing that could be said out loud. Or at least not when the others were here, what would she think, that I was making fun of her?

"What the hell are you lot doing here?" I said.

Jøgge smiled. "What are *you two* doing here?"

I glared at him. He was doubled up with laughter on the bed.

Harald passed Lisbeth a beer. She took it and smiled at me.

"How funny that your friends came too," she said.

What? Did she mean that?

She looked around. "Anyone got a cigarette?"

"We're soccer players," Harald said. "Only Karl Ove smokes."

"Here," said Bjørn, tapping out a Prince Mild from his packet and passing it to her.

Such a wonderful opportunity as this would not come up again for several years. And they had ruined it out of pure devilry.

Lisbeth put her hand in my back pocket and moved close to me. My dick was like a crowbar again. I sighed.

"Have a beer, Karl Ove," Jøgge said. "Can't you take a joke?"

"Yeah," I said. "Very funny."

He writhed with laughter again.

We stayed there for half an hour. Lisbeth chatted with all of them. After we had finished the beer, we went back to the restaurant. Lisbeth left at one, the rest of us stayed until early morning. The next day I met her briefly, we exchanged addresses, and she started to cry. Not much, there were only a few tears running down her cheeks. I hugged her. Lisbeth, I said. We can meet in Løkken before very long. It's only a ferry trip away for me. Can you make it, do you think? Yes, she said, and smiled through the tears. I'll write to you so that we can organize the details, OK? Yes, she said. We kissed, and when I turned around she was standing there watching me.

The Løkken idea was nonsense of course, just something I had said to lighten the atmosphere. She was nothing to me, I was in love with Hanne and had been all winter and spring. Everything had been about her, all I wanted was to be close to her, not to sleep with her, not even in the hope of a kiss or a caress, no, that wasn't it, it was the light and the excitement I was filled with when I saw her that attracted me and which I occasionally thought was not of this world, it came down to us from another world. How else could it be explained? She was a normal girl, there had to be thousands of girls like her, but she alone, by being exactly the way she was, could make my heart tremble and my soul glow. Once that spring I had knelt down on the road before her and asked her to marry me. She was pushing a bicycle, it was dark and raining, we were walking up by the blocks of flats in Lund, and when I did it she just laughed. She thought I was playing the fool.

"Don't laugh," I said. "I mean it. In all seriousness. We can get married. We can move to a house on an island and stay there, just you and me. We can do that! *No one* can stop us if that's what we decide to do."

She laughed again, that wonderful trilled laugh of hers.

"Karl Ove!" she said. "We're only sixteen!"

I got up.

"I know you don't want to," I said. "But I mean it. Do you understand? You're the only girl I think about. You're the only girl I want to be with. Should I act as if this didn't exist?"

"But I'm going out with someone else. You know that very well!"

"Yes, I do," I said.

I didn't need reminding. She only went on these walks with me because she felt flattered and because I was so different from the other boys she knew. Any hope that one day I would be going out with her was gone, nevertheless I didn't give up, I never would. So, standing on the deck of the Danish ferry, with the wind blowing in my hair, squinting into the low afternoon sun, surrounded by blue sea on all sides, I was thinking about Hanne, not Lisbeth.

In fact, I wasn't going to go home when we arrived in Kristiansand, I was off to a class party in a cabin on an island, and Hanne would probably be there too. I had written a few letters to her over the summer, two of them from Sørbøvåg, where I walked along the river alone with my Walkman, without a soul in sight, thinking only of her, and where I got up in the night and went outside, under the starry sky, walked up the river valley to the waterfall, climbed up alongside to sit high on a plateau beneath the stars, and thought of her.

She had answered my letters with a postcard.

But after Lisbeth my confidence was high, and even the sight of the vast sea could not dent it, or the urges in me, which were so vast that I was driven outside at night and tears formed in my eyes at all the beauty that existed in the world, but I couldn't turn these urges to any use, nor could I sublimate them.

"Hi, Elk," Jøgge said behind me. "Would you like a last beer?"

I nodded, and he passed me a can of Tuborg and stood next to me.

I opened it, foam squirted over the shiny lid. I slurped it up. Then I tipped my head back and took a real swig.

"There's nothing like drinking for four days in a row!" I said.

He laughed in that strange manner of his, it was almost ingressive, which was so easy to imitate and indeed everyone did.

"She's really something, that Lisbeth," he said. "How did you catch her?"

"Catch? I've never caught a girl in my life," I said. "You're asking the wrong guy."

"You were making out for a week. She went back home with you. If that's not catching, I don't know what is."

"But that wasn't me! It was her! She just came up to me! Then she put her hand on my chest. Like this."

I placed my hand flat against his chest.

"Hey, stop that!" he shouted.

We laughed.

"I don't know," he said, looking at me. "Do you think I'll ever get a girl? Honestly?"

"*Ever? Honestly?*"

"Cut the crap. Do you think there's someone who will have me?"

Jøgge was the only person I knew who could ask questions like that and really mean them. He could be completely open. He was as kind as could be. But handsome? Maybe not many would call him that. Nor elegant. Robust, that was perhaps the word. Solid. A hundred percent reliable. Intelligent. A good person. A sense of humor. But he was no male model.

"There's got to be someone," I said. "You aim much too high. That's your problem. You want . . . well, who do you want?"

"Cindy Crawford," he said.

"Now you cut the crap," I said. "Come on. Which girls do you usually talk about?"

"Kristin. Inger. Merethe. Wenche. Therese."

I spread out my arms.

"There you are. The cream! You'll never get any of them! You've got to understand that!"

"But those are the ones I want," he said with his broadest grin.

"Same here," I said.

"Oh?" he said, turning his head toward me. "Thought it was just Hanne with you?"

"That's something else."

"What's that then?"

"Love."

"Oh my God," he said. "I think I'll join the others."

"I'll come with you."

They were playing cards around a table in the café, drinking Coke now, we were approaching land. I sat down with them. Harald, his protégé, Ekse, Helge, and Tor Erling were there. They didn't like me, I had no real relationship with any of them, except on occasions like this. I was tolerated, but no more than that. A sarcastic comment was never far away. It didn't matter though, I couldn't give a shit about them.

Jøgge was different. We had been in the same class for two years, discussed politics until smoke came out of our ears, he was a Fremskrittsparti man, a right-winger of all things, I was a Sosialistisk Venstreparti supporter, the left. He liked good music, strangely enough, out there in farming country, he was the only person I knew who had an ounce of good taste. He had lost his father when he was little, lived at home with his mother and younger brother, he had always had big responsibilities. Now and then people tried to tease him, he was an easy target, but he just laughed and so they gave up. The crowd we were sitting with used to bait him in a good-natured way and if he reacted they would just imitate his laugh, then he went quiet or laughed along with them.

Yes, he was a good man. He went to the business gymnas, as a couple of others on the team did, the rest went to the technical school, and I had written a few essays for him and been paid for it, he'd been concerned that they shouldn't be too good, the teachers would never swallow that. Once, when he had been in the danger zone, I'd written a poem for him to hand in and his teacher considered that way out of character for Jøgge. But he scraped through; he was asked to interpret this poem, which he managed to do and was awarded a passing grade.

I had been a little disappointed because I'd put my heart and soul into that poem and I'd had a top grade in mind. But this was the business gymnas, so what could you expect?

In town, in one of the cafés, I would have probably looked in a different direction if Jøgge had walked in, he was a different breed, the wrong breed, but he may have known that himself. At any rate, I never saw him in such surroundings.

"Hey, Casanova, want another beer?" he said now.

"Why not," I said. "But then who are you? Anti-Casanova?"

"My name is Bøhn, Jørgen Bøhn," he said, and laughed.

An hour and a half later I walked ashore in Kristiansand with my big seaman's kitbag over my shoulder. The others were going up to Tveit, I was going to a party with Bassen, who was waiting for me when I came out of customs.

"Hi," he said.

"Hi," I said.

"Have a good summer?"

"So-so. And you?"

"Good."

"Any women?" I said.

"Of course. A couple, I guess."

He laughed, and we headed for the bus station to catch a bus to the ferry quay. We had a kind of competition running that year, to see who could make out with the most girls in our class, we chatted about that as we sat drinking beer and waiting for Siv to come in her boat and pick us up. The approaching night was the last chance to change the score, which was heavily weighted in Bassen's favor: he had been with seven; me, only four.

Occasionally I wondered what school would be like in the autumn. He was going down the science route, I was doing social subjects, until now we had been in the same class, which meant it was natural to hang out together.

In one of the first lessons we'd sat next to each other, and after the home-room teacher had handed out slips of paper for us to write down three personal qualities we had, Bassen had looked at my answer. *Somber, torpid, and serious*, I had written.

"Are you a complete idiot?" he had said. "You should add *lacking in self-knowledge*! I've never seen anything like it. Somber and torpid, you've got to be kidding! Who's put these ideas in your head?"

"So what did you write?"

He showed me.

Down to earth, honest, horny as hell.

"Throw that away. You can't write that!" Bassen said.

I did as I was told. Then on a new piece I wrote, intelligent, shy, but not really.

"That's better," he said. "Jesus! *Somber and torpid!*"

The first time I went to his house, late that autumn, I was filled with respect, I could hardly believe it, he was all I wanted to be, and even later, when we saw more of each other, that thought was never far away. Also now. His presence pervaded every part of me, I admired everything he did, I noticed every look he cast, even across the sea in boredom, and reflected on it.

Why did he want to meet me? I had nothing that was of any use to him.

When we were together I always left early so that he wouldn't discover how boring I really was. There was a kind of fever in me, two conflicting emotions, such as on the spring morning when we ditched school and went by moped back to his place and listened to records on the lawn. It was fantastic, yet I had to cut it short, something told me I wasn't worthy or couldn't fulfill his expectations. So I lay on his lawn with my eyes closed, like a cat on hot bricks, listening to Talk Talk, whom we had discovered at the same time. "It's your life," they sang, and everything should have been great, it was spring, I was sixteen years old, had ditched school for the first time, and was lying on the grass with my new friend. But it wasn't great, it was unbearable.

He probably thought I feared a reprimand for skipping school and that was why I got up to go. How could he have known that it was because it was much too good? Because I liked him too much.

Now we hadn't said anything for maybe five minutes.

I rolled a cigarette to fill the silence with a normal activity. He glanced at me. Took a packet of Prince Mild from his shirt pocket, poked a filter tip in his mouth.

"Got a light?" he said.

I passed him a yellow Bic lighter. He lit up and blew out a cloud of smoke, which hung in the air for a few seconds in front of him before dissolving.

"How's it going with your mom and dad?" he said, passing me the lighter. I took it, lit my rollie, crushed the empty can with my free hand and threw it down into the rocks by the water.

Dusk fell over the islands in front of us, heavy with the low-pressure system. The sea was calm and gray. The can clattered against the rocks below.

"It's going OK, I think," I said. "Dad's living in Tveit now with his new girlfriend. Mom's in Vestland. She'll be home in a few days."

"Is it still the two of you living up there?"

"Yes."

Around the headland came a boat. The person at the helm had long blond hair that shone against all the gray, and when we got up and lifted our rucksacks she waved and screamed something, which was reduced to a faint squeal across the hundred meters between us.

It was Siv.

We loaded our rucksacks on board, sat down, and ten minutes later we moored beneath her cabin.

"You're the last," she said. "So now finally we can eat."

Hanne was there. She was sitting at the table. Dressed in a white shirt and jeans. Her bangs had grown, I noticed.

She smiled, a touch embarrassed.

Probably caused by the letters I had sent.

We ate shrimp. I drank beer, and the intoxicating effect on me was greater and more deeply seated than I had ever experienced before, presumably because of all the drinking over the previous days. It affected not only my head and my thoughts, it started in the depths of my body and slowly spread, and I knew that the wave that was coming would be long lasting.

And so it was. We cleared the sitting room and danced as night fell over the archipelago, we went outside and swam in the darkness, gingerly I walked along the diving board, above me the sky was black, below me the sea was black, and when I dived it felt as if I would never reach the water, I fell and fell and fell and then suddenly I was enveloped by cold, salty water, I saw nothing, everything was black, but it was not dangerous, a few strokes and I broke the surface and could see the others standing on land like small, pale trees in the darkness.

Hanne was waiting for me with a towel, which she wrapped around my shoulders. We sat high up the mountainside. Some of the girls below were swimming naked.

"They're skinny-dipping," I said.

"I can see," Hanne said.

"Don't you want to join them?"

"Me? No! That's the last thing I would do."

Silence.

She looked at me.

"Would you like me to?"

"Yes."

"Thought so!" she said with a laugh. "What about you?"

"The water's so cold. It would disappear."

"It?" she said, and smiled at me.

"Yes," I said.

"You're a strange boy," she said.

There was another silence. I gazed at all the islets, a touch blacker than the sky above. A ribbon of light hung over the horizon. Surely day couldn't be coming already?

"It's great sitting here with you," I said. "I love you."

She shot me a rapid glance. "I'm not so sure about that."

"How can't you be? I don't think about anyone but you. When I was in Vestland – oh, by the way, it was fantastic, even though you weren't there – I was full of you, in a way. Absolutely drunk."

"You drink too much," she said. "Couldn't you be a bit more careful? For my sake?"

"Drunk with you," I said.

"I know that! But seriously. You don't have to drink so much, do you?"

"Happy clappy Christian? Intoxicated by Jesus?"

"No, don't make jokes. I *am* a bit worried about you. Is that a problem?"

"No."

We fell quiet. On the diving board there were two figures fighting. One was Bassen, I guessed.

Both fell in the water. Those watching on land screamed and clapped.

Somewhere in the distance a lighthouse flashed. Music blared out from an open door in the cabin behind us.

"Actually you know nothing about me," she said.

"I know enough."

"No, what you see is something else. It's not me you see."

"You're wrong there," I said. "You're actually wrong there."

We stared at each other. Then she smiled.

"Well, shall we join the others?" she said.

I sighed and got up. "For a bit more to drink, if nothing else," I said.

I held out my hand and pulled her up.

"You promised!" she said.

"I promised nothing. Hanne?" I said.

"Yes?"

"Can I hold your hand the short distance to the cabin?"

"Yes."

I put on my trousers and jacket and danced to "Don't You (Forget About Me)" by Simple Minds with Bassen while Hanne sat at the table chatting to Annette and watching us.

I stood next to her and poured vodka and juice into a glass.

"You're so sexy when you wear a jacket," she said.

"Do you think so too?" I said, looking at Annette.

"No," she said. "Of course I don't. Aren't you two going to kiss soon?"

"Not in this life by the look of things," I said.

"Perhaps in heaven then?" she said.

"But I don't believe in God," I said.

Hanne laughed, and I went over to Bassen, who was poring over the record collection.

"Find anything?"

"Well," he said. "There's some Sting. But I need some sleep. I'm off to England tomorrow. I don't want to miss the boat."

"You can sleep on the boat," I said. "You don't need to go to bed now."

He laughed. "Why not? You'll have a free hand when I'm out of the way."

"OK, you win. I didn't stand a chance."

He took out the inner sleeve and held it at an angle so the record slid out. With his thumb on the edge and his other fingers on the label in the center, he placed it on the turntable.

"How's it going with you and Hanne?" he said, swinging the pick-up arm to the first groove and lowering it with the little lever.

"It's not," I said.

"You looked pretty happy out there on your rock."

"That's as far as it goes," I said.

Then "If You Love Somebody Set Them Free" streamed out of the loud-speakers, and soon everyone inside was dancing.

We slept in the loft, I lay dozing till late in the morning and dragged out the time for as long as I could after that, I didn't want it to end, I wanted to be there, in the happiness I had felt, but then Siv had to take the last group back, and I jumped on board, sat quietly in the bow on the way across, found a seat to myself right at the back of the bus, pressed my forehead against the window and gazed out at the rolling Sørland countryside, which gradually became more and more urban until we reached the bus station and I got onto a bus that would take me home, to where Dad was living now with Unni.

I had caught this bus almost every day for three years, but it felt like a whole life. I knew every bend, indeed every tree on the route, and I was on such familiar terms with many of the people who got off or on that we nodded to one another even though we had never exchanged a word.

It had been good on the island. Perhaps I'd never had such a good time.

On the other hand, it was only a class party.

Then there was Hanne.

Each in our own sleeping bag, we had lain face-to-face, whispering for maybe an hour before we fell asleep. She had also tried to whisper when she was laughing, and when she did I had thought, I can die now, it won't matter.

"Can I give you a goodnight kiss?" I said as we were about to go to sleep.

"On the cheek!" she said.

I levered my way forward a few centimeters on my elbows, she half turned her cheek to me, I moved my head slowly toward it, changed direction at the last minute and gave her a juicy kiss on the mouth.

"You cheat!" she said with a laugh.

"Goodnight," I said.

"Goodnight," she said.

That was how it had been.

And surely it is impossible for that whole evening and night not to mean something?

She had to feel something for me.

She had to feel something.

She had said several times that she wasn't in love with me. She liked me, she said, very much even, but it was no more than that.

Now she was going to change schools and start at Vågsbygd Gymnas, where she lived.

At least that would release me from the torment of seeing her every day!

The bus indicated it was going to Kjevik, and at that moment a plane flying low thundered over us, touched down, and screamed along the runway at a speed that made it seem as if we were standing still.

Flashing lights, roaring engine. We were living in the future.

I might bump into her now and then in town, we could have lunch together, go to the cinema, I could take her swimming with me on Saturday mornings. Gradually she would realize she was in love with me. She would finish the other business, tell me with a glow in her eyes that now there was nothing to stop us anymore.

But then?

When we were together?

Visit each other in the evenings, kiss, and eat pizza? Go to the cinema with her friends?

That was not enough.

I *wanted* her. Not as part of a gymnas existence, a gymnas girlfriend, she meant more than that. I wanted to move in with her. Be with her day and night, share everything with her. Not in town, with everything that went on there constantly around us, but in the skerries or perhaps in the forest, no matter where, as long as it was a place where we could be completely alone.

Or in Oslo, a large town where no one knew us.

Then I could go shopping after returning from lectures because I would study, and make dinner for her, there in our own flat.

Then we could have a child.

The bus stopped in front of the tiny terminal building, and a man wearing a cap and carrying a little suitcase got on board, paid, and walked down the bus whistling as he went. He sat down in the seat in front of me.

I threw my arms in the air. The whole bus was empty! And he has to sit right there!

He smelled of sweet aftershave. His neck was covered in a scattering of thin hairs. His earlobes were fat and red. A farmer from Birkeland.

Child?

I didn't want one, I didn't want to work from nine to four, that was a trap I would steer clear of, but it was different with Hanne, that was about something else.

Jesus, no, of course we wouldn't get married, of course we wouldn't live in the skerries, of course we wouldn't have children!

I smiled. It had to be the wildest idea I'd ever had.

On the other side of the runway, across the road, was Jøgge's house. There was light in the windows, and I leaned forward to see if I could catch a glimpse of him. But, if I knew Jøgge, he would be lying on his waterbed listening to Peter Gabriel.

I woke up the next morning to the drone of a vacuum cleaner in the room underneath. I didn't move. The vacuuming stopped and other sounds became more prominent: the clink of bottles, the hum of the dishwasher, water running into a bucket. They had been having a party when I arrived. The last I had seen of them before sneaking up to my room the night before had been his contorted face and her laying a hand on his shoulder. That was the first time I had seen him drunk and the first time I had seen him cry. After a while the door was opened, footsteps crunched on the gravel outside, and then I heard their voices just under my window.

There was a bench with a table where Dad used to sit in the summer in that characteristic way of his, one leg crossed over the other, his back bent slightly forward, often holding a newspaper in his hands and a smoking cigarette between his fingers.

They laughed. Her voice was high-pitched, his deeper.

I got up and tiptoed over to the window.

The sky was a little misty, it softened a tone, but the sun shone and the air in the garden was perfectly still and quivered.

I opened the window.

And they were indeed sitting on the bench beneath, leaning against the wall with their eyes closed to the sun. Both tipped their heads back and looked up at me.

"Well, isn't that our Kaklove?" Dad said.

"Good morning, early bird!" Unni said.

"Good morning," I said, securing the window with the latch. I didn't like the way their voices seemed to embrace me, as though it was us three now. It wasn't true; it was the two of them and me.

But I liked the role of the rebellious teenager even less. The last thing in the world I wanted was to give them any reason at all to blame me for anything.

I ate a few slices of bread in the kitchen, carefully cleaned up afterward, brushed the crumbs on the plate and table into the trash bin under the sink, fetched the Walkman from my room, tied my shoes up, and went down to see them.

"I'm off for a walk," I said.

"You do that," Dad said. "Are you going to visit a buddy?"

He didn't know the name of a single one of my friends, not even Jan Vidar, whom I had been friends with for three years. But now he was sitting beside Unni and wanted to show that he was a good father who knew his son's habits.

"Yes, guess so," I said.

"Tomorrow I'll start moving my stuff down. It would be good if you were here. I might need some help carrying."

"Of course," I said. "OK, bye."

I wasn't going to a friend's. Jan Vidar was working at a bakery in town this summer, Bassen was on his way to England, Per was probably grafting at the floor factory, and what Jøgge was doing I had no idea, but it wasn't, and never had been, natural for me to get on my bike without a specific aim. I felt like being alone though, and I put on my headset, pressed play, and allowed myself to be engulfed in music as I walked downhill. The countryside lay serene before me, and the few clouds, above the ridges on the other side of the river valley, were motionless. I followed the road down, it was quiet too, because, apart from a farm a kilometer farther up, there was barely a house on this side for some distance. Only forest and water.

The green of the spruce needles shone brightly in the sunshine, it was almost black in the shadows, but there was something light about all the trees, it was the summer that did that, they weren't brooding or turned into themselves as in winter, no, they let the warm air filter through and stretched toward the sun, like everything else living.

I walked along the old forest path. Even though it was only a couple of hundred meters above our house I hadn't been there more than two or three times, and then only in winter, wearing skis. Nothing happened there, it was deserted and none of the kids up here gravitated toward that path: down at the bottom was where it all happened, that was where people lived.

If I had grown up here, I might have been familiar with every bush and rock, as I was with the countryside around our house in Tybakken. But I had lived here for only three years and no roots had developed, nothing meant anything, not really.

I turned off the music, pulled the headset down over my neck. Above me the air was so full of birdsong that it felt as if I could *see* it. Now and then there was a rustle in the undergrowth beside the path, that must have been birds too, I mused, but I didn't see any.

The path rose gently, in constant shadow from the high trees growing on both sides. At the top there was a small lake, I lay down on my back on the grass not far away and stared at the sky, listening to music, I played *Remain in Light*, and thought about Hanne.

I had to write another letter to her. It had to be so good that she wouldn't be able to think about anything else but me.

Dad didn't need much help from me with moving the following afternoon. He carried all the boxes himself, loaded them onto the big white rental van, and drove off to town, three trips was all it took; it was only when it came to the furniture that he needed a helping hand. With it aboard he slammed the doors shut and shot me a glance.

"Let's keep in touch," he said.

Then he laid a hand on my shoulder.

He had never done that before.

My eyes went moist and I looked down. He removed his hand, clambered up into the driver's seat, started the engine, and drove slowly downhill.

Did he like me?

Was that possible?

I wiped my eyes on my T-shirt sleeve.

That was that, I thought. I would never live with him again now. From the edge of the forest came the cat, his tail held high. He stopped by the door and looked at me with his yellow eyes.

"Do you want to go in, Mefisto?" I said. "Are you hungry too?"

He didn't answer, he rubbed his head against my leg as I went to open the door, darted in toward his dish, and stood there staring up at me.

I opened a new can, dumped a large pile in the dish, and went into the living room, where a faint trace of Unni's perfume hung in the air.

I opened the terrace door and stood on the step outside. Even if the sun no longer shone on the house, it was still warm out there.

Per came up the hill, walking with his bicycle at his side.

I went to the edge of the slope.

"Have you been working?" I shouted.

"By the sweat of my brow!" he shouted back. "Not like some people I know who sleep all day!"

"How much did you earn for your pension today?"

"More than you'll ever earn in the course of your whole life."

I watched him chuckling. He was the type that chuckled and had always been older than his years.

He raised a hand in salute, I did the same and then I went inside.

Two of the pictures on the living-room wall had gone. Half the records, I assumed, and half the books. All his papers, the desk and the office equipment. The sofa in front of the TV, the two Stressless leather chairs. Half of the kitchen utensils. And of course all his clothes.

But the house didn't seem to have been stripped.

In the room beside the hall the telephone rang. I hurried over.

"Hello, this is Karl Ove," I said.

"Hi, Yngve here. What's new?"

"Dad's just left with the last load. Mom will be here soon. So I'm on my own with the cat. Where are you?"

"I'm at Trond's still. I was thinking of coming over. Tomorrow actually, but if Dad's gone, I might come tonight."

"Could you? That would be great."

"I'll see. Arvid would have to drive me. He might have time. Anyway, maybe see you tonight then!"

"Fantastic!"

I cradled the phone and went to see what there was in the fridge.

When Mom drove up the hill an hour later, I had fried some sausages, onions, and potatoes, sliced some bread, put out the butter and set the table.

I went to meet her. She drove the car into the garage, got out, stretched up on her toes, grabbed the door, and closed it.

She was wearing white slacks, a rust-red sweater, and sandals. She smiled when she saw me. She seemed tired, but then she had been driving all day.

"Hi!" she said. "Are you alone?"

"Yes," I said.

"Did you have a nice time in Denmark?"

"Yes, great. And what about you? Did you have a nice time in Sørbøvåg?"

"Yes, I did."

I leaned forward and gave her a hug. Followed her into the kitchen.

"Have you made some food?!" she said.

I smiled.

"Take the weight off your feet. You've been driving all day. I'll put some water on for tea. I didn't know exactly when you would get here."

"No, of course. I should have called," she said. "Tell me then. How was it in Denmark?"

"It was really good. Some fantastic fields. We played a couple of games. And then we went out on the last night. But the best part was the class party. That was really great."

"Did you meet Hanne there?" she said.

"Yes. That was the great part."

She smiled. I smiled too.

Then the phone rang. I went in and answered it.

"Dad here."

"Hi," I said.

"Is Mom there now?"

"Yes. Do you want to talk to her?"

"No, what should I talk to her about? We were wondering if you would like to visit us on Monday. A little housewarming party."

"Love to. When?"

"Six. Have you heard anything from Yngve?"

"No, I think he's on Tromøya."

"Tell him he's invited too if you hear from him."

"OK, will do."

"Good. See you."

"See you."

I put down the phone. How could his voice be so cold now when he'd put his hand on my shoulder only a few hours ago?

I went into the kitchen, where Mom was pouring hot water into the teapot.

"That was Dad," I said.

"Oh?" she said.

"He invited me to dinner."

"That's nice, isn't it?"

I shrugged.

"Have you heard from him this summer?"

"No, only from his solicitor," she said, putting the teapot on the table and sitting down.

"What did the lawyer have to say?"

"Well . . . it's all about how to share the house. We can't agree, but it's nothing you have to worry about."

"Have to? I can worry about it if I want, can't I?" I said as I put the spatula in the pan and transferred some sausages, potatoes, and onions onto a plate.

"You don't have to take sides. I suppose that's what I mean," she said.

"I took sides years ago," I said. "When I was seven I took sides. So that's nothing new. Or a problem."

I stuck the fork into a bit of sausage that had curled up in the heat, put it to my mouth, and sank my teeth into it.

"But if things go the way it looks as if they're headed, we won't have much money in the future. That is, you'll get your payments from Dad of course. They're yours to dispose of as you like, I suppose. But as I've got to buy his share of this house, it's going to be tough economically for me."

"That doesn't matter," I said. "It's only money. That's not what life's about."

"True enough." She smiled. "That's a good attitude to have."

Yngve and Arvid arrived at about ten. Arvid just poked his head around the door to say hello before leaving again while Yngve dragged a suitcase and a big bag up to his room, which he had hardly used in the three years we'd lived there.

"You're not going tomorrow, are you?" I said when he came back down.

"Nope," he said. "The plane leaves the day after. Perhaps. I've got a standby ticket."

We went into the living room. I sat down in the wicker chair, Yngve sat beside Mom on the sofa. Outside, two bats flitted to and fro, disappearing completely in the darkness of the mountains across the river, then reappearing against the lighter sky. Yngve poured coffee from the Thermos.

"Well," he said. "I suppose it's debriefing time."

Throughout our childhood we three had sat chatting, that was what I was used to, but this was the first time we had done it without Dad living in the house, and the difference was immense. Knowing that he couldn't walk in at any moment, forcing us to think about what we were saying and doing, changed everything.

We had chatted about everything under the sun then too, but never so much as a word about Dad, it was a kind of implicit rule.

I had never thought about that before.

But we couldn't talk about him now, that would have been inconceivable. Why?

Perhaps it was bound up with loyalty. Perhaps with a fear of being overheard. But irrespective of what had happened during the day and irrespective of how upset I was, I never talked to them about it. To Yngve on his own, yes, but not when the three of us were together.

Then it was as though a dam had burst. Everything suddenly flowed into the same channel, into the same valley, which was soon full of something that excluded everything else.

Yngve began to talk about himself, and it wasn't long before we were going through one incident after the other. Yngve told us about the time the B-Max supermarket opened and he was sent off with a shopping list and some money, under strict instructions to bring back a receipt. He had done that, but the sum in his hand hadn't tallied with the till receipt and Dad had marched him into the cellar and given him a beating. He told us about the time his bike had had a puncture and Dad had beaten him. I, for my part, had never been beaten; for some reason Dad had always treated Yngve worse. But I talked about the times he had slapped me and the times he had locked me in the cellar, and the point of these stories was always the same: his fury was always triggered by some petty detail, some utter triviality, and as such was actually comical. At any rate we laughed when we told the stories. Once I had left a pair of gloves on the bus and he slapped me in the face when he found out. I had leaned against the wobbly table in the hall and sent it flying and he came over and hit me. It was absolutely absurd! I lived in fear of him, I said, and Yngve said Dad controlled him and his thoughts, even now.

Mom said nothing. She sat listening, looking at me then Yngve. Sometimes her eyes seemed to go blank. She had heard about most of these incidents before, but now there was such a plethora of them she might well have been overwhelmed.

"He had such chaos inside him," she said at length. "More than I realized. I saw him angry of course. I didn't see him hitting you. He never did when I was around. And you didn't say anything. I tried to compensate for his bouts of anger. To give you something else . . ."

"Relax, Mom," I said. "We got through it. That was then, not now."

"We always talked a lot, didn't we," she said. "And he was manipulative. He was. Very. But he did also have some self-awareness. He made that clear to me. So I . . . well, I always saw it from his side, what happened. He said he had so little communication with you, and it was because I stood between you and him. And in a way that's true. You always turned to me. When he was there you left. I had a bad conscience about that."

"What happened happened, and it's fine," Yngve said. "But what I have a problem with is that when you moved here I was left to cope on my own. You didn't help me. I was seventeen years old, at gymnas, and had no money."

Mom took a deep breath.

"I know," she said. "I was loyal to him. I shouldn't have been. That was wrong of me. It was a big mistake."

"Come on," I said. "It's over, all of it. It's just us now."

Mom lit a cigarette. I looked at Yngve.

"What shall we do tomorrow then?"

He shrugged.

"What do you feel like doing?"

"Swimming maybe?"

"Or we could go to town? Check out some record shops and cafés?"

He turned to Mom. "Can I borrow your car?"

"Yes, you can."

Mom went to bed half an hour later. I knew all she was thinking about was what we had been saying and she would be lying awake and reflecting. I didn't want her to feel like this, to be so tormented by it, she didn't deserve that, but there was nothing I could do.

When we heard the creaks in the ceiling on the other side of the living room, Yngve looked at me.

"Coming out for a smoke?"

I nodded.

We walked quietly into the hall, put on shoes and jackets, and crept out to the opposite side of the house from where she was sleeping.

"When are you going to tell her you smoke?" I said, watching the flame from the lighter flicker across his face, the glow that came to life when the lighter died.

I heard him blowing out the smoke.

"When will *you*?"

"I'm sixteen. I'm not allowed to smoke. But you're twenty."

"All right, all right."

I was a little offended and walked a few steps into the garden. There was a heavy aroma coming from the big bush with white flowers at the end of the potato patch. What was it called again?

The sky was light, the forest beyond the river dark.

"Did you ever see Mom and Dad hug?" Yngve said.

I walked back to him.

"No," I said. "Not that I can remember. Did you?"

He nodded in front of me in the semidarkness.

"Once. It was in Hove, so I must have been five. Dad was yelling at Mom so much she burst into tears. She was standing in the kitchen crying. He went into the living room. Then he went back and put his arms around her and consoled her. That's the only time."

I started to cry. But it was dark, and not a sound came from me, so he didn't notice.

Before we left for town I went to find Mom. She was wandering around the garden with a pair of large gloves on, trimming the edges of the beds with shears.

"Could you give me some money?" I said. "I spent all I had in Denmark."

"I'll see what I've got," she said, and went indoors to get her bag. I followed.

"Is fifty OK?" she said, taking a green banknote from her purse.

"Have you got a hundred? I was thinking of buying a record or two."

She counted her coins.

"Ninety. That's all, I'm afraid."

"It'll have to do then," I said, went back to the car, which stood idling on the gravel drive, and got in beside Yngve, who was wearing his Ray-Bans.

"I'm going to buy myself a pair when I get the money," I said, pointing to the sunglasses.

He set off down the hill.

"Buy them when you get your first student loan," he said.

"That's *two* years away."

"You'll have to get a job then. Piling planks at Boen or whatever it is you do there."

"I was thinking of doing record reviews," I said. "And interviewing bands, that sort of thing."

"Oh?" he said. "That sounds like a good idea. Who for?"

"*Nye Sørlandet.*"

We drove along the narrow road under the deciduous trees, past the old white houses, the river glinting beneath us. When we reached the waterfall and I saw some figures lying on the cliff beside it, I turned to him.

"Let's go swimming afterward. We can fit in both," I said.

"We could," he said. "At Hamresanden?"

"Ye-es."

"Do they sell ice cream there?"

"Of course they do. They may even have soft ice cream."

I took Yngve to Platebørsen, the record shop in the town's old *børs*, the stock exchange, a situation I relished, now I was the one who knew where everything was and what was good.

He held up a record. "Have you got this one?"

"No? What is it?"

"The Church. *The Blurred Crusade*. You've *got* to have this one."

"OK. I'll get it."

I also had enough money for a Nice Price record and bought the Talking Heads' *77*. Yngve was going to wait until his student loan came through before he bought any records.

We sat down in the café outside the library and smoked and drank coffee. I hoped someone I knew would come by, so that Yngve wouldn't think I had no friends in town and because the ones I had would see me sitting with Yngve.

But there didn't seem to be anyone in town today.

"Where did Mom buy the records at Christmas?" Yngve said. "Do you remember?"

For Christmas Yngve had been given The The's debut album by Mom while I got *Script of the Bridge* by the Chameleons. I had never heard of the Chameleons, but they were absolutely fantastic. Yngve thought the same about The The. We couldn't figure out how she had managed this. There was hardly anyone here in town who followed the indie scene more closely than Yngve and me. Well, she said, she had gone into a record shop and then she had described first Yngve, then me, and the assistant had pulled out these two records.

I asked which shop it was, she told me, and over the Christmas period I popped in. Harald Hempel was behind the counter. So now I understood. He played with Lily and the Gigolos, and what he didn't know about good music wasn't worth knowing.

"It's in Dronningens Gate," I said. "Shall we head down there?"

"Do a little tour?"

As we drove away from the last shop I pointed to a building in the next block.

"That's *Nye Sørlandet*. The paper I was talking about."

Yngve glanced up as we passed. "Looks small," he said.

"Well, it's the second biggest newspaper here. Like *Tiden* in Arendal, more or less."

I cast an eye up and down Elvegaten, where Dad lived now, to see if I could see him. But I couldn't.

"What's better, do you think?" I said. "Writing an application or going to speak to them?"

"Going to speak to them."

"OK. I'll do that then."

"Have you heard that Simple Minds are coming, by the way? To Drammenshallen."

"Really?"

"Yes. It's not for a while yet, but the tickets are on sale soon. You should go and see them."

"OK. And you?"

"It's too far away and too expensive. But for you it's only a train ride."

"OK," I said, and leaned back in the seat. As we drove I tried to imagine what it would have been like here without a road, without the housing estates, as it must have been once. Untouched bays and coves, vast, perhaps impenetrable, forests. The beach at Hamresanden no more than a strip of sand along the riverbank and the sea inlet. No caravans, no tents, no cabins, no stalls, no people. No shops, no petrol stations, no houses, no chapel, nothing. Just forest, mountain, beach, sea.

It was an impossible image.

"Let's forget about Hamresanden," Yngve said. "Mom'll probably have dinner ready soon anyway."

"OK," I said. "I feel like listening to the Church record anyway."

I was never upset when people left, the way that Mom always was. Except when it was Yngve. And then I wasn't upset, there were no strong emotions at play, it was more a kind of melancholy.

So I didn't join Mom when she drove Yngve to Kjevik, instead I cycled down to see Jan Vidar and went with him to the river, where we swam and stayed for an hour. We paddled across the rapids, then we slid down over the smooth algae-slippery overhang into the current beneath, which it was impossible to fight, all you could do was let yourself be carried along, swim a couple of strokes, and steer patiently toward the bank.

Afterward we lay on a rock, our arms down by our sides, drying in the sun, our sneakers beside us, Jan Vidar's folded glasses in one of his.

On this particular day, Merethe and Gunn were there too. They lay on the bare rock in the middle of rapids, both in bikinis. It excited us that they were there, our pulse rates shot up sky high, even though we were lying quite still. The effect was contrary to nature. At least that was how it felt to me.

Merethe was wearing a red bikini.

She was two years younger than we were, still in the eighth grade, about to start the ninth, but what did that matter?

I couldn't go out with her, but what did my body care about that?

Oh, how unbelievably frustrating it was to lie there ogling her. Seeing her thighs, which spread as she lay on the rock, seeing that little area between her thighs, the red material nestling against her, just there. And, oh yes, her breasts.

When we got up we hoped they would see us and perhaps be thinking the same as we were. But they were so blasé, so worldly wise, that not even we, Jan Vidar and Karl Ove, were good enough for them.

We climbed up the waterfall above them, swam into the current, were carried down into the rapids and into the broad deep river beyond.

They didn't bat an eyelid.

We were used to that though. We had spent three summers like that now. My insides ached and I presumed the same was true for Jan Vidar. At any rate, like me, he was squirming on the rock where we lay.

We could no longer tell each other that our chance would come because we didn't believe it would.

Why had they ruined my opportunity in Denmark?

What a dirty trick that had been. They had got so little out of it, an extra little laugh maybe, while what they had ruined for me meant everything.

I told Jan Vidar about it.

He laughed.

"You had it coming to you. How could you be so foolish as to tell Bjørn and Jøgge?"

"It was all planned," I said. "Absolutely everything! It was perfect! And then . . . nothing."

"Was she good-looking?"

"Yes, she was. Very good-looking."

"Better looking than Hanne?"

"No, no, no comparison. Like apples and pears."

"What?"

"It's impossible to compare Hanne with some Danish girl I want to fuck. Surely you can see that?"

"What are you going to do with Hanne?"

"Well, I'm not going to talk about her in this way for starters."

He smiled and closed his eyes.

The following afternoon I went to Dad's. I had put on a white shirt, black cotton trousers, and white basketball shoes. In order not to feel so utterly naked, as I did when I wore only a shirt, I took a jacket with me, slung it over my shoulder and held it by the hook since it was too hot outside to wear it.

I jumped off the bus after Lundsbroa Bridge and ambled along the drowsy, deserted summer street to the house he was renting, where I had stayed that winter.

He was in the back garden pouring lighter fluid over the charcoal in the grill when I arrived. Bare chest, blue swimming shorts, feet thrust into a pair of sloppy sneakers without laces. Again this getup was unlike him.

"Hi," he said.

"Hi," I said.

"Have a seat."

He nodded to the bench by the wall.

The kitchen window was open, from inside came the clattering of glasses and crockery.

"Unni's busy inside," he said. "She'll be here soon."

His eyes were glassy.

He stepped toward me, grabbed the lighter from the table, and lit the charcoal. A low almost transparent flame, blue at the bottom, rose in the grill. It didn't appear to have any contact with the charcoal at all, it seemed to be floating above it.

"Heard anything from Yngve?"

"Yes," I said. "He dropped by briefly before leaving for Bergen."

"He didn't come by," Dad said.

"He said he was going to, see how you were doing, but he didn't have time."

Dad stared into the flames, which were lower already. Turned and came toward me, sat down on a camping chair. Produced a glass and bottle of red wine from nowhere. They must have been on the ground beside him.

"I've been relaxing with a drop of wine today," he said. "It's summer after all, you know."

"Yes," I said.

"Your mother didn't like that," he said.

"Oh?" I said.

"No, no, no," he said. "That wasn't good."

"No," I said.

"Yeah," he said, emptying the glass in one swig.

"Gunnar's been round, snooping," he said. "Afterward he goes straight to Grandma and Grandad and tells them what he's seen."

"I'm sure he just came to visit you," I said.

Dad didn't answer. He refilled his glass.

"Are you coming, Unni?" he shouted. "We've got my son here!"

"OK, coming," we heard from inside.

"No, he was snooping," he repeated. "Then he ingratiates himself with your grandparents."

He stared into the middle distance with the glass resting in his hand.

Turned his head to me.

"Would you like something to drink? A Coke? I think we've got some in the fridge. Go and ask Unni."

I stood up, glad to get away.

Gunnar was a sensible, fair man, decent and proper in all ways, he always had been, of that there was no doubt. So where had Dad's sudden backbiting come from?

After all the light in the garden, at first I couldn't see my hand in front of my face in the kitchen. Unni put down the scrub brush when I went in, came over and gave me a hug.

"Good to see you, Karl Ove." She smiled.

I smiled back. She was a warm person. The times I had met her she had been happy, almost flushed with happiness. And she had treated me like an adult. She seemed to want to be close to me. Which I both liked and disliked.

"Same here," I said. "Dad said there was some Coke in the fridge."

I opened the fridge door and took out a bottle. Unni wiped a glass dry and passed it to me.

"Your father's a fine man," she said. "But you know that, don't you?"

I didn't answer, just smiled, and when I was sure that my silence hadn't been perceived as a denial, I went back out.

Dad was still sitting there.

"What did Mom say?" he asked into the middle distance once again.

"About what?" I said, sat down, unscrewed the top, and filled the glass so full that I had to hold it away from my body and let it froth over the flag-stones.

He didn't even notice!

"Well, about the divorce," he said.

"Nothing in particular," I said.

"I suppose I'm the monster," he said. "Do you sit around talking about it?"

"No, not at all. Cross my heart."

There was a silence.

Over the white timber fence you could see sections of the river, greenish in the bright sunlight, and the roofs of the houses on the other side. There were trees everywhere, these beautiful green creations that you never really paid much attention to, just walked past; you registered them but they made no great impression on you in the way that dogs or cats did, but they were actually, if you lent the matter some thought, present in a far more breathtaking and sweeping way.

The flames in the grill had disappeared entirely. Some of the charcoal briquettes glowed orange, some had been transformed into grayish-white puffballs, some were as black as before. I wondered if I could light up. I had a packet of cigarettes inside my jacket. It had been all right at their party. But that was not the same as it being permitted now.

Dad drank. Patted the thick hair at the side of his head. Poured wine into his glass, not enough to fill it, the bottle was empty. He held it in the air and studied the label. Then he stood up and went indoors.

I would be as good to him as I could possibly be, I decided. Regardless of what he did, I would be a good son.

This decision came at the same time as a gust of wind blew in from the sea, and in some strange way the two phenomena became connected inside me, there was something fresh about it, a relief after a long day of passivity.

He returned, knocked back the dregs in his glass and recharged it.

"I'm doing fine now, Karl Ove," he said as he sat down. "We're having such a good time together."

"I can see you are," I said.

"Yes," he said, oblivious to me.

Dad grilled some steaks, which he carried into the living room, where Unni had set the table: a white cloth, shiny new plates and glasses. Why we didn't sit outside I didn't know, but I assumed it was something to do with the neighbors. Dad had never liked being seen and definitely not in such an intimate situation as eating was for him.

He absented himself for a few minutes and returned wearing the white shirt with frills he had worn at their party, with black trousers.

While we had been sitting outside Unni had boiled some broccoli and baked some potatoes in the oven. Dad poured red wine into my glass, I could have one with the meal, he said, but no more than that.

I praised the food. The barbecue flavor was particularly good when you had meat as good as this.

"*Skål*," Dad said. "*Skål* to Unni!"

We held up our glasses and looked at each other.

"And to Karl Ove," she said.

"We may as well toast me too then." Dad laughed.

This was the first relaxed moment, and a warmth spread through me. There was a sudden glint in Dad's eye and I ate faster out of sheer elation.

"We have such a cozy time, the two of us do," Dad said, placing a hand on Unni's shoulder. She laughed.

Before he would never have used an expression such as *cozy*.

I studied my glass, it was empty. I hesitated, caught myself hesitating, put the little spoon into a potato to hide my nerves and then stretched casually across the table for the bottle.

Dad didn't notice, I finished the glass quickly and poured myself another. He rolled a cigarette, and Unni rolled a cigarette. They sat back in their chairs.

"We need another bottle," he said, and went into the kitchen. When he returned he put his arm around her.

I fetched the cigarettes from my jacket, sat down and lit up.

Dad didn't notice that either.

He got up again and went to the bathroom. His gait was unsteady. Unni smiled at me.

"I teach my first course at gymnas in Norwegian this autumn," she said. "Perhaps you can give me a few tips? It's my first time."

"Yes, of course."

She smiled and looked me in the eye. I lowered my gaze and took another swig of the wine.

"Because you're interested in literature, aren't you?" she continued.

"Sort of," I said. "Among other things."

"I am too," she said. "And I've never read as much as when I was your age."

"Mm."

"I plowed through everything in sight. It was a kind of existential search, I think. Which was at its most intense then."

"Mm."

"You've found each other, I can see," Dad said behind me. "That's good. You have to get to know Unni, Karl Ove. She's such a wonderful person. She laughs all the time. Don't you, Unni?"

"Not all the time." She laughed.

Dad sat down, sipped from his glass and as he did so his eyes were as vacant as an animal's.

He leaned forward.

"I haven't always been a good father to you, Karl Ove. I know that's what you think."

"No, I don't."

"Now, now, no stupidities. We don't need to pretend any longer. You think I haven't always been a good father. And you're right. I've done a lot of things wrong. But you should know that I've always done the very best I could. I have!"

I looked down. This last he said with an imploring tone to his voice.

"When you were born, Karl Ove, there was a problem with one of your legs. Did you know that?"

"Vaguely," I said.

"I ran up to the hospital that day. And then I saw it. One leg was crooked! So it was put in plaster, you know. You lay there, so small, with plaster all the way up your leg. And when it was removed I massaged you. Many times every day for several months. We had to so that you would be able to walk. I massaged your leg, Karl Ove. We lived in Oslo then, you know."

Tears coursed down his cheeks. I glanced quickly at Unni, she watched him and squeezed his hand.

"We had no money either," he said. "We had to go out and pick berries, and I had to go fishing to make ends meet. Can you remember that? You think about that when you think about how we were. I did my best, you mustn't believe anything else."

"I don't," I said. "A lot happened, but it doesn't matter anymore."

His head shot up.

"YES, IT DOES!" he said. "Don't say that!"

Then he noticed the cigarette between his fingers. Took the lighter from the table, lit it, and sat back.

"But now we're having a cozy time anyway," he said.

"Yes," I said. "It was a wonderful meal."

"Unni's got a son as well, you know," Dad said. "He's almost as old as you."

"Let's not talk about him now," Unni said. "We've got Karl Ove here."

"But I'm sure Karl Ove would like to hear," Dad said. "They'll be like brothers. Won't they. Don't you agree, Karl Ove?"

I nodded.

"He's a fine young man. I met him here a week ago," he said.

I filled my glass as inconspicuously as I could.

The telephone in the living room rang. Dad got up to answer it.

"Whoops!" he said, almost losing his balance, and then to the phone, "Yes, yes, I'm coming."

He lifted the receiver.

"Hi, Arne!" he said.

He spoke loudly, I could have listened to every word if I'd wanted to.

"He's been under enormous strain recently," Unni whispered. "He needs to let off some steam."

"I see," I said.

"It's a shame Yngve couldn't come," she said.

Yngve?

"He had to go back to Bergen," I said.

"Yes, my dear friend, I'm sure you understand!" Dad said.

"Who's Arne?" I said.

"A relative of mine," she said. "We met them in the summer. They're so nice. You're bound to meet them."

"OK," I said.

Dad came back in and saw the bottle was nearly empty.

"Let's have a little brandy, shall we?" he said. "A digestif?"

"You don't drink brandy, do you?" Unni asked, looking at me.

"No, the boy can't have spirits," Dad said.

"I've had brandy before," I said. "In the summer. At soccer training camp."

Dad eyed me. "Does Mom know?" he said.

"Mom?" Unni said.

"You can have one glass, but no more," Dad said, staring straight at Unni. "Is that all right?"

"Yes, it is," she said.

He fetched the brandy and a glass, poured, and leaned back into the deep white sofa under the windows facing the road, where the dusk now hung like a veil over the white walls of the houses opposite.

Unni put her arm around him and one hand on his chest. Dad smiled.

"See how lucky I am, Karl Ove," he said.

"Yes," I said, and shuddered as the brandy met my tongue. My shoulders trembled.

"But she has a temper too, you know," he said. "Isn't that true?"

"Certainly is," she said with a smile.

"Once she threw the alarm clock against this wall," he said.

"I like to get things off my chest right away," Unni said.

"Not like your mother," he said.

"Do you have to talk about her the whole time?" Unni said.

"No, no, no, not at all," Dad said. "Don't be so touchy. After all, I had him with her," he said, nodding toward me. "This is my son. We have to be able to talk as well."

"OK," Unni said. "You just talk. I'm going to bed." She got up.

"But Unni . . ." Dad said.

She went into the next room. He stood up and slowly followed her without a further look.

I heard their voices, muted and angry. Finished the brandy, refilled my glass, and carefully put the bottle back in exactly the same place.

Oh dear.

He yelled.

Immediately afterward he returned.

"When does the last bus go, did you say?" he said.

"Ten past eleven," I said.

"It's almost that now," he said. "Perhaps it's best if you go now. You don't want to miss it."

"OK," I said, and got up. Had to place one foot well apart from the other so as not to sway. I smiled. "Thanks for everything."

"Let's keep in touch," he said. "Even though we don't live together anymore nothing must change between us. That's important."

"Yes," I said.

"Do you understand?"

"Yes. It's important we keep in touch," I said.

"You're not being flippant with me, are you?" he said.

"No, no, of course not," I said. "It's important now that you're divorced."

"Yes," he said. "I'll ring. Just drop by when you're in town. All right?"

"Yes," I said.

While putting on my shoes I almost toppled over and had to hold on to the wall. Dad sat on the sofa drinking and noticed nothing.

"Bye!" I shouted as I opened the door.

"Bye, Karl Ove," Dad called from inside, and then I went out into the darkness and headed for the bus stop.

I waited for about a quarter of an hour until the bus arrived, sitting on a step smoking and watching the stars, thinking about Hanne.

I could see her face in front of me.

She was laughing; her eyes were gleaming.

I could hear her laughter.

She was almost always laughing. And when she wasn't, laughter bubbled in her voice.

Brilliant! she would say when something was absurd or comical.

I thought about what she was like when she turned serious. Then it was as if she was on my home ground, and I felt I was an enormous black cloud wrapped around her, always greater than her. But only when she was serious, not otherwise.

When I was with Hanne I laughed almost all the time.

Her little nose!

She was more girl than woman in the same way that I was more boy than man. I used to say she was like a cat. And it was true there was something feline about her, in her movements, but also a kind of softness that wanted to be close to you.

I could hear her laughter, and I smoked and peered up at the stars. Then I heard the deep growl of the bus approaching between the houses, flicked the cigarette into the road, stood up, counted the coins in my pocket, and handed them to the driver when I stepped on board.

Oh, the muted lights in buses at night and the muted sounds. The few passengers, all in their own worlds. The countryside gliding past in the darkness. The drone of the engine. Sitting there and thinking about the best that you know, that which is dearest to your heart, wanting only to be there, out of this world, in transit from one place to another, isn't it only then you are really present in this world? Isn't it only then you really experience the world?

Oh, this is the song about the young man who loves a young woman. Has he the right to use such a word as "love"? He knows nothing about life, he knows nothing about her, he knows nothing about himself. All he knows is that he has never felt anything with such force and clarity before. Everything hurts, but nothing is as good. Oh, this is the song about being sixteen years old and sitting on a bus and thinking about her, the one, not knowing that feelings will slowly, slowly, weaken and fade, that life, that which is now so vast and so all-embracing, will inexorably dwindle and shrink until it is a manageable entity that doesn't hurt so much, but nor is it as good.

Only a forty-year-old man could have written that. I am forty now, as old as my father was then, I'm sitting in our flat in Malmö, my family is asleep in the rooms around me. Linda and Vanja in our bedroom, Heidi and John in the children's room, Ingrid, the children's grandmother, on a bed in the living room. It is November 25, 2009. The mid-'80s are as far away as the '50s were then. But most of the people in this story are still out there. Hanne is out there, Jan Vidar is out there, Jøgge is out there. My mother and my brother, Yngve – he spoke to me on the phone two hours ago, about a trip we are planning to Corsica in the summer, he with his children, Linda and I with ours – they are out there. But Dad is dead, his parents are dead.

Among the items Dad left behind were three notebooks and one diary. For three years he wrote down the names of everyone he met during the day, everyone he phoned, all the times he slept with Unni, and how much he drank. Now and then there was a brief report, mostly there wasn't.

"K.O. visited" appeared often.

That was me.

Sometimes it said "K.O. cheerful" after I had been there.

Sometimes "good conversation."

Sometimes "decent atmosphere."

Sometimes nothing.

I understand why he noted down the names of everyone he met and spoke to in the course of a day, why he registered all the quarrels and all the reconciliations, but I don't understand why he documented how much he drank. It is as if he was logging his own demise.

Starting school again after the holidays was like being sent back to Go: it turned out that everything was as it had been when I started gymnas the previous year. The class was new, the pupils and teachers unknown. The sole difference was that there had been twenty-six girls in the sophomore class while there were only twenty-four in the junior class.

I sat on the same seat, in the left-hand corner at the back, seen from the front, and I behaved in the same way: spoke up during lessons, discussed what teachers said, got into fights with other pupils over political or religious issues. When the breaks came everyone in the class joined the crowd they belonged to or the friends they had from before, and I invested all the physical and mental strength I possessed into avoiding the humiliation it was to be left standing somewhere on your own.

I went up to the library and read books such as *The Falcoln Tower* by the twenty-year-old writer Erik Fosnes Hansen, only four years to go until I am twenty, I thought, perhaps my name will be on the front of a book then? I sat in the classroom on my chair pretending I was doing homework. I walked up to the gas station opposite the school premises and bought something, anything, more often than not an Oslo newspaper because I couldn't read it with others around and so that was a plausible reason for sitting alone in the canteen during the endlessly long lunch break. Or I acted as if I was searching for someone. Up and down the stairs, through the long corridors, sometimes to Gimlehallen or over to the business school, in pursuit of a fictional person whom I searched for high and low. But usually I stood smoking by the entrance, because that act by its very nature determined where I should be, where I was entitled to be, where there were also others, my "friends" to those who wondered.

My fear of being seen as friendless was not without some justification. One day there was a new note on the notice board. A student who had recently moved to the town and didn't know anyone at the school wanted someone to be friends with, if anyone was interested they could meet him by the flagpole at twelve the next day.

The area around the flagpole at twelve the next day was packed with pupils. Everyone wanted to observe this friendless creature, who naturally enough didn't show up.

Had it been a hoax? Or had this friendless creature got cold feet when he saw the crowd?

I suffered with him, whoever he was.

One day I went to *Nye Sørlandet* and asked to speak to the person responsible for the newspaper's music section. I was shown into the office of someone called Steinar Vindsland. He was young with dark, big hair that was cut short at the back and on the sides, much in the style of the bass player in Simple Minds, and had a bristly chin and a gleam in his eye. I said who I was and what I wanted.

"Well, we don't have a regular record reviewer," he said. "I usually do the reviews, but I've got so many other jobs to do it would be great if someone else could do that."

He studied me.

I had dressed for the occasion, put on my black and white checked shirt, which was like the one The Edge wore, studded belt, and black trousers.

"So who do you like?"

I told him, and he nodded.

"We'll give you a spin. Look," he said, rummaging through the piles of records spread across the desk. "Take these with you and write about them. If it's good, you're our new record reviewer."

I sat down and wrote all weekend, draft after draft, and when Monday came round I walked down to the newspaper after school and delivered six handwritten pages. He read them standing up in his office, at a disconcertingly fast tempo. Then he fixed me with his gaze.

"I'm looking at our new record reviewer," he said.

"Did you like it?"

"It's good. Have you got a few minutes?"

"Yes."

"I'll take a few shots of you and do a little profile. Ask you a couple of questions. Are you at Katedralskolen?"

I nodded. He grabbed a camera from the table, lifted it to his face, and pointed it at me.

"Sit down there," he said, indicating the corner of the room.

My spine ran cold as I heard the clicks of the camera.

"Here," he said. "Grab these records and hold them up facing me."

He passed me three LPs and I held them up while staring into the lens with as serious an expression as I could muster.

"You like U2, you said. Who else?"

"Big Country. Simple Minds. David Bowie. And Iggy, of course. Talking Heads. R.E.M.'s *Chronic Town*, have you heard it? Fucking great."

"Oh yeah. Do you have a mission statement?"

I could feel my cheeks burning.

"Nooo," I said.

"Any particular axes to grind? Musically speaking? The gigs we get in town? Music programs on NRK? Any views on that?"

"Yes, well, it's shocking that there's only one good music program on the radio and nothing on TV."

"Great!" he said. "You're still sixteen, right?"

"Yes."

"That's it then. We'll run it tomorrow. You start next week. Is that all right?"

"Yes."

"Pop in on . . . say Thursday and we can discuss the nitty-gritty."

He shook my hand.

"And by the way," he said on the way out.

"Yes," I said.

"You can't write in longhand. That won't work. If you don't have a typewriter, get one!"

"OK," I said. "Thank you."

Then I was outside on the street.

It was too good to be true. I was *the* record reviewer for a *newspaper*! Sixteen years old!

I lit a cigarette and set off. The dry asphalt, the windows darkened in places with exhaust fumes, all the cars made me think I was in a city. I was a music journalist on my way through the streets of London. Coming hotfoot from a hectic editorial office.

Steinar Vindsland had been exactly as I had imagined a journalist to be. Unbelievably fast. Everything happened fast. They had deadlines, that was why they had to nail their articles at breakneck speed.

And he knew about music. Probably knew Harald Hempel. Maybe some of the bands in Oslo.

Now I could meet them!

I hadn't even thought about that. But now that I was a music reviewer I could hang out with the bands when they came to town.

No joke!

Fifteen meters in front of me was the crossroads between Dronningens Gate and Elvegaten. Since I was in the area I ought to go and see either Dad or Grandma and Grandad.

There was just one problem: I didn't have more than seven kroner on me and after five o'clock my student card was no longer valid on the bus.

But I ought to be able to borrow what I needed. After all, I had a job now.

I stopped by the traffic lights, which were red, pressed the button on the blue box and closed my eyes to get an impression of what it would be like for a blind person to be standing here.

Perhaps it was more important to visit Grandma and Grandad? I hadn't been to see them since Dad moved out. Perhaps now that Dad was divorced they were afraid they might lose contact with me or that I might stick with Mom.

I could see Dad on Tuesday after the meeting with Steinar.

Steinar!

At that moment the ticking started. The signal for the blind. I opened my eyes and walked over the pedestrian crossing, past the large square building with the supermarket and onto Lundsbroa Bridge, where the smell of sea was always stronger and the light also seemed stronger, probably because it reflected off the water, which widened out at this point.

A couple of white sails were visible in the distance. A double-ender was on its way in. I stopped, placed my hands on the brick parapet and leaned over. The water around the columns was a deep green.

Once Dad had fallen in here. This was about the only story he had told us about his childhood. He had been given a sound beating by Grandad, he had said, and had been put under the stairs, where he stayed for several hours.

Whether that was true or not, I didn't know. Dad had also said he had once been a promising soccer player and played for IK Start, which turned out to be a lie. Another time he had said that everything the Beatles did was plagiarism, they had stolen the songs from an unknown German composer and when I, twelve years old and a big Beatles fan, asked him how he knew, he said he had played the piano when he was young, and one day he had played some tunes by this German composer, whose name he couldn't remember, and discovered they were the same as the Beatles' songs. He still had the music at home. I believed him, of course; it was Dad who had told me. The next time we go there, could you find the sheets of music and play them on the piano? I had asked. No, they were stored away in the loft, it would take too long to find them. And then the realization dawned on me! He was lying! Dad was lying!

This insight was a relief, not a burden, because it was a face-saver for the Beatles.

I kept walking, took the shortcut to the right, came out in Kuholmsveien and walked up the gentle slope, from there I saw the sea widen out, so desolate and blue.

But why had he said we were so poor?

What did that have to do with anything?

I shook my head and passed a garden surrounded by wire fencing, inside which there were three trees groaning with dark red apples. A blue station wagon parked in the adjacent drive glinted in the sunlight.

Grandma poked her head out the window when I rang the bell, disappeared and reappeared a minute later at the door.

"Well, look who it is," she said. "Come in!"

I leaned forward and gave her a hug. She stiffened slightly. I was too old for this now, I thought, and straightened up.

She had the same fragrance as always, and it was as though the whole of my childhood opened inside me as I smelled it. We were going to Grandma's! Grandma's coming! Grandma's here!

"What's that in your ear?" she said.

I had forgotten it!

The two previous times I had been here I had taken the cross out. But not today.

"It's just a cross," I said.

"Yes, times are changing," she said. "Boys wearing jewelery in their ears! But that's how it is nowadays."

"Yes, it is," I said.

She turned and I followed her up the stairs. Grandad was sitting where he always did, in the kitchen chair.

"Well, look who it is," he said.

Under the clock on the wall I saw the tall blue step chair I had always loved, and on the table the coffeepot on the small wire stand that had always been here as well.

"Got your ear pierced?" he said.

"Yes, that's what's in nowadays," Grandma said. She smiled and shook her head. Came over and ruffled my hair.

"I got myself a job today," I said.

"Did you now?" Grandma said.

I nodded.

"At *Nye Sørlandet*, the newspaper. As a record reviewer."

"Do you know anything about music?" Grandad said.

"A little," I said.

"How time flies," he said then. "You're so big now."

"He goes to the gymnas," Grandma said. "He's probably got a girlfriend too, don't you think?" She winked at me.

"No, I'm afraid I haven't," I said.

"You will," she said. "Good-looking fellow like you."

"If you take that cross out of your ear," Grandad said, "the girls'll come running."

"You don't think it's the cross they want then?" Grandma said.

Grandad didn't answer, he picked up the newspaper that he had put down when I arrived. He could spend hours reading it. He absorbed absolutely everything, every little ad.

Grandma sat in the chair and reached for the pouch of menthol tobacco on the table.

"But you haven't started smoking yet, I bet!" she said.

"In fact, I have," I said.

She scrutinized me.

"You have?"

"Not much. But I have tried."

"You didn't inhale though?"

"No."

"Because you mustn't inhale, you know."

She looked at Grandad.

"Hey, Grandad!" she said. "Do you remember who got *us* started?"

He didn't answer, she licked the edge of the paper and shaped the cigarette.

"It was your father," she said.

"Dad?"

"Yes, we were in our mountain cabin. He had brought some cigarettes along. And he told us to try one. So we did. Didn't we, Grandad?"

When she didn't get an answer this time either, she winked at me.

"He's getting senile, I think," she said, put the cigarette between her lips, lit up and then blew a huge cloud of smoke out through her mouth.

No, she didn't inhale. I had never thought about that before.

She looked at me.

"Are you hungry? We ate a little while ago, but if you like I can heat something up for you?"

"Oh, please," I said. "Actually I'm ravenous."

She placed the cigarette on the edge of the ashtray, got up and shuffled over to the fridge in her slippers. She was wearing a blue dress, it went down to her midcalves, which were light brown under her tights.

"If it's in the *fridge*, you don't need to warm it up," I said.

"Don't worry. It's no trouble," she said.

She began to clatter around. I watched Grandad. He was interested in politics and soccer. I was too.

"Who do you think will win the elections?" I said.

"Eh?" he said, lowering the newspaper.

"Who do you think will win the elections?"

"Hard to say. But I'm hoping it will be Willoch. We can't take much more socialism in this country, that's for sure."

"I'm hoping it'll be Kvanmo," I said.

He studied me. With a stern, solemn expression. No, no, that wasn't how it was, because the next moment he smiled.

"You're like your mother there," he said.

"Yes," I said. "I don't want money to control people's lives. Or us to be focused only on ourselves in our own backyards."

"Who should we focus on if not ourselves?" he said.

"People in wretched situations. The poor. Refugees."

"But why should they come here and be maintained by us? You explain that to me," he said.

"Don't listen to him," Grandma said to me, and put a pot on the stove. "He's just teasing you."

"But we have to help those who are less well off, don't we?" I said.

"Yes," he said. "But we have to look after our own first. Then we can help the others. But what they want is to live here. Help is not what they want. We've slogged our guts out and we've done well, and now they want to take over. Without lifting a finger. Why should we allow that?"

Grandma sat down on her chair.

"Why did the man from the laboratory refuse to enter the labyrinth?" she said.

"I don't know," I said, although I knew what was coming.

"Because it was too laborious!" she said, and laughed.

Grandad picked up the newspaper again.

There was a silence. The pot crackled on the hotplate. Grandma lit another cigarette, placed one hand on her other arm and whistled softly to herself.

Grandad turned over a page.

I had exhausted all my conversational topics. We had spent less time on my new job than I had anticipated.

Did I dare take out the cigarettes from my jacket pocket?

Would the cross plus smoking be too much for them? I wondered.

An image of Dad entered my head. Perhaps smoking had been the link, my having smoked twice in his presence without him saying a word.

If it was fine by him, it should definitely be fine by them, shouldn't it?

I took out the packet.

Grandma eyed me.

"Have you got your own cigarettes?" she said.

I nodded. I didn't want to use her lighter, somehow that would be too intimate, or too obtrusive, so I put my hand back into my pocket and took out my own. I lit up.

"I was at Dad's a few days ago," I said. "Things are going well for him."

"Yes, he dropped by yesterday," Grandma said.

"We're trying to maintain the amount of contact we had, even if we live separately," I said. "I think he must have been under a lot of pressure this summer, with the divorce and everything."

"Do you think so?" Grandma said, looking at me as she blew out smoke.

"Ye-es," I said. "They were married a long time. Getting separated is no laughing matter."

"No, it certainly isn't," Grandma said.

"I'll try to keep in touch with you as well," I said. "It's easy enough for me to come by after school. And now that I've got a job I can have dinner here every so often."

Grandma smiled at me. Then she turned, glanced at the pot, which was making some muffled gurgling noises, got up and moved it to the side, switched off the burner, fetched a plate and cutlery, which she placed in front of me on the table.

I stubbed out my half-smoked cigarette in the ashtray. She lifted the pot, held it by one handle, dipped the ladle inside, and served three meatballs, two potatoes, and some onions onto my plate.

"I did it the easy way and heated the potatoes in the sauce," she said.

"Looks fantastic," I said.

No one talked while I ate. I was soon finished.

"Thank you!" I said when I had eaten everything and placed the knife and fork on my plate. "That was fantastic!"

"Good," Grandma said, got up and carried the plate to the sink, rinsed it, opened the dishwasher lid, pulled out the little basket with the tiny fishbone-like plastic spikes, slotted the plate in, and closed it again.

The wall clock said two minutes past five.

If I was going to ask to borrow some money it mustn't look as if I had planned it or even counted on it. After all I could have stayed a shorter time and caught the bus home using my card. It would have to seem spontaneous.

But I didn't need to do it yet.

Could I smoke another cigarette?

My intuition told me that would be a mistake. Too much.

"What's so interesting in the newspaper?" Grandma said. "I read it this morning and there wasn't a damn thing in it."

"I'm reading the obituaries," Grandad said.

"And they're interesting now, are they!" Grandma said, glancing at me as she laughed. "The obituaries!"

I smiled.

"Have you met Dad's new girlfriend?" I said.

"Unni? Yes. We have. Nice girl."

"Yes," I said. "I think she's right for Dad. But it's a bit odd for me, I have to admit."

"I can imagine," Grandma said.

"It doesn't matter though," I said.

"Goodness, no," Grandma said. "I'm sure it doesn't."

She whistled again, turned her hand over to form a little rake and inspected her nails.

"Is there a lot of fruit this year?"

"Yes, it's not bad at all," she said. "Would you like to take some apples with you?"

"Is that OK? They remind me of my childhood."

"I can imagine," she said. "I'll put some in a bag for you." I raised my eyes and stared pointedly at the clock.

"Oh no!" I said. "Is that the time? Ten past five?"

I got up and rummaged through my pockets for money. Took it out, counted it, pursed my lips.

"The last bus went at five," I said. "My travel card isn't valid after five. And I don't have enough money."

I glanced at Grandma, then lowered my eyes.

"I could hitchhike though," I said.

"I'll see if I've got some you can have," Grandma said. "It's such a long way. You really should take the bus."

She got up.

"I'll be off then," I said to Grandad.

He put down the newspaper.

"Bye then," he said.

"Bye," I said, following Grandma down to the hall. She took a small purse from an off-white coat hanging up, opened it, and looked at me.

"How much does the bus cost?"

"Fourteen kroner," I said.

She passed me two twenty-krone notes.

"So you can buy yourself something nice with the rest," she said.

"I'm just borrowing it," I said. "You'll get it back next time."

She snorted.

For a moment we stood in the hall without moving. I could feel she was waiting for me to go.

Had she forgotten the apples?

For a few seconds I was at a loss to know what to do. She had said I could take some with me, so surely it wouldn't be unreasonable to remind her?

But she had just given me some money for the bus. I didn't want to bother her.

She turned her head, saw her reflection in the mirror, put a hand on top of her hair and patted it in place.

"Did you say you had some apples? I could take a few with me and Mom could try some. I'm sure she misses them too."

"Oh, that's right," she said. "The apples."

She opened the door beside the staircase that led down to the cellar.

In the meantime I inspected myself in the mirror. Pulled at the back of my T-shirt to straighten the neck. Ran my fingers through my hair to make it stand up more. Smiled. Put on a serious face. Smiled.

"Here you are," Grandma said, coming up the steps. "You've got a few here."

She passed me a bag, I took it, went out onto the front doorstep and turned to Grandma.

"Bye then!" I said.

"Bye," she said.

I turned and set off. The door shut behind me.

At the Rundingen shop I lit a cigarette while waiting for the bus. There was only one every hour, but I was lucky: the next one arrived after only a few minutes.

I boarded and while I was waiting for my ticket and change, I squinted down the bus.

Wasn't that Jan Vidar?

Yes, it was.

He was sitting gazing out the window, his chin resting on his hand. Didn't notice me until I reached his seat. He removed the small Walkman earplugs.

"Hi," he said.

"Hi," I said, plumping down onto the seat. "What are you listening to?"

"B.B. King actually," he said.

"B.B. *King*!" I said. "Have you gone nuts?"

"He's a damn good guitarist," he said. "Believe it or not."

"Him?" I said.

Jan Vidar nodded.

"He's so fantastic that when he plays, his guitar is *horizontal*," I said. "Haven't you seen? It's like he's playing a steel guitar."

"Where do you think Led Zeppelin got everything from?" he said. "They're old blues boys."

"Yes, of course. I know that," I said. "But that doesn't mean *we* should listen to it. Blues is a pile of shit, if you ask me. Fine for inspiration for something else, but on its own? It's just the same old song again and again."

"If you can play like him, you can play anything," Jan Vidar said. "You were the one who always talked about feeling. Who said that was why Jimmy Page was better than Ritchie Blackmore or Yngwie Malmsteen. I agree with you now. We don't need to discuss the point any more. But for feeling, brother, just listen to this guy!"

He passed me the earplugs, I put them in, he pressed play. I listened for two seconds before taking them out.

"Same song," I said.

He looked a bit annoyed.

"Are you annoyed or what?"

"No, why should I be? I know I'm right."

"Ha ha," I said.

The bus stopped at the lights before the E18.

"Why were you at Rundingen?" Jan Vidar said. "Have you been visiting your grandparents?"

I nodded.

"But before that I was at *Nye Sørlandet*."

"What were you doing there?"

"I've got work there."

"Work?"

"Yes."

"What as? Paperboy?" He laughed.

"Ha ha," I repeated. "No, as a music journalist. I'm going to review records."

"Are you? Fantastic! Really?"

"Yes, I start next week."

There was a silence. Jan Vidar drew up his knees and put his feet on the seat opposite.

"And you?" I said. "Where have you been?"

"Out with a friend. We've been jamming."

"Where's the guitar then?"

He tossed his head back.

"On the seat behind."

"Is he good?"

"Better than you anyway."

"That's not saying much," I said.

We smiled. Then he gazed out the window. I glanced behind us, in case someone I knew was sitting there and I hadn't noticed them. But there was just a boy I hadn't seen before, perhaps a seventh year, and a woman of around fifty with a white shoe-shop bag on her lap. She was chewing gum, which was a mistake, chewing gum didn't go with her glasses and hair.

"Do you remember when you stood in for me?" Jan Vidar said.

"Of course," I said.

He had been a paperboy. Over time he had built up a long, challenging route. Then he had to have a holiday and I was given his job for a week. He didn't go anywhere, just lazed around while I was working, and then we went swimming or biked out to a friend's. But after three days there were so many complaints from people on the route that he had to take over. One hell of a holiday that was, he had said. But he didn't look too upset.

"I still can't understand how you could make such a mess of it," he said now.

I shrugged. "Actually I did the best I could."

"Unbelievable," he said.

He had gone over the route with me twice, there were two or three quirks to watch out for – some wanted the newspaper through the door, others had boxes with identical names on them – and I couldn't remember these nuances when I was standing there, even though he had repeated them several times, so I improvised and followed my gut instinct.

"That was only last year!" I said. "At first I thought it was several years ago!"

"That was a good summer, that was," he said.

"Yes, it was."

We entered the forest after the Timenes crossroads. The sun was shining on the hilltop trees but completely absent here. I associated the bus stop we passed with Billy Idol, we had been to one of those half-baked parties we sometimes ended up at and as we had been going home in the freezing cold I had been humming "Rebel Yell."

"I think I can associate some memory with every damn bus stop from here to home," I said.

He nodded.

Topdalsfjord opened in front of us on the right. The water was a gleaming blue close to the shore, but farther out it was foam-tipped in the breeze. A couple of families were sitting on the beach and children were wading in front of them.

It would soon be autumn.

"Any nice girls at school?" I said.

"Not that I've seen. And at Katedralskolen?"

"Actually, there's a great one in my class. But she's a Christian, first of all."

"That's never deterred you before."

"No, but she's the perfection type. Pentecostalist. Well, you know the type, down jackets and Bik Bok and Poco Loco clothes."

"Second of all?"

"She doesn't like me."

"Seen much of Hanne?"

I shook my head. "Spoke to her on the phone a couple of times, that's all."

I wondered whether Jan Vidar wasn't sick of hearing about Hanne, so I didn't follow up, even though I was burning to talk about her. Instead we sat silent for the last ten minutes, lulled into the regular drone of the bus that we both knew so well. It felt as if we had been catching the bus for the whole of our lives. Up and down, back and forth, day after day. Bus, bus, bus. We knew all about buses. We were bus experts. In the same way that we were experts on pointless cycling and endless footslogging, not to mention the very center of our existence, something we knew very well: using the grapevine to stay up to date with what was happening. What? Someone had *The Texas Chainsaw Massacre* on video? Right, over we cycled, a tumbledown house with piles of garbage outside, and a complete stranger, a dubious but also dopey-looking twenty-year-old, who was just standing there when we arrived, in the middle of the yard, with no discernible aim, he was just standing there, and when we showed up he turned toward us.

The house was situated right in the middle of a field.

"Heard you'd got a copy of *The Texas Chainsaw Massacre*," Jan Vidar said.

"That's right," he said. "But I've just lent it to someone."

"Oh," said Jan Vidar, looking at me. "Better head back then, eh?"

An eighth grader who was alone at home and had invited a few friends round? Right, off we trudged, knocked on the door and were invited in, they were watching TV, had nothing to drink, there were no girls and they were just some twats with nothing in their heads, we stayed nevertheless, the alternative was no *better*, that was the point, if we were completely honest.

And we frequently were.

Oh! Someone somewhere had got a new guitar.

Right, onto our bikes and off we pedaled to see it.

Yes, we were good at using the grapevine. But what we were best at, what we were really the kings of, that was buses and sitting around in bedrooms.

No one could beat us at that.

None of this led anywhere. Well, we probably weren't very good at doing things that led somewhere. We didn't have particularly good conversations, no one could say we did, the few topics we had developed so slowly we ourselves assumed they had nowhere to go; not one of us was a great guitarist, although that is what we would have loved to be, more than anything else, and as far as girls were concerned, it was rare we came across one who wouldn't object if we pulled up her sweater so that we could lower our heads and kiss her nipples. These were great moments. They were luminous shafts of grace in our world of yellowing grass, gray muddy ditches, and dusty country roads. Yes, that was how it was for me. I assumed it was the same for him.

What was this all about? Why did we live like this? Were we waiting for something? In which case, how did we manage to be so patient? Because nothing ever happened! *Nothing* happened! It was always the same. Day in, day out! Wind and rain, sleet and snow, sun and storm, we did the same. We heard something on the grapevine, went there, came back, sat in his bedroom, heard something else, went by bus, bike, on foot, sat in someone's bedroom. In the summer we went swimming. That was it.

What was it all about?

We were friends, there was no more than that.

And the waiting, that was life.

Jan Vidar jumped off the bus at Solsletta, guitar case in hand, I continued as the sole passenger to Boen, where I also jumped off and plodded home with my rucksack on my back and the bag of apples in my hand.

Mom had been waiting for me with dinner.

"Hi," she said as I went in through the door. "I just got home too."

"Look," I said, holding out the bag. "Apples from Grandma."

"Did you pop in?"

"Yes, they send their love."

"Thanks," she said.

I lifted the lid off the pot. Tomato sauce and chunks of fish, probably pollock.

"I had dinner there," I said.

"That's fine," she said. "But I'm starving."

She put the cat down on the floor, straightened up and took a plate.

"And how did you get on at *Nye Sørlandet*, Karl Ove?" I said.

"Oh!" she said. "I'd completely forgotten."

I smiled. "I got the job! He just skim-read the reviews and I was home and dry."

"You worked hard on them," she said, placed some bits of pollock on the plate, lifted the lid of the second pan and spooned out a potato. It wobbled around as she lowered the spoon and rolled off when she turned it.

"And they're going to make a little article about it," I said. "It'll run tomorrow."

"Run" was a genuine journalistic expression.

"Very nice, Karl Ove," she said.

"Yes, but there's a snag."

She put the plate on the table, took cutlery from the drawer and sat down. I took a seat opposite her.

"A snag?" she said, digging in.

"He said I had to get hold of a typewriter. Writing by hand is taboo. They don't accept it. So I'll have to buy one."

"A new typewriter costs quite a bit of money."

"Come on. We *must* be able to afford one. It's an investment. I'll earn some money doing this. Surely you can understand that?"

She nodded as she chewed.

"Perhaps there's one there you can borrow?" she said.

I snorted.

"First day at work? And then you walk in and ask to borrow a typewriter?"

"Well, maybe that isn't such a good idea," she said.

The cat rubbed against my leg. I bent down and scratched his chest. He closed his eyes and began to purr. I picked him up, he stretched out on my lap with his paws on my knees.

"How much will one cost, do you think?" Mom said.

"No idea."

"When I get my salary next month it should be OK. But for now, I'm afraid I'm flat broke."

"But that's too late, don't you understand?"

She nodded.

"I know what you're going to say," I said. "If there's no money, there's no money."

"That's how it is, sadly," she said. "But you can ask your father as well, you know."

I said nothing. It was true, I could. He had enough money. But would he give some to me?

If he wouldn't, there would be an embarrassing situation. He would feel I was demanding something from him, and if he said no, or felt forced to say no, it would be me who had put him in this predicament. And by then it would be too late, he couldn't suddenly say yes after saying no.

"I'll ask him," I said, caressing the cat behind the ear. He writhed in pleasure with his eyes closed.

"There's a letter for you, by the way," Mom said. "I left it on the dresser in the hall."

"A letter?"

I put the cat down on the floor, I didn't like to have to do that when he had been having such a good time, but the little twinge in my conscience was gone the very next second because I didn't get letters that often.

My name on the envelope, written in a girl's hand.

The postmark was almost unreadable.

But it was airmail, and the stamps were Danish.

"I'm going to my room," I said. "Are you OK eating alone?"

"Yes, of course!" Mom said from the kitchen.

In my bedroom I sat down on the chair by the desk, tore open the envelope, took out the letter and started reading.

Nyk M 20 August 85
Hi, Karl Ove,
*Hope you're fine. I don't know if you are because you haven't written, although
you promised you would. Why not? I wish you could see me running to our post
box when I get up. Well, if you don't want to write I won't be annoyed, I love
you too much for that, but I have to admit I will be upset if I never hear from
you again. Are you coming to Denmark? And if so, when? It has been boring
here since you left. During the day I'm with my friends. In the evening I go to
the disco. But this will soon be over as I'm moving to Israel on 14 September. I'm
really looking forward to that. I would just love to see you before I go.*

*Perhaps you think I'm stupid to make so much of the short time we had
together? That's probably because you're the only boy I've ever fallen in love with.
So, don't disappoint me, write to me now.*

A girl who loves you,
Lisbeth

I pushed the letter aside. My chest was riven with despair. I *could* have slept
with her. She had been willing! She wrote that she was in love with me, that
she loved me, of course she would have said yes.

She knew where we were heading and what I was thinking, of that I was
sure.

Bloody Jøgge!

Those *fucking* dickheads!

A sudden inspiration made me pick up the envelope and look inside.

There was a photo.

I took it out. It was Lisbeth. She wasn't smiling, she was looking into the
camera with her head tilted. She was wearing a yellow sweatshirt with NIKE
emblazoned across it in big red letters. Her bangs hung over her forehead on
one side, covering one eye. A stray lock of hair hung down behind one ear
on the other.

Her neck was bare. She had a nice long neck.

Her lips were also beautiful, full, almost disproportionately full compared with her narrow face.

Oh, she looked seriously displeased.

But I could remember what it was like to hold her. How she had laughed when she put her hand up my shirt, against my chest, and I straightened up and took a deep breath.

"You're pumping yourself up!" she said. "Relax. I like you as you are. You're fantastic."

And she was Danish.

I put the picture and the letter back in the envelope, tucked it into the diary that I kept in the drawer, and got to my feet.

Mom was washing the dishes when I went to the kitchen.

"Karl Ove," she said. "I've just had a thought. Dad had a typewriter once. It's probably still around. I can't imagine he would have taken it with him. Have a look up in the barn, in the cardboard boxes."

"*He* had a typewriter?"

"Yes, he did. He used it to write letters for a few years."

She rinsed a glass in cold water and placed it upside down on the grooves in the drainer.

"During the first few years we were together he wrote poems as well."

"*Dad?*"

"Yes, he was very taken by poetry. Obstfelder was his favorite. He liked Vilhelm Krag as well, I remember. The Romantics."

"*Dad?*" I repeated.

Mom smiled.

"They weren't very good though."

"I can believe that," I said, and went into the hall, put on my shoes, and walked up to the back of the barn, which actually was the front because this was where the great barn door was, and inside was where the hay was stacked. The floor beneath, which Dad had used, consisted of small rooms which had been converted into a flat in the 1970s. But here nothing had been done.

I went in and thought, as I had done so many times before, it was strange that we owned such a large room. And that we didn't use it for anything.

Well, except for storage, that is.

All the old farming implements hung on the wall: cart wheels, harnesses, rusty scythes, mucking-out forks, and hoes. In some places Dad had written the nicknames he had used for me, in chalk, he did that when we moved in and when he was so happy about everything.

They were still there.

Kaklove

Loffe

Love

Klove

Kykkeliklove

Boxes were stacked against the wall facing me. I had never looked inside them. That would have been inconceivable when Dad lived here, he often sat in the flat beneath the old floorboards and would definitely have come up to check if anyone had been walking around. And then I would have had to have an *extremely* good reason for being here, let alone rummaging through our old possessions.

I found clothes I remembered Mom and Dad wearing when I was smaller: flared trousers they must have bought the winter they had been in London together because you couldn't get such big bell-bottoms in Norway, even in the 1970s, Mom's white coat, Dad's large orange jacket with the brown lining he had worn to go fishing, shawls and skirts and scarves, sunglasses, belts, boots and shoes. Then there was a box of pictures we used to have on the walls. A couple of boxes containing old kitchen utensils.

But no typewriter!

I opened a couple more boxes, flicked through them. Came to one containing what looked like magazines in plastic bags.

Comics I had forgotten I had?

I opened the top one.

They were porn mags.

I opened the next.

Also porn mags.

A whole storage box full of pornographic magazines?

Whose were they?

I laid some of them on the floor and began to leaf through. Most were from the '60s and '70s. The centerfolds had bikini marks; all the breasts and bottoms were white. Many of the women were posing outdoors. Standing behind trees, lying in fields, all the colors of the '70s, big breasts, some sagging, with big nipples.

I sat there with an erection, turning the pages. A couple of the magazines were from the '80s and there was nothing strange about them. The ones from the '60s had no shots of girls with their legs open.

Had he had all these magazines at home during all that time? Down in his office?

And, not least, had he actually bought them?

I put them in a pile and stood musing. I ought to hide them. First of all this wasn't anything Mom should see. Second I would like to go through them again.

Or would I?

He had read them. *He* had pored over them.

I couldn't do that. It was too disgusting.

I decided to put them all back as they had been. Mom would never go through these boxes anyway.

I couldn't make this add up. All the years when I had been small, indeed, oh God, from the time before I was born until last year, he had been buying porn mags and keeping them at home.

Shit.

I opened the other boxes, and in the penultimate one I found the typewriter. It was an old manual model, I should have known, and if I had seen it before the magazines I would have been disappointed, I might even have rejected it and insisted on Mom or Dad buying me another one, but now, after finding his magazines, it didn't matter.

I carried it back and showed it to Mom, who was resting on the sofa.

"That's good enough, isn't it?" she said, her eyes half closed.

"Yes, it'll have to do," I said. "Are you going to sleep?"

"I'll just have forty winks. Can you wake me in half an hour if I'm not up?"

"OK," I said, and went up to my room, where I read Lisbeth's letter once again.

She had written unequivocally that she loved me.

No one had ever done that before.

Was that how it was with Hanne? When I said I loved her? Because I didn't love Lisbeth. I liked her writing that she loved me, but it meant no more than that. It was nice, and I was happy that she had written it, but it existed outside me, she existed outside me. Not like Hanne.

Was that how Hanne felt about me?

That was what she said.

Was she playing with me?

Why didn't she want me? Want to be with me?

Oh, how I wanted her!

That was all I wanted. She was all I wanted!

Really.

But if she didn't want me, I wasn't going to get any further. So it didn't matter.

I decided to give her a taste of her own medicine. It wouldn't matter anyway.

I stood up, went downstairs to the telephone, lifted the receiver and dialed all the numbers except the last. Gazed out the window. Two blackbirds were in the bush across the drive, pecking at the small red berries growing on it. Mefisto watched from a crouch position, his tail wagging to and fro.

I dialed the last number.

"Yes, hello," Hanne's father said.

I hated it when he answered because his daughter was going out with someone else, not me, and he knew what I was trying to do. Sometimes we chatted for more than an hour on the phone. So he probably didn't like me phoning.

"Hello, Karl Ove here," I said. "Is Hanne in?"

"Just a moment, Karl Ove, and I'll have a look."

I heard his footsteps going down the stairs and watched Mefisto creep closer to the two birds, which continued to jerk their heads and peck at the red berries undeterred. Then came the sound of light steps and I knew it was Hanne, and my heart beat faster.

"Hi!" she said. "Funny you should ring. I was just thinking about you!"

"What were you thinking?" I said.

"About you, that was all."

"What are you doing this evening?"

"I'm studying. French. It's a level up from last year. Quite difficult. How's it going with your French?"

"Same as last year. I knew nothing then, and I know nothing now. Do you remember the test I got a Good in?"

"Yes, I do. You were proud of that."

"Was I? Well, usually I got Poor. So, of course I was pleased. But what I did was incredibly simple. The text was long, right, with lots of French words in it. So I just used them in my answer, adapted them a bit and added a few of my own. And, hey presto, a Good."

"You're so smart!"

"Yes, aren't I."

"What are you doing?"

"Well, nothing special actually. I've received a letter I've read a few times."

"Oh? Who from?"

"A girl I met in Denmark."

"Oh? You didn't tell me about her!"

"No. So much happened I thought . . . well, it wouldn't be of any interest to you."

"It certainly is!"

"Right."

"What does she say?"

"She says she loves me."

"But you were only there a week!"

"A lot happened in that week, as I said. We slept together."

"Did you?" she said.

"Yes," I said.

Silence.

"Why are you telling me this, Karl Ove?"

I didn't reply at first. Then I said, "I told you this wouldn't interest you. Then you said it would. So I thought I may as well tell you."

"Mm," she said.

"And then . . . Well, when it was happening I thought a lot about us. That perhaps it wasn't . . . well, you know. Perhaps I don't feel all the things I have said I do. For you, I mean. The letters this summer . . . I think somehow I was in love with love. Do you know what I mean? When I met Lisbeth . . ." I said, and paused to let the name achieve maximum impact ". . . it was somehow real. Flesh and blood. Not just thoughts. Then I got her letter and I realized I was in love with her. And it's fantastic! There wasn't anything between you and me anyway. And there's nothing now. So, yes, just thought I had to say that."

"Yes," she said. "It's good you told me. It's good to know."

"But we're still friends."

"Of course we are," she said. "You can fall in love with whoever you like. We're not in a relationship."

"No."

"But I am a bit sad nevertheless. It was so wonderful in the cabin. With you."

"Yes," I said. "It was."

"Yes."

"Well, you'd better get back to your French."

"Yes," she said. "Bye. Thanks for ringing."

"Bye."

I rang off.

Now it was ruined. That was what I wanted. And now it had happened.

In the first break the next day I jogged up to the petrol station over the E18 to buy the latest *Nye Sørlandet*. Grabbed a copy from the stand and thumbed through the pages at the back.

My cheeks burned when I spotted a photo of myself.

There was a big spread, almost a page, and the photo took up two-thirds of the space. I was sitting and looking straight at the reader with three records fanned out in front of me.

I skimmed through the text. It said I was a young man who was passionate about music and that I was critical about society's marginalization of rock. Personally, I liked British indie bands best, but I promised to be open to all genres, even the Top Twenty.

I hadn't said that, not in so many words, well, I probably hadn't said it at all, now that I thought about it, but I had *meant* it and Steinar Vindsland had understood.

The photo was brilliant.

I paid, folded it, and walked back down to the school with it in my hand. In the classroom, which was filling up, I placed it on my desk, leaned back in my chair, tipping it against the wall as I usually did, and watched the others.

I doubted any of them read *Nye Sørlandet*, except on rare occasions, hardly anyone did. The only newspaper that was any good was *Fædrelandsvennen*. So having it there spread out on my desk might therefore cause a few eyebrows to be raised. Why have you brought *Nye Sørlandet* with you to school?

They would imagine I had brought it from home! To show off!

I rocked forward again and folded the newspaper. No, I hadn't brought it from home to show off. I had bought it at the petrol station and where else would you go with it? That was why I had it with me.

But what the hell. Shouldn't I just say?

Straight out?

As long as it didn't seem as if I was bragging?

But it wasn't bragging, it was true, I was a record reviewer now, and today there was an interview with me in the newspaper I had bought at the petrol station opposite the school.

There was no point hiding it either.

"Hi, Lars," I said. He was the least dangerous boy in the class. He turned to me. I held up the newspaper.

"I'm the record reviewer," I said. "Do you want to see?"

He got up and came over; I opened it at the right page.

"Not bloody bad," he said, straightening up. "Hey! Karl Ove's in the paper!" he shouted across the room.

It was more than I could have hoped for, the very next moment he was standing with a crowd around him, all staring at the photo of me and reading the article.

In the evening I browsed through my old music magazines and studied the record reviews and articles. There were three kinds of writer, I concluded. There were the witty, smart, often malicious writers like Kjetil Rolness, Torgrim Eggen, Finn Bjelke, and Herman Willis. There were the serious, ponderous types like Øivind Hånes, Jan Arne Handorff, Arvid Skancke-Knutsen, and Ivar Orvedal. And then there were the knowledgable, clearheaded writers who went straight to the point, like Tore Olsen, Tom Skjeklesæther, Geir Rakvaag, Gerd Johansen and Willy B.

It was as though I knew them all. I really liked Jan Arne Handorff. I understood virtually nothing of what he wrote but sensed his passion, somewhere deep in the wilderness of all those foreign-sounding words, while every second reader's letter accused him of being incomprehensible, although he didn't seem to care, he steered a straight line, further and further into the impenetrable night. I also had huge respect for those who could puncture opponents with a killer comment. I adopted it, to deal with my opponents. Its sole importance was that it worked. And many reviewers were vicious.

When a band changed direction and became more commercial, such as Simple Minds was doing for example, taking the easy route, they didn't think twice about confronting the band and asking for an explanation. Why? You were so good, you had everything, so why sell out? Playing at stadiums? What are you doing? What is in your heads? And if the band wouldn't respond, often they didn't, Norway was not exactly the most important country for groups on the up, they still peppered them with caustic remarks.

I had written only three record reviews, the ones Steinar Vindsland had read. In them I had tried to be impartial while also being hard, and I had dismissed one record with a couple of sarcastic comments at the end. That was the new Stones' single, I had never liked them, they were terrible, apart from the *Some Girls* LP, which wasn't bad. Now they were over forty and as pathetic as it was possible to be.

I had it in me. I just had to let it out.

Outside it was dark, autumn was wrapping its hand around the world, and I loved it. The darkness, the rain, the sudden cracks in the past that opened when the smell of damp grass and soil rose up at me from a ditch somewhere or when car headlights illuminated a house, all somehow caught and enhanced by the music in the Walkman I always carried with me. I listened to This Mortal Coil and thought about when we used to play in the dark in Tybakken, a feeling of happiness grew in me, but not a happiness of the bright, weightless, carefree kind, this happiness was rooted in something else, and when it met the melancholic beauty of the music and the world that was dying around me, it was like sorrow, beautiful sorrow, romantic sorrow, beauty and pain in one impossible mix, and from there sprang a wild longing to live more. To leave this, to find life where it was really lived, in the streets of cities, beneath skyscrapers, at glittering parties with beautiful people in unfamiliar apartments. To find the one great love and all the restlessness that involved, and then the acceptance, the relief, the ecstasy.

Discard her, find a new one, discard her. Rise and be ruthless, a seducer of women, a man they all wanted but none could have. I put the music magazines in a heap on the bottom of my bookshelves and went downstairs. Mom was sitting and talking on the telephone in the clothes room, the door was open, she smiled at me. I stood still for a few seconds to hear who she was talking to.

One of her sisters.

In the kitchen I took a slice of bread, ate it leaning against the worktop and drank a glass of milk. Went back upstairs and started a letter to Hanne. I wrote that I thought it was best if we never saw each other again.

It felt good to write that, for some reason I wanted to avenge myself on her, to hurt her, to make her think of me as someone she had lost.

I put the letter into an envelope and dropped it into my schoolbag, where it lay until I bought some stamps after school the following day.

I posted it before catching the bus, convinced this was the right course of action.

In the evening, lying on the sofa and reading a book I had borrowed from the school library – Bjørneboe's *Ere the Cock Crows* – it suddenly struck me what I had done.

I loved her, why would I say I never wanted to see her again?

Regret exploded inside me.

I had to get it back.

I rested the book on the sofa arm and sat up. Should I write another letter and say I didn't mean what I had written in the previous one? That I wanted to see her despite what I had written.

It would look absolutely idiotic.

I had to ring her.

Before I had time to change my mind, I went into the room where the telephone was and dialed her number.

She answered.

"Hi," I said. "I just wanted to apologize for the last time I called. I didn't mean to behave as I did."

"You've got nothing to apologize for."

"Yes, I have. But there's something else. To cut a long story short, I sent you a letter today."

"Did you?"

"Yes. But I didn't mean what I wrote. I don't know why I wrote it. Anyway, it's nonsense. So now I'm wondering if you could do me a favor. Don't read it. Just throw it away."

She laughed.

"Now you've really whetted my appetite! Not read it? Do you really imagine I could do that? What did you write?"

"I can't say. That's the whole point!"

She laughed again.

"You're strange," she said. "But why did you write whatever it was you wrote if you didn't mean it?"

"I don't know. I was in a funny mood. But, Hanne, please promise me you won't read it. Throw it away and pretend it doesn't exist. Actually it doesn't really exist anyway, because I don't mean any of what I wrote."

"I'll see what I can do," she said. "But it is addressed to me. It's me who decides what to do with it, right?"

"Yes, of course. I'm just asking you to be extra nice to me."

"Is there anything that's not nice in the letter? Yes, there must be of course."

"Now you know at any rate," I said. "But if you'd like me to go down on my knees and beg, I will. I'm doing it now. I'm on my knees now. Please throw the letter away!"

She laughed.

"Up on your feet, boy!" she said.

"What are you wearing?" I said.

Seconds passed before she answered.

"A T-shirt and jogging pants. I didn't know you would ring. What are you wearing?'"

"Me? A black shirt, black trousers, and black socks."

"I don't know why I asked," she said, and laughed. "I'm going to give you such a brightly colored bobble hat for Christmas that you'll be embarrassed to walk down the street wearing it, but you'll have to because I gave it to you. When you see me anyway."

"That's pure evil," I said.

"Yes, you don't have a monopoly on it," she said.

"What do you mean by that? Surely I'm not evil just because I don't believe in God?"

"I'm just teasing you. No, you're not evil at all. But now they're calling me. I think they've cooked something they want me to taste."

"So you'll throw the letter away?"

She laughed.

"Bye!"

"Hanne!"

But by then she had hung up.

The meeting with Steinar Vindsland was brief and was basically him showing me how to write the reviews, there were special forms they used at the newspaper, some boxes at the top had to be filled out in a special way, and I was given a stack of them. Then he said I should choose three new releases a week from a record shop with whom they had an arrangement. I could keep the records, that was my fee, OK? Of course, I said. You deliver the reviews to me, he said, and I'll fix the rest.

He winked and shook my hand. Then he turned and started to read some papers on the desk, and I went into the street, still with the tension from the meeting in my body. It was only half past three and I went to see if Dad was at home. I stopped outside the door and rang, nothing happened, I stepped to the side and looked through the window, the house looked empty and I was about to head for the bus stop when his car, a light green Ascona, appeared.

He pulled in by the curb.

Even before he got out of the car I could see he was the way he used to be. Rigid, severe, controlled. He undid his seat belt, grabbed a bag beside him, and placed a foot on the ground. He didn't look at me as he crossed the road.

"Waiting for me?" he said.

"Yes," I said. "Thought I'd stop by."

"You should call in advance, you know," he said.

"Yes," I said. "But I was in the neighborhood, so I . . ." I shrugged.

"There's nothing happening here," he said. "So you may as well catch the bus home."

"OK," I said.

"Call next time, OK?"

"All right," I said.

He turned his back on me and inserted the key in the lock. I started to trudge toward the bus. It was right what he had said: I may as well go. I hadn't visited him for my sake but for his, and if it wasn't convenient, it didn't bother me. Just the opposite.

He phoned at half past ten in the evening. He sounded drunk.

"Hi, Dad here," he said. "You haven't gone to bed?"

"No," I said. "I'm up late."

"You dropped by at an inconvenient moment, I'm afraid. But it's very nice of you to come and visit us. It wasn't that. Do you understand?"

"Yes, of course."

"Don't give me *yes, of course*. It's important we understand each other."

"Yes," I said. "I know it's important."

"I'm sitting here making a few calls to hear how people are, you know. And I'm relaxing with a *pjall*."

He used the Østland expression *pjall*, which he had recently started to say. Another was *slakk*, off color. He had it from Unni. I'm feeling a bit *slakk*, he had said once, and I had looked at him because it was as though it wasn't him who had used the word but someone else.

"We're having people round for dinner tomorrow evening, a few colleagues, well, you met them up in Sannes, and it would be nice if you had time."

"Yes, I'll come," I said. "What time?"

"Six, half past, we thought."

"Fine," I said.

"Yes, but we don't have to hang up yet. Or do you want to?"

"No," I said.

"I think you do. You don't want to talk to your old dad."

"I do."

There was a brief pause. He took a swig.

"I heard you visited Grandma and Grandad," he then said.

"Yes."

"Did they say anything about Unni and me?"

"No," I said. "Nothing special, anyway."

"Now you have to be more precise than that. They said something, but it was nothing special?"

"They said you'd been there the day before, and then they said they'd met Unni and that she was nice."

"Oh, so that was it?"

"Yes."

"Have you thought about where you want to spend Christmas? Here with us or with your mother?"

"No, haven't given it any thought. It's not for a while yet."

"Yes, that's true. But we have to make plans, you know. We were wondering whether to go south to the sun or celebrate it here. If you come, we'll stay here. But we have to know soon."

"I'll give it some thought," I said. "Maybe I'll talk to Yngve about it."

"You can come on your own, you know."

"Sure, I could. Can we wait and see? I haven't given it any thought at all."

"By all means," he said. "You need time to think. But you'd probably prefer to be with Mom, wouldn't you?"

"Not necessarily," I said.

"All right," he said. "Well, see you tomorrow then."

He hung up and I went into the kitchen and boiled some water.

"Do you want some tea?" I shouted to Mom, who was sitting in the living room, her legs tucked up underneath her, the cat on her lap, and knitting while listening to classical music on the radio.

It was almost pitch black outside.

"Yes, please!" she replied.

When I went in five minutes later, with a cup in each hand, she put her knitting on the arm of the sofa and the cat down beside her. Mefisto placed his paws in front of him, extended his claws, and stretched. Mom swung her legs down onto the floor and rubbed her hands a couple of times, which she often did after she had been sitting still for any length of time.

"I think Dad might be drinking a lot," I said, sitting down on the wicker chair under the window. It creaked under my weight. I blew on the tea, took a sip, and glanced at Mom. Mefisto stood in front of me and a moment later jumped onto my lap.

"Was that who you were talking to just now?" Mom said.

"Yes," I said.

"Was he drunk?"

"Mm, a bit. And he was pretty drunk when I was there for dinner the last time."

"How do you feel about that?" she said.

I shrugged. "I don't know. Feels a little strange maybe. When I went to the party they had here, that was the first time I'd seen him drunk. Now it's happened twice in a very short space of time."

"That's perhaps not so strange," Mom said. "There have been such big changes in his life."

"Yes," I said. "That's true. But he's becoming very hard work. He keeps asking me if he did things wrong when we were growing up, then he gets all sentimental and talks about the time he massaged my leg when I was very small."

Mom laughed.

It was such a rare occurrence. I looked at her and smiled.

"Is that what he says?" she said. "He might have massaged you once. But he did feel a lot of tenderness for you. He did."

"But not later?"

"Yes, of course. Of course he did, Karl Ove."

She looked at me. I lifted Mefisto and stood up.

"Anything you want to listen to?" I said, kneeling in front of the small record collection I'd stacked against the wall. Mefisto walked slowly, the way he did when he was offended, into the kitchen.

"No, play whatever you want," Mom said.

I switched off the radio and put on Sade, which was the only record I possessed that there was the remotest chance she would like.

"Do you like it?" I said after the music had filled the room for a few minutes.

"Yes, it's very nice," she said, putting her cup down on the table beside the sofa and resuming her knitting.

After school the next day I went to Platebørsen, spoke to the assistant, said I had an arrangement with Steinar Vindsland at *Nye Sørlandet* to pick up three records, he nodded, I spent half an hour choosing the ones I would write about, the trick was to choose someone I already knew, preferably someone who had been reviewed elsewhere, so that I had a pattern to follow.

I also bought one with my own money, which Mom had given me that morning. To still my hunger I went to Geheb and bought a cardamom and custard bun, strolled up Markens Gate munching, bun in one hand, records in the other, dropped the paper bag onto the street and was brushing off my hands when a slightly plump but well-dressed elderly man shouted after me.

"Hey, you!" he yelled. "We don't litter in this town! Pick it up!"

I turned, my heart pounding, and eyed him as coldly as I could. I was frightened, but I defied my fears and took a few steps toward him.

"Pick it up yourself if it's so important to you," I said.

Then, my legs trembling with fear and my chest quivering with emotion, I turned my back on him and continued up the street.

I half expected him to come running after me, grab me and shake me, even punch me in the stomach, but nothing happened.

Nevertheless, I walked quickly for several blocks before daring to turn around.

No one there.

How had I dared!

To answer back like that!

Now I had given him something to think about. What the hell was he doing, ordering me around? Who gave him the right?

Wasn't I a free person? No one was going to tell me what to do and what not to do. *No one!*

This bubbled inside me as I walked past the Hotel Caledonien. It was around four o'clock, I had two hours to kill, and I headed for the library, through the side streets so that there was no chance of bumping into him again. Once there, I sat down in the reading room, studied my records for a while before going to find a book from the shelves behind me, there was the first volume of Bjørneboe's trilogy about the history of bestiality, which Hilde from our class had talked about with such enthusiasm. All I had read by Bjørneboe, apart from the few pages of *Ere the Cock Crows* that I had managed yesterday, was *The Sharks*, which I had read when I was twelve as if it were Jack London. But now, perusing the first few pages of this trilogy, I realized that I hadn't understood a thing. This was deep, and it was painful. The opening, with the föhn wind, was fantastic.

Did evil come from outside?

Like a wind dragging people along with it?

Or did it come from inside?

I gazed at the square outside the church, where there were already yellow and orange leaves on the ground. In the street behind, people were walking under umbrellas.

Could I become evil? Find myself borne along by a wind of inhumanity and torture someone?

Or *was* I evil?

Torture wasn't so relevant really, not now, I thought, and continued to read. But this was a book you had barely glanced at before you raised your eyes again. The torture was extreme, the annihilation of the Jews extreme. But it was carried out by regular people! Why did they do it? Didn't they know it was wrong? Yes, of course they did. Is this what they wanted, in their heart of hearts? While they were walking around in their elegant little picture-perfect towns, making sure that everyone was doing what they should and believing that they were so utterly good, was evil what they really wanted if they got the chance? Without realizing it themselves? Was it just something they carried within them, an evil without form, as it were, which emerged when the opportunity arose?

Oh, how stupid it was that they went around believing in a god and a heaven. It was so conceited! So unbelievably conceited! Why would God have selected *them*, people who were so preoccupied with ensuring everyone did the right thing all the time? Those petty-minded fools, why would God bother about *them* of all people?

I almost laughed out loud in the library, but managed at the last moment to stifle it to a giggle.

Looking around me, I saw that no one had noticed. Then, to disguise the fact that I had been looking around, I gazed out through the window again, with my head slightly tilted, so that it resembled an active decision, as if I was searching for something.

Wasn't that Renate?

Yes, it was.

She was going into Peppe's Pizza. And that was probably Mona with her, wasn't it?

For one wild moment I considered going in after them. Bump into them as if by chance, ask if I could join them, sit down, turn on the charm, all casual, catch the bus home with them, it was Friday, they were popular, they were bound to be going to a party, we could have a few beers, I could accompany Renate home, she might hold my hand and ask if I wanted to come in, I would say yes and once inside I would pull off her T-shirt and jeans and spread-eagle her on the bed and fuck her senseless.

Ha ha.

Fuck her senseless, oh sure, Karl Ove.

I went weak at the knees even thinking about it. Yes, I could probably undress her, on a very, very good day I might be able to do that, but that was all I could do. That was where it stopped, then I went weak at the knees.

Renate was two years younger. And had a body that made everyone drool. Where I lived she was *the* body.

Once, on the bus, they had teased me. Not her, she had only been listening, but Mona. And she was *three* years younger!

"You're so good-looking, Karl Ove," she had said. "But you never say anything. Why don't you say anything? What is it with your cheeks? They're so red! Are you coming with us? We're going to Renate's. That would be great, wouldn't it? Or are you a homo? Is that why you're so quiet?"

She was a cheeky little brat with a great big mouth and an even greater belief in herself.

I had been in love with her sister all through the eighth grade and had absolutely no chance. I was so much older than them and couldn't find an answer, she would tie me in knots. Renate was also there, and at least she wasn't three years younger, only two, she was in ninth grade, and she . . . yes, but no, she was listening to all this and saw me rigidly staring out the window, red-cheeked, as though I imagined it was possible to get out of this situation by pretending I could neither see nor hear them.

So hopeless. Couldn't I just fuck them? Well, not Mona, but Renate?

No. That was exactly what I couldn't do.

I lowered my gaze and continued reading. Not many seconds passed before all words other than the ones Bjørneboe had written were gone from my mind. Thank goodness.

Six other guests came to dinner at Dad and Unni's. They had set the big living-room table, there was a white cloth, there were candlesticks, napkins, and silver knives, forks, and spoons. Have a glass of red wine with the food, Dad said, and I did. I said very little, sat watching for the most part, saw their spirits rising as they chatted and laughed. After I had finished one glass I reached out for the bottle and lifted it. Dad saw me and shook his head once. I put the bottle back down. One of them said he had a six-month-old baby at home and now they were discussing whether to have her christened or not. Neither he nor his wife was a believer, but tradition was important for both of them. Was that enough? he asked.

My heart beat faster.

"I got confirmed for money," I said. "And the day I turned sixteen I left the state church."

Everyone looked at me, most with a soft smile on their lips.

"Have you left the church?" Dad said. "Secretly? Who gave you permission?"

"Everyone has permission when they're sixteen," I said. "And, as you know, I am sixteen."

"It may be legal," Dad said, "but that's not the same as right."

"But you left the church too!" Unni said, laughing. "So you can't say your son shouldn't do the same."

He didn't like that.

He hid it behind a smile, but I knew him. He didn't like it. I could feel his chill. She didn't notice. She went on chatting and laughing.

Slowly he warmed up, he drank and his stiffness evaporated, what had been important was important no longer, nor that I was allowed to drink only one glass of wine, I speculated, and I was right, I took the bottle, he didn't notice, I poured, and a completely full glass stood before me.

Dad let go, his aura was great, indeed immense in the room. He was the person you noticed, he was the person eyes sought. But not in a warm way. There was no warmth in their eyes. He was too much, he was too loud, he interrupted in the wrong places, laughed at nothing, uttered inanities, didn't listen. Took offense, went absent for a while, returned as if nothing had happened. Gave Unni a lingering kiss in front of everyone. The others retreated with their eyes and expressions, they didn't want to know what he had to say, it was over the top for their taste, he was inappropriate, I could see that, and I found myself thinking that the idiots knew nothing, understood nothing, they were petty and didn't know it, and that was the worst of it, their bloated opinions of themselves while all they were was petty.

A pattern began to emerge that autumn. Dad drank every weekend, it made no difference whether I visited in the morning or the afternoon or the evening, on Saturday or Sunday, although at the beginning of the week he didn't drink, or at least he drank much less, apart from perhaps the odd blip one evening a week, when he phoned everyone he knew, including me, and rambled on about something or other. I tried to see him at least once, preferably twice a week, and when he wasn't drinking he was stern and formal, exactly as he'd always been, asked me a couple of questions about school and maybe Yngve, and then we would watch TV, not a word was spoken until I got up and said I had to go. He didn't want me there, I could feel that, but I continued to call and ask if I could come at such and such a time, and he said, I'm home then, yes. When he was drunk everything was a mess, he would talk about what a great time he was having with Unni and he didn't spare me the details about his life with Mom, how it had been compared with the life he had with Unni. Then he would cry, or else Unni would make a thoughtless remark and he would leave the room extremely upset, she only had to mention a man's name and he could be on his feet and gone, and the same applied to her, if he mentioned a woman's name she would stand up and leave.

At least once during the course of these evenings, he would talk about my childhood, which then merged into his, Grandad had beaten him, he said, and even though he might not have been a good father to me, he had always done the best he could, this he said with tears in his eyes, there were always tears in his eyes then, when he said he had done the best he could. Often he would mention how he had massaged my leg and how poor they had been in those days, they'd had almost no money, he mentioned that a lot.

I told Mom about some of this. With her I lived a completely different life, my real life; with her I discussed every thought that went through my head, apart from anything to do with girls, and the terrible feeling of being on the outside at school, and what Dad was doing. I told her everything else and she listened, occasionally with a genuinely surprised expression on her face, as though she hadn't thought about what I was saying. Although she had, of course, it was just that her empathy was so immense that she forgot herself and her own thoughts. Sometimes it was as if we were like minds. Or equals at least. Then something changed and the distance between us became apparent. Such as the weeks when I was reading Bjørneboe and for several evenings in a row I went on about the meaninglessness of all things until she burst into an uncontrollable fit of laughter, and with tears in her eyes, exactly the same as her father, said that wasn't what life was like, look around you! How offended I was for the rest of the week. But she was right, and what was strange was the fact that we had switched positions. Usually I was the one who said life was about enjoyment and that I would never fall into the traps known as duty and the nine-to-four working day, and she said life was a slog, that was the way it was. I subscribed to Bjørneboe's pessimism and the wall of meaninglessness you saw as soon as you started thinking along these lines, I acknowledged the world's misery; however, this did not apply to my own life and the plans I had, which were positive and robust. There was a connection though, since an alternative life, life outside bourgeois values, brought with it some insight into the meaninglessness, was this not the basis for all the thinking about enjoying yourself, not working, not giving a damn, and not conforming to duty? The diary I kept in my gymnas years was full of this kind of reasoning. Was there a god? I wrote at the top of one page, no, there probably wasn't, I concluded three lines later. I wasn't an anarchist in the punk "fuck 'em all" way, I was more structured, there should never be anyone above anyone else, no national state but more of a loose federation of individuals at a local level, in my opinion. No multinational companies, no capitalism, and definitely no religion. I stood for freedom, free people performing free acts. Who would take care of the sick? Mom would counter. We-ell, that could be done locally, couldn't it? Who would pay for it then and in what currency? she would respond. Surely you would need some national institutions? Or would you like to abolish the whole financial system? Why not? What's wrong with the barter system? I would say. But why on earth would we do that? How could all your records be produced in that kind of system? Then I was on shaky ground, two of my worlds were colliding, one that contained everything that was good and cool and one that contained principles. Or, expressed in a different way, what I wanted and what I believed in. I was no eco-vegetarian, for Christ's sake! That wasn't what this was about. However, it was where I ended up if I followed the logic of my basic principles.

A couple of times she received visits from friends in Arendal, a couple of times from old student friends in Oslo, and a couple of times friends she had made in Kristiansand. For them I was the grown-up son, I joined them and chatted away to surprise and impress them, he's so grown-up they said to Mom after I had gone and it was ridiculously easy to make them believe I was.

I spent most of my time outside school writing the three weekly record reviews, but since I wasn't paid in kroner and øre I also worked several evenings at the floor factory. During these months I was especially careful to drop in on Grandma and Grandad because they knew what Dad was doing and it was up to me to show that I was my old self while also, in a way, representing Dad, if life was going well for me this helped to offset the impression that Dad's life gave.

At school I made a few new acquaintances. Bassen hung out with a junior called Espen Olsen, an arrogant kid from Hånes with self-confidence that bordered on the insufferable and who knew everyone it was worth knowing. I was aware of his existence, he was one of those you noticed, the way he mounted the speaker's platform without a second thought when it was election time and spoke to a packed canteen, the self-assurance he had as chairman of Idun, the gymnas association. I stood next to him one break. "See you review records for *Nye Sørlandet*," he said. "Yes," I said. "I saw you once in sophomore year and I had to laugh," he said. "You were wearing a

Paul Young pin next to one of Echo and the Bunnymen! How is that *possible*? Paul fuckin' *Young*?" "He's underrated," I said. He scoffed, loudly. "R.E.M. are good though," he said. "Have you heard Green on Red?" "Of course." Had he heard Wall of Voodoo? Are you joking? Stan Ridgway is the king!

A few weeks later, out of the blue, he invited me to a pre-loading session at his house. Why had he invited me? I wondered. I had nothing to offer; there was nothing he could conceivably need. But I said yes anyway. He would get some beer, don't worry about it, he said, you can pay for it when you're there, and I caught the bus early one Saturday evening, jumped off at the Rebel Yell stop, and plodded up the hill to Hånes, where he lived, not so far from the shopping center where we'd had the catastrophic gig the year before.

It turned out he lived in a terraced house. A man who must have been his father opened the door.

"Is Espen home?" I said.

"Yes," he said, stepping aside. "Come in. He's upstairs."

A woman who must have been his mother was a bit farther back in the hall, bending over, putting on her shoes.

"I don't think we've met, have we?" the father said.

"No," I said, shaking his hand. "Karl Ove."

"So you're Karl Ove," he said.

The mother smiled and shook my hand as well.

"We're going out, as you can see," she said. "Have a nice evening!"

They left and I went up the stairs with some hesitation, this wasn't a house I knew.

"Espen?" I called loudly.

"In here!" his voice answered, and I opened the door to where I had heard it.

He was lying in the bath, his arms down by his sides, with a broad grin on his face. The second I saw him there, naked, I mustered the utmost concentration to look him in the eyes. I couldn't – not for anything in the world – look down at his dick, which was floating on the surface of the water, even though that was my first impulse. Do not look at his dick. Do not look at his dick. And I steeled my gaze, looked him straight in the eye, thinking as I stood there, I had never looked anyone in the eye for such a long time before.

"So you found your way here?" he said with a smile. Lying totally at ease in the bath, as though he owned the whole world.

"Yes, it was easy enough," I said.

"You seem ill at ease," he said, laughing. "Is there something wrong?"

"No," I said.

He laughed again.

"You're looking at me strangely."

"No, I'm not," I said, staring him in the eye.

"Have you never seen a cock before? Is that what it is?"

"When are the others coming?" I persisted.

"At eight, of course. That's what I told you. But you would show up early."

"You told me seven."

"Eight."

"Seven."

"Listen, you pig head. Toss me the towel, will you?"

I grabbed the towel and threw it to him. Before he had a chance to stand up, I turned and went out. My forehead was covered in sweat.

"Is it all right if I wait downstairs until you're ready?" I said.

"Be my guest," he said from inside. "Don't sit down anywhere though!"

I knew he was teasing, but I still didn't sit down anywhere, just wandered around carefully examining everything.

He *had* said seven, hadn't he?

There were pictures of him on one wall, as a baby and a teenager, with another boy who must have been his brother.

When he came down, wearing blue jeans and a white T-shirt, no socks on his feet, he went straight to the stereo and put on a record. Sent me an arch glance as the first chords resounded in the room.

"Do you know who this is?" he said.

"Naturally," I said.

"Who is it then?" he said.
"Violent Femmes."
He nodded and straightened up.
"Aren't they fucking great?" he said.
"They are."
"Beer?"
"Sure, sounds good."

I didn't know any of the others who came, although I had heard about them at Katedralskolen. Trond, tall, thin, fair-haired with a triangular face, an impressively large mouth and equally impressive verbal skills, he knew how to express himself and was never, as far as I could ascertain, tongue-tied. Gisle was his polar opposite, small, black-haired, with dark, intelligent eyes, he didn't say much but what he did say was direct rather than eloquent. Then there were the twins, Tore and Erling, whom it took me several months to tell apart. They were obsessed by music and were always happy, always up for anything, talking over each other and looking at people around them with warmth in their eyes. They had seen me on the train to Drammen the winter before, they said, on the way to the U2 concert. They said nothing about me going on my own to see them or that it was pretty strange. Bassen already knew everyone and belonged to the same group, but something had happened between Espen and him, they barely tolerated each other, although I never found out what had happened.

Tonight Bassen wasn't there, and as I didn't know the others and had barely spoken to Espen, I sat silent for a long time.

Espen was full of jibes, trying to rouse me into action, I understood that, but the sole result was that I became aware of my silence, which lay like a low-pressure system over my thoughts.

I drank though, and the more I drank the more it eased my discomfort. When at last I was drunk I was *there*, in the room with them, babbling away, singing along to the songs at the top of my voice, groaning aloud, oh that one's great! Oh shit, what a terrific song! That is one fantastic band!

This was where I wanted to be, this was how I wanted to be, getting drunk and singing, staggering out to a bus stop, staggering into a discotheque or a bar, drinking, chatting, laughing.

The next day I woke up at twelve. I couldn't remember a thing about what had happened after we caught the bus from Espen's, apart from a few fragments which fortunately were long and specific enough for me to be able to place them, if not in time then at least in space.

But how had I got home?

Tell me I hadn't taken a taxi! It cost 250 kroner, in which case I would have spent all the money I possessed.

No, no, I hadn't, I had been on the night bus because I had been looking at the light on the little slalom slope beneath the school in Ve.

The alcohol was still in my body, and, feeling equal amounts of distaste and delight, which I recognized from previous occasions when I had been drunk, I went down to the kitchen. Breakfast was still on the table and Mom was preparing her lessons at the desk in the living room.

"Did you have a nice time yesterday?" she said.

"I did," I said, put some water on for tea, found some rissoles in the fridge, which I fried, fetched the previous day's paper, and sat at the table eating, reading, and gazing out on the almost completely yellow and orange countryside for two hours. Waking up still drunk wasn't quite as good as getting drunk, but it wasn't far off, I reflected, because that feeling of catching up with yourself, of your body slowly regaining its energy, dynamic energy at that, could have its exultant moments.

The sky above the yellow deciduous trees and the green conifers was dense and gray. The grayness, and the fact that all visibility stopped there, just a few meters above, increased the intensity of the colors; the yellow, the green, and the black were hurled into space, as it were, yet blocked by the gray sky, and that must have been why the colors shone with such abandon. They had the power to lift off and disappear into eternity but couldn't, and so the energy was burned up where they were.

The telephone rang.

It was Espen.

I was happy, he had never called me before.

"Did you get home OK?" he said.

"Yes, but don't ask me how."

He laughed. "I won't. Christ, we were drunk."

"Yes, that's for sure. How did you get home?"

"Taxi. God knows I don't have money for taxis, but it was still worth it."

"Yeah."

"What are you doing up there in farming country?"

"Nothing. Have to write a record review afterward, so I'm staying at home."

"Oh? Which band?"

"Tuxedomoon."

"Them, oh yes. That's just European avant-garde crap, isn't it?"

"It's pretty good actually. Very atmospheric."

"Atmospheric?" he sneered. "You can pan them then. See you on Monday."

At around four, as darkness was drawing in, I sat down at the living-room desk and worked on the review until eight, when I got up and sat beside Mom on the sofa and watched TV for a couple of hours. I shouldn't have, since one of the characters in the British series we were following was a homosexual, and when this was mentioned or referred to, I blushed. Not because I was homosexual and unable to tell her, but because she might have thought I was. And that was ironic because if I blushed whenever the word "homosexual" was mentioned, she definitely would have thought I was, and the idea of that made me blush even more.

In my absolutely worst hours I used to imagine that I really was homosexual.

Sometimes, just before I fell asleep, I would begin to wonder whether I was a boy or a girl. I didn't know! My consciousness struggled furiously to clear this matter up, but the walls of my mind were slippery, I didn't know, I could equally well have been a girl as a boy, until finally it found firm ground and, eyes wide open, fear deep in my chest, I knew for certain I was not a girl but a boy.

And if that could happen, if such doubts could appear, who knew what else might be there? What else could be hidden inside me?

So strong was this fear that I seemed to be watching over myself when I dreamed, it was as though there was something in me that was present in the dream to see what I was dreaming about, to see whether it was a boy or a girl I was lusting after while I slept. But it was never a boy, it was always girls I dreamed about when I was asleep and when I was awake.

I wasn't homosexual, I was fairly sure about that. The doubt was minuscule, a tiny fly buzzing in the vast landscapes of my consciousness, but its existence was enough. Great therefore was the torment when homosexuality was mentioned at school. If I had reddened then, it would indeed have been a catastrophe so terrible that I didn't even dare consider it. The trick was to do something, anything at all really, even if only to rub an eye or scratch your head. Anything that could distract attention from reddened cheeks or explain them.

In football, "homo" was one of the most common terms, are you a homo or what, or you fucking homo, but this did not present a threat and because everyone used it constantly, no one would have ever dreamed that someone actually was one.

And of course I wasn't one either.

When the program was over, Mom made some tea and brought two cups into the living room, where we sat chatting about this and that. Mostly about family matters. She had phoned her sisters – Kjellaug and Ingunn – in the course of the day and now she was telling me what they had said about their jobs, the jobs of their husbands, and everything their children were doing. She had also phoned Kjartan, her brother. We spent most of the time talking about him, he'd had four poems accepted by a literary journal, they would be published in the spring, and he was still thinking of moving to Bergen and studying philosophy. But Grandma wasn't doing well, Grandpa couldn't possibly manage on his own, and Kjellaug lived too far away to help much more than on weekends, she had her own family and farm to take care of, as well as a job.

"But he's studying philosophy at home anyway now," Mom said. "Perhaps that's not such a bad idea. Kjartan's not twenty anymore. I'm not sure university life is as easy as he imagines."

"No," I said. "But you've just studied for a year, haven't you? And you're not twenty anymore either."

"I suppose so," she laughed. "But I have a family. I have you. My identity isn't dependent on student life, if you know what I mean. Kjartan has such immense expectations."

"Have you read his poems?"

"Yes, he sent them to me."

"Did you understand anything?"

"I think so, a bit."

"He showed me one this summer. I understood *nothing*. Someone was walking on the edge of heaven. What does that mean?"

She looked at me and smiled. "Well, what could it mean?"

"Haven't got the foggiest," I said. "Something philosophical?"

"Yes, but the philosophy he reads is about life. And everyone knows something about that."

"Why can't he just write it as it is, straight?"

"Some do," she said. "But there are things you can't say straight."

"Such as?"

She sighed and stroked the cat on the head, which he immediately raised, his eyes closed in ecstasy.

"When I was a student I studied a Danish philosopher called Løgstrup. He's very taken by the philosopher who means so much to Kjartan: Heidegger."

"Yes, I remember the name," I said with a laugh.

"He uses a concept Heidegger writes about," Mom continued. "*Fürsorge*. Care. It's at the heart of nursing science of course. Nursing is about caring for people. But what actually is care? And how do we provide care? It's about being human with another human. But what is it to be human?"

"I suppose that will depend on who you ask?" I said.

"Yes, exactly," she said with a nod. "But is there a feature that is common to us all? It's a philosophical question. And it's important for the job I do too."

"I understand *that*," I said. "But I don't understand why he walked on the edge of heaven for that."

"Are we meant to understand?"

"Why should I read it if I don't understand?"

"Perhaps you should ask Kjartan the next time you meet him."

"About what it means?"

"Yes, why not?"

"No, I can't talk to Kjartan. He's always so angry. Or maybe not angry but grumpy. Or peculiar."

"Yes, he is, but he's not dangerous, if that's what you were thinking."

"No, no," I said.

There was a silence.

I racked my brain for something else to say because it was late and I knew the silence would make Mom wonder about going to bed, and I didn't want that, I wanted to continue talking. On the other hand, I had a review to write, and the longer I sat here doing nothing, the later into the night I would have to work.

"Well," she said. "It's late again now."

"Yes," I said.

"Are you going to stay up and work?"

I nodded.

"Don't stay up too long."

"It'll take the time it takes," I said.

"I suppose it will," she said, getting up. "Well, goodnight."

"Goodnight."

As she walked through the living room the cat stood next to the sofa and stretched. Stared up at me.

"Oh no, Mefisto," I said, shaking my head. "I've got to work, you know."

With the record I was reviewing playing on the turntable, I wrote draft after draft, scrunched up the rejects and threw them into the growing heap on the floor. It was a little after two before I was happy, scrolled the paper out of the typewriter, pushed back my chair, and read through what I had written for the final time.

Tuxedomoon
Holy Wars (Cramboy)
reviewed by Karl Ove Knausgaard

Tuxedomoon hail from San Francisco but are now based in Brussels. The band is scheduled to play in Norway this winter; they will be playing Den Norske Opera in Oslo on 1 December.

Blaine Reininger, Tuxedomoon's front man, has left the band to pursue a very promising solo career, and Holy Wars *is their first LP without Reininger. It never scales the dizzy heights of* Desire, *but is not a bad LP for all that.*

The members of Tuxedomoon are classically trained and have grown up with rock music. The result is impossible to classify, but avant-garde rock, futurism, and modernism are handy cues.

The band explores uncharted territory and discovers new musical paths. Holy Wars is a beautiful, atmospheric album, although at times I do find it rather inaccessible. It embraces diffuse moods of the past mixed with the future, synthesizer instruments mixed with acoustic. One of the songs on the LP is a medieval poem translated from the French. In my opinion, this track, "St. John," is the strongest offering, with an infectious organ intro and an equally infectious melody.

Along with "In a Manner of Speaking" it displays the band's lighter side. Other tracks I would pick out for special mention are "Bonjour Tristesse" and the instrumental "The Waltz."

Before I went to bed I wrote a note for Mom to say I had worked till late and she shouldn't wake me. Usually she got up an hour before me, had breakfast, drank coffee, and smoked a cigarette while listening to the radio. Then she woke me and, on the days when our timetables coincided, gave me a lift to school. Her school was only a kilometer farther down the road. We wouldn't say much during the half hour the journey took, and it often struck me how different the lull in conversation was from the one I endured with Dad, when the silence burned like a fever inside me. With Mom the silence was painless.

This morning I woke up half an hour late for the bus, saw that I'd had a nocturnal emission, took off my sticky underpants, and walked naked to the closet, where to my horror I discovered that there were no clean underpants.

Why hadn't she washed them? She'd had the whole fucking weekend to do it!

As I entered the bathroom I saw the laundry rack in the middle of the floor covered in clothes, but they were wet. I realized she had washed them the previous evening but had forgotten to hang them up, so she had done it at top speed in the morning.

Oh, how absentminded she was!

This meant I had a choice between finding a pair of dirty underpants in the laundry basket or wearing wet ones off the rack.

I hesitated. It was pretty cold out and it would be no fun walking the kilometer down to the bus wearing wet underpants.

On the other hand, you never knew how close you might be to people in the course of the day. Not that I imagined I smelled, but if I suspected I did, it would make me behave in an even stiffer and more unnatural manner than usual.

What if Merethe, in my class, who could be very flirty, what if she decided today of all days to clap her light blue eyes on me and perhaps come so close that she could stroke me fleetingly on the shoulder or even the chest with one of her exquisite hands?

No, it would have to be the wet ones then.

I showered, had breakfast, saw that I wouldn't make the next bus without rushing, so I decided I might as well catch the one after.

Outside, the sky was blue, the sun hung low, and in the shadow beneath the trees along the riverbank the frozen mist drifted across the tranquil water.

When the bus pulled up at the stop by the school the third lesson was drawing to a close, and since there was no point going now I took the bus to town and went to *Nye Sørlandet* with the three reviews. Steinar was in his office.

"Are you ditching school?" he said.

I nodded.

"Tut-tut," he said, and smiled. "Have you got something for me?"

I produced the sheets of paper from my bag.

"Just leave them there," he said, pointing to the table.

"Aren't you going to look at them?"

He usually skimmed through them before I left.

"No. I trust you. You've done a good job so far. Why should it be any different today? See you!"

"See you," I said, and left. My insides were glowing at what he had said, and to celebrate I went to buy a couple of records, sat down in Geheb and ate a cardamom and custard bun and drank a Coke while carefully scrutinizing the covers. Once I had finished, it was so late it would have been senseless to go to school so I wandered around the streets for a while, then caught an early bus home. I stopped by the postbox down at the crossing; apart from the newspaper, there were three letters in it. Two for Mom, window envelopes: bills. And an airmail letter for me!

I recognized the writing on the envelope and saw from the postmark that it was from Israel. Waited until I was sitting at the desk in my room to open it. Opened it, took out the letter, stood up, put on a record, and sat down again. Began to read.

Tel Aviv, 10/9/1985

Hi Karl Ove,

I arrived in Tel Aviv a month ago. It's great but also hard. I've never done so much cleaning in my whole life as in the last four weeks. It's thirty degrees here and I'm lying on the terrace writing this letter. I've been to the Mediterranean twice and some Israeli boys have taught me how to play Frisbee and surf. But it's impossible to trust the boys here if you've got blond hair. They assume you're on holiday and so, aha, they think, she'll be easy. But I can't forget you. And I don't understand myself. But I think it's because you were/are the boy I've loved most in all my life. So, Karl Ove, no matter how many girls have come into your life, don't forget me, and come to Denmark next year. And if you are nice and write back quickly this time you are très bien.

I'm your fan,
Lisbeth

I got up, went over to the window, opened it, placed my forearms on the frame, and leaned out. The air was cold and crisp, the heat of the sun shining on me barely evident.

She meant it. She was serious.

I stood up, went outside with the letter, sat down on the bench under the window, and read it through once again. I put it down beside me and lit a cigarette.

I could go to Denmark in the summer. And I didn't need to return.

I didn't need to return.

The thought had never occurred to me before, and it changed everything.

With the cold sharp light in my face, beneath the dark blue autumnal sky, in the midst of the forest above the river, it was as though the future was opening itself to me. Not as what I was expected to do, what everyone did, military service in Northern Norway first, then university in Bergen or Oslo, stay there for six years, go home during the holidays, find a job, get married, and have children who became your parents' grandchildren.

But instead go out and disappear from sight. Vanish. Not even "in a few years" but *now*. Say to Mom in the summer: Listen, I'm off and I won't ever be coming back. She wouldn't be able to stop me. She couldn't. I was a free spirit and she knew it. I was my own man. The future, like a door, was open.

The beech trees in Denmark. The low brick houses. Lisbeth.

No one would know who I was, I was just someone who appeared on the scene and would soon leave again. I didn't need to return! No one ever needed to know any more about me, I could go, vanish.

I really *could*.

A car came around the bend below the house, and I recognized the sound of Mom's Golf. I stubbed out my cigarette, buried it under some grass, and got to my feet as the car drew up on the gravel in front of the house.

She jumped out, opened the trunk, and removed two shopping bags.

"Have you come into some money?" I said.

"Yes, it's payday," she said.

"What did you buy for dinner?"

"Fish cakes."

"Great! I'm starving."

Dad's inquiry about Christmas had been a smoke screen, actually he hadn't wanted us there, and he had booked a trip to Madeira for himself and Unni without waiting to hear what Yngve and I wanted to do.

We would go with Mom to stay with her parents in Sørbøvåg. It was the first Christmas without Dad, and I was looking forward to it: everything had been free and easy the few times all three of us had been together after the divorce.

The day school finished I ambled down to Grandma and Grandad's to wish them Merry Christmas; Mom and I would fly to Bergen the following day, meet Yngve there, and catch the boat to Sørbøvåg together.

Grandma unlocked the front door as always.

"Oh, well look who's here," she said with a smile.

"Yes, I was nearby and thought I would come and wish you Merry Christmas," I said, following her up the stairs without hugging her first. Grandad was sitting in his chair, and his eyes lit up for a brief instant when he saw me. At least that was what I imagined.

"The meal's not ready yet," Grandma said. "But I can heat up some rolls for you, if you're hungry."

"Yes, that would be nice," I said, and sat down, took my cigarettes from my shirt pocket, and lit up.

"You haven't started inhaling, have you?" she said.

"No," I said.

"That's good. It's dangerous, you know."

"Yes," I said.

She put the little metal rack on the hotplate and switched on the stove, placed two rolls on top, and took out some butter, a mild white cheese, and brown goat cheese.

"Dad left for Madeira this morning," I said.

"Yes, we heard," Grandma said.

"I'm sure they'll have a nice time there," I said. "You've been there, haven't you?"

"No, we haven't," Grandma said. "No, we've never been to Madeira."

"Perhaps he's thinking of Las Palmas," Grandad said. "We've been there."

"Yes, we've been to Las Palmas," Grandma said.

"I can remember that," I said. "We each got a T-shirt from there. Light blue with dark blue letters. Las Palmas, it said, and there were some palm trees, I think."

"Can you remember that?" Grandma said.

"Yes," I replied.

Because I did. Some events stood out from that time and were etched in my consciousness. Others were more vague. I thought I remembered Grandma once saying there had been a man downstairs in the hall, a stranger, perhaps someone who had broken in. Later I mentioned it to her and Grandma stared at me in surprise, shaking her head. No, there had never been a man in the hall. So where had I gotten that idea from? Other stories I seemed to remember were similarly dismissed as soon as I mentioned them.

A forefather or a forefather's uncle, I thought I had been told, emigrated to America and remarried there, although he hadn't been legally divorced from his wife back home and was, in other words, a bigamist. I mentioned this during a meal we were having that autumn, sitting in the dining room one Sunday, Grandma, Grandad, Dad, Unni, and I. But no one had ever heard this story before, and Grandma looked almost angry as she shook her head. There was also something about a stabbing, I seemed to remember. But if the story hadn't happened and it was just something I believed had happened, how could it have formed in my mind? Had someone told me it in my dreams? Had it been in one of the countless novels I had read when I went to *ungdomsskole*, which in some mysterious way I had superimposed on vague characters in the family and thus drawn myself into the heart of the narrative?

I didn't know.

But it was no fun because I gained a reputation for being unreliable, I was someone who made things up; in other words, I was like Dad. This was ironic because if there was one resolution I had made it was never to lie, precisely on account of him. Well, yes, I might resort to white lies if there was some matter I didn't want others, Mom more often than not, but Dad too, to know. But whatever I hid, I hid for their sake, not for mine. So that at least was not immoral.

"It's good to have a few days' vacation now," I said.

"I'll say," Grandma said.

"Is Gunnar coming here with the others on Christmas Eve?" I said.

"No, they're staying at home. But I imagine we'll pop over."

"All right," I said.

"There we are. They're done," Grandma said, and placed two rolls on a plate she put on the table in front of me. Then she sat down.

She had forgotten to bring a knife and the cheese slicer.

I got up to get them.

"What's the matter?" she said. "Have I forgotten something?"

"Knife and cheese slicer," I said.

"You stay put. I'll get them!"

She went to the drawer and placed them next to me.

"There we are," she said again. "*Now* you've got everything you need."

She smiled. I smiled back.

The crust on the rolls was so crispy that I had crumbs all around my mouth. I ate quickly, not only because this was a habit, but also because they weren't eating, they were sitting quietly while I munched away, so that every slightest movement I made, even if it was only to brush the crumbs off the table, was somehow emphasized.

"Mom's looking forward to the holidays too," I said as I spread margarine over the second roll.

"Yes, I can imagine," Grandma said.

"She hasn't been to Sørbøvåg since the summer, and her parents are getting on now. Especially her mom. She's not doing well, as you know."

"No," said Grandma, shaking her head. "No, she's not."

"She can't even walk anymore," I said.

"Can't she?" Grandma said. "Is it that bad?"

"She's got a walker though," I said, swallowed, and wiped a few crumbs off my lips. "So she can get around at home. But she doesn't go out anymore."

I had never thought about that. She didn't go out anymore, she was always indoors in those small rooms.

"She has Parkinson's, doesn't she?" Grandad said.

I nodded.

"But Mom's enjoying her job," I said. "There's not *so* much new stuff anymore."

Grandma suddenly got up, lifted the curtain, and looked out.

"Thought I heard someone," she said.

"You were just imagining it," Grandad said. "We're not expecting anyone."

She sat down again. Ran her hand through her hair, looked at me.

"Oh yes," she said and got to her feet again. "We mustn't forget the Christmas presents!"

She was gone for a moment, and I looked at Grandad, who had his eyes on the folded soccer paper on the table beside him.

"Here you are," Grandma said from the hall, and came in with two envelopes in her hand. "Well, it's not much, but it'll help a bit. One for you and one for Yngve. Do you think you can carry them both all the way up to Sørbøvåg?"

She was smiling.

"Yes, of course," I said. "Thank you very much!"

"Our pleasure," Grandma said.

I got up.

"Have a good Christmas," I said.

"And a good Christmas to you too," Grandad said.

Grandma walked downstairs with me, gazed into the air while I put on my black jacket and wound the black scarf around my neck.

"Is it OK if I spend some of my present on the bus fare home?" I said, looking at her.

"No, it isn't," she said. "The whole idea is for you to buy something nice. Haven't you got any money?"

"I'm afraid not."

"I'll have a look to see if I've got some coins somewhere," she said, taking her purse from the pocket of the coat hanging in the wardrobe, and passed me two ten-krone coins.

"Merry Christmas," I said.

"Merry Christmas," she said, smiled at me, and closed the door.

As soon as I was out of sight of the house I opened the envelope with my name. There was a hundred-krone note inside. Perfect. I could hurry and buy two records before going home.

In the shop it struck me that actually I could buy four. Yngve had been given a hundred as well, hadn't he? Yes, he had.

I could give him the hundred from my own money. It wasn't as if the note was marked.

We arrived at Sørbøvåg in the evening. Rain, a couple of degrees above freezing, the darkness as solid as a brick wall as we carried our luggage up the road to the illuminated house. The countryside around us was saturated, everywhere water dripped and trickled.

Mom stopped, put down her suitcase, and opened the brown wooden door with the grooves and the window at the top. The smell, a bit musty from Grandpa's cowshed gear hanging in the hall, wafted toward me, and together with the sight of the door and the white wall at the end of the hall, unlocked my whole childhood in an instant.

In those days they would have met us on the drive or at least come out the second the door was opened, but now nothing happened: we deposited our cases on the floor and removed our jackets to the sound of our own breathing and the rustle of our clothes.

"So," Mom said. "Shall we go in?"

Grandpa, who was sitting on the sofa, stood up with a smile to greet us.

"The Norwegian population is going through a growth spurt, I can see!" he said, looking up at Yngve and me.

We smiled.

Grandma was sitting on a chair in the corner looking at us. Her whole body trembled and shook. She was completely in the grip of the illness now. Jaws, arms, feet, legs, everything twitched.

Mom sat down on a stool beside her and held her hands in hers. Grandma tried to say something, but all that came out was a hoarse whisper.

"We'll just carry up our bags," Yngve said. "We'll be sleeping upstairs, I guess?"

"You can do whatever you like," Grandpa said.

We went up the creaky staircase. Yngve took Kjartan's old room, I took the old children's room. Switched on the main light, put my backpack down by the old cot, drew the curtain, and tried to peer through the darkness outside. It was impenetrable, but I sensed the landscape there nevertheless, the wind gusting through seemed to open it up. The windowsill was covered with dead flies. In the corner under the ceiling hung a spider's web. The room was cold. It smelled old, it smelled of the past.

I switched off the light and went downstairs.

Mom was standing in the middle of the floor. Grandma was watching TV.

"Shall we make some supper then?" Mom said.

"OK," I said.

It was Grandpa who did the cooking in this house. He had learned to cook when his mother died, he had been twelve years old and the responsibility had fallen on him. Not many men of his generation had experience of this kind and he was proud that he could cope. But he wasn't very fussy about washing pots and pans and ladles and so on. The grease that had collected in a thick yellowish-white layer at the bottom of the frying pan appeared to have melted and solidified countless times, the saucepans in the cupboard bore scum marks around the top from boiling fish, and there were bits of overcooked potato stuck to the bottom. Otherwise the kitchen wasn't dirty, a cleaner came twice a week, but it was run-down.

Mom and I scrambled some eggs, made some tea, and took in a selection of sliced meats and cheese while Yngve set the table. When supper was ready I went to get Kjartan, who had built himself a house beside the old one a few years ago. Light droplets of rain settled on my face as I walked the three meters to his door and rang the bell. I opened the door, went into the hall, and shouted up the staircase that supper was ready.

"OK, OK, I'm coming!" he called down.

When I went back Mom was standing next to Grandma in the middle of the floor, holding her arm and guiding her slowly toward the table, where Grandpa and Yngve were already seated, Grandpa was telling him all about the various types of salmon breeding. If he had been younger, that is what he would have done, he said. One of the neighbors had done it, down below in the fjord there was a small breeding station, he was earning so much money it was as if he had won the lottery.

I sat down and poured myself a cup of tea. Kjartan came into the hallway, closed the door after him, went straight to a chair and sat down.

"Are you studying political science?" he asked Yngve.

"Hi, Kjartan," Yngve said. As Kjartan didn't respond to the discreet reproof, Yngve simply nodded. "Or comparative politics, as it's called in Bergen. But it's the same thing," Yngve said.

Kjartan returned the nod.

"And you're at gymnas?" he said to me.

"Yes," I said.

I stood up and pulled back a chair for Grandma. She slowly lowered herself onto it, Mom pushed the chair into the table, sat down on her other side while Kjartan started talking. He didn't look at us. His hands transported bread and meat, buttered bread and raised it to his mouth, poured tea and milk into a cup and raised it to his mouth, all somehow independently of himself and what he was saying, this long unstoppable stream of words that issued from his lips. Occasionally he corrected himself, he laughed a little, he even peeked up at us, but otherwise it was as though he had disappeared in order to let the speaker in him speak.

He talked about Heidegger, held a ten-minute monologue about the great German philosopher and his struggle with him, then stopped in midstream and fell quiet. Mom picked up on something he had said, asked whether that was what he meant, had she understood him correctly? He looked at her, smiled briefly, and then continued his monologue. Grandpa, who had previously dominated the conversations around this table, said nothing as he ate, stared down at the table in front of him, occasionally glanced around the table, a cheery expression on his face as though he had remembered something and was about to tell us what, but held back and lowered his eyes again.

"Not everyone here has heard of Heidegger," Yngve said in an unexpected lull. "Surely there must be other topics we can discuss apart from some obscure German philosopher."

"Yes, I suppose there are," Kjartan said. "We can talk about the weather. But what shall we talk about then? The weather is what it always is. The weather is what existence reveals itself through. Just as we reveal ourselves through the mood we are in, through what we feel at any given moment. It's

not possible to imagine a world without weather or ourselves without feelings. But both elements automate *das Man*. *Das Man* talks about the weather
as though there is nothing special about it, in other words he doesn't see it,
not even Johannes," Kjartan said, nodding toward Grandpa, "who spends
an hour every day listening to the weather forecast, and always has done,
who absorbs all the details, not even Johannes sees the weather, he just sees
rain or sun, mist or sleet, but not as such, as something unique, something
which reveals itself to us, through which everything else reveals itself in
these moments of, well, grace perhaps. Yes, Heidegger is close to God and
the divine, but he never fully embraces it, he never goes the whole way, but
it's there, in close attendance, perhaps even as a prerequisite for the thinking.
What do you say, Sissel?"

"Well, what you say sounds quasi-religious," she said.

Yngve, who had rolled his eyes when Kjartan had started talking about
the weather, speared a piece of salmon with his fork and put it on his plate.

"Is it going to be lamb ribs and pork belly this year as well?" Yngve said.

Grandpa looked at him.

"Yes, it is. We've dried the lamb in the loft. Kjartan bought the pork
yesterday."

"I've brought some aquavit with me," Yngve said. "You need that."

Mom raised a glass of milk to Grandma's mouth. She drank. A white
stream ran from the corner of her mouth.

The countryside was like a tub filled to the brim with darkness. The next
morning the bottom slowly became visible as the light was poured in and
seemingly diluted the darkness. It was impossible, I reflected, to witness this
without feeling it involved movement. Wasn't Lihesten, that immense verti-
cal wall of rock, creeping closer with the daylight? Wasn't the gray fjord rising
from the depths of darkness in which it had been hidden all night? The tall
birches on the other side of the meadowland, where the fence to the neighboring property was, weren't they advancing meter by meter?

The birches: five or six riders who had kept watch on the house all through the night and now had to pull hard on the reins to curb the restless horses beneath them.

During the morning the mist thickened again. Everything was gray, even the winter-green spruces growing on the ridge beyond the lake were gray, and everything was saturated with dampness. The fine drizzle in the air, the droplets collecting under the branches and falling to the ground with tiny, almost imperceptible, thuds, the moisture in the soil of the meadow that had once been a marsh, the squelch it gave when you stepped on it, your shoes sinking in, the mud oozing over them.

At eleven I walked with Yngve to Kjartan's car, he had borrowed it, we were going to Vågen to buy the last bits and pieces for the Christmas dinner. Sauerkraut, red cabbage, some more beer, nuts and fruit, and sodas to quench the thirst that lamb ribs always produced. And some newspapers, if there were any, I needed them to kill the time until the evening, for childhood Christmases were so deeply rooted in me that I still looked forward to them.

With the wipers swishing back and forth across the windshield, we drove across the yard, through the gate, and down to the road in front of the school, where we turned right and set out on the narrow two-kilometer carriage-way to Vågen, which had seemed an interminable distance to me as a child. Almost every meter along the road constituted a special place, the most exciting by far however was the bit leading to the bridge over the river, where I used to hang over the railings for hours just looking.

By car, it took three, maybe four minutes. If I hadn't had my previous attachment to the area, I wouldn't have noticed anything. The trees would have been any trees, the farms any farms, the bridge any bridge.

"Kjartan's incredible," Yngve said. "He doesn't take any account of others at all. Or does he believe everyone's as interested in what he says as he is?"

"I don't know," I said. "Me, I have no idea what he's talking about. Do you?"

"A bit," Yngve said. "But it's not as impressive as it sounds. It's just a question of reading."

He turned in and parked, we walked toward the co-op shop. A woman in a long raincoat came out the door clutching a small child. She was startled to see us.

"Goodness, Yngve! Is that you!" she said.

Who was she?

They hugged.

"This is my brother, Karl Ove," Yngve said.

"Ingegerd," she said, sticking out a hand.

I smiled. Her child clung to her.

"You have grandparents here," she said. "Now I remember. How funny to see you here!"

I wandered across and gazed over Vågen. The water was perfectly still. Some boats were moored to buoys that glowed red in the middle of the fjord in all the gray. When we were little, the Bergen boat used to dock here. Once we had caught it at night, slept on a hard bench, there had been a smell of gasoline and coffee and sea, what an adventure it had been. *Kommandøren* it had been called. Now the *hurtigbåt*, the express boat, had superseded it. The boat didn't stop here anymore.

"Are you coming?" Yngve said from behind me. I turned. The woman and the child were on their way to a car.

"Who was that?" I said.

"Someone I know from Bergen," he said. "She lives with Helge."

On our return, the house smelled of green soap. Mom had washed the floors. Now she was turning her attention to the windowsills. Grandma was asleep in the chair nearby. Mom wrung the cloth over the bucket, straightened up, and looked at us.

"Will you put some porridge on?" she said.

"Yes, I can do that," Yngve said.

"Are we going to put up the tree soon?" I said.

"You can bring it in, if you like," she said.

"Where is it?"

"Actually, I don't know," she said. "Ask Kjartan."

I slipped my feet into a pair of much too small clogs and shuffled over to the other house. Rang the bell, opened the door, shouted hello.

No answer.

I walked carefully up the stairs.

He was leaning back in his Stressless chair and taking in the fjord. He had those big headphones on. Tapping his foot to the music.

Obviously he hadn't heard me. If I walked into his line of vision I would startle him. There was no other option though. Shouting was no good; the music was so loud I could hear it from where I was standing.

I went back out.

Grandpa was walking from the barn to the house. A cat sauntered along behind him.

"Any luck?" Mom asked when I went back in.

"He was busy," I said. "He was listening to music."

Yngve sighed. "I'll go and see him," he said.

Five minutes later he was wrestling with a large straggly Christmas tree in the hallway. We screwed it into the rusty metal stand and then set about hanging decorations on it from a box Mom had located in the meantime. After we had eaten I went for a stroll around the farm, over to the old derelict mink sheds, down to the black mere, past the place where the beehives had been. Farther on, by the remains of the foundations of the house that had once stood there, I smoked a cigarette. There wasn't a sound to be heard, nor a soul to be seen. I threw the stub into the wet grass and walked back to the house. My shoes glistened. In the downstairs bathroom Mom was helping Grandma to take a shower. Yngve sat listening to Grandpa, who was bent forward on the sofa, his arms resting on his knees, and chatting the way he always did.

I plopped down in the other chair.

Grandpa was talking about the time he had fished for herring in the 1920s with his father, how you could hit the jackpot with one cast of the net and how that had actually happened once. His eyes gleamed as he recalled those times. He told us about the skipper who had stood in the bows as they approached

Trondheim one evening, like a baying dog, he said laughing, because what
he was baying for was women. He had spent a long time smartening himself
up, now he stood at the very front of the boat sniffing the wind as they glided
into the illuminated town. Then he talked about the time he had been the
explosives boss on a road-building project: in the evenings they had played
poker in the workmen's hut and he had won time and time again, but he
couldn't spend the money, he had to buy a wedding ring for Grandma and
didn't want the money for it to come from gambling, so he kept putting all
the money back in the pot and sat watching the sweat pouring from the others' foreheads. He laughed so much he had tears in his eyes as he described
how the others had looked, and Yngve and I laughed too, Grandpa's laughter
was so infectious it was impossible not to. He was bent double with laughter,
unable to speak and tears were streaming down his cheeks. But he not only
entertained us with stories of the past, he wasn't given to nostalgia, for as
soon as he had regained his composure, he started to tell us about a trip he
had made to America to visit his brother, Magnus. About how he had sat
alone at night zapping through the endless variety of channels Magnus had,
it was incredible, a miracle, and I smiled because he couldn't speak English
and understood nothing of what was being said as he sat there mesmerized
in front of the television night after night.

Yngve shot me a look and got up. "Are you coming for a breath of fresh
air?"

"Yes, you boys do that," Grandpa said, leaning back against the sofa.

It was raining and we stepped under the overhang by Kjartan's front door
and lit up.

"How's it going with Hanne then?" he said. "It's been a long time since
you mentioned her."

"It's going nowhere," I said. "We chat on the phone now and then, but it
won't work. She doesn't want to go out with me."

"I see," Yngve said. "Might just as well forget her then, eh?"

"That's what I'm trying to do."

He ground his heel into the soft gravel. Stopped, looked across at the barn. It was falling to pieces, the paint was peeling off here and there and the ramp to the hayloft was overgrown with grass, but even though the barn was decrepit, it still stood out because the background – the green meadows, the gray fjord, and the leaden gray sky – somehow thrust it forward, somehow elevated it.

Or else it was because the barn had been so important when I was young, it had been one of the most pivotal buildings in my young life.

"By the way, I've met a girl," Yngve said.

"Really?" I said.

He nodded.

"In Bergen?"

He shook his head, took such a deep drag his cheeks were hollow.

"In Arendal actually. It happened this summer. I haven't seen her since then, but we've exchanged letters. And I'm going to meet her on New Year's Eve."

"Are you in love?"

He eyeballed me. Such a direct question could go both ways; he didn't always want to talk about things like this. But he *was* in love of course, he glowed in that peculiarly introverted way at any mention of her and probably wanted to talk about her all the time, at least if he was like me he would, and he was.

"Yes, basically," he said. "That's what it boils down to! To so few words! To one word, in fact!"

"What does she look like then? How old is she? Where does she live?"

"Can we start with her name? That's the most practical."

"All right."

"Her name's Kristin."

"Yes?"

"She's two years younger than me. She lives on Tromøya. She's got blue eyes. Blond curly hair. She's quite small . . . You went to the same school as her. She was in the class two years above you."

"Kristin? Doesn't exactly ring any bells."

"You'll recognize her when you see her."

"You'll have to get together with her then."

"That was the idea." He looked at me. "Why don't you come to the party? At the Vindilhytta cabin? If you're not going to another party, that is."

"I don't have any special plans," I said. "Perhaps I should."

"I'll be going anyway. Come with me!"

I nodded and looked away so that he wouldn't see how happy I was.

When we went back in, Grandpa was asleep with his chin resting on his chest and his arms folded.

It was five o'clock, *The Silver Boys* was starting on TV, I went downstairs from my room dressed and ready. White shirt, black suit, black shoes. The whole house smelled of lamb. Grandma was wearing her finest dress and her hair was brushed. Grandpa was in a blue suit. Kjartan a 1970s-style gray suit. The table was set, a white cloth, the best dinner service, green napkins next to the plates. Four bottles of beer, room temperature, the way it was drunk here, and a bottle of aquavit in the middle. All that was missing was the food, which Yngve had gone to bring in. Grandpa had cooked it.

"There are only five potatoes," Yngve said. "There isn't even enough for one each!"

"I can go without," Mom said. "Then you can have one each."

"Even so," Yngve said. "One paltry potato for Christmas dinner . . ."

I helped him to carry in the dishes of food. Steaming lamb ribs, square pieces of roast pork with crackling, some with tiny bristles intact, mashed swede, sauerkraut, red cabbage, five potatoes.

The lamb was delicious, Grandpa had cured it, soaked it in water, and cooked it to perfection. The sole criticism of the meal, the most important in the year, was the lack of potatoes. You should never skimp on anything, and certainly not the potatoes! But I recovered from my disappointment and no one else seemed to give it a thought. Grandma sat hunched over the table trembling, but her mind was clear, her eyes were clear, she saw us and she was pleased to have us there, I could see. Just the fact that we were there, that was enough for her and always had been. Grandpa wolfed down the meat, his chin glistening with fat. Kjartan hardly touched the food, he rambled on about Heidegger and Nietzsche, a poet called Hölderlin and someone called Arne Ruste, to whom he had sent poems and who had made some kind comments. He mentioned several other names in his monologue and all of them were spoken with a familiarity he seemed to assume everyone shared.

When the meal was over Yngve and I carried the plates and dishes out while Mom whisked the cream for the rice pudding. Kjartan sat in silence alone with his parents.

"I suggest we institute a Heidegger-free zone," Yngve said.

Mom laughed. "But it is quite interesting," she said.

"Perhaps not on Christmas Eve?" I said.

"No, you're probably right there," she said.

"Shall we have the dessert a bit later?" Yngve said. "I'm absolutely full."

"Me too," I said. "The lamb was good this year."

"Yes, it was," Mom said. "A bit salty though maybe?"

"No, no," Yngve said. "It was just right. It was perfect."

"So shall we start on the presents?" I said.

"We could," Yngve said.

"Will you do the honors?"

"OK."

I was given an EP by Yngve, The Dukes of Stratosphear, a sweater and Wandrup's Bjørneboe biography by Mom, a torch by Kjartan, and a big slice of salmon by my grandparents, as well as a check for two hundred kroner. I gave Mom a cassette of Vivaldi she could listen to in the car, Yngve the solo LP by Marty Willson-Piper, the guitarist in the Church, Kjartan a novel by Jan Kjærstad. Yngve read out the names in a confident voice and distributed the presents with a firm hand, I scrunched up the wrapping paper, threw it into the roaring wood burner, and took occasional sips from the cognac Grandpa had brought in. Yngve passed him a present from Kjellaug and Magne's youngest daughter, Ingrid, born many years after her siblings, and when he opened it and saw what it was he stiffened. Suddenly he was on his feet and heading for the wood burner.

"What did you get?" Mom said. "Don't throw it away!"

Grandpa opened the stove door. Mom hurried over.

"You can't burn it," she said, and took the present from him.

Grandpa looked hostile and bewildered at the same time.

"Let me see," I said. "What is it?"

"It's a plaster cast of her hand," Mom said.

The impression of a small hand in plaster, why would he want to burn that?

Kjartan laughed. "Johannes is superstitious," he said. "It means death, that does."

"Yes, it does," Grandpa said. "I don't want to see it."

"We'll put it here then," Mom said, putting the plaster cast out of sight. "She made it at the nursery and sent it to you. You can't throw it away, you know that."

Grandpa said nothing.

Was that a smile on Grandma's lips?

Yngve passed Kjartan a present from him. A bottle of wine.

"Bull's-eye," Kjartan said. He was sitting on a chair at the back of the room with a glass of cognac in his hand, wearing a milder, more conciliatory expression on his face now.

"Perhaps we could listen to our records on your stereo tomorrow, could we?" I said.

"Yes, help yourselves."

Kjartan was sitting by the Christmas tree, which wasn't quite straight, it was leaning toward him, and then while I was looking him in the eye I saw on the margins of my vision that it had started to move. He turned his head. His eyes lit up in panic. The next second the tree crashed down on top of him.

Grandpa burst into laughter. Yngve and Mom and I laughed too. Kjartan jumped up from his chair. Yngve and I straightened the tree, screwed it into position again, and moved it against the wall.

"Even the tree won't leave me in peace," Kjartan said, running a hand through his hair, and then sat down again.

"*Skål*," Yngve said. "And Merry Christmas!"

After Christmas, we took the express boat to Bergen and flew from there to Kjevik. Mefisto was ecstatic to see us when we arrived, almost clawing my trousers to pieces when I let him lie on my lap during supper.

It was good to be home and it was good to have Yngve there.

The next day he wanted to visit our grandparents on Dad's side, he hadn't seen them since the summer, and I went with him.

Grandma beamed when she saw us standing on the doorstep. Grandad was in his office, she said as we were going upstairs, and Yngve immediately sat down in his chair. With him the atmosphere with Grandma was not as humdrum as it was when I was there on my own; Yngve was much better at hitting the right tone in our family: he joked, made Grandma laugh, and had fun with her in a way that I would never be capable of, even if I practiced for a hundred years.

Suddenly, completely out of the blue, she looked at Yngve and asked him if he had bought something nice with the money.

"What money?" he said.

I flushed scarlet.

"The money we gave you," Grandma said.

"I haven't been given any money," Yngve said.

"I forgot to pass it on to you," I said. "Sorry."

Grandma stared at me as if she couldn't believe her ears. "You didn't give it to him?"

"I'm really sorry. I forgot."

"Did you spend it?"

"Yes, but I only borrowed it. I was going to give him the money back in Sørbøvåg and then I forgot."

She got up and went out.

Yngve sent me a quizzical look.

"We were given a hundred kroner each," I said. "I simply forgot to give you yours. You'll get it later."

Grandma came in with a hundred-krone note in her hand and gave it to Yngve.

"There we are," she said. "Now let's forget all about it."

Yngve did in fact get together with Kristin on New Year's Eve. I saw it all. From the moment they met and she looked up at him with her head tilted and a smile. He had said something and seemed strangely shy. I laughed inwardly. He was in love! Afterward they didn't talk but they did cast occasional glances at each other.

Suddenly they were sitting opposite each other at a long wooden table. Yngve was talking to Trond; she was talking to one of her friends.

They sent each other furtive looks.

Still talking.

Then Yngve got up and was gone for a short while, sat back down, continued to chat with Trond. Picked up a slip of paper and a pen, wrote something.

And then he pushed the slip of paper over to Kristin!

She looked at him, looked at the piece of paper and read what he had written. Looked at him, pinched her thumb and first finger together several times, and he passed her the pen.

She wrote something, pushed the sheet across, he read it. Got up and went over to her, and then suddenly they were immersed in deep conversation, there were only the two of them in the room, and the next time I saw them they were kissing. He had managed it!

After that evening for him everything was about Kristin. He went to Bergen on January 2 and the house felt empty, but only for a day or two until I was used to it, and life continued as it had before with its minor developments in one direction or another, all the unforeseen events that fill our lives, some of which lead to a locked door or a deserted room while others might have consequences that only come to fruition many years later.

I started doing local radio with Espen. We broadcast one program a week, it was live and the basic format was that we played records by our favorite bands and talked about them. I told everyone I knew they should listen, and many of them did, now and then, it was not uncommon for people at school or on the bus to comment on something we had said or some of the music we had chosen. Radio 1 was a small station, there were not many listeners on a normal weekday evening, and *Nye Sørlandet* was not a big newspaper, but between them they gave me a sense that I was on my way.

The radio program meant that I had to stay in town after school, there was no point going home, turning round, and going back, and I made it a habit to pop in to see Grandma and Grandad, they were a safer bet than Dad for food, and I also avoided the uncertainty that a visit to Dad entailed: would he ask me in or not, would it be too much for him or not?

After these long evenings in town, having dinner with my grandparents first, then meeting Espen at the radio station, planning the program with him, and then doing it, I would get on the bus and listen to music the whole weary way home, including the last kilometer, locked inside myself, hardly noticing the white world I was passing through until I removed my headset, opened the door, untied my boots, hung up my jacket, and went into the kitchen to have a bite of supper.

Mom was on the first floor watching TV. When she heard me she switched it off and came down.

"Did you hear it?" I said.

"Yes," she said.

"Was it embarrassing when we got the giggles or was it OK?"

"No, it wasn't embarrassing. Just funny. Karl Ove, Grandma rang while you were out."

"Oh?"

"Yes. It wasn't a pleasant conversation, I'm afraid. She said . . . well, she said you weren't to go there anymore. She said you'd never had anything to

eat whenever you turned up, you were shabbily dressed, and were always asking them for money."

"What?!" I said.

"Yes," Mom said. "She said it was my job to look after you and not theirs.
It was my responsibility. So now they don't want you to go there."

I started crying. I couldn't help myself, the tears came with such force. I
turned away from her, my face contorted into ugly grimaces, I covered it with
my hands, and even though I didn't want to, I sobbed.

I took a saucepan from the cupboard and filled it with water.

"This has got nothing to do with you," Mom said. "You have to understand that. This is about me. It's me they want to hurt."

I put the pan on the stove, barely able to see through all the tears, raised
my hand in front of my face again, bowed my head. Another loud sob rolled
out.

She was wrong, I knew that, this was about me. I had been there, I had
physically felt all the silences and all the unease I carried with me, and in a
way I understood them.

But I said nothing. The convulsive twitches in my face let up, I took a few
deep breaths, wiped my eyes with the sleeve of my sweater. Sat down on a
chair. Mom didn't move.

"I'm so angry," she said. "I don't think I've ever been so angry before.
You're their grandchild. It's difficult for you now. It's their *duty* to support
you. No matter what."

"It isn't difficult," I said. "I'm fine."

"You have hardly anyone around you. The few people you have cannot
turn their backs on you."

"I'm absolutely fine," I said. "Don't give it a second thought. I'll manage
fine without them."

"I'm sure you will," Mom said. "But they're turning their backs on their
own grandchild! Can you imagine! No wonder your father struggles."

"You don't think he's behind this then?" I said.

She looked at me. I had never seen her so furious before. Her eyes were blazing.

"No, I truly don't. Well, not unless he has changed *totally* in these last six months."

"He has," I said. "He's a completely different person."

She sat down.

"And there's one more thing," I said. "That you don't know. Yngve and I were given a hundred kroner each for Christmas. I was supposed to pass the money on to Yngve, but I spent it. Afterward I forgot all about it. When we were there over Christmas it all came out."

"But, Karl Ove," Mom said with a sigh, "even if you'd *stolen* the money that's no reason for them to turn their backs on you. It's not up to them to punish you."

"You've got to understand," I said. "It's obvious they were angry. And what Grandma said is right. I eat whenever I'm there and they give me money for the bus."

"You've done nothing wrong. Don't even think it," she said.

But I did, of course. I lay awake for the first hours of the night as the cold took a grip on the countryside and caused the timber walls of the house and the ice in the river below to creak. Then, in the darkness, I was able to see the matter in a colder, clearer light. If they didn't want to see me, well, then they wouldn't see me. I hadn't gone to visit them for my benefit, I lost nothing by staying away. And there was a sweetness in my decision never to see them again. Not even when they lay on their deathbeds would I go and see them. Indeed, even when they had died and were about to be buried, even then I wouldn't go and see them. Unlike Dad, who during my childhood years had boycotted them for periods, cut off all contact for a month or two, only to resume relations as though nothing had happened. No, I would stand firm. I would never see them again, I would never talk to them again.

If that was how they wanted it, that is how they would get it. I didn't need Grandma or Grandad, they were the ones who needed me, and if they didn't understand that, well, good luck to them.

One afternoon I caught the train alone to Drammen, where Simple Minds were playing at the same venue that U2 had played the year before. I loved their new record, the sound was so monumental and the songs so brilliant I played them again and again that autumn. It was perhaps a bit commercial and the tracks were perhaps not as strong as those on *New Gold Dream*, but I loved it nevertheless. Leaving the concert, I was however somewhat disappointed, not least with Jim Kerr, who had become pretty flabby and actually stopped the gig when a fan ran onto the stage and snatched his red beret. He crouched down at the edge of the stage and said they wouldn't play any more unless he got his hat back. I couldn't believe my ears and from then on it didn't matter how good the songs were, for me Simple Minds were a thing of the past.

I arrived back in Kristiansand by train in the middle of the night. There were no buses and it was too expensive to take a taxi home, so I had arranged with Unni that I would sleep in her flat. She had given me a key; all I had to do was let myself in. So half an hour after I had clambered off the train I inserted the key into the lock, warily opened the door and carefully stepped into the flat. It was a 1950s or '60s build, consisted of two rooms, a kitchen and a bathroom, and had a view of the town from the sitting room. I had been there two or three times before, for dinner with Dad and her, and I liked it, it was an elegant flat. The pictures on the wall were nice, and even though I didn't care much for the Sosialistisk Venstreparti-style ceramic cups and woven fabrics, it was her style, and that was indeed what I noticed about the room, the harmony.

She had made up a bed on the sofa with a sheet and a duvet, I found a book in the bookcase, Johan Bojer, *The Last of the Vikings*, read a few pages, then switched off the light and fell asleep. Next morning I woke to the sound of her clattering around in the kitchen. I got dressed, she set the table in the sitting room and brought in a plate of bacon and eggs, some tea and hot rolls.

We sat chatting all morning. Mostly about me, but also about her, about her relationship with her son, Fredrik, who was having difficulty accepting that our dad had come into her life, about her job as a teacher and life in Kristiansand before she met Dad. I told her about Hanne and my plans to write after I had finished gymnas. I hadn't said anything to anyone because I hadn't formulated the thought before, not in so many words anyway. But now the words just poured out of my mouth. I want to write, I want to be a writer.

When I left it was too late to go to school, so I caught the bus home. The sun was cold and hung low in the sky, the ground was bare and damp. I was happy but not unreservedly so, because chatting with Unni, being open and honest with her, felt like betrayal. Whom I was betraying I wasn't quite sure.

A couple of months later, at the beginning of April, Mom went away for the weekend, to visit a friend in Oslo, and I was left alone at home.

When I returned from school I found a note in the kitchen.

Dear Karl Ove
Take care of yourself – and be good to the cat.
Love,
Mom

After frying some eggs and meatballs for dinner, drinking a cup of coffee and smoking a cigarette, I sat down in the living room with a history book and started to read. The countryside had not yet emerged from the strange interlude between winter and spring when the fields are bare and wet, the sky is gray and the trees leafless, nothing in themselves, everything charged with what will be. Perhaps it has already started to happen, unseen in the darkness, for isn't the air slowly warming up in the forest? Isn't there scattered birdsong coming from the trees after these long months of silence, which had been broken only by the occasional hoarse screams of a crow or a magpie? Had spring not stolen in, like someone wanting to surprise his friends? Wasn't it there, ready any day now to explode into a blaze of green, spewing out its leaves and insects everywhere?

That was the feeling I had, spring was in the offing. And perhaps that was why I was so restless. After reading for an hour or so I got up and walked around the house, opened the door for the cat, which headed straight for the food dish, I thought of Hanne and before I could change my mind I was standing by the telephone and dialing her number.

She was happy to hear from me.

"Are you at home on a Friday evening?" she said. "That's not like you. What are you doing?"

In fact, it was very much like me, but I had probably exaggerated my social life so much that she had integrated it into her perception of me.

"I'm cramming for an exam. And I'm on my own here. Mom won't be home until tomorrow. And so, well . . . I was a bit bored. And I thought of you. What are you doing?"

"Nothing special. I'm a bit bored too."

"Oh good," I said.

"I could stop by," she said.

"Stop by?"

"Yes, I've got my driver's license now, you know. Then we can drink tea and talk until late."

"That sounds perfect. But can you do that?"

"Why wouldn't I be able to?"

"I don't know," I said. "So come over. See you."

An hour and a half later she rounded the bend in the old green Beetle she borrowed from her sister. I shuffled into my shoes and went out to meet her. She looked completely out of place behind the wheel of a car, it struck me as she drove up the hill, driving required a set of movements and actions that I found irreconcilable with her somewhat gauche girlish charm. She performed every maneuver as it had to be done, it wasn't that, but there was something extra which injected a stream of effervescent happiness into my blood. She parked outside the garage door and stepped out. She was wearing the black stretch pants I had once commented on, I had said they looked incredibly sexy on her. She smiled and gave me a hug. We went indoors, I made some tea and put on a record, we chatted for a while, she talked about what was happening at school and I told her what was going on at mine. Some anecdotes about mutual friends.

But we weren't quite in sync.

We looked at each other and smiled.

"I hadn't imagined this when I woke up this morning," I said. "That you would be sitting here this evening."

"Me neither," she said.

A plane came in over the ridge behind our place, the whole house seemed to shake.

"That was low," I said.

"Yes," she said, getting up. "I won't be a minute."

I lit a cigarette, leaned back against the sofa, and closed my eyes.

When she returned she stopped by the garden door and gazed out. I got to my feet, went over to her, stood behind her and gently placed my hands on her stomach. She put her hands on mine.

"It's so lovely here," she said.

The river flowed past, shiny and black, it had flooded the soccer field, only the two homemade goals were visible. The air over the valley had thickened with the dusk. Lights shone in the houses across the valley. Droplets of rain ran down the pane in front of us.

"Yes, it is," I said, moving away from the window. She was in a relationship, she was a Christian, I was just a good friend.

She sat down in the wicker chair, swept the hair hanging over her forehead to one side, and raised the cup of lukewarm tea to her mouth. Her lips were perhaps her finest feature, they formed a gentle curve and at the top seemed to crimp as though not wishing to adapt to the otherwise clean lines of her face. Unless it was her eyes, which I sometimes imagined were yellow, because there was something feline about her face, but of course they weren't. They were gray-green.

"It's getting late," she said.

"You don't have to go yet, do you?" I said.

"Not really," she said. "I don't have anything special on tomorrow. Do you?"

"No."

"When's your mama back?"

Your mama. Only Hanne could say something like that, as though there was still a remnant of childhood in her that hadn't been eroded yet.

I smiled.

"My mama? You make me feel like a ten-year-old."

"Your mother then!" she said.

"She won't be back until tomorrow night. Why's that?"

"I was thinking I might sleep here. I don't like driving in the dark much."

"Can you do that?"

"What?"

"Sleep here?"

"Why shouldn't I be able to?"

"You're in a relationship for starters."

"Not anymore."

"What! Is that true? Why didn't you say?"

"I don't tell you everything, young man," she said, laughing.

"But I tell you everything."

"Yes, you certainly do. But my splitting up has got nothing to do with you."

"Of course it has! It's got everything to do with me!" I said.

She shook her head.

"No?" I said.

"No," she said.

That was a no to me, there was no other way of interpreting it. However, I had given up on her ages ago. She no longer filled my every waking thought, it was several months since she had.

The chair creaked as she shifted position and drew her legs up underneath her.

I liked her. And I liked her being here, in the old house. That was enough, wasn't it?

We sat there for an hour, until the darkness outside was complete and all you could see through the windows was the reflection of the living room.

"It's starting to get late," I said. "Where would you like to sleep?"

"I don't know," she said. "In your room?" She smiled. "I don't like sleeping alone in a house I don't know," she said. "Especially not here. We're almost in the middle of the forest!"

"That's fine," I said. "I'll get a mattress."

I took the mattress off Yngve's bed and laid it on the floor next to mine. Fetched a pillow, sheet, duvet, and cover and put it on while she brushed her teeth downstairs in the bathroom.

She came into the room wearing panties and a T-shirt.

My throat constricted.

Her breasts were so clearly outlined under the T-shirt that I didn't know where to look.

"There we are," she said. "I'm ready. Aren't you going to brush your teeth?"

"Yes, of course," I said, holding her gaze. "I'll do it now."

When I returned she was sitting on the chair by the desk and looking at some pictures Yngve had sent me, which I had left lying around. They were dramatic, in black and white, some of them with me in exaggerated poses.

"How good you look!" she said, holding up one of the photos.

I rolled my eyes. "Shall we go to bed?" I said.

A shudder went through me as she got up.

Her naked thighs.

Her small bare feet.

Her beautifully formed breasts beneath the thin T-shirt.

She lay down on the mattress on the floor, I lay next to her on the bed. She pulled the sheet up to her chin and smiled at me. I smiled back. We chatted a little, she sat up and pushed the mattress closer until it was right under me.

I thought about lying next to her. Lying close to her. Stroking her breasts, stroking her thighs, stroking her bottom.

But she was a Christian. And she was completely innocent, she didn't know who she was or what effect she had on others, she could ask the strangest of questions and that side of her, which I loved, was also the reason I had to stay where I was.

"Goodnight," I said.

"Goodnight," she said.

We lay there, breathing, utterly still.

"Are you asleep?" she said after a while.

"No," I said.

"Can you stroke my back a little? I just love it."

"Of course," I said.

She flipped the duvet to the side and bared her back. I gulped and ran the palm of my hand over her back, back and forth, back and forth.

I don't know how long I was doing it for, a couple of minutes perhaps, but then I had to stop, otherwise I would have gone mad.

"Can you sleep now?" I said, withdrawing my hand.

"Yes," she said, pulling her T-shirt back down. "Goodnight again."

"Goodnight," I said.

She left the next morning, I read all day on the sofa, ate pizza and watched TV with Mom in the evening. She sat with the cat on her lap and a cup of coffee on the table in front of her. I had eaten most of the pizza, then sat with my feet on the table and a glass of Coke in my hand watching *Albert and Herbert*, a Swedish series, it was totally meaningless, it must have been for Mom too, but now that we were sitting there it required an effort to move.

Hanne filled me to the brim. I had thought about her all day. It was a long time since I had erased her from my mind, she didn't want to be with me, but now the whole rusty funfair, once shiny and gleaming, returned once more.

What would have happened if I had snuggled up to her last night?

Suddenly I saw everything in a new light. Suddenly I saw what had really happened.

Oh my God.

That was what she had wanted all along.
Oh, how obvious it was.
Oh my God. Oh my God.
Or was it? Was it only in my mind?
I half sat up, I had to ring her, then I slumped back on the sofa.
"What is it?" Mom said.
"Nothing," I said. "A thought just struck me."

Down at Dad's the dinners had come to a complete halt, at the weekend he generally sat alone drinking, apart from the occasional afternoon when he was sober and received visits from relatives. I had told him that Grandma had rung, yes, he knew, he said, and they're right, your mother should take better care of you. I pay huge sums in child maintenance, you know. Yeah, yeah, I knew. But the fact that I was so upset about not being allowed to go there anymore must have passed him by, or else that was precisely what hadn't happened, for I had said I would pop by on his birthday, he was turning forty-two, and Grandma and Grandad were there. I could smell her perfume in the hallway, but by then it was too late, I couldn't run off now, instead I opened the door to the living room where Grandad's brother Alf and his wife, Sølvi, were sitting, as well as Grandma and Grandad, Gunnar and Tove and their children. I didn't look at Grandma when I said hello, nor when I sat down at the table. I kept my eyes cast down as I ate a piece of cake and drank a cup of coffee. The gathering dispersed, some sat on the sofa, some took their plates out, the conversation swung this way and that. No alcohol was served, of course. I got up and went to the bathroom, when I got back Grandma was in the kitchen.
    "That wasn't how we meant it, Karl Ove," she said. "Not like *that*."
    "I see," I said, and walked past her.
    So now all of a sudden she hadn't said it?
    I suppose she hadn't called Mom either.
    It then struck me that everyone here had heard about what had happened.

They might have discussed it. Me and my behavior. What the most appropriate way of dealing with it was.

While Dad, who drank himself senseless several times a week, he could just invite them here and pretend nothing had happened and everything was hunky-dory.

Oh shit, why wasn't Yngve here?

Why did I have to deal with all this on my own?

I stood my ground against Grandma and Grandad for a few more weeks, but then, one afternoon when I was down at Dad's, he asked me to go there with him and told me I shouldn't be so childish, I was too old for that, of course I should visit them.

I did, and everything was as it had always been.

Dad formal, Grandad formal, Grandma who kept the wheels in motion, Grandma who winked mischievously, who served us food and who took Dad with her into the garden afterward. It didn't matter to me that Dad had clearly split into two different personalities, one when he was drinking and one when he wasn't, which was the one I was used to and knew, this was just how it was, it wasn't something I gave much thought.

For the whole year, from when he moved out, through all the sentimental drunken babble, all the arguments and reconciliations, through all the jealous spats and all the chaos he created, Dad never tired of telling us about the day when his separation from Mom would become a divorce and he would finally be free to do what he wanted. The moment it happened he would marry Unni. I have such a good relationship with Unni, he said, I'm so happy when I wake up with her beside me, I want to do this for the rest of my life, so we're going to get married, Karl Ove, you may as well prepare yourself for that. Had it not been for the damned law we would have done it a year ago. That's how much it means to me.

That's fine, I said in response, unless I was drunk myself and just smiled stupidly, perhaps even with tears in my eyes because that happened too, I was as sentimental as he was, and we sat there in our chairs, each with moist eyes.

When the day came he was true to his word. It was July. In the morning Yngve, Kristin, and I caught the bus to Dad's flat, where they were walking around nervously, Dad in a flamboyant white shirt, Unni in a white dress made from coarse material. They weren't quite ready; Unni asked if we wanted something to drink while we were waiting. I glanced across at Dad. He was standing with a beer in his hand. Help yourselves to anything in the fridge. I'll get it, I said. I went into the kitchen and returned with three beers. Dad looked at me. Perhaps you might wait a bit with that, he said. It's early yet and it's going to be a long day. But you've got a bottle in your hand yourself! Unni said, and Dad smiled, yes, well, I suppose there's no harm in it.

Getting ready took longer than they had anticipated, I had time for two beers before we went to wait for the taxi to take us to the registry office. The sky was overcast and it was cold. I could feel the effect of the alcohol, it lay like a thin membrane over my thoughts, a canopy of mixed feelings. Yngve and Kristin had their arms around each other. I smiled at them, lit a cigarette, and gazed down at the river, which also seemed heavy beneath the somber sky, but the taxi arrived before I had even taken the first drag. We couldn't all fit in, no one had considered that. Dad said he could walk, it was only around the corner. No, Unni said, not on your wedding day.

"We can walk," Kristin said. "Can't we, Yngve?"

"Of course," he said.

And so it was decided. I went with Unni and Dad to the registry office, where the witnesseses were waiting. I vaguely remembered them from the party at our house the summer before. A small bald man and a large buxom woman with a thick shock of hair. I shook hands, they smiled, we stood waiting in a room, Dad looked at his watch impatiently, soon it would be their turn, but it would be quite a few minutes before Yngve and Kristin arrived.

They came rushing in through the hall, red-cheeked, ready for anything. Dad stared at them blankly, we went in, they stood in front of the official conducting the ceremony with a witness on either side, both said yes, passed each other the rings, after which Dad was married again. They chose a name that was new to both of them, or rather two names, each of which was fine and elegant on its own, but in combination sounded ridiculously stilted and pretentious.

On our way to the Sjøhuset restaurant, where we were going to have lunch, Dad said that one of the names, which was originally Scottish, had some connection with our family as actually in the distant past we had come from Scotland. Unni, for her part, said that the name existed in the ancestral past of her family. I could believe that, but what Dad had said was just nonsense, that much I did know.

Yngve shared my opinion, for our eyes met when Dad started talking.

We were shown to a table at the back of the maritime-themed restaurant and ordered shrimp and beer. Dad and Unni smiled and *skål*-ed, this was their day.

I had five beers there. Dad noticed, he told me to take it easy, not in a particularly unfriendly way, and I said I would, but I was in control. Yngve had the flu, so he wasn't going at it like me. Besides, Kristin was there, he kept turning to her, they sat there laughing and talking about something or other.

I was alternately flying – that must have been because of the alcohol, at least I was able to take the initiative and talk to everyone with ease in that lofty manner that occasionally but not very often took hold of me – and completely on the fringes, when everyone around the table, even Yngve, appeared alien to me, indeed not only that, but also totally irrelevant.

Kristin must have spotted this for she often broke out of her twosome with Yngve and said something to draw me into the conversation. She had done that ever since they got together, she had become a kind of big sister to me, someone whom I could talk to about everything, someone who understood. Yet she wasn't much older than me, so the big-sister role could vanish without warning and we would face each other as equals in age, almost as peers.

Eventually we left Sjøhuset and went back to Dad's. The witnesses didn't join us, they would be coming to the dinner in the evening, which had been booked at the Fregatten restaurant in Dronningens Gate. I continued drinking at Dad's place and was starting to get quite drunk, it was a wonderful feeling and slightly odd as it was light outside and all the passersby on the street were pursuing their everyday activities. I sat there, getting more and more pie-eyed, without anyone noticing, as far as I could judge, since the sole manifestation of my drunkenness was that my tongue was looser than usual. As always, alcohol gave me a strong sense of freedom and happiness, it lifted me onto a wave, inside it everything was good, and to prevent it from ever ending, my only real fear, I had to keep drinking more. When the time came Dad ordered a taxi, and I staggered down the stairs to the car that would take us the five hundred meters to Fregatten, and this time there was no question of there not being enough space. Once there we were shown to our table, close to the window in the big room, which was otherwise completely empty. I had been drinking since ten o'clock, now it was six, and it was only by the grace of God that I didn't fall through the window as I went to pull out my chair and sit down. I barely registered the presence of the others, no longer heard what they said, their faces were blurred, their voices a low rustle as though I was surrounded by faintly human-like trees and bushes in a forest somewhere, not in a restaurant in Kristiansand on my father's wedding day.

The waiter came, the food had been pre-ordered, what he wanted to know now was what we were going to drink. Dad ordered two bottles of red wine, I lit a cigarette and gazed at him through listless eyes.

"How's it going, Karl Ove? Are you all right?" he said.

"Yes," I said. "Congratulations, Dad. You've got a lovely wife, I have to say. I really like Unni."

"That's good," he said.

Unni smiled at me.

"But what should I call her?" I said. "She's a kind of stepmother, isn't she?"

"Call her Unni, of course," Dad said.

"What do you call Sissel?" Unni asked me.

Dad looked at her.

"Mom," I said.

"Then you could call me mother, couldn't you?" Unni said.

"I'll do that," I said. "Mother."

"What *nonsense!*" Dad snapped.

"Was the wine good, Mother?" I said, staring at her.

"Yes it was," she said.

Dad fixed his eyes on me. "That's enough of that now, Karl Ove," he said.

"OK," I said.

"So where are you going on your honeymoon?" Yngve said. "You haven't told us."

"Well, there'll be no honeymoon right away," Unni said. "But we've got a room booked at this hotel tonight."

The waiter came and held a bottle in front of Dad.

Dad nodded, not interested.

The waiter poured a little into his glass.

Dad tasted it, smacked his lips. "Exquisite," he said.

"Excellent," the waiter said, and filled all the glasses.

Oh, how welcome that warm dark taste was after all the sharp, cold, bitter beers!

I knocked it back in four long gulps. Yngve sat with his head supported on one hand staring out the window. He must have had his other hand resting on Kristin's thigh, judging by the crook of his arm. The two witnesses sat silent on either side of Unni and Dad.

"We've ordered the food for half past six," Dad said. He looked at Unni. "Perhaps we should inspect the room in the meantime?"

Unni smiled and nodded.

"We won't be long," Dad said, getting up. "You just relax and enjoy yourselves."

They kissed and left the room hand in hand.

I looked at Yngve, he met my gaze, then turned away. Dad's two colleagues were still silent. Usually I would have felt responsible for them and asked them some trivial question in the hope that it might interest them, if not me, but now I couldn't care less. If they wanted to sit there eyeing us, let them.

I filled my glass with red wine and drank half of it in one swallow, and then I went for a piss. I found myself in a long corridor, which I followed to the end without seeing a toilet anywhere. I walked back and down some stairs. Now I found myself in a cellar of some kind, completely white with a dazzling light and some sacks piled against the wall. Back up I went. Was it here? Another corridor, carpeted this time. No. I came out by the reception desk. Bathroom? I said. Beg your pardon? said the receptionist. Sorry, I said. But do you know where the bathroom is? He pointed to a door on the other side of the room without looking at me. I lurched toward it, had to insert an extra step to stop myself falling, opened the door, leaned against the wall, here it was, thank God. I went into one of the cubicles and locked the door, changed my mind, unlocked it, the toilet was empty, wasn't it? Yes, no one around. I hurried over to the washstand, unzipped, pulled the thing out and pissed in the sink. The yellow stream filled the whole basin for a brief instant before being sucked down the drain. Once I had finished I went back into the cubicle, locked the door, sat down on the toilet seat, rested my head on my hands, and closed my eyes. The next second I was gone.

At one point I seemed to hear someone calling my name, Karl Ove, Karl Ove, I heard, as though I was on some mountain plateau, I thought, and someone had been sent out in the mist to find me. Karl Ove, Karl Ove. Then I was gone again.

Next time I came around it was with a jolt. I hit my head against the cubicle wall. The toilet was completely silent.

What had happened? Where was I?

Oh no. This was the wedding day! Had I fallen asleep? Oh no, I had fallen asleep!

I hurried out, washed my face in cold water, walked past reception and into the dining room.

They were still there. They stared at me.

"Where on earth have you been, Karl Ove?" Dad said.

"I think I dozed off," I said, sitting down. "Have you eaten?"

"Yes," Unni said. "We've just finished. Would you like to have something now? We're waiting for dessert."

"Dessert's fine," I said. "I'm not that hungry."

"There"ll be coffee and brandy afterward," Dad said. "You'll pick up then, you'll see."

I finished the wine in my glass and refilled it. My head ached a bit, not much, it was as if a door had been opened a fraction, out streamed the pain, and I knew the wine was doing me good, it seemed to be closing the door again.

When we left it was no later than half past nine. I was drunk, but not as drunk as when I arrived, the sleep had diminished the effect of the alcohol, which the wine and brandy had not managed to replenish. But Dad's drunkenness had escalated prodigiously, he was standing with his arms around Unni waiting for the taxi, the notion of walking five hundred meters had not occurred to him, and it was only with great difficulty that he managed to squeeze himself onto the black leather seat.

Dad went to get some beer from the fridge when we got home. Unni put out some peanuts in a bowl. Yngve had taken a turn for the worse, he had a temperature and was lying on the sofa. Kristin was sitting in the chair next to me.

Unni brought a blanket and spread it over Yngve. Dad stood some distance away watching.

"Why are you wrapping the blanket round him?" he said. "Isn't he big enough to do it himself? You've never wrapped a blanket round *me* when *I've* been feeling a bit off color."

"Oh yes, I have," Unni said.

"Oh no, you haven't!" Dad almost shouted.

"Calm down now," Unni said.

"That's something, coming from you," Dad said, and went into the kitchen, where he sat down in a chair with his back to us.

Unni chuckled. Then she went in to pacify him. I drank half the beer in one go, belched up the froth, and realizing that Kristin was there, swallowed a couple of times with my hand in front of my mouth.

"Sorry," I said.

She laughed. "That's definitely not the worst thing that has happened this evening!" she said, so low that it could only be heard around the table, and then laughed in an equally muted tone.

Yngve smiled. I went to get another beer from the fridge. As I passed the newlyweds Dad got up and went back into the living room.

"I'm going to ring Grandma," he said. "They didn't even send me so much as a single flower!"

I opened the fridge door, took out a beer, and then, suddenly, I was back in the living room reaching for the opener on the table.

Yngve and Kristin were staring awkwardly into the middle distance. Dad was speaking in a loud voice.

"I got married today," he said. "Have you two realized? It's a big day in my life!"

I threw the bottle top onto the table, took a swig, and sat down.

"You could at least have sent some flowers! You could at least have shown that you care about me!"

Silence.

"Mother! Yes, but, Mother, please!" he shouted.

I turned.

He was crying. Tears were streaming down his cheeks. When he spoke his face contorted into an enormous grimace.

"I got married today! And you didn't want to come! You didn't even send any flowers! When it was your own son's wedding!"

Then he slammed down the receiver and stared into space for a few moments. Tears continued to run down his cheeks.

Eventually he got up and went into the kitchen.

I belched and looked at Unni. She got to her feet and ran after him. From the kitchen came the sound of sobbing and crying and loud voices.

"What do you think?" I said after a while, looking at Yngve. "Shall we go out on the town while we're at it?"

He sat up.

"I'm not well," he said. "I think I might have a high temperature. I should probably go home. Let's ring for a taxi."

"Without asking Dad first?" I said.

"Without asking Dad what?" Dad said from the doorway between the two rooms.

"We were thinking of slowly making a move," Yngve said.

"No, stay for a while," Dad said. "It's not every day your father gets married. Come on, there's more beer. We can enjoy ourselves a bit longer."

"I'm not well, you know," Yngve said. "I think I'll have to go."

"What about you then, Karl Ove?" he said, gazing at me through his glazed, almost completely vacant eyes.

"We're sharing a taxi," I said. "If they go, I have to go."

"Fine," Dad said. "I'll go to bed then. Goodnight and thanks for coming today."

Straight afterward we heard his footsteps on the stairs. Unni came in to see us.

"That's how it is sometimes," she said. "Lots of emotions, you know. But you go. We'll see you soon and thanks for coming!"

I got up. She gave me a hug, then she hugged Yngve and Kristin.

Outside I had to sit down on the curb, I was much too tired to stand up for the minutes it would take the taxi to arrive.

When I woke up in bed the next day there was something surreal about all that had happened, I wasn't certain of anything, other than that I had been more drunk than I had ever been before. And that Dad had been drunk. I knew how drunkenness appeared in the eyes of the sober and was horrified, everyone had seen how drunk I had been at my father's wedding. That he had also been drunk didn't help because he hadn't shown it until right at the end when we were alone in his flat and all his emotions were flowing freely.

I had brought shame on them.

That was what I had done.

What good was it that I only wanted the best?

I spent the last weeks of the summer in Arendal. Rune, the program director at the radio station, ran a kind of agency, he sold cassettes to local gas stations, and when one evening I complained that I didn't have a summer job, he suggested I sell his cassettes on the street. I bought them from him for a fixed sum, he didn't care about only making a small profit, and so I could sell them at whatever price I liked. The towns in Sørland were full of tourists in the summer, purse strings were loose, if you were selling music from the charts you were bound to be in with a chance.

"Good idea," I said. "My brother's living in Arendal this summer. Perhaps I can set up there?"

"Perfect!"

And so one morning I loaded a bag of clothes, a camping chair, a camping table, a ghetto blaster, and a box of cassettes into Mom's car, which Yngve had at his disposal all summer, sat in the passenger seat, put on my new Ray-Bans, and leaned back as Yngve engaged first gear and set off down the hill.

The sun was shining, which it had done all July, there was very little traffic on this side of the river, I rolled down the window, stuck out my elbow, and sang along with Bowie as we raced through the spruce forest, the gleaming river appearing and disappearing between the trees, occasionally alongside sandbanks where children were swimming and screaming and shouting.

We talked about Grandma and Grandad, whom we had visited the previous day, about how time seemed to stand still there compared with the house in Sørbøvåg, where in the past two years it seemed to have accelerated and caused everything to go into decline.

We drove through the tiny center of Birkeland to Lillesand and from there onto the E18, the stretch I knew inside out after all the journeys back and forth in my childhood.

I put on a cassette by the Psychedelic Furs, their most commercial LP, which I loved.

"Have I told you about the girl who came up to me in London?" Yngve said.

"No," I said.

"'You're the spitting image of the lead singer in Psychedelic Furs,' she said, and then she wanted someone to take a photo of us together."

He looked at me and laughed.

"I thought it was Audun Automat from Tramteatret you looked like?" I said.

"Yes, but that's not quite as flattering," he said.

We drove past Knut Hamsun's Nørholm property, I leaned forward to look past Yngve and into the grounds, I had been there once, on a class trip when I was in ninth grade, we were shown round by Hamsun's son and saw the cottage where he wrote and a few pieces of furniture he had made.

Now it was empty and looked overgrown.

"Do you remember Dad saying he had seen Hamsun on the bus to Grimstad once?"

"No," Yngve said. "Did he say that?"

"Yes, an old man with a stick and a white beard."

Yngve shook his head. "Imagine all the lies he's told us over the years. There must be tons we still believe without realizing it."

"Yes," I said. "I can't say I'm sorry he's moving."

"No," Yngve said. "Me neither."

Dad and Unni had gotten jobs in Northern Norway, they were going to work at the same gymnas and during recent weeks had packed everything they owned and sent it north. They would be driving up in a couple of days.

"Has Kristin recovered from the wedding?" I said. "I assume it must have been a bit of a shock?"

"It was somewhat special, yes," he said.

We drove down to Grimstad, past the Oddensenter Mall, the old Hotel

Norge, where Hamsun had done some of his writing, up the steep incline, and onto the wide plain.

"And what was that business with the hotel?" I said. "They booked a room at the hotel where we ate, they even went up to see it. But did they sleep there?"

Yngve shrugged. "Perhaps they went back there after we left?"

"Didn't look like it."

"No, but there are a few things in their lives they don't plan. Such as when they said, if you remember, they wouldn't be having a honeymoon. But the day after they caught the boat to Denmark and stayed at a hotel in Skagen."

"That's true," I said.

We drove past Kokkeplassen, Mom's old workplace, where I had been at a nursery for a year, and I craned my neck, there had been a cliff there, we had climbed up a tree over the cliff every day, I seemed to remember. But it wasn't a cliff, it was just a little slope, I could see now. And the tree must have been chopped down. Then we motored down the hill with Arendal below us and beyond it the island of Tromøya, in all its nostalgic splendor, flooded with sunshine.

"Well?" Yngve said. "Are you going to find a spot right now?"

"May as well," I said.

Nothing had been arranged in advance; Rune thought all you had to do was ask in a shop whether they minded if you set up outside in the street and used their electricity, and then hope they didn't charge you a commission. Offer them a couple of hundred if they dithered was his advice.

Yngve parked the car, we walked down the pedestrianized street, I popped into a randomly chosen boutique and asked whether it was all right if I sold cassettes in the street outside and if they had a socket I could use. Might attract customers for them, too.

No problem.

Once that was arranged we drove up to his studio. He had taken his prelims that spring, after finishing the foundation year in comparative politics before Christmas, and now he was working at the Central Hotel in town to earn some money for a trip to China he and Kristin were planning later in the autumn.

The studio he rented was by Langsæ, outside Arendal, and I would be staying for three weeks, sleeping on an inflatable mattress on the floor.

We hadn't spent so much time together since we were little.

The next day he drove me to the town center with all my paraphernalia. It was fantastic standing there in the quiet morning streets, with the sea so blue and heavy and still before us, erecting the old yellow '70s camping table, arranging the cassettes on it – Genesis, Falco, Eurhythmics, Madonna, and anything else that sold well in those months – pulling the cable from the shop, plugging in the cassette recorder, sitting down on the chair, putting on my shades, and pressing play.

The King of Arendal, that was me.

Beside my table was an ice cream stand, and soon after I arrived a girl started work there. She swept the street in front, carried in a few boxes, came out with a rag in her hand and wiped the outside of the window, went back in, and stayed there.

She looked great. Reddish hair, freckles, big curves. When I saw her next, half an hour later, she was wearing a white apron.

Terrific!

But she didn't look in my direction, not once.

That could be arranged.

Gradually people began to trickle by, they walked up and down the small pedestrian street, passed my table several times, I kept a careful eye on them and was quick to recognize faces and bodies. Some of them stopped and examined my selection of cassettes, and if they pointed to one, I jumped up, took an unopened one from the box beside the table, pocketed the money they passed me, thanked them, registered a cross on a sheet of paper I kept handy and sat down.

What a job!

At eleven, sales began to take off with a vengeance. Through to one I sold loads of cassettes, then business flagged until I shut up shop at a few minutes to four, when Yngve came to pick me up.

At his place I counted out the money due to Rune and put it in a plastic bag. The rest I spent when we went out in the evening. I bought bottles of white wine in ice buckets, danced, chatted to whoever came over to Yngve's table. White wine, that was the discovery of the summer for me, it slid down like water, and the buzz it produced made me feel light and happy.

The next day the girl in the ice cream stand smiled at me when she arrived. A little smile, it was true, but unmistakeable.

I knocked on her window at eleven and asked if I could have a glass of water.

She handed me one.

"We're neighbors," I said. "What's your name?"

"Sigrid," she said.

Her accent was curious. The "r" was hard. She also pronounced the "d."

"Where are you from?"

"Iceland," she said with a beam.

That was as far as we got, she didn't come over to exchange a word or two, a little smile and a nod sufficed: the day had begun.

A couple of evenings later she was suddenly standing in front of me at the disco. I was so drunk that everything except her face was blurred. When I woke up in her bed the next morning I couldn't remember how I had got there, was mystified as to how I had managed it, everything was black apart from a couple of scenes from her room: she is lying on the bed wearing only panties and I'm on top of her, we're making out, I kiss her magnificent breasts, I put my hand between her legs, no, she says, absolutely no way, and I get up and take off my underpants and stand in front of her in all my glory, which can't have impressed her as much as I must have imagined it would because she laughed at me and said no again.

I held my head in shame. I had of course registered long ago that she wasn't there, but I hadn't considered where she was until the next second, when I sat up and said hello into the empty room.

No answer. Was she in the toilet perhaps?

I stood up.

Oh no, I was *still* naked.

On the table in the middle of the room there was a note.

Hi, King of Arendal!
I've gone to sell some ice cream.
See you again, underline{maybe}.
S.
(Put the door on the latch when you leave.)

Why on earth had she underlined *maybe*?

I got dressed, stuffed the note in my back pocket, put the door on the latch as she had requested, and went down the narrow, gloomy, and musty-smelling staircase. I hadn't the slightest idea where I was. For all I knew, I could have been kilometers out of town.

The sunlight hit me in the eyes as I emerged.

A street, a house on the other side.

Where was the town?

I followed the street down, rounded a corner and suddenly saw where I was. Somewhere up by Skytebanen!

I strolled down to the center, gave the ice cream stand a wide berth, and sat down in Pollen with a Coke and a bag of rolls. The mere smell of seawater put me in a good mood.

After watching the boats entering and leaving the harbor, the gulls circling, and the cars heading along Langbrygga on the other side, all beneath a deep-blue, motionless sky, I went to see Yngve at the hotel. He was dealing with some guests, I sat down on the sofa and observed him, his patient smile and polite nod, speaking in English, dressed in his not quite immaculate hotel uniform.

When they had gone he came over to me.

"Where did you get to then?"

"I went back to the ice cream girl's place," I said, and could hear what a wonderful sentence that was to say.

"How was it? Are you two together now?"

"Don't think so. She wasn't there when I woke up. But she left me a note and underlined the word *maybe*. *See you again, maybe.* What do you think that means?"

He shrugged, suddenly uninterested.

"Kristin will be at my place tonight, by the way."

"Where should I sleep then?"

"In the bathroom."

"Seriously?"

"It's no problem, is it?"

"No, of course not. I was thinking of you two."

"Don't worry, it'll be fine. I've warned her. Anyway, I stayed at her place last night."

It was fine too, though it felt a little strange lying on the mattress in the bathroom listening to Yngve and Kristin giggling and laughing and chatting in subdued voices in the bed.

As I walked down the pedestrian street the next morning I was excited. I had got up extra early to be there before her, I thought that would give me an edge. She arrived, smiled her little smile, and went into her stand. I stayed where I was, sold loads of cassettes, and when I finally did go over to her it was to ask for a glass of water.

I was given one.

"Thanks for the other night," I said.

"Thank *you*," she said.

"I was thinking of going out tonight. Would you like to come?"

She shook her head.

"Tomorrow night then?"

She shook her head again. "You're not my type," she said with a smile. "We could meet though."

"When?"

She shrugged and smiled again.

I went back to my table and the days passed. She attended to her business in her stand, I attended to mine, once in a while our glances met and we smiled.

That was all.

I bought a felt pen and some cardboard from a bookshop and hung a sign on the tree beside the table. ORGINAL CASSETTES, I wrote, then the price and the names of some Top Twenty artists. It wasn't long before a man in his midforties stopped and said it was "original," not "orginal." I was good at writing, my spelling was perfect, so I said no, you're wrong, that's how it's spelled. There's not another "i" in "orginal." I stuck to my guns, he stuck to his, and eventually he walked away shaking his head.

The money was rolling in. People were crazy about my cassettes, buying four or five at a time, so when evening came and I went out with Yngve I didn't stint myself. I drank as I had never drunk before. If I ran out of cash all I had to do was sell some more cassettes the next day. Once a week Rune dropped by in his red car with fresh stock. And now and then someone I knew from the old days happened by. Dag Lothar, for example, who had a summer job in a bank and was the same as always. Geir Prestbakmo, who was at vocational college and rode around on a brand-new moped, he was his old self as well. And then John, the class tough guy, who just loafed around, as he put it.

Yngve and I went to the other side of Tromøya one day, to the place where Dad had always taken us swimming. Yngve parked the car by the rifle range, we walked down through a dense prickly thicket, I relished the incomparable smell of heather, pine needles, and salt water, the massive gray ridge that had been there for so many million years, and then the sight of the sea below. The air was thick with insects. I stamped my foot down hard at every step, the area was full of adders, at least it had been when I was growing up.

Once Dad and I had encountered one only a few hundred meters from where I was walking now, it was spring, the snake had been stretched out on a stone slab in the sun. I must have been about ten. Dad went crazy, started throwing stones at it, I watched as they seemed to sink into the snake's body as they struck, the adder tried to get away, it was hit again and again until it lay still beneath a pile of stones. But as we were about to walk on, out it wriggled again. Dad went closer, continuing to throw stones at it, he wanted me to do the same, I was on the point of throwing up, the snake was still now, Dad ventured closer and crushed its head with the big rock he was holding in his hand.

I turned. Yngve was behind me. We walked along the spine of sea-smoothed rocks and found a warm spot by the water's edge. I went down to examine the great sinkhole in the rock, which wasn't so big anymore, dived into the foaming water, swam out to the long island maybe a hundred meters away and then back again. Lay down to dry in the sun, ate biscuits and oranges, smoked and drank coffee. Yngve suggested going with him to Kristin's place afterward, so that would save him having to take me to the town center. Is that all right? I said, of course, he said, they're incredibly open and kind. Anyway, the rest of the family's on holiday, so she's the only one there.

A few hours later he pulled up outside their house. We watched a video and ate pizza. Yngve had been there a lot over the past six months, he liked her parents, her brother and sister, and they liked him. He was like a son in the house, I could see.

Her sister's name was Cecilie and she was one year younger than me, I saw some photos of her and was impressed. Her brother was much younger than them, he was still at primary school.

I stayed the night and slept in Cecilie's bed. We decided to go out together the following night, Kristin would bring along some girlfriends, but first we would eat in a restaurant, just us three.

I drank two bottles of white wine with the food, and when we went to the discotheque I had three more.

And who should I meet there but the girl from the ice cream stand!

The four of us took a taxi to Tromøya. I sat in the front seat. We had stood wrapped around each other making out while we waited for it to come, and, still dazed by that, I stretched my arms back toward her. She took my hands and caressed them. Her hands were very rough, I noticed.

"Oh, Karl Ove," Yngve said from behind me.

They laughed.

Furious, I retracted my arms.

"How much have you had to drink, actually?" Yngve said.

"Five," I said.

"Five *bottles* of wine?" Yngve said. "Are you kidding?"

"No," I said.

"No wonder you're behaving so weirdly. If it had been me, I would have been lying in the street snoring."

"True," I said.

The taxi stopped, I paid, we went into the house.

The same thing happened there, with the sole exception that this time she was *absolutely* naked. But no, she didn't want to. Alabaster skin, full-bosomed and beautiful, she lay there saying no, no, no.

When I awoke next morning she was gone.

Still drunk, I went upstairs and into the kitchen, where Yngve and Kristin were having breakfast.

"She caught the bus a while ago," Kristin said. "She said to say hello and thank you for yesterday."

For a change, the sky was overcast. I decided to give this day a miss, lie on the sofa and read until Yngve went in to do his evening shift. The next day she wasn't there. There was a girl in her twenties at the hatch. I asked her where Sigrid was, she said she had finished, yesterday had been her last day. Did she have any idea where she was? No, she didn't.

I went to Kristin's a couple more times, and on the last evening the family had returned from their holiday. I said hello, they were as nice as Yngve had said they were, we rented a video of *Apocalypse Now*, Kristin sat leaning against Yngve while I sat beside Cecilie, we exchanged occasional glances and smiled, we were so clearly the little brother and sister on the floor below our two siblings, who, if they had decided to get married, would not have surprised anyone.

There was a tension in the air, I felt it all evening, but what kind of tension was it?

We were a bit shy with each other, was that what it was?

I saw how Cecilie sometimes tried to wrest the initiative, as though wanting to make it clear that she was not only on an equal footing with her sister but also very distinct from her.

I liked to see that. Her will, how that led the way and she followed.

She did ballet, and she was good, Kristin had said; after leaving school she was going to take the ballet school entrance exams.

The way she threw herself onto the sofa. The way her face could suddenly become quite open and artless when she smiled.

But this was no good. There was no point even thinking about it.

Yet I did.

There was only a week left of the summer job and I joined Yngve whenever he drove to Kristin's, I enjoyed being in her home too, there was such a nice atmosphere, they were good people and it was reflected everywhere in the house.

I saw how Yngve was treated and how happy he was. I thought to myself, come on now, don't be an idiot, just let him have it all.

But I also thought about Cecilie, because when she was in the room, I could feel her presence with the whole of my body.

And I knew it was the same for her too.

First of all her parents left and went to bed. Then Yngve and Kristin left and went to bed.

We sat alone in the big living room, on opposite sides of the table. We made conversation, for we couldn't talk about or show anything of what we felt, or rather of what I felt and of what I imagined she also felt.

"I was there when they got together," I said. "At Vindilhytta. You should have seen it. It was really sweet."

"Yes, they are sweet," she said.

"Yes," I said.

What kind of situation was this I suddenly found myself in? In a house on Tromøya alone with the sister of Yngve's girlfriend?

Nothing wrong with the situation. Only with my feelings.

"Well," she said with a yawn. "Time to go to bed."

"I'm going to stay up for a bit," I said.

"See you at breakfast then."

"Yes, goodnight."

"Goodnight."

She disappeared down the stairs, moving in that self-assured elegant way she had. Thank God I was going home soon and could put all this behind me.

The following evening, which was the last, I went to see Yngve, he was on the evening shift and served me an enormous pizza, which I ate at the table in the lobby while he worked and came over for a chat whenever he could. He said Cecilie and Kristin were in town. Kristin was coming over soon. He didn't know what Cecilie was doing. But she came as well, I joined them, it was the last night, in just a few hours I would be home again. Nevertheless, even though I knew it was stupid, I stayed close to Cecilie, we walked side by side, we had nothing to say to each other, we just walked and listened to each other's breathing, which was deep and tremulous, and then we hugged and kissed, again and again.

"What are we doing?" I said. "Can we do this?"

"I've been thinking about that ever since I first saw you," she said, holding my face between her hands.

"Me too," I said.

We stood wrapped in each other's arms for a long time.

"At the last moment," Cecilie said.

"Yes," I said.

"Now you mustn't have any regrets," she said. "Or rather, of course you can. But tell me if you do. Do you promise?"

"I won't have any regrets," I said. "I promise. Are you at home next weekend?"

She nodded.

"Can I come and see you?"

She nodded again, we kissed for a last time and then I went, turned, she waved, I waved.

Yngve was standing behind the counter studying a sheet of paper when I went into the hotel to get the keys. I said nothing about what had happened. Were we going out together now? I wondered as I walked up Arendal's steep hills in the hazy darkness of the late-summer night. In which case how strange it would be for Yngve and me to be going out with two sisters! Wasn't there something a bit circus-like about this? Roll up, roll up, come and see the two brothers who go out with two sisters! But why should I care? He lived in Bergen while I lived in Kristiansand, and soon he and Kristin would be in China.

This had completely bowled me over.

She was walking home now too, also bowled over.

Yngve drove me to the bus the following morning. I didn't say anything then either. When I sat down in a window seat and looked for him, he was already on his way up the street.

I closed my eyes and could feel how thoroughly exhausted I was. As the bus turned into Grimstad town center I was asleep and didn't wake until it passed Kristiansand Zoo. I jumped off at the Timenes intersection and caught a different bus for the last part up to Boen. Out of habit I looked for a glimpse of Jan Vidar in his window as the bus crossed Solsletta, but he wasn't there and his car wasn't in the driveway either.

I took out a cigarette and looked down at the waterfall, the last kilometer home was a drag, but I did finally manage to motivate myself and set off with my bag on my back.

As I came up the last hill I saw Mom by the barrel we used to burn paper in. A thin, almost transparent flame flickered back and forth over the edge. She caught sight of me and walked down.

"Hi," she said with a smile. "How was it?"

"Fine," I said. "How's everything here?"

"I've been fine," she said.

"Good," I said. "Think I'll have a shower and change."

"You do that," she said. "I've made dinner. Just have to heat it up. Are you hungry?"

"Yes, starving."

In the evening I sat at my desk reading, but I couldn't settle down, my thoughts raced this way and that, and everywhere they went they confused me, none of them were as they had been. Now and then I looked out the window, saw the garden merge imperceptibly into the dense forest behind the little potato patch, felt the trees close to us waiting or listening, darkness always gave me this sense, and as the gentle gusts of wind grew stronger the leaves trembled and the branches swayed. A week ago I had never seen her, hardly knew who she was. Now we were going out.

What about Hanne?

And the girl in the ice cream stand, what had that been?

It was as though I was faced with a jigsaw puzzle made of pieces from several sets. Nothing fit, nothing made any sense.

I went downstairs to Mom in the living room.

"Are you sure you've been fine while I've been away?" I said.

She put down the book she was reading on the table.

"Yes," she said. "I really have been."

"You weren't lonely?"

She smiled. "Not at all. I was at work. There was a lot to do. And then it was wonderful to come up here afterward."

Presumably roused by our voices, the cat padded across the floor with a sleepy face. He jumped straight into my lap and rested his heavy head on my thigh.

"How about you?" she asked.

I shrugged.

"It was fine," I said. "I liked selling the cassettes on the street. In a way I lived from hand to mouth. Earned money during the day and spent it at night."

"Oh?" Mom said. "What did you spend it on?"

"Well, different things," I said. "I went out for meals a lot. That costs money. And then I had a beer once in a while with Yngve. But I've saved a bit too. I've brought a bag of money back with me. Nearly three thousand kroner."

I hadn't counted the money, in fact I had forgotten all about it, so now I got up and went into the hall to check and keep it in something more suitable than a plastic bag.

But the bag wasn't there.

I had dropped it on the floor just inside the door, hadn't I?

Yes. On top of the shoes. A white Beisland bag it had been. Full of creased notes.

Had Mom put it away?

I went back into the living room.

"The bag that was in the hall," I said. "Did you move it?"

She looked up at me, her index finger keeping her place on the page.

"A plastic bag in the hall?" she said. "I threw it away."

"Chucked it away? Are you crazy? There was three thousand kroner in it!"

And it wasn't even mine, it was Rune's. In fact, he should have had more than that because I had spent quite a chunk of his money during the past few days there.

"You had money in it?" Mom said. "And you left it on the floor? How was I supposed to guess?"

"Where did you throw it?"

"In the barrel. Where we burn paper."

"Have you burned it? How could you? Have you burned the money?"

I shook my hands in the air. Then I dashed into the hall, slipped on a pair of shoes, and ran up the slope.

There was the bag.

But was the money in it?

I snatched at it and looked inside.

Oh, thank God. There it was.

I took the bag, emptied the money onto the floor of my room, counted it, there was a bit more than three thousand two hundred kroner, put it in a drawer, and went down to the living room.

"You found it?" Mom said.

I nodded. Put on a record, ran my eye along a bookshelf, eventually picked out Hamsun's *Pan*, sat down on the sofa, and began to read.

There was a week left before school began and I decided to spend it writing some reviews, went down to town, dropped in on Steinar Vindsland, it was good I came, he said, he had been trying to get hold of me, had called a couple of times without any luck.

"Thing is I'm finishing here. I've got a new job on *Fædrelandsvennen*. You can probably keep going here, but I can't guarantee it, after all it was me who hired you."

"That's a shame," I said.

"Yeah, well," he said. "Anyway, I have an offer for you. I'll be responsible for the young adults and music sections. How would you feel about writing for *Fevennen*? It wouldn't be record reviews, Sigbjørn Nedland does that, as I'm sure you know. But material for young adults, and then maybe reviews of gigs and interviews with bands."

"That would be good," I said.

"Great," he said. "So I'll see you!"

Nye Sørlandet was a sinking ship, that was common knowledge, so this was good news. *Fædrelandsvennen* was a paper everybody read. If I wrote something there, everyone would see it.

I went to Platebørsen and bought five LPs to celebrate my promotion, which was how I considered it. I had taken the money from the plastic bag, the odd couple of hundred kroner wouldn't make any difference anyway, somehow I would have to find the money to pay Rune.

When I returned home Yngve rang, eager to know what had happened on the last evening. Cecilie had been so strange and secretive and was writing a letter to me.

I told him.

"So you're going out with Cecilie?"

"Yes, I guess you could say that."

"Isn't that a bit weird?"

"Yes. Does it matter?"

"No . . . maybe it doesn't."

"Good!"

But it made no sense to me. Two days later the letter arrived. She was confused, it had been like a dream, she wrote, and she shouldn't tell me, but when she had left me that evening, tears had been streaming down her cheeks. On the Friday I went to see her, we were alone, we had to edge our way forward. We talked about what had actually taken place. She said she had been so intrigued by me after all the things that Kristin had told her and the photos she had seen. She had wondered whether perhaps something might happen, and after she had seen me she wanted something to happen, but it couldn't, after all we were just the younger siblings. I said I had felt the same. She said Yngve had looked at us one evening, first at her, then at me, then at her again. It had been in the air. Yes, I said, and I ached. We didn't know each other, didn't know what it was, but then it happened again, suddenly we were embracing, kissing each other, and then we went to bed . . .

But we didn't make love. I thought she was so young, we didn't know each other, and I ought to tread carefully . . .

No, that wasn't the real reason.

The real reason was that I came before anything had happened.

I was so ashamed that I lay totally still so as not give myself away.

And not only then, it happened every time we were together in the ensuing weeks.

At the first editorial meeting I attended at *Fædrelandsvennen* I suggested writing an article about the Sissel Kyrkjebø phenomenon. She was lauded by all the newspapers, had sold an unimaginable number of records, but why actually? I asked.

"Good idea. Go for it," Steinar said.

"Why does Sissel sell?" I called the article. "Savor the name," I wrote. "Sissel Kyrkjebø . . ." And then I made fun of all the associations you could make, with Christianity, the farming community and nationalism, she was even wearing traditional dress on the LP cover. She stood for everything I disliked, it was false, manipulative, clichéd, a dreadful picture postcard of the world, who could bear the beauty of it, and on top of everything in such an undemanding form?

There were lots of letters to the editor over the following days. One opened with the words "Karl Ove Knausgaard. Savor the name," then feasted on its associations with the sterility of rocks (*knaus*) and the scant yield of a farm (*gaard*). *Fædrelandsvennen* was a popular newspaper, it was loyal to its readers, the qualities that I preferred – innovation, the avant-garde, provocation – were not for the likes of them, and in the months that followed there was a conspicuously large number of glowing articles about Sissel Kyrkjebø.

I loved it, finally my name had been raised above the anonymous ranks of the crowd, not much, though not so little either.

The weekend after the article appeared Yngve came to visit, and as usual we dropped in on Grandma and Grandad. On this occasion Gunnar was there. He rose to his feet and stared straight at me as we entered the kitchen.

"Well, here he is, the world champion," he said.

I smiled at him inanely.

"Who do you think you are?" he said. "Do you realize what an idiot you've made of yourself? No, you don't, do you? You think you're something special."

"What do you mean?" I mumbled, even though I knew all too well what he was talking about.

"What makes you think that you of all people are right and everybody else is wrong? You, a seventeen-year-old schoolkid! You don't know anything. Yet you assume the lofty position of an arbiter of taste. Oh, it's so pathetic!"

I said nothing, studied the floor. Yngve did the same.

"Sissel Kyrkjebø is a popular artist loved by everyone. And she gets good reviews. Then you come along and say everyone's wrong! You! No!" he said, and shook his head. "No, no, no!"

I had never seen him so angry or worked up before, and I was shaken.

"Well, I was actually on my way," he said. "Good to see you, Yngve. You're still in Bergen, right?"

"Yes, for the time being," he said. "But I'm going to China in the autumn."

"There you go," Gunnar said. "Off to see the world!"

Then he left, and we turned to Grandma and Grandad, who had been sitting at the kitchen table minding their own business during this little interlude.

"I agree with you anyway," Yngve said as we got into the car to go home. "I think what you wrote was perfectly reasonable."

"Yes, of course it is," I said, laughing, there was something exhilarating about all this.

Cecilie and I talked for hours on the telephone. She trained hard, was enormously disciplined and determined, things came to her easily and she was open to life. But there was also something closed inside her, or silent, I didn't know quite what, but I noticed it. At the weekend I hitchhiked to her place, unless she came to mine. I preferred to be there because I too was treated like a son of the house, though not with the same acceptance as Yngve, I sensed, we were younger and siblings of the other two, something to do with that meant we weren't taken as seriously, I felt, as though we were imitations, as though we weren't ourselves or people in our own right.

When we were alone, we *were*, of course. Autumn descended upon us, we walked into the deepening gloom, hand in hand or entwined, Cecilie delicate yet strong-willed, open yet closed, full of platitudes yet passionately herself.

One evening we went to the primary school I had once attended, not so far from their house. I had been twelve when I left, now I was seventeen. The five years felt like an eternity, there was almost nothing that connected me with the person I had been, and I remembered next to nothing of what I had done then.

But when I saw the school before us, hovering in the mist and darkness, my memories exploded inside me. I let go of Cecilie's hand, approached the building, and pressed my hand against the black timbers. The school really existed, it wasn't merely a place in my imagination. My eyes were moist with emotion, it was as though the whole bounteous world that had been my childhood had returned for an instant.

And then there was the mist. I loved mist and what it did to the world around us.

I remembered Geir and me running around with Anne Lisbet and Solveig in the mist, and the memory had such power that the thought was painful. It tore me to pieces. The soft gravel, the trees glinting with humidity, the lights shimmering, shimmering.

"Strange to think that you actually went to this school," Cecilie said. "I don't connect you with Sandnes at all."

"Neither do I," I said, gripping her hand again. We walked alongside the building, toward the annex, which in my imagination was brand new. I craned my neck the whole way, running my gaze over everything I could, absorbing it all.

"We must have been here at the same time, no?" I said as we clambered down the slope to the football field.

"Yes," she said. "When you were in the sixth grade, I was in the fifth."

"And Kristin was in eighth grade and Yngve his first at gymnas," I said.

"And now I'm in the second at gymnas," she said.

"Yep, the world is tiny," I said.

We laughed, walked across the empty field, and followed the gravel path through the forest to Kongshavn. Only a few hundred meters farther on, the sensation of coming home, of recognizing, was gone, we were stepping into the outer zone of childhood, where I had been only a few times and where the scenery assumed a dreamlike quality which I both recognized and discovered anew.

Everything was so odd. It was so odd to be here, and it was odd to be with Cecilie, the sister of Yngve's girlfriend. It was also odd to go home to Mom and our life there, which differed so starkly from the life I lived away from home.

I had started at another local radio station, it was bigger, all the equipment was new, the rooms were fantastic, they had asked if I wanted to work for them and I did. I still played football, I still wrote for the newspaper, and I went out more and more often. When I wasn't with Hilde, Eirik, and Lars, I drank with Espen and his friends, or with colleagues from the radio station, unless I was hanging out with Jan Vidar. It was hard to take Cecilie into this world. She was something different for me. When I sat in Kjelleren drinking she was infinitely distant; when I was sitting next to her she was infinitely near.

One problem was her devotion to me, it placed me in a superior position, which I didn't want. Yet I was inferior to her, indeed as low as anyone can be, that was where I was for the weeks that became months because what I was slowly realizing, the terrible truth that my relationship with her had revealed, was that I couldn't make love to anyone. I couldn't do it. A naked breast or a hurried caress across the inside of a thigh was enough, I came long before anything had begun.

Every time!

So there I lay, beside her, this girl who was such a delight, and I was pressing my groin against the mattress in an attempt to hide my humiliating secret.

She was young, and for a long time I hoped she wouldn't realize, she probably did though, but I doubted she could imagine it was a permanent condition.

One evening she mentioned that her mother had asked whether she had considered going to the doctor for the contraceptive pill.

She said this with a smile, but there was expectation in her voice, and I, trying to repress it, or deceiving myself into believing this really wasn't happening, began to look for a way out. Not that I didn't want it, I did too of course, no, there were other problems, greater ones, for example, that we lived in separate towns and that I couldn't spend *all* my weekends with her.

Those were my thoughts, at the same time I thought about her devotion, it was immense, she would do anything for me, I knew that, not least through her letters, which were permeated with longing even though they were written barely hours after we had last seen each other.

No, I had to get out of this relationship.

She came over one Saturday morning at the beginning of December, intending to stay until the following day, when her parents would come to pick her up, they wanted to meet Mom, after all she was the future mother-in-law of both of their girls. It was a kind of endorsement of our relationship, and perhaps I didn't want this. We went for a walk, the countryside was frozen, the grass in the meadow below the house glittered with rime in the light from the street lamps, afterward we had dinner with Mom, and then we caught the bus down to the Hotel Caledonien, Cecilie was wearing a red dress, we danced to Chris de Burgh, "Lady in Red," and I thought, no, I can't finish this, I don't want to finish it.

We caught the night bus home, walked hand in hand over the last part, it was cold, she snuggled up to me. We entered the house, took off our coats and I thought: I'm going to do it now. We went upstairs, Cecilie first, she opened the door to my room.

"What are you doing?" I said.

She turned and gaped at me in surprise.

"Going to bed?" she said.

"You're sleeping in there," I said, pointing to Yngve's room, which was adjacent to mine.

"Why?" she said, looking at me with big eyes.

"It's over," I said. "I'm breaking it off. I'm sorry, but it's not working out."

"What did you say?"

"It's *over*," I said. "You have to sleep in there."

She did as I said, her every movement leaden. I undressed and went to bed. She was crying, I could hear her clearly, the wall was thin. I put my fingers in my ears and went to sleep.

The next day was torture.

Cecilie cried, Mom was wondering what was wrong, I could see, but she didn't ask, and neither of us wanted to say anything. After a while her parents drove up. Mom had laid out a big brunch, now we had to sit there and have a nice time, both families. But Cecilie was silent, her eyes were red. Our parents made conversation, I chimed in with an occasional comment. Of course they knew something was wrong, but not what, and probably thought we'd had an argument.

But we had never argued. We had laughed, played, chatted, kissed, gone on walks together, drunk wine together, and lay naked in bed together.

She didn't cry while they were there, she sat quietly and ate very slowly, her movements constrained, and I could sense her parents were very concerned, it was as though they were embracing her with their presence and their actions.

Then at last they left.

Thank God they were going to Arendal. It was far away, and the bridge Yngve represented between the two families was even farther away.

Sometime between Christmas and New Year Dad phoned. He was drunk, I could hear that from the slur. He didn't quite have full control of his voice, there was an added timbre, although the tone didn't sound any more resonant or complex as a result.

"Hi," I said. "Merry Christmas. Are you still in the Canaries?"

"Yes," he said. "We're here for a few more days. It's wonderful to get away from the darkness, you know."

"Yes," I said.

"We're going to have a baby," Dad said. "Unni's pregnant."

"Is she?" I said. "When will she give birth?"

"Just after the summer."

"That's good news," I said.

"Yes, it is," he said. "Now you'll have another brother or a sister."

"That'll be strange," I said.

"I don't think it'll be strange," he said.

"Not in that sense," I said. "Just that there'll be such a large difference in age between us. And we won't be living together."

"No, you won't. But you'll be siblings anyway. That's as close as you can get."

"Yes," I said.

In the kitchen Mom was setting the table. The coffee machine was chugging away with small puffs of steam rising from it. I quickly rubbed my arm several times.

"Is it nice where you are?" I said. "Can you swim there?"

"Oh yes, you bet you can," he said. "We lie by the pool all day. It's wonderful to get away from the darkness in Norway, we think."

There was a silence.

"Is your mother there?" he said.

"Yes," I said. "Would you like a word with her?"

"No, what would I have to talk about with her?"

"I don't know," I said.

"Don't ask such stupid questions then."

"All right."

"Did you go to Sørbøvåg at Christmas?"

"Yes, we've just got back. Half an hour ago in fact."

"They're still alive?"

"Oh yes."

"And Grandma was ill?"

"Yes."

"You know that's a hereditary illness she has, don't you? Parkinson's."

"Is it?" I said.

"Yes, so you're vulnerable. You could get it. And then you'll know where it came from."

"I'll cross that bridge when I come to it," I said. "Dad, food's ready here. Have to go. Say hello to Unni and congratulations!"

"Give me a call sometime, Karl Ove, when we're back. You hardly ever call."

"Will do. Bye."

"Bye."

I put the phone down and went into the kitchen. The cat had settled on the chair under the table, I could see his bushy tail hanging over the edge. Mom opened the oven door and put some frozen rolls on the shelf.

"There wasn't a lot of food in the house," she said. "But I found some rolls in the freezer. How many do you want?"

I shrugged.

"Four maybe."

She added one more and closed the door.

"Who was it on the phone?"

"Dad."

I pulled out the chair beside the cat and sat down.

"He's in the Canaries, isn't he?" Mom said, crossing the floor to the fridge.

"Yup," I said.

She took out one white and one brown cheese, fetched a chopping board from the counter, put it on the table, and placed the cheeses on it.

"What did he have to say? Were they having a good time?"

"He didn't say much. Just wanted to talk. He was a little drunk, I think."

She put the slicer on top of the white cheese. Removed the pot from the coffee machine, filled the cup on the other side of the table.

"Do you want some?" she said.

"Yes, please," I said, passing over my cup. "But he said one thing that was a bit strange. He said Parkinson's was hereditary. And that I was in the danger zone."

"Did he say that?" Mom said, meeting my eyes.

"Yes, that's precisely what he said."

I cut the rind off the white cheese, moved it to the edge of the plate, changed my mind and threw the rind in the bin under the counter.

"Not much is known about that," Mom said.

"Don't worry," I said. "You don't think I'm worried about it, do you?"

She sat down. I opened the fridge, took the juice from the door and looked at the date: December 31. Shook it. There was a drop left.

"Did he really say that?" Mom said.

"Yes," I said. "But don't give it another thought. He was a bit drunk, as I said."

"Have I ever told you about the first time he met Grandma and Grandpa?" she said.

I shook my head. Opened a cupboard and took out a glass.

"They made a deep impression on him, both of them. But especially Grandma. He said she was like nobility."

"Nobility?" I said, sitting down and pouring the juice into my glass.

"Yes. He saw something special in her. Dignity, he said. You know, it was tough, very different from what he was used to. We weren't poor in any real sense, we always had food and clothes, but things were tight, they were. At least, compared with his childhood home. I don't know what he'd been expecting. But he was surprised. Perhaps also because they dealt with him in a way he was unused to. They took him seriously. They took everyone seriously. Perhaps it was as simple as that."

"How old was he then?"

She smiled.

"We were nineteen, both of us."

"Do you want some juice by the way?" I said. "There's a drop left."

"No, you take it," she said.

I emptied the carton and threw it into the sink. A perfect aim. The sudden noise made the cat stir.

"He talked about her eyes," Mom said. "I can remember that. He said they were piercing yet gentle at the same time."

"That's true," I said.

"Yes, he's always been good at observing others, your father," she said.

"You wouldn't believe it now, the way he behaves," I said, taking a sip of the juice.

The acid taste made me grimace.

"That's partly why I'm telling you," she said. "So you can appreciate that he's more than what he's showing at the moment."

"I realize that," I said.

Some steam escaped from the gap at the top of the oven door and from the outlet at the back of the stove. How long had they been in now? Six minutes? Seven?

"He was a very gifted person. There were so many sides to him. Much more so than any of the others around him – when I met him anyway. And there can be no doubt that it was a problem that his talents were never really appreciated when he was growing up. Do you understand what I mean?"

"Yes, of course."

"Mm."

"But if he was as gifted as you say he was, how could he do to us what he did when we were growing up? I was petrified of him. All the time."

"I don't know," she said. "Perhaps he was confused. Perhaps he was driven by external demands incompatible with what was inside him. He grew up with so many demands on him, so many rules and regulations, and when he met me I brought along other demands that probably didn't suit him at all. Well, obviously they didn't."

"Yes, he mentioned something about that," I said.

"Did he?"

"Yes."

"So you talk about all this?"

I smiled.

"I wouldn't exactly say that. It's more him sitting there and moaning. But I think the rolls are done now."

I got up, walked around the table, opened the oven door, took out the burning-hot rolls one by one as quickly as I could, put them in the bread basket, and set it on the table.

"Lots of external rules and monumental internal chaos, is that your diagnosis?" I said.

She smiled.

"You could put it that way," she said.

I split open a roll and then handed her the bread knife. The butter I spread melted the second it made contact with the grayish surface, which was partly

285

doughy from the heat. I cut myself two slices of brown cheese and placed them on top. They melted too.

"Why didn't you just leave?" I said.

"Leave Dad?"

I nodded with my mouth full.

"I've wondered about that many times myself," she said. "I don't know."

We ate for a while without speaking. It was odd to think we had been in Sørbøvåg only this morning. It seemed like much longer. It was a different world.

"Well, I don't have a good answer to that," she said at length. "There were so many reasons. Divorce would have been a defeat. And then we'd been together all our lives. That creates a lot of bonds of course. And I loved him, that goes without saying."

"I don't quite understand that," I said. "But I hear what you're saying."

"You can say what you like about your father," she said. "But he wasn't boring to live with."

"No," I said, and stood up to get my tobacco pouch from my jacket in the hall.

"What about Kjartan then?" I said as I returned. "Surely there's a kind of inner chaos in him too?"

"Is there?" Mom said.

"Isn't there?" I said, and opened the pouch, took a rolling paper, filled it with tobacco, and plucked a bit out to create better air flow.

"Maybe," she said. "At any rate, he's searching for something. He's been searching all his life, I would say. Now he's found it he's holding on to it."

"You're thinking of communism?"

"For example."

"What about you?" I said, rolling the paper back and forth around the tobacco. "Are you searching?"

She laughed.

"Me, no! I'm trying to survive. That's what I'm doing."

I licked the gum on the edge, stuck it down, and lit up.

The next evening I went out, first of all I sat around drinking with a few others in a gymnas friend's house, we pinched a few beers from the cellar and were thrown out, ran downhill to town, everywhere was covered with snow, it cracked and creaked beneath our shoes, and the freezing-cold wind was all around us, buffeting against our faces as we walked, we forced our way through, it was endless. At the Shell station in Elvegate we flocked around a little man who had been talking to one of the girls there and laughed at him, we sang, "Here comes toughie, toughie, toughie, tough," and then, "Here comes dickie, dickie, dickie, dick" to the tune of "Here comes Pippi." I kicked him in the ass as he turned and everyone laughed. After we had paid and left, he was standing there waiting for us all, with a pal. The pal was much bigger than him. Who could possibly have guessed? "Him," the little man said, pointing at me over by the pumps. The big pal came over to me, said nothing, then looked me straight in the eye. A second passed, perhaps two, then he punched me. I collapsed in a heap. Hot blood ran from my nose down onto the concrete. What happened? I thought. Had he punched me? It didn't hurt.

Behind me I heard Hauk. I'm only sixteen! he was shouting. I'm only sixteen! I'm only sixteen! I sat up. They ran down the hill. Hauk and two others in front of him, the big man at the back. He was brandishing a knife. I got up and went over to the girls, whom no one had threatened. Marianne dashed into the toilet and emerged with an armful of paper, and I wiped off the blood. Not long afterward, Hauk and the others returned from the opposite direction, they were still frightened, went into the kiosk and asked the assistant to call the police. The sparkle went out of the evening, the group dispersed, suddenly I was the only person left who wanted to keep going, and I had to catch a taxi home, sitting on the back seat while my nose and head pounded and throbbed.

The moment I opened the door, I knew that Yngve had come home. Luggage scattered across the floor, his jacket on a hook, his sturdy boots. I decided to surprise him. My joy at the idea made my chest bubble with excitement, and when I opened the door, switched on the light and shouted,

"Da-da!" and he sat up in bed, utterly bewildered, I burst into laughter. I completely lost control, just kept on laughing, he looked at me, what happened, he asked, what's up with your nose, I was laughing so much I couldn't answer, he said, go to bed, Karl Ove, we can talk tomorrow.

"Did you just get back from China?" I said, continuing to laugh, closed the door behind me, and went into my room, where I undressed and climbed into bed still cracking up. My head felt as if it were a box full of objects swaying to and fro whenever I moved it. Now they were continuing to sway even though my head was still, I noticed, and then I fell asleep.

I woke up with my face aching. I remembered what had happened and sat up in horror.

Then I remembered Yngve was here.

Great.

There was a faint smell of smoke, they had lit the fire. Their low voices could be heard from the floor below, they were probably sitting in the kitchen having breakfast.

I put on a T-shirt and a pair of jeans and went downstairs.

They looked at me. Yngve smiled.

"Just need to wash up," I said, and went into the bathroom.

Oh dear, oh dear, oh dear.

My nose was slightly crooked, the bone beneath the bridge. In addition, it was extremely swollen and my nostrils were full of crusted blood. I washed it carefully and went back into them.

"What happened to you yesterday?" Yngve said.

"Someone punched me," I said, sat down and put a roll on my plate. "I didn't do anything. A guy at the gas station came over and just punched me. Then he ran after the others I was with and chased them down the hill with a knife. Thugs."

Mom sighed, but she said nothing and in a second it was over because Yngve talked about China, which I assumed he must have been doing for a long time. He was full of it. He talked and talked, and I could visualize it:

throngs of people swarming around Kristin when they arrived, attracted by her blond hair, what fun it had been on the Trans-Siberian Railway, how wild it had been in Tibet and how foreign the colors were. Big yellow rivers and tree-clad cliffs, the alien cities and cheap hotels, the Great Wall of China, ferries and trains, crowds of people everywhere, dogs, hens, as far from the deserted snow-covered frozen countryside as it was possible to be.

Two days later, on New Year's Eve, Yngve went to Vindilhytta while I went down to Bassen's wearing shiny new shoes and a suit I had rented. Hanne was there. I drank vodka and juice, I wanted to dance with her, we did, I drank more, I said we should get together even though it was ages since I had last seen her, it was almost an obsession, she laughed off my suggestion, I was offended, danced with other girls, got more and more drunk, and at twelve when everyone gathered together on the road, including people from the other houses in the vicinity, things degenerated, people lit rockets and held them until the very last second so that they whizzed around the ones standing there, people screamed and shouted, there were bangs and explosions, and I watched Hanne, she was shivering, and she was so beautiful, she really was, why couldn't I be hers and stand there with my arm around her? I thought, and then a rocket landed by her feet.

People screamed and ran away.

But this was my chance, so I ran forward, I went to kick it away and just as I did, it exploded. It was a bizarre feeling, my calf went all hot, and looking down I saw my trousers in tatters. Blood was flowing. There was even a big hole in my shoe! I refused to go to the emergency room, someone washed the blood off with a cloth and wound a bandage around my leg, I shouted that I was Hamsun's Lieutenant Glahn and had shot myself in the foot so that Hanne would realize how much I loved her, jumped around in tattered trousers and with the bandage soaked in blood, I'm Lieutenant Glahn, I yelled, and I have a vague memory of sitting on a chair in a corner and crying, but I am not absolutely sure. At any rate I got home at five, I remember asking the taxi driver to stop by the mailboxes, as I always did, so the engine noise wouldn't wake Mom, and I put my trousers and shoes at the back of the wardrobe before going to sleep. The next morning I took off the bandage, put it in a plastic bag and shoved it to the bottom of the rubbish bin, washed the wound, which was quite deep, put a plaster over it, and went in to have a hearty breakfast.

We don't live our lives alone, but that doesn't mean we see those alongside whom we live our lives. When Dad moved to Northern Norway and was no longer physically in front of me with his body and his voice, his temper and his eyes, in a way he disappeared from my life, in the sense that he was reduced to a kind of discomfort I occasionally felt when he called or when something reminded me of him, then a kind of zone within me was activated, and in that zone lay all my feelings for him, but he was not there.

Later, in his notebooks, I read about the Christmas when he called from the Canary Islands and the weeks that followed. Here he stands before me as he was, in midlife, and perhaps that is why reading them is so painful for me, he wasn't only much more than my feelings for him but infinitely more, a complete and living person in the midst of his life.

It was Yngve who found his notebooks. A few weeks after the funeral he rented a large car, drove back to Kristiansand and got Dad's things from the garage, and then he drove to the Østland town where Dad had lived for his last years and collected the little that was left there, then he had it all sent to Stavanger, and he put it into the loft until I arrived and we could go through it together.

When he called that evening in the autumn of 1998, he said that for a moment he had been convinced Dad was alive and was following him in a car on the motorway.

"There I was, in a car full of his things," he said. "Can you imagine how furious he would have been if he'd found out? It's absolutely absurd of course, but I'm *sure* it was him following me."

"It gets me in the same way," I said. "Whenever the phone rings or some-one buzzes at the door, I think it's him."

"Anyway," Yngve said, "I've found some diaries he'd been keeping. Well, actually, they're notebooks. He jotted down a few notes every day. From 1986, 1987, and 1988. You've got to read them."

"Did he write a diary?" I said.

"Not exactly. Just some notes."

"What does he say?"

"You'll have to read them."

When I went to Yngve's some days later, we threw away nearly everything Dad had left behind. I took his rubber boots, which I still wear ten years later, and his binoculars, which are on my desk as I am writing this, and a set of crockery, as well as some books. And then there were the notebooks.

Wednesday 7 January
Up early, 5:30. Pjall.
The shower was cold.
Bus 6:30 from Puerto Rico. Took a quick swig here too.
At the airport. Bought a Walkman. Dep. 9:30. Delayed – Kristiansand 16:40.
Flight to Oslo 17:05. Problem.
The same in Alta. Met Haraldsen here. Via Lakselv (−31°C)
Taxi home. Cold house. Warmed myself on duty-free. <u>Hard</u> day.

Thursday 8 January
Tried to get up for work. But had to call Haraldsen and throw in the towel.
Grinding abstinence – stayed in bed all day . . . I made an attempt to read Newsweek. Managed a few TV progs. School tomorrow?

Friday 9 January
Up at 7:00. Felt lousy at breakfast.
Work. Survived the first three lessons. Had terrible diarrhea in lunch break and had to give the HK class a free. Home for repair – rum and Coke. Incredible how it helps. <u>Quiet</u> afternoon and evening. Fell asleep before TV news.

Saturday 10 January
Slept in. Downed the sherry in the kitchen. Evening spent in the company of blue Smirnoff!

Sunday 11 January
Had a feeeling when I woke up it was going to be a bad day. I was right!

Monday 12 January
Slept badly. Tossing and turning and hearing voices. Work. Started with English background. Hard going when you're out of shape. Evening classes even more stressful!

Tuesday 13 January
Another sleepless night. My body won't accept being without alcohol. Went to work.

Tuesday 20 January
Another bad night. Always like that when you don't take any "medicine." After an hour and a half you're too exhausted to do a good job. Lutefisk for dinner – my favorite. I had a siesta after dinner – a very long nap – up at 10. Worked till 3. Working through the night is the norm now!

And so it goes on. He drinks every weekend, but also more and more often during the week, and then he tries to stop, to have some alcohol-free days or even weeks, but it doesn't work, he can't sleep, he is restless, hears voices, and is so worn out it's almost a relief when he finally goes to the liquor store or buys beer and comes home, and all his inner conflict eases.

Under "Wednesday 4 March" his notebook just says *Yngve, Karl Ove, Kristin.* We went up north in the winter vacation to visit them. Dad paid for us all. Unni had invited her son, Fredrik, who was there when we arrived. I flew with Kristin from Kristiansand to Bergen, I was a bit nervous about it of course, because of what had happened between Cecilie and me, but she didn't say a word about it and treated me as she always had. Yngve joined us in Bergen, then we flew up to Tromsø, where we changed to a propeller plane for the last part.

The terrain beneath was wild and deserted, there was barely a house or a road to be seen, and when we reached the airport there was no pilot announcement of a slow descent, no, the plane simply swooped down like a bird of prey that had seen its victim, I thought, and the moment the wheels touched down on the runway, we braked and were hurled forward toward the seat in front.

The passengers filed out of the plane across the tarmac to the tiny terminal building. It was cold and overcast, the countryside was white with a scattering of shiny black patches where the rock was too steep for snow to settle.

Dad stood waiting in the arrivals hall. He was formal and tense. Asked us how the trip had been, didn't listen to the answer. His hands shook as he inserted the key into the ignition and let go of the hand brake. He was silent for the whole journey through the vast misty desolate terrain to the town. I observed his hand, he rested it on the gearshift, but as soon as he raised it, it shook.

The building he parked under was outside the center, facing the sea, on an estate that must have been built in the 1970s, judging by the shape of the houses. They had rented the entire upper floor and had a big balcony outside the living room. The windows were gritty, I supposed the salt from the spray had caused that, even though it was several hundred meters to the sea from there. Unni met us in the doorway, smiled, and gave everyone a hug. A boy who must have been Fredrik was sitting in a chair watching TV and got up to say hi.

He smiled, we smiled.

He was tall, had dark hair, and was a distinct presence in the room. When he sat down again I went into the hall for my backpack and caught a glimpse of Dad as I passed the open kitchen door. He was standing by the fridge and knocking back a beer.

Unni showed us where we would be sleeping. I left my things there. When I got back the first bottle was on the table while he was attending to the second. He belched quietly and put the bottle down next to the first, wiped the froth from his beard, and turned to me.

The tension was gone.

"Are you hungry, Karl Ove?" he said.

"I guess I am," I said. "But there's no hurry. We can eat when it suits you."

"I've bought steaks and red wine today. We can have that. Or shrimp. They've got good shrimp up here, you know."

"Both fine by me," I said.

He took another beer from the fridge.

"It's good to have beer on a holiday," he said.

"Yes," I said.

"You can have some later, with the food," he said.

"Great," I said.

Yngve and Kristin had sat down on the sofa. They were looking around the way you do when you are somewhere new, discreetly absorbing their surroundings, constantly aware of each other, not necessarily with their glances but in the total way that lovers can be when everything is about the two of them. Kristin was a miracle of joy and naturalness, and that rubbed off on Yngve, he was fully open to it and wore an almost childish glow that he only had when he was with her.

Fredrik sat in his chair on the other side of the table and shyly answered the questions Yngve and Kristin asked him. He was a year younger than me, lived somewhere in Østland with his father, played soccer, was interested in fishing, liked U2 and the Cure.

I sat down in the chair beside him. On the wall above the sofa hung the blue picture by Sigvaldsen that Dad had taken with him after the divorce, on the two longer walls there were more pictures we used to have at home. The suite of furniture in the other corner was the one Dad had always had downstairs in his office, one of the carpets on the floor came from there, too. I recognized the furniture from Unni's flat.

Dad sat down on the sofa. He put one arm around Unni, in his other hand he held a bottle of beer. I remember thinking I was glad Yngve and Kristin were here.

Dad asked Yngve a question, which he answered briefly but not in an uncivil tone. Kristin slowly tried to bring harmony to the situation with questions about the town and the school where they worked. Unni answered.

After a while Dad turned to Fredrik. His tone was light and good-natured. Fredrik's body language was dismissive, it was obvious he didn't like Dad, and I could understand why. Only an imbecile would not have heard the false ring to Dad's voice, as though he were talking to a child, and not realized that he was doing this for Unni's sake.

Fredrik gave a surly response, Dad stared into the middle distance for some seconds, Unni said something kind but reproachful to Fredrik, who writhed with discomfort.

Dad sat motionless, drinking. Then he got to his feet, hitched up his trousers, and went into the kitchen, where he started making dinner. We stayed in the living room chatting with Unni. By the time the food was on the table, at about eight, Dad was drunk, he wanted to calm the waters but his efforts were too bumbling and he made a fool of himself. Fredrik in particular suffered. We were used to Dad, we had nothing else, but Fredrik had lost his mother to this idiot.

Dad sat silent for a long time with a stupid, disgruntled expression on his face. Then he got up and went into the bedroom. Unni followed him, we heard their voices, they came back as though nothing had happened, chatted about the holiday they'd had and the dispute they were having with their travel company. It transpired that Dad had collapsed in Gran Canaria, fallen over in the room, and had been taken to the hospital by ambulance. He said it was heart failure. At any rate he had sued the tour operator because there had been several incidents – arguments with the reps, arguments with other tourists at the hotel – and now they were sure that everyone had been against them, indeed bullied them almost, and that had led to Dad's heart problem. He had been kept at the hospital for two days. He showed us photos, and some of them were an unpleasant sight: we saw photos of a couple on a terrace, the camera zoomed in, the couple got up, shook their fists, and walked toward the camera. What were they doing? See how nasty they were, Dad said. What fatheads. They're as bad as Gunnar. What's wrong with Gunnar then? Yngve said. Gunnar? Dad repeated. OK, I'll tell you. For a whole summer he was snooping round the flat in Elvegate. He was supposed to be keeping an eye on me, you know, making sure I wasn't drinking. He's so self-righteous, that brother of mine. He told me so too, that perhaps I ought to cut down, can you imagine? Is he his brother's keeper? I was an adult when he was only knee-high to a grasshopper. Can't a man have a beer in his own garden? He really went too far. And just look how he ingratiates himself with Grandma and Grandad. He's after the cabin. He's always wanted the cabin. And he'll get it in the end. He'll inject them with his poison as well.

I didn't say anything. Met Yngve's gaze.

How could he stoop so low? They were brothers, Gunnar was his younger brother, and he not only had some order in his life, the children he brought up were close to him, they trusted him, I could see that whenever I saw them, there was not a trace of fear in their eyes, on the contrary, they liked their father. If he had told Dad he was drinking too much, he was perfectly within his rights, who else was going to tell him? Me? Ha ha, don't make me laugh. And the cabin? Gunnar was the only one of the brothers who used it and always had, he loved living out there. Dad didn't. If Dad got his hands on the cabin, he would sell it.

I watched him, he sat there with his eyes brimming and the slightly stupid expression around his mouth he always had when he was drunk.

"Perhaps it would be best to show the slides tomorrow," Yngve said. "It's already late."

"What slides?" Dad said.

"Of China," Yngve said.

"Oh, that's right, yes," Dad said.

Unni stretched her arms above her head.

"Well," she said. "Now I really *do* have to go to bed."

"I'm coming too," Dad said. "I'll just have a few words with my two boys, who have come a long way to see their dad."

Unni ruffled his hair and went into their bedroom. As soon as the door was closed Fredrik got up.

"Goodnight," he said.

"Are you off, too?" Dad said. "You aren't pregnant, are you?"

He laughed, I looked at Fredrik and raised my eyebrows to indicate to him that he wasn't alone in what he thought.

"I'm beat too," Kristin said. "Either it's the journey or it's the sea air. Whichever it is, it's goodnight anyway!"

After she had gone the three of us sat there saying nothing. Dad gazed into the air and finished his beer, then went to get another. I wasn't drunk, but I could feel the alcohol.

"So here we are," Dad said.

"Yes," I said.

"Just like in the old days. Do you remember, in Tybakken? Yngve and Karl Ove. Sitting in the kitchen and having breakfast."

"How could we ever forget?" Yngve said.

"Yes," said Dad. "It wasn't an easy time for me either. I'd like you to know that."

"Times aren't easy for lots of people," Yngve said. "But it's not everyone who takes it out on their children."

"No," Dad said.

He started crying.

"I'm so happy to have you here," he said.

"Do you have to get so sentimental?" Yngve said. "Can't we talk about this in a normal way?"

"Unni's got a new life in her belly now. It'll be either your brother or your sister. Think about that."

He smiled through the tears, dried them, emptied the bottle, and rolled himself a cigarette.

Yngve and I exchanged glances. It was hopeless, you got nothing from him but hot air.

"I'm going to bed," Yngve said.

Dad said nothing as he left. I didn't want him to be on his own and stayed a little while longer, but when he made no sign of either leaving or speaking, and just sat there staring into the room, eventually I got up too and went to bed.

After breakfast the next day Yngve, Kristin, Fredrik, and I went to town and wandered through the snow-covered, windblown, night-black streets. While Yngve and Kristin went into a clothes shop I sat in a café chatting with Fredrik. We exchanged a few names of bands, established a kind of base, and then we started talking about what we could actually do in this godforsaken town. We couldn't just sit on our hands in the flat. He said there was a swimming pool not far away, perhaps we could go there later in the day? That's a good idea, Unni said when we went home. Yes, a great idea, Dad said from inside the living room. I haven't been to a pool in years. Are you going to join them?! Unni said. Yes, why not? he said. I could see Fredrik wasn't happy, but I thought it might be OK, the evening was a long time away. Unni drove us because Dad had drunk a couple of beers. We went into the changing room with our gear and sat down on the bench.

Dad started undressing.

I turned away. I had never seen him undress, I had never been in the same room as him before when he was doing something so intimate. Sitting on the bench, he folded his trousers, rolled his socks in a ball, and undid his shirt.

I felt myself getting hot and flustered, didn't know where to look or what to do with myself, because now he was taking off his underpants and for a few seconds he was completely naked.

I had never seen him naked before, and a shudder went through me as I cast my eyes over him.

He looked at me and smiled.

Everything else had been removed, there was just the smile he sent me before turning away to put on his trunks.

I put on mine and together we walked into the spacious swimming area.

When we returned home, Unni had made dinner, a fondue, Dad drank a bottle of red wine on his own, afterward Yngve and Kristin showed their slides of China. Unni had borrowed a projector from school. They talked and explained, Dad sat and looked on with no interest at all, I could see Yngve was getting annoyed, why did it bother him, I thought, he should give up on Dad.

Fredrik was ironic with Dad, who got angry and rebuked him, which made Unni furious, she went to her room, he struggled to his feet and followed, they shouted at each other while, in the living room, we pretended everything was fine. Something smashed against the wall, a shout became a scream, then there was silence. Dad emerged, said nothing, had a drink, suddenly looked up at us and grinned that inane grin of his, looked at Fredrik and said they could go fishing tomorrow if he wanted, his sons weren't interested in fishing.

Of all the days Dad described in his notebooks this is the only one I have a clear memory of, presumably because I saw him naked for the first and only time in his life.

In the notebook he wrote:

Friday 6 March
With K.O. and Fredrik in the swimming pool.
Nice to swim again. Home for fondue and slides of China.
Talk after. Too much to drink. Scenes. Unni fed up – broke clock.
Shame.

On the last evening in Northern Norway I was alone again in the living room after the others had gone to bed. I smoked, made myself some tea, read a book I found, got up and found their photo album, wanting to see the disconcerting pictures once more, and at the back I came across some papers from which it emerged that the travel company had been informed by the hospital where Dad had been admitted that the heart problems had been induced by an excess of medicine and alcohol.

I read this with a chill that ran through my whole body.

Medicine?

What sort of medicine was he taking?

There were several documents, I flicked through them, some were connected with a lawsuit he had clearly been involved in that spring. The trigger was an incident with a Securitas guard at the bus station in Kristiansand, and as I read it I remembered that he had mentioned something about it once, he had been harassed, but I knew nothing about him taking the matter to the law courts. However, he had lost resoundingly and had been ordered to pay the costs.

What was he doing?

I put the photo album back, brushed my teeth, and went into the narrow room where my bed was, undressed, got into bed, switched off the light, and rested my head on the pillow.

But I couldn't sleep. After a while I got up, sat down on the sofa closest to the little telephone table, picked up the receiver, and dialed Hanne's number.

I would do this on occasion, call her in the night. If her father answered, I would put down the receiver, but he never did, she had a phone next to her room and was always quick to answer. Also this time.

We chatted for an hour. I told her about what was going on here, that I would have a brother or a sister by the end of the summer and I wasn't sure what that would be like. I told her about my father and about Yngve and Kristin. She listened, laughed when I said something funny, and somehow the heaviness in me lifted and we began to talk about other things, the exams that were in the offing, all my ditched classes, her choir, what we would do after we left school.

Suddenly the door burst open and Dad charged in.

"I have to hang up," I said, and put down the receiver.

"What on earth are you doing?!" he said. "Do you know what the time is?"

"Sorry," I said. "I was trying to speak as softly as I could."

"And who said you could use the phone? How long have you been talking?"

"An hour."

"An hour! Do you have any idea how much that costs? I paid for your ticket here! And this is how you thank me? Go to bed, now."

I lowered my head so that he wouldn't see the tears in my eyes, got up, my body half-turned away from him, and walked to my room. My heart was pounding, terror had spread to every part of me, I was shaking as I lifted a leg to pull off my jeans.

I waited until I was sure he had gone to sleep, then tiptoed out again, found a pen, some paper, and an envelope, wrote an ironic note about how sorry I was for having used his precious phone, anyway here was the money for the call. Then I put a hundred-krone note in the envelope, sealed it, wrote his name on it, and slipped it onto the bookshelf, where he would probably find it after I had gone.

At home I seldom gave Dad a thought, apart from when he called or his name came up. But there were still problems. I had gradually begun to live a double life. I liked being at home in the evening with Mom, we either drank tea and chatted, listened to music, watched TV, or did our own work, but I also liked being out at night and drinking. I didn't have a driver's license and buses were few and far between, but Mom always said she would pick me up, it wasn't an issue, all I had to do was call, even if it was in the middle of the night. I called, she answered, an hour later I opened the car door and hopped in. She had no objection to me having a glass, but she wasn't happy if I was drunk, to put it mildly, so I had to hide that from her. I solved this by sleeping at people's houses or I said she didn't need to pick me up, there were people around with a car, and sometimes there were, then I got a lift, sometimes I took a taxi, sometimes the night bus. She didn't wait up, she trusted me, from my behavior at home she had every reason to. And it was the real me when I was with her. It was also the real me when I was with Hilde. It was also the real me when I got drunk with Espen or any of the others at school. I was the real me, but the real *me*s were irreconcilable.

There were other matters I hid from Mom. For example, my missing school. I did it more and more, I was absent almost more often than I was present. She caught me one day, I hadn't gone to school, I was at home relaxing, she turned up earlier than usual and we had a fight. She said I had to go to school, it was important, I had to get a grip on what was important. She said I'd had a strict upbringing, much too strict, and now she was trying to give me some freedom, but I was abusing it. This was all about norms and they had to come from me. I said school wasn't the most important thing in my life, she said that was all well and good, but now you're at school, this is what you do and you have to fulfill your obligations. Can you promise me that? Yes, I could. I didn't keep the promise, but I camouflaged what I did better. I had a more-than-understanding homeroom teacher, he had realized I was having a difficult time, on a school trip he had been sitting on the seat next to me and said, I know you're having a difficult time at the moment, Karl Ove, say if there is anything I can do to help or if there is anything you want to talk to me about. I smiled and said I would, and for a few seconds tears were imminent, the concern for me had come out of the blue, but the next moment they were gone. Naturally enough it wasn't because I was going through a difficult time that I had been ditching school, on the contrary it was because I liked doing it so much, drifting around, meeting people in cafés, stopping by the radio station, buying records, or just lying around at home and reading. I had decided ages ago that I would not continue my education after school, what we learned was just nonsense, basically what life was about was living, and living in the way you want, in other words, enjoying your life. Some enjoyed their lives best by working, others by not working. OK, I was aware that I would need money, which meant that I would also have to work, but not all the time and not on something that would deplete all my energy and eat into my soul, leaving me like one of the middle-aged

half-wits who guarded their hedges and peered across at their neighbors to
see if their status symbols were as wonderful as their own.

I didn't want that.

But money was a problem.

Mom had started working overtime to make ends meet. As well as her
job as a teacher at the nursing college she had agreed to do extra shifts at Eg
Hospital on weekends and holidays. The house must have been making deep
inroads into her money. She had bought Dad out and taken on big loans. I
barely noticed, I had the money I earned from the newspaper and Dad's child
support, and when that was gone it was still possible to get something out
of Mom, so that was fine. She did occasionally criticize my priorities, how
could I buy three new LPs one Friday afternoon when I was walking around
in shoes with the sole flapping off? They're just material things, I responded,
objects, while music was completely different. This was the spirit, for Christ's
sake. This is what we need, really, and I do mean *really*, and it's important
to prioritize it. Everyone prioritizes. Everyone wants new jackets and new
shoes and new cars and new houses and new caravans and new mountain
cabins and new boats. But I don't. I buy books and records because they say
something about what life is about, what it is to be a human here on earth.
Do you understand?

"Yes, you're probably right, in a way. But isn't it terribly impractical to walk
around with your soles coming off? And it doesn't look very good, either."

"What do you want me to do? I don't have any money. I prioritized music
this time."

"I'll have a little surplus this month. You can have it to buy some shoes.
But you'll have to promise me you'll spend it on shoes and nothing else."

"I promise. Thanks very much."

And so from her office in the nursing college I went to town and bought
some sneakers and a Nice Price LP.

At Easter the soccer team was going to a training camp in Switzerland, of
course I wanted to go with them, but it was quite expensive and Mom said

no, she was sorry, she wished it didn't have to be like this, but that was how it was, we didn't have the money.

A week before the departure date she slapped the money on the table in front of me.

"Hope it's not too late," she said.

I called the coach, not too late, no, he said, you can come along.

"Wonderful!" Mom said.

During the days before we were due to leave I finished an article on Prince that I had been mulling over for ages. His new record, *Sign o' the Times*, was absolutely brilliant and I wanted everyone to know.

Then we left. Bus through Denmark and Germany, spirits were high, we were drinking duty-free beer on the way, and when we got to the hotel, Bjørn, Jøgge, Ekse, and I jumped off while the bus continued over the border to Italy, where a Serie A match was on the program. We preferred to be in a bar drinking. When they came back at ten we were in a fantastic mood while they were exhausted after the journey and everyone wanted to go to bed early. I shared a room with Bjørn, it was on the fourth floor and more luxurious than any room I had ever slept in, with attractive furniture, mirrors, and a carpet on the floor. We reclined on the beds, bottles of beer in hand. It was eleven at the latest, what about a trip into town to have a look? The rule was no noise after ten, by eleven everyone was supposed to be in bed, but they hadn't exactly posted guards on the doors. We waited for a while, not wishing to risk meeting anyone in the corridors, then we went out, hailed a taxi, mumbled, "Downtown," leaned back, and were driven along unfamiliar streets with the soft light from the street lamps shining down over us. The driver stopped in a square, we paid, got out, and strolled toward the center. Soon we came across a large building, we could hear music inside, there were bouncers on the door, we went in. There were discotheques, bars, an enormous casino, and a stage where beautiful women stripped and other scantily clad women, equally beautiful, wandered around the audience.

Bjørn and I exchanged glances. What was this fantastic place?

We drifted round, looking and drinking, hung around the stage and watched the striptease, discovered to our horror that the scantily clad girls who were walking between the tables were the same ones as those dancing on the stage, hardly had we watched one go up than she was down and walking past us on the floor. We went into a disco, bar-hopped there, wandered around the room with the roulette tables, where the men were dressed in dark suits and all the women wore evening gowns, ended up in front of double doors at the other end and saw a hall beyond, with groups of people standing around chatting while waiters dressed in black and white carried trays of wineglasses and canapés. We didn't talk to anyone else, drank non-stop, left at about half past three in the morning, and six hours later were running around a field in a semiconscious state. Slept for a couple of hours before the next round of training, had dinner, drank a few beers in the bar, and then it was off to find a taxi to go to this palace, where we floated around like in a dream until the following morning. Then we had to get up and go skiing in the Alps, there was something dreamlike about that too, for the sky was completely blue, the sun was shining, everywhere we looked white mountains towered in the air, and after a few minutes on the lift, with our skis dangling beneath us, everything was perfectly still. As though we had passed into another state. All that could be heard was the low hum of the lift close to us, otherwise it was completely and utterly still. A sense of jubilation filled me, for the silence was as vast as an ocean, while there was also something painful about it, as there is in all joy. The silence high up in the mountains, surrounded on all sides by beauty, allowed me to see myself or become aware of myself, not in relation to my psyche or my morality, this had nothing to do with my personal qualities, this was all about being here, this body which was ascending, I was here now, I was experiencing this, and then I would die.

I slept on the bus back, had a headache when I awoke, drank a few beers in the bar, had dinner, downed a few more because tonight everyone was going out, there was a disco near the hotel, we were there until one in the morning. I danced and drank and had a good word for everyone I saw. On the way back Bjørn and I climbed up onto a roof. It wasn't any old roof, it was a Swiss roof, turret after turret soared upward, we shinned up, climbed and sweated and finally stood aloft, roughly thirty meters above the parking lot, where a small crowd had gathered. Our legs trembled as we shouted into the night, then we crouched down and began the descent. When there were only a few meters left two men with flashlights ran over. The beams wandered back and forth in the blackness. *Polizei*, they said, and came to a halt beneath us. One was holding his ID card and shining the flashlight on it. That must be Chief Inspector Derrick, I giggled. We jumped down. Our football coach came over to us, he could speak some German, and explained the situation to the two police officers, who, despite their skeptical glares, let us go. On our way down the hill to the hotel one of the players from the senior team came over to us. He said he thought we were so courageous, we were so tough, going out and drinking every night and climbing up that roof, he really looked up to us, he said, and wished he could do things like that, he didn't dare, he wasn't as brave as we were and, he said, I admire you.

That was the word he used. Admire.

I would never have believed it, I said to Bjørn after he had disappeared into the group behind us. No, said Bjørn. That wasn't bad, I said. He admires us. Bjørn looked at me. Shit, I said, the police coming and shining their flashlights on their badges. *Polizei! Polizei!* We laughed. Then it struck me that he knew we had been out drinking at night. Did that mean everyone knew? What did it matter anyway? The worst that could happen was that we would be barred from playing, but this was the fifth division we were talking about and the end-of-school festivities were in sight, so it wasn't a big deal.

When we returned everyone had gathered in our room. Some of the senior team had brought girlfriends with them on the trip, a couple were here, and I saw Bjørn talking to one of them, Amanda, who went out with Jøran. She was around twenty-five. Was Bjørn really trying it on with her? Here?

Yes, he was. As people began to withdraw he did too and I was left alone on my bed, I fell asleep fully clothed, only to be awoken an hour later by Bjørn shaking me.

"Amanda's coming," he said. "Could you go somewhere else? For half an hour?"

Befuddled by sleep, I got up.

"OK," I said, went to the window and opened it.

"You're not going to go out there, are you? This is the fourth floor or have you forgotten?"

"No," I said. "It'll be fine."

Beneath the window, all the way, ran a brick ledge almost the width of my feet. Two meters above it there was another. I stood on the lower one, gripped the upper one tightly and then shuffled along centimeter by centimeter. Bjørn watched me with his head out the window.

"Don't do this," he said. "Come back."

"Now you're with Amanda and I'm here. I'll be back in half an hour."

He eyed me for a moment. Then he closed the window. I looked down. There was a large fountain outside the entrance, around it an open square, on the margins a few parked cars. A high brick wall separated the hotel grounds from the road beyond. There was no one around, but that wasn't so strange, it had to be three in the morning at least.

I slowly shuffled toward the window of the room adjoining ours. The curtains were drawn, there was nothing to see. I edged back, stopped by the window, leaned forward and peered in. They were lying on Bjørn's bed and kissing, their legs intertwined, Bjørn's hands were sliding up and down her thigh under her dress. I straightened up, took a few steps to the side, squinted down again. Still deserted. How long had I been there now? Ten minutes? I let go of the ledge with one hand, patted my jacket for cigarettes and my lighter, succeeded in knocking one out, sticking it in my mouth, and lighting it without swaying once. When the cigarette was finished and lay like a small glowing eye on the tarmac far below, I shuffled sideways and banged on the window. Bjørn jumped to his feet. Amanda sat up. Bjørn came over to the window, Amanda ran out the door, Bjørn turned, ready to give chase, or so it seemed, but then he reconsidered and opened the window for me.

"Five more minutes," he said. "Couldn't you have given me five more minutes?"

"How was I supposed to know?" I said. "From where I was standing it didn't look like you were making much progress."

"Were you watching?"

"Not at all," I said. "I was just kidding. But now I want to get some sleep. You should too, if you ask me. You've got a tough day with Jøran ahead of you."

Bjørn snorted. "He's too conceited to believe she would want anyone else."

"He's all right, I think," I said.

"Sure, I do too," Bjørn said. "But Amanda's more than all right."

He laughed. I lay down on the bed and fell asleep in an instant, without having found the answer to the enigmatic and somewhat vexing question: why would Amanda want Bjørn? What had he done to deserve that?

On the last evening in Lucerne the bus stood with its engine idling outside the hotel after dinner. Everyone was going out on the town. The destination was a secret. It turned out, however, to be our casino. While the other juniors wandered around slack-jawed, Bjørn and I sat nonchalantly at a table in the striptease venue drinking white wine.

"I got her number today," Bjørn said. "She said I should phone her when we were home."

"Why on earth would she do that?" I said. "Has she left Jøran?"

Bjørn shook his head. "No. They're together. But aren't you happy for me?"

"Yes, she's nice."

"Nice? She's great. Absolutely great. And she's twenty-four!"

We finished our wine and went for a look round. I lost sight of Bjørn fairly soon and cruised around on my own. By the door to the big hall, on a sudden impulse, I looked in. What's going on in here? I asked a small bald man with glasses. It's a conference, he answered. Who for? I said. Biologists, he said. OK, I said. Interesting! He withdrew, I went in, people were gathered around the small tables, but far fewer than earlier in the week. On one of them lay a little green and white card. I went over and inspected it. It was a name tag. I pinned it to my lapel and walked toward the big door. It opened onto a

conference hall, rows of seats in a wide, gradually ascending semicircle
around a speaker's podium. A man was talking below. Stills were being
shown on a screen behind him. The room was slightly more than half full.
I walked down past a few rows, entered one, people stood up just as in the
cinema, and I sat down, crossed my legs, and concentrated on the speaker.
Now, I said to myself in a low voice. Imagine that. Fascinating! After twenty
minutes, during which I spent as much time looking at the other people in
the audience as the speaker, whose grating microphone voice filled the whole
auditorium and hung like a constant annoying thought in the background,
I got up and went back to the disco. Most of the junior players were inside
watching the striptease, it appeared. I went in too and when Jøgge spotted
me he came rushing over.

"Can I borrow some money?"

"How much do you need? I have some but not much."

"A thousand? Have you got that much?"

"What are you going to do with a thousand kroner?"

"Actually I need two thousand. That's what champagne costs."

"Two thousand for champagne? Are you out of your mind?"

"If you buy an expensive drink for one of the women, you're allowed to
talk to them. And if you buy champagne, you can go off with them."

"And that's what you want to do?"

"Of course. If only I had the money! Have you got it or not?"

He looked around.

"Come on. Please. I need two thousand kroner. I've never slept with
a woman. I'm eighteen years old and I've never had sex. You have. But I
haven't. And it costs two thousand kroner. Come on. Please, please."

He went down on his knees in front of me. Held up his hands in sup-
plication.

And, even worse, he was serious.

"I want to sleep with a woman. That's all I want. And I can do it here. I
don't give a shit if they're prostitutes. They're unbelievably beautiful, all of
them. Come on. Show some mercy. Harald! Ekse! Bjørn! Karl Ove!"

"I don't have that much," I said. "I may have enough for a little chat . . ."

"This is serious!" Jøgge said, back on his feet. "This is my chance. There aren't any places like this in Kristiansand."

"Sorry, Jøgge. Would have liked to help you," said Bjørn.

"Same here," said Harald.

"For Christ's sake, come on," Jøgge said.

"You'll have to try the old-fashioned method," Bjørn said. "Hit on someone. The place is full of girls."

"Easy for you to say," Jøgge said.

"Come on. Let's go in and see the action," Bjørn said, dragging Jøgge with him.

I had never experienced such an alcoholic high as the one I had that night. It was like a cool green river flowing through my veins. Everything was in my power. As we stood at the bar I noticed a girl on the dance floor, she might have been a year or two older than me, with blond hair and a beautiful, yes, an unbelievably beautiful face. When her gaze met mine a second time I didn't hesitate, I trotted down the two steps to the dance floor. At that moment the music she had been dancing to changed and, along with three other girls, she walked over to a wall. I followed her. I stopped and said I had seen her dancing and she looked fantastic. You looked amazing, I said. She smiled and said thank you and looked at me with her head tilted. I asked her if she was American. Yes, she was. Did she live in the town here? No, she lived in Maine. They all came from Maine. Where was I from? A small barbaric country up north, I said. We are in fact the first generation to eat with a knife and fork. I turned and nodded to the other members of the team, who were watching me from the bar. I'm with them, I said. We're soccer players at a training camp here. Do you want to dance?

She nodded.

She wanted to dance!

We glided onto the floor. I put my arms around her. The feeling of her body against mine provoked an electric storm in my head. Round and round we went, sometimes I pressed her close to me, sometimes I held her away from me and looked into her eyes. What's your name? I whispered. Melody, she whispered. Melody? I repeated. No, Melanie! she said with a smile.

When the song was over I thanked her and joined the others, who were still hanging around the bar.

"How did you manage that?" Bjørn said.

"I just asked. Had no idea it was so easy. It's crazy."

"Go back to her. You can't stay here!"

"OK. I'll just have a little drink. Just my luck this is our last night."

The bus was supposed to be outside waiting at three. It was half past two. I had no time to lose. Nevertheless I hesitated, although I could still feel her, a kind of phantom joy, her breasts, oh, her breasts, the feeling of them against my body, the light pressure, the arousal, I had all that inside me, and if I went down there now it would disappear in a new situation, which might not go that well. I knocked back two glasses of wine in quick succession and walked over again. Her eyes lit up when I appeared. She wanted to dance. We danced. Afterward we stood in the corner chatting, the others were beginning to make tracks toward the exit, I said I had to go, she wanted to go with me, I took her hand, we stopped outside, a stone's throw from the bus, which was waiting with the engine running. Where do you live? I asked. She said the name of a hotel. No, not here, but in Maine, I said. I'll write to you. May I? Yes, she said. Then she told me her address. I had nothing to write with. Did she? No. Hurry up, came shouts from the bus, we're going now. I'll memorize your address, I said. Say it again. She said it, I repeated it twice. You'll get a letter, I said. She nodded and looked at me. I leaned forward and kissed her. Put my arm around her and pressed her into me. Now I have to go, I said. All the best to you in your barbaric country, she said with a smile. I paused by the bus door and waved to her, then clambered on board.

Everyone clapped. I bowed to the right, then the left and sat down next to Bjørn. Drunk, happy, and confused, I waved to her as the bus drove past.

"Damn it – if only it could have happened on the first evening," I said.

"Did you get her address?"

"Yes, I've memorized it. She lives in . . ."
I had forgotten. I couldn't drag it up for the life of me.
"Didn't you write it down?" Bjørn said.
"No. I relied on my memory."
He laughed. "You idiot," he said.

We carried on drinking in my room. Bjørn accidentally broke a lamp, he was turning around with a bottle in his hand and hit the glass dome, which shattered. Someone else, I don't recall who, smashed the other one out of pure devilry. Then I took down the big picture hanging on the wall, which had irritated me all week, and threw it out the window. It exploded into smithereens on the street five floors down. Lights came on in the room beneath us. Shit, what was the point of that? Bjørn said, no problem, I said, we can just take one of the pictures in the corridor and hang it here, they'll never notice. What about the picture downstairs? I'll get it, I said, and did as I promised. Took the elevator down, went past the unmanned reception into the square, where I collected all the fragments I could find and put them in the pool around the fountain, close to the nearest wall, so that you could only see them if you were standing over them. On my way back along the corridor I grabbed one of the pictures hanging on the wall. The incident must have sobered people up, because the room was empty when I returned, apart from Bjørn, who was lying on his back with his mouth open and his eyes closed. I got into bed and switched off the light.

The next day was all about packing, having breakfast, and getting ready to leave. The hotel manager came out as we were stowing the baggage in the bus, he wanted to know who had been in Room 504, that was Bjørn and I, we went over, and he, the little man, was so angry that he was jumping up and down in front of us. People like you shouldn't be allowed to stay in a hotel! he yelled. You have to pay for this! It was all very unpleasant. We apologized, said we hadn't meant anything by it and we would pay. I think we even bowed to him. The others stood around grinning. The team coach, Jan, came over, said he would handle this, the hotel would be properly compensated for any damage we had caused, he was extremely sorry, they were young, anything could happen, we bowed again and got on board, people like you shouldn't be allowed to stay in a hotel! he yelled again. Jan took out his wallet and passed him a wad of notes, the bus started up, he jumped on, we drove slowly onto the road while the hotel manager glowered at us with hatred in his eyes.

Once at home, I quickly fell back into my old self, or it fell back into me. At school, where teachers focused on exams, I stayed in the shadows, I skulked around in the breaks and in class filled my notebooks with my scribblings. The trip to Switzerland had been a procession of triumphs, and I hoped the *russ* – graduation – celebrations would be the same. At home I wrote the social studies special paper in one night, a twenty-page comparison of the Russian revolution with the Sandanista revolution in Nicaragua, which I had followed with interest for several years, and I wrote a letter to a hotel in Switzerland asking them for the address of a guest, if at all possible, as in my possession I had a purse I would like to return, belonging to an American girl, whose name was Melanie, surname unknown, but she had stayed at the hotel over Easter.

At the end of April I had a party at home. As editor of the *russ* newspaper, a duty I shared with Hilde, I probably should have been on the *russ* committee, as had always been the case, but for some reason we were excluded. Perhaps because Hilde and I didn't really fit in there, or because we hadn't accepted our posts with the requisite nonchalance, what did I know? Whatever the reason, I invited the whole of the committee, as well as many others, home one Saturday evening. Mom was sleeping at a friend's and would be home in the afternoon, so I had told everyone that they must not under any circumstances arrive before six. But at three a red *russ* camper chugged up the hill. In it were Christian and two girls. He wanted to drop off the beer, he said. But I told you six o'clock, I said. Yes, but now we're here, he said. Where can I leave it?

Ten minutes later there was a stack of beer crates in the kitchen. The stack went from the floor right up to the ceiling. It was fair to say the ceiling was low, but Mom, whom Christian barely greeted when he entered the kitchen, was not enamored of the sight. What's this? she said after they had gone. Are you going to drink all of this? You're not going to have some drunken orgy here, are you? I won't allow it. Relax, I said. This is a *russ* party. Everyone's eighteen. There'll be quite a bit of drinking. But I'll take responsibility for everything. I promise you. It'll all be fine. Are you sure? she said, eyeing me closely. There's enough beer here for a hundred people. How many crates are there actually? Yes, but take it easy. There's a lot of drinking at *russ* parties. But that's the whole point. Is it really? she said. Not the whole point, I said. But it is an important element. I know you don't like the idea, and I'm sorry it's here, but everything will be fine, I promise you. Well, anyway, it's too late to do anything about it now, she said. But had I known what I know now, you wouldn't have had my blessing. Promise me you won't drink much yourself now. You're responsible for everything going well, you know. Yeah, yeah, I said.

We had dinner beside the yellow beer-crate tower, Mom got in her car and drove to town, I put on a record, grabbed a beer, and lounged on the sofa waiting for the others to come.

A few hours later the drive was full of *russ* vehicles. Everywhere there were screaming girls and boys in red *russ* outfits, all holding bottles of beer. Music was pounding from several of the cars, and in the living room the stereo was so loud that the music coming from the speakers was distorted. Three or four times more people had come than had been invited.

At one in the morning everything seemed to build up to a climax. Christian screamed and kicked a big hole in the bathroom door. Trond was sitting in the kitchen beating out the rhythm of the music on the edge of the table with two large knives, every beat was a new notch. People were throwing up on the doorstep outside the living room, people were throwing up on the path between the cars, people were throwing up in Yngve's bed. Behind the lilac bush a couple was going at it standing up. Others were jumping up and down to the music, roaring for all they were worth. People stood on car hoods and roofs, one of them naked, swirling his sweater around his head. Even though I had made up my mind not to give a damn, and had succeeded by getting drunk, I carried a constant horror within me that, at various points, would surface in my consciousness, no, oh no, I thought then, only to recede as I got wrapped up in one of the many incidents going on around me.

At three the tempo began to slow down. Some people were still dancing, some were fooling around, some were asleep, lying across the table, hunched in corners, outside under bushes. I sat on the sofa in front of the TV making out with a girl, we had hardly exchanged a word, she had been sitting there, I sat down beside her, we started to kiss. She was dark-haired, everything about her was dark, even her clothes, she was the only one not dressed in a red outfit but in a black sweater, black skirt, and black tights. Want to come with me to the room over there, I whispered, she nodded, I had drunk a lot and was thinking this will make everything different because now I didn't give a shit about anything, wasn't nervous about anything, and I took out my keys and unlocked the door to my room, held my arm around her, she pulled off the little handbag she wore diagonally across her chest, lay down on the bed, *my* bed, it reverberated through my brain, I rolled her sweater over her head, kissed her dark nipples, rubbed my face between them, lovingly and lingeringly, here we go, I thought, now I've got a girl here, now it's going to happen, and my legs were trembling as I sat up to pull down her tights, she let me do it, I took off my trousers, this is it, she was naked, her skin shone white in the dark, I put my hand between her legs and felt the curly though still smooth hair, and I was naked, and I squirmed a bit, she said you're so heavy on top of me, I pushed down with my arms and then my dick was in her pubic hair, I thrust, farther down, she said, I moved and there it was, wet and soft and then, no, no, oh for Christ's sake, no.

Long shudders like electric shocks went through me as she lay there, her eyes wide open, staring up at me.

No, no, no.

I hadn't even penetrated her. A couple of centimeters maybe, no more. And then it was over. I fell on top of her and kissed her neck. She pushed me away and half sat up. I reached out for her, touched her breasts, but she just got up, pulled on her panties and tights, and left the room.

In the morning I woke to a discussion outside my half-open door. I recognized the voices of Espen, Trond, and the girl from the night before. No, she said, it wasn't me. Yes, it was. I saw you. You went into his bedroom. No, it wasn't, she said. But we saw you. Yes, I went in with him, he was going to sleep, but I came out again *right away*, she said. Nothing happened. Ha ha ha! said Espen. You were doing it in there. No, we weren't, she said. And where were you going just now? Were you going in? Why would you go in if you hadn't slept together? You know him, don't you? No. I was going to get something I'd left in there. What's that? My bag.

I hastily got up, put on a pair of jeans and a T-shirt, grabbed her bag, and went out to them.

"Here you are," I said, passing her the bag. "You forgot this."

"Thank you," she said without meeting my eyes, and went downstairs.

"What a disaster this house is," Espen said.

"I can imagine," I said.

"I'll help you clean up."

"Great."

"I'll get Gisle and Trond to give a hand." He looked at me. "Did you sleep with Beate then?"

"Was that her name?" I said. "Yes, I did."

"She says you didn't."

"I heard."

"Why?"

"How should I know?" I said.

Our eyes met.

"Well," I said. "Better go down and inspect the hell."

There was nothing that could be done about the door, it would have to be replaced. Nor about the slashes to the table. But all the rest? Couldn't that be scrubbed clean? We cleaned the house all morning. Espen, Gisle, and Trond went home at one, I continued on my own with a steadily increasing sense of panic in my chest because no matter how much I cleaned things up, the place still looked as if a party had hit it.

Mom came at five. I went out to meet her so that it wouldn't come as a shock. I didn't want her to see it before I had told her.

"Hi," I said.

"Hi," she said. "How did it go?"

"Not so well, I'm afraid," I said.

"Oh?" she said. "What happened?"

"It got a bit out of control. Someone kicked in the bathroom door, among other things. And there are a lot of other bits and pieces. You'd better see for yourself. I'm really sorry."

She looked at me.

"I had a feeling," she said. "We'd better go in and see."

When the inspection was over, she sat down at the kitchen table, ran both hands over her face, and looked up at me.

"It's dreadful," she said.

"Yes," I said.

"What will we do about the door?" she said. "We can't afford a new one."

"Are we so hard up?"

"I'm afraid so. Who kicked it in?"

"Someone called Christian. An idiot."

"Surely he should replace it?"

"I can tell him to."

"Please do that."

She got up with a sigh.

"I suppose we'd better eat," she said. "I think there are some pollock fillets in the fridge. Shall we have those?"

"OK."

She went to the hall and hung up her coat, I found the two packs of fish, she started washing some potatoes while I sliced the frozen blocks into pieces.

"We've had this conversation before," she said.

"Yes," I said.

"You have to make your own decisions. And if they're bad ones, you have to live with the consequences."

"Of course," I said, and sprinkled flour, salt, and pepper onto a plate, turned the by now soft fish in the mixture, put the frying pan on the burner, and watched the knob of butter slide across the black surface as the heat took hold, not unlike a house, it struck me, when the clay base it stands on starts slipping. Slow, erect, with a final dignity before it subsides.

"A year's wear and tear in one night," she said. "Or even more."

"The house was built in 1880," I said. "One year's not so much."

She ignored me.

"You're eighteen years old. I can't tell you what to do anymore. I can't control you. All I can do is be here for you and hope you will turn to me if you need help."

"OK."

"I could have tried to stop you, but why should I? You're an adult and you have to take responsibility for your actions. I trust you. You're free to do what you want. But you have to trust me too. And treat me like an adult. What we share is this house. We share the responsibility for it."

She squirted some soap onto one hand, rubbed both of them together under the running tap, and dried them on the kitchen towel.

"You're washing your hands of me, I can see," I said.

She raised a smile, but it was mirthless.

"This is serious, Karl Ove. I'm worried about you."

"You have no reason to be," I said. "What happened here, well . . . it was a *russ* party, no more, no less."

She didn't answer, I put the fish fillets into the pan, diced an onion, and added the little cubes, poured in a can of tomatoes, sprinkled in spices, and sat down with the Saturday newspaper, flipped through to the page where my Prince article, which I had handed in several weeks ago, had finally appeared in print. I held it up for her.

"Have you seen it?" I said.

That Monday I went to Christian and told him the door was smashed beyond repair. Oh yeah, he said. You kicked it in, I said. Yes, it was me, he said. So you should replace it, I think, I said. No, he said. What do you mean *no*? I said. I mean what I said, he replied. No. It was your party. But it was you who broke the door, I said. Yeah, he said. So you won't replace it? I said. No, he said. And then he turned and left.

When I got back home from school there was a letter with a foreign stamp in the post box. I opened it at once and read it walking up the hill. It was from the manager of the Grand Hotel in Lucerne. He wrote that, unfortunately, all the rooms were registered by surnames and therefore he couldn't help me with Melanie's address, but I could try the two travel bureaus involved, whose addresses he added afterward: one in Philadelphia and one in Lugano.

I put the letter back in the envelope and went in. Bang went my plan to write letters for a year and then make a surprise visit, with the exciting possibility that it was there, in America, that my future lay.

For the rest of the spring I was drunk almost all the time. The first thing I did when I woke up in the *russ* van or on a sofa at a friend's or on a bench in the park was to get my hands on something to drink and continue where I had left off. And there was little that beat starting the day with a beer and walking around drunk in the morning. What a life. Going here, there, and everywhere, having a drink, sleeping whenever an opportunity offered itself, eating something maybe, and then just carrying on. It was fantastic. I loved being drunk. I came closer to the person I really was and dared to do what I really wanted to do. There were no limits. I only went home for a shower and a change of clothes, and once, when I was sitting in the living room with a six-pack of Carlsberg, which I drank while waiting for the *russ* van to come and pick me up, Mom suddenly flew into a rage. She had tolerated so much, but she drew the line here, at this, sitting alone and drinking in the living room, she would not put up with it. I could choose: either I stopped drinking or found myself somewhere else to live. It was a simple choice, I got up, grabbed the beer, said good-bye, and went out, down the road, where I sat on the slope, lit a cigarette, and opened a beer while waiting for the van. If she didn't want me to live at home, well, I wouldn't live at home.

"What are you sitting there for?" Espen said when the van pulled up in front of me.

"I've been thrown out," I said. "Actually, it doesn't matter."

I got in, we drank what we had on the way to town, bought some more crates of beer at a supermarket, went on toward Vågsbygd, where we were meeting that night, a grass plain by the sea with an ancient deciduous forest sloping upward, where we sat drinking, where I disappeared into myself and walked around without a thought in my head. It was great, as always. The interpersonal shit I usually got bogged down in meant nothing, I was footloose and free, everything was as cold and clear as glass. I asked after Geir Helge, a lean, sociable guy with glasses and a Mandal dialect. He smoked hash, everyone knew that, and now I wanted to try it too. I had been considering it for a long while. Smoking hash was a stigma, if you did you were on the outside, you were no longer a decent person, you were on the way to becoming a junkie. In any case that was how it was in Kristiansand. And the idea of it being the beginning of a road that would lead me to a life as a junkie was incredibly appealing and filled life with destiny and meaning. Being a junkie, just living for drugs, renouncing everything else, for me that was the worst of the worst. Junkies had abandoned their humanity, they were a kind of devil, it was terrible, terrible, the worst, hell. I laughed at those who associated hash with heroin, it was propaganda, nothing else, smoking hash was a bid for freedom for me, but although hash was completely harmless, it was in the same category as harmful drugs, in a way, smoking it made me a drug addict, and what an immense and exhilarating thought that was.

I wanted to steal, drink, smoke hash, and experiment with other drugs –

cocaine, amphetamines, mescaline – to get high and live the great rock-and-roll lifestyle, to feel to the last drop of my blood that I couldn't give a flying fuck about anything. Oh, what appeal there was in that! But then there was all the rest of me inside that wanted to be a serious student, a decent son, a good person. If only I could blow that to smithereens!

This was an attempt to do that. The thought of smoking hash, the thought that I could actually do it, that I could actually become a junkie, if I ever dared, it was only a question of *doing* it, making the move, this simply made my insides explode with happiness and excitement as I walked up the slope under the leafy trees to where Geir Helge hung out. I asked if he had any-thing to smoke, I said I had never done it before, he would have to show me, which he was more than happy to do. After we'd finished I walked slowly down the slope and into the crowd. At first I didn't notice anything in par-ticular, perhaps I was too drunk, Geir Helge had said something about this, that it didn't always work the first time and it didn't always work if you were too drunk. But when I got into the back of the *russ* van, which was empty, something happened. I moved my shoulder and it was as though the joint had been lubricated with oil, yes, as though the whole of me was full of oil. A tiny, tiny movement anywhere was enough to fill my body with sensual pleasure. So I sat there wagging a finger, lifting one shoulder, shaking a hip, and wave after wave of pure sensuality washed through my body.

Espen stuck his head in.

"What are you up to? Are you feeling OK?"

I opened my eyes and straightened up. The movement was so vigorous that a jolt of pleasure rippled through me.

"I'm fine," I said. "I'm having an absolutely fantastic time. But I want to be alone. I'll be out afterward."

I wasn't, I fell asleep, and in the following days I smoked as much hash as I could, as well as drinking. The last nights before Constitution Day, May 17, I was so stoned and drunk that I didn't know where I had been, and when I woke up that morning I was in a *russ* van, we were parked in some square, and outside the windows, the streets were lined deep with people. Vaguely I remembered we had been to Tresse and that at some point we had been sitting under a tarpaulin in a double-ender moored to the pontoons, together with some uncommunicative and inert man, and that Espen had later run over and dragged Sjur and me away, the man was dead, he said, but when we stood by the boat it was empty. Espen desperately ran up and down, and then I remembered nothing else. How many minutes of the long night were left? Ten maybe?

Once we came across a tramp, he was sitting on a bench in the park, we stood around him talking. He said he had sailed with Leif Larsen during the war, running refugees and agents between the Shetlands and Norway. From then on I called him the Shetland Shit. Laughed and repeated it as often as I could. Hey, Shetland Shit! After a while I went behind him to have a piss, and then I pissed on him, up and down his back. Then we drifted on through the night, settling here, settling there, there was always someone with a beer or a bottle of spirits. I laughed, danced, drank, and made out with whoever was there. I could go over to a girl in the class and tell her she had always been on my mind, I had always stolen furtive glances at her, it was a lie, but it did the trick, everything had opened up. Everything was open.

When I woke up in the *russ* van on the seventeenth of May and saw I was surrounded by festively dressed people on all sides, I was frightened. But not even that mattered, I just had to drink a couple more beers and the fear was gone, and we would go out and sell more *russ* newspapers so that we had the money for more beer, and when it was midnight I was as free as could be after several days' drinking, running through the streets and shouting, chatting to strangers, joking with some, harassing others, happy but also extremely tired, and it was in this state, racing back and forth through the procession, streets on both sides packed with people, all wearing their best clothes, suits, and national costumes, and Norwegian flags everywhere, that I suddenly heard someone shout my name.

It was Grandma and Grandad.

I pulled up in front of them with a grin on my face. Gunnar's son was there too, and it wouldn't have surprised me if I was the first drunk he had ever seen. They stared at me through icy eyes, but it didn't matter, I laughed and carried on, there were two days left to the exams, and I didn't want them to end. The final party was held at the Fun Senter, and the atmosphere was on the wane, however much I tried to resist it, and I and two others caught a taxi to Bassen's late at night. He wasn't at home, the house was empty, and we leaned a ladder against the first floor where there was a window ajar. Once inside we sat on the living-room carpet and smoked hash from perforated Coke cans. When Bassen turned up the following morning, he was furious, naturally enough, but not so much so that we couldn't catch a couple of hours of sleep, but we all knew that the fun was definitively over. I was still drunk when I woke up, but this time there was no hair of the dog, and I was already beginning to sink deeper and deeper into myself on the bus home, it was terrible, everything was terrible. Mom said nothing about having thrown me out, we barely spoke, I lay in the bath with a layer of scum on the surface of the water. I was tired and went to bed early, we had the Norwegian exam the following day, but I couldn't sleep. My hands were trembling, but that wasn't all that trembled, the flex on the lamp writhed back and forth like a snake whenever I looked at it. The floor sloped, the walls leaned, I sweated and tossed and turned with my head full of random images. It was dreadful, a night of hell, but then morning came and I got up, dressed, and caught the bus to school. I was unable to concentrate, every twenty minutes I signaled to the proctor, who accompanied me to the toilet, where I washed my face.

Of all the things I had done and that would come back to haunt me during these days the encounter with my grandparents was the worst. But surely they couldn't know that I had drunk *so* much, could they? Surely they couldn't know that I had not only been drinking but also smoking hash, could they? No, they couldn't. And in my diary for the beginning of June that year I wrote that the months I had been a *russ*, celebrating the end of school, were the happiest in my life. I used those words: the happiest in my life.

Why did I write that?

Oh, I was so happy. I laughed and was free and friends with everyone.

At the end of June, I left home, Mom drove me to a flat at the hospital, I worked there for a month, was together with Line, drank wine in the evenings and on weekends, smoked hash whenever I could get my hands on it. Espen rejected it point-blank, it was filth, he said, and he continued to insist that the story about the man he had found dead the night before May 17 was true. One afternoon he called up to say there had been an article in the newspaper about a man discovered floating in the harbor. "That's him!" Espen said. I didn't know if he really meant it or was just trying to get as much mileage from the joke as he could. He said he had a vague memory, as if in a dream, of him dumping the body overboard. Why would you have done that? I said. I was drunk, he answered. No one else but you saw any dead man. It's just a fantasy. No, he said, it's true. What about the man sitting with us in the boat? Don't you remember him? Yes, I do. You saw him then? Yes. He was dead. Now, come on, Espen, if he'd been dead, why would you have heaved him over the side and then run to get us? I don't know.

The month had been packed with such incidents, I wasn't sure whether they had happened or not, and this combined with the feeling I had that everything was possible, that there were no limits, and the enormous tracts of time of which I remembered nothing caused me to begin to lose sight of myself. It was as though I had disappeared. In part I liked this, in part I didn't. The routines at the hospital, where I was mostly responsible for setting and clearing the tables at mealtimes and otherwise helping with anything of a practical nature, neutralized this feeling but didn't erase it because in the evening I always went out, drank with the people I met, it was summer and there was always someone around I knew. One evening we were refused admission to Kjelleren, so Bjørn and I climbed up on the roof of the block behind, ran all the way across the rooftops, found a skylight, crawled in, went down to Kjelleren, which was absolutely empty, it must have taken us an hour. We went up a few floors, entered a flat, someone woke up and shouted at us, we said we had gone in the wrong door, walked amid gales of laughter to Tresse, a square in the center of town where Bjørn's dad had a flat and we could sleep. In the morning I rang the hospital and said I was ill, they probably didn't believe me, but what could they do?

That night I drank with a radio technician, Paul, who had driven us to an Imperium concert in Oslo, and on the way home, in the middle of the night in Telemark, at twenty degrees below, the car skidded, left the road doing a hundred kilometers an hour, brushed against a lamppost, flew through the air, and landed in a ditch. We're going to die, I thought, and the idea of it didn't bother me in the slightest. We didn't die, the car was a write-off but we were in good shape. It was a great story, one we could tell others, also the sequel, the old house whose door we knocked on, the rifle standing in the hallway, the feeling of being in another, nastier world than our own, and the incredible cold outside as we hitched for more than two hours wearing sneakers and suit jackets. We hung around talking about that at Kjelleren, Paul and I and his girlfriend, she was wonderful, perhaps twenty-three, twenty-four, I had secretly had my eye on her for ages, and when she suggested taking a taxi back to her place to smoke some dope, of course I said yes, we smoked, and when I smoked I sometimes became so unbelievably horny, and sitting next to her on the sofa it hit me at once, I grabbed her, she laughed and wriggled away, saying she loved Paul, and then she put her hand between my legs and laughed even more and said you've grown up. Downstairs in Kjelleren she had been quiet most of the time, Paul had smiled at us, he trusted her, which he was right to do.

At work the next day they said nothing, but I noticed of course, I wasn't someone they were interested in keeping however much effort I made to mollify them. I had the job for only a month, and when the time was up, I went back to our house, which was no longer ours, Mom had sold it, for the next two days we packed everything into boxes, and then a big removal van came and took it all.

Except for one thing, and that was the cat.

What should we do with the cat?

Mefisto?

Mom couldn't have the cat where she was going to live, and I definitely couldn't take him to Northern Norway.

We would have to have him put down.

He wound around our legs, Mom put a tin of liver paste in his carrier, he ran in, Mom closed the door, put the carrier on the passenger seat, and drove to the vet in town.

That afternoon I lay on the rocks beneath the waterfall and swam. When I got back, Mom's car was in the garage. She was sitting in the kitchen drinking coffee. She got up when I entered, walked past me without saying a word, her eyes downcast.

"So is Mefisto dead now?" I asked.

Mom didn't answer, just shot me a glance, then opened the door and went out. Her eyes were brimming.

That was the first time I had seen Mom cry.

Eight days later, in a fetal position on the sofa in Håfjord, I lay asleep after emptying the contents of my stomach into the toilet, so wonderful. My sleep was light, the revving of a car engine somewhere was all it required for me to open my eyes. But I didn't have anything to do, I had no duties, I could lie in bed and sleep all Saturday and Sunday. Monday was an eternity away, I mused as I lay there feeling sleep steal over me again.

There was a ring at the door.

I went to answer it, surprised at how light my body felt.

It was Sture.

"It's soccer practice," he said. "In fifteen minutes. Had you forgotten? Or are you too muzzy after yesterday?"

"I'm a bit fuzzy," I said with a smile. "But not muzzy."

I ran my hand through my hair.

"I haven't brought any cleats with me. I was thinking of buying some but I forgot. So I suppose you can count me out."

Sture brought his arm forward from behind his back. Two pairs of cleats hung from his hand.

"Forty-five?" he said. "Or forty-six?"

"Forty-five," I said, taking them.

"See you up there then?"

"OK, see you there."

I hadn't played soccer for a couple of months, and it felt strange to run around on a field again, especially this field, for there was something about the spot, squeezed in under the gleaming green mountain slopes, the sea straight ahead, which went against everything I associated with soccer. It didn't improve matters that the team I was playing on were all fishermen, the whole bunch of them. A couple of them were good, particularly one called Arnfinn, who resembled one of the English midfield players we used to see on Saturday afternoon TV in the 1970s, balding and red-haired, relatively short, stocky with a paunch, not the quickest in the world, but he made things happen around him as soon as he had the ball, whether he was flicking it on, hitting a cross, or threading a forward through, without even raising his head, as though he didn't have to see, he could sense everything. He tackled me a few times, it was like running into a tree. He was good. Their striker was good, a tall, thin guy who was surprisingly fast, and their goalie, Hugo, was also decent. The rest were like me, perhaps a bit worse, with the exception of Nils Erik, who could hardly have played before and warmed up by doing the kind of knee bends that had probably last been witnessed in the '50s.

After the game we went to the changing rooms by the swimming pool, showered, and sat in the sauna. Everyone apart from Nils Erik and me was as white as snow. Many had freckles on their shoulders and backs, many were very hairy, and when they walked around, strutting naked and teasing one another, I had the impression they almost belonged to a different race. I still had a tan after the summer, with a white patch where my trunks had been, I didn't have a single hair on my arms or chest or shoulders, just some barely visible down, and my back was as straight as a pillar, not broad and bulging like theirs. Not to mention my biceps, which were as thin as twigs while their arms were the width of tree trunks. And as for my chest, it was as flat as could be, like a board, and looked nothing like the kegs they walked around with. Not that their bodies were magnificent specimens, they weren't, many had spare tires and flab, no one had a chest arched into two well-defined halves from muscle training, no one had six-pack abs, that was another world for them. What they respected, I could see, was strength. So it made no differ-ence to them if a belly hung over a belt or the odd double chin rolled over a collar.

We sat on the three benches in the sauna, someone had opened some beer; Hugo, the goalie, passed one over.

"Actually I have to work this evening," I said, "but one can't hurt."

"Good," he said, and gave it to me.

Froth streamed out of the bottle. The glass was green and cold.

"It was fun last night!" he said.

"Yes, it was," I said.

"That was Irene you were all over, wasn't it?"

I smiled and paused.

"We saw you! Not bad, one week in Northern Norway and Karl Ove's got himself a girlfriend!"

"Coming up here and taking our women! You stay down south, you south-ern bastard!" someone else said.

They laughed. I laughed too.

"But old Pinocchio here just wanted to dance," Hugo said, looking at Nils Erik.

Pinocchio! *That* was who he looked like!

"Yes," Nils Erik said. "I really like dancing. I used to dance a lot at Horten's Dance Academy!"

They looked at him and smiled uncertainly. I had to laugh. At that moment, Sture came in, he flicked his towel at one of the players to make room for him. He was slim and not as well built as the others, but slight he was not, there were muscles on him too. In addition, he had a beard and was bald and confident. I had been a bit nervous that, as a teacher, he wouldn't be able to cope with them, but within seconds I saw that this was not the case.

He turned and looked up at me.

"We've got a match on Tuesday evening. You're in, aren't you?"

I nodded.

"You'll be the center back."

"Center back?" I echoed.

"Yes," he said. "That's what I said."

He winked and turned away. I finished the beer and belched, got up, and went into the shower. Nils Erik followed and stood beside me.

He had a big dick, it hung down and smacked against his thighs.

Why would someone with such red cheeks who liked to go on long walks in the forest have such a big cock? I wondered. What would he do with it?

"Did you used to do outdoor calisthenics or what?" I said.

"Calisthenics? No."

"Looked like it with your warm-up exercises," I said.

He laughed and did a few knee bends in the shower.

"Was that what you meant?" he said.

"Exactly," I said. "Don't teach my class that in the gym lessons, just so you know. It would totally destroy their self-confidence."

Two or three more came in and turned on the showers. In seconds the air was full of steam again.

"Are you coming up to my place afterward?" Hugo said. "There's a gang of us having a drink."

"I'd love to," I said, "but I can't."

"Me neither," Nils Erik said. "Two nights in a row is too much."

"What wimps!" Hugo said.

That stung, I didn't want to be a wimp and I could drink him under the table any day of the week, but I couldn't go, I had to write.

I said good-bye to Nils Erik at the crossroads and walked down to my flat. Slung the bag down on the floor in the hall, stopped by the mirror and ran my fingers through my hair to make it stand up, sniffed the air a couple of times: what was that smell? Perfume? Had someone been here?

There was a folded piece of paper on the sitting-room table I was sure I hadn't left there.

I opened it. It was from Irene.

Hi Karl Ove,

Well, Hilde and I've been here on a big surprise visit. While you were at soc-cer practice we sat here making ourselves comfy. We've had a look at all your records. Wow, what a collection! We can see you've got a few more now than when we were here last. Good for you.

You seem like an all-right guy and I hope to get to know you better. I've missed you. I've just been waiting to see you again. But it'll have to be another time because we've gotta go now.

Hugs and kisses from Irene

Had they just come in and sat down?

Yes, they must have.

And then left again?

I opened the door and stepped out to look for them, in case we had just crossed paths.

Nobody.

Just the sound of the sea, the vast gray sky, a couple of tiny figures walking along the road at the bottom of the hill.

I went back in and boiled a whole packet of spaghetti, fried all the old potatoes I had in the fridge, and soon I was in the sitting room with a steam-ing mountain of spaghetti and browned potatoes on a plate in front of me, I applied ketchup liberally and wolfed it down. Wonderful. Then I made some coffee, put Led Zeppelin's first LP on the record player, turned the volume up almost full, and walked up and down clenching my fists and nodding my head. Now I'll show them. And then, pumped up with adrenaline and anger, I sat down and started to bang away on the typewriter.

The short story I wrote was based on a dream I'd had that summer. I had been doing exercises in some kind of net that stretched endlessly into the darkness on all sides, it was slippery but thick and strong, like an enor-mous sinew. This net turned out to be in my own brain. In other words I had turned the relationship around: my thoughts didn't exist in me, I existed in my thoughts. The dream had been a sensation, but when I wrote it down it dissipated into nothing, so I crumpled up the paper and threw it away, turned the record over and started afresh. This too was based on a dream, and in this too what I was standing on stretched into the darkness on all sides, however, unlike in the first dream, this darkness was broken by bonfires. Bonfire after bonfire burned around me as I walked. To my right there was a mountain, ahead of me the sea, that was all, nothing happened, there were just these elements, and I wrote it all down.

Oh shit, this was no good either!

All the fires in the darkness, the tall mountain and the immense plain, it had been so extraordinary!

On paper it was nothing.

I moved to the sofa and started writing my diary instead. "Have to work on transferring the moods from inside to outside," I wrote. "But how? Easier to describe people's actions, but that's not enough, I don't think. On the other hand, Hemingway did it." I raised my head and looked out at the mountains above the fjord. "But I'm happy here anyway. Who would have thought it? And I've met someone. Very pretty. Think I might have a chance. Rock 'n' roll!"

Early that evening the upstairs front door opened. The footsteps that followed across the floor were heavier and more solid than Torill's, and I remembered she had said her husband was coming home today. Life in the rooms above me now was completely different. They were laughing, music was blaring, and when I went to bed they were at it above my head.

Oh, it went on for ages.

She screamed, he groaned, something was thumping to a regular, rhythmic beat, perhaps the bed knocking against the wall.

I thrust the pillow over my head and tried to think about something else.

But it didn't work, how could it, I knew who she was and what she looked like.

All went quiet. I dozed off.

I'll be damned if they didn't start up again.

I went to the sofa and lay down there. It was as though a shadow had fallen over me. The anticipation I had felt when I had thought that something might happen with Irene collapsed like an old mineshaft and tumbled in on me.

I couldn't do it.

I was eighteen years old, I was a teacher, I had my own place and an enormous record collection for my age with almost exclusively good music. I was good-looking, I could occasionally pass for someone in a band with my coat, black jeans, white basketball shoes, and black beret. But what good was that if I couldn't do the only thing I really wanted to do?

At last they finished, for the second time, and like a child I fell asleep on the sofa, lost to the world.

I wrote all the next day, started work listening with clenched fists to Led Zeppelin, then sat tapping away for four hours without a break. I returned to the style of the first short story, and this time I had the two boys smashing a shed window on the estate where they lived and stealing the porn mags. The writing went well, except that I couldn't find an ending. One boy couldn't go home to his enraged father, something else had to happen, but what?

In the evening I walked up to the school. I still suffered pangs of conscience at being there alone, it felt as if I was snooping, but I wasn't, I thought, and dropped the big bunch of keys on the staff-room table with a clatter, opened the door to the small telephone cubicle, and dialed Mom's number.

She answered at once.

"How's it going?" I said.

"Very well," she said. "In fact, I was thinking of writing to you this evening."

"Did you get the short story?"

"Yes. Thanks for that."

"So what do you think?"

"I think it's very good. I was surprised. I thought, really, this is *literature!*"

"Is that true?"

"Yes. You tell a story, there are two wonderful characters, and the writing is so alive. It's as though I'm there when I'm reading it."

"Was there anything you particularly liked?"

"Well . . . no, not really, no. I think everything's very good."

"The ending?"

"You mean the part with the father?"

"Yes."

"That's what the story is about, isn't it?"

"It is, yes. As well."

There was a silence.

"What about Kjartan? Have you heard anything from him? Actually, I sent it to him too."

"No, I usually call him on Sundays. I'll talk to him afterward."

"Say hello from me."

"I'll do that. How are you?"

"Fine. Yesterday I went to soccer practice. Tomorrow I'm back in harness."

"Is it hard work?"

I blew out my cheeks.

"No, in fact it's quite easy. I honestly don't understand why teachers have to go to college for three years. It might be different with big classes though. There are only five or six students in each class here."

"Are you absolutely sure?"

"About what?"

"That it's so easy," she said.

I smiled. "Typical of you to be skeptical," I said. "But, no, of course there are problems, too."

"Have you gotten to know anyone?"

"Yes, some of the teachers. Especially one, Nils Erik. People up here are unbelievably open. They drop by and ring your doorbell all the time."

"Oh?"

"Yes, all sorts of people. Even my students!"

"Sounds as if you're having a good time."

"Yes, that's what I said."

We chatted for another half an hour, then I hung up and sat on the sofa to watch *Sportsrevyen* on TV. IK Start had lost again, things were beginning to look grim for them. If they didn't get their act together, they would be relegated.

Two days later Richard came into my lesson and beckoned to me.

"There's a call for you," he said. "I'll take your class in the meantime."

A call?

I hurried into the staff room and grabbed the receiver, which was lying next to the phone.

"Hello?" I said.

"Hi, this is Irene."

"Hi!"

"Are you working?"

"Yes."

"Did you get my note?"

"Yes. A bit of a surprise, I can tell you!"

"That was the idea! Listen, Karl Ove, would you like to see me? There's someone going to Håfjord on Friday, and I can get a lift."

"Yes, that would be great."

"I'll be over then. Bye."

"OK, bye," I said, and hung up.

Richard hadn't only kept an eye on the class, I could see, he was drawing something on the board and explaining it. He smiled at me, but there was a cold expression in his eyes, wasn't there?

In the break he took me aside.

"Just a moment, Karl Ove. No personal calls when we're teaching."

"It wasn't my fault she called," I said. "Couldn't you have taken a message? Then I could have called her back in the break."

He eyed me. "She said it was important. Was it?"

"Yes," I said.

He winked and went into his office.

Jesus.

When I opened my box at the post office after school there were three letters in it. One from a debt-collection agency threatening legal action if I didn't pay. That was the dinner suit I had rented on New Year's Eve, it had been damaged, and since I didn't have the money to replace it, I had tossed it, hoping that, in time, they would forget the whole business. I still didn't have the money, so the case would have to run its course. What could they do if I didn't pay? Put me in prison? I didn't have any money!

The other letters were from Hilde and Mom. I didn't open them until I got home, letters were a party, everything had to be perfect when I read them.

Steaming coffee in a cup, music on the stereo, a rollie in my hand, and one ready on the table.

I started with the one from Mom.

Dear Karl Ove,

You're probably waiting for more feedback, so here's Kjartan's: he was enthusiastic about your story – "it's literature and he has talent" was one of the comments I remember. He considers you his peer and sends you (via me) his latest piece of work, he's having a crack at prose now. And he urged you to push ahead with your writing but thought you probably lacked someone to discuss matters with and wondered if there were any writing courses/seminars in the area you could attend. Which is what he does. He also suggested getting in touch with a reader (publishing house). (I'm less certain about that – think it's too early in your personal development – but I'm passing on his thoughts.)

It sounds to me as if you've made the transition from "the warm nest of home" to the "great wide world" without any problems as you can see the positive sides of life. The transition isn't always painless. But then again maybe home wasn't that warm a nest either. Maybe you are less exposed where you are now; your music must help.

Other news from my end? My mind is mainly on the psychiatric nursing school. Recently, though, I have been out and about and I found an old house, an abandoned school with large, attractive, grand rooms complete with acquired wisdom and knowledge. I could imagine teaching my psychiatric nurses there!

In Sørbøvåg the patients are as fragile as ever – helpless, destitute, with an indomitable will to live, an inextinguishable determination to cope, to manage at all costs. It's good to be there in the sense that it's good to have people close to me. But the conditions there eat away at your own will and zest for life. I don't know how they keep going. Their lives are full of difficulty just managing their daily existences – like getting up, putting their clothes on, cooking, etc. – and yet they have this energy and determination.

Grandpa thinks he's going to live to be a hundred. That makes him happy! Grandma, even with her physical and mental problems, continues to follow what's going on, or perhaps more what went on, she mixes up the past and the present. The distinction is not always that clear for Grandpa either. It's depressing to witness their frailties, but without them life would be very empty. Talking to Auntie Borghild is often a solace though, she is sharp and wise, has experienced a lot in life, and is secure – on top of that, she's a good talker. I've been thinking about going to see her one evening this week for a chat.

I can see writing is an earnest business for you. It must be good to have found something you want to invest time and effort in. The possibilities are endless if you have the courage. That's what I believe.

As for the sweater, I've bought a pattern that can be adapted to suit you. But at the moment I have no desire to either knit or crochet. I might buy one here or send you the money. We'll see. Good luck with everything!

Love, Mom.

Could it be true that Kjartan had said I had talent? And that I should send my short story to a publisher?

She would never have written it if it wasn't.

But what did she mean by my *personal development*? Either the texts were *good* or they *weren't*?

I opened the letter from Hilde. As expected, I was showered with superlatives. She was looking forward to reading more, she wrote in that open-hearted passionate way only she had.

I put it aside and sat down in front of the typewriter. As soon as I had plugged it in, I knew what should happen in the bonfire stories.

They were burning dead bodies! All the fires across the whole of the unending plain were funeral pyres! At first he didn't understand, but then he went closer and that was when he saw. They were pushing a kind of flat wooden spade under each body and *lifting* it into the flames.

I finished the story in an hour, *tore* the sheet of paper out of the typewriter, and hurried up to the school to copy it.

Three days later Irene stood at my door.

I invited her in.

The mood was tense, she tried to handle it as well as she could, we drank tea and chatted, nothing happened.

When she was about to go, she put her arms around me and as she looked up at me I bent down and kissed her.

She was warm and soft and full of life.

"When will we see each other again?" she said.

"I don't know," I said. "When would be good for you?"

"Tomorrow?" she said. "Are you home then? I can get someone to drive me here."

"Yes," I said. "Come tomorrow."

I stood in the doorway and watched her walk toward the car. My member ached with desire. She turned and waved, then she got into the car and I closed the door, went in, and sat on the sofa. I was full of feelings for her, but they were not unambivalent, I liked her and wanted her, but did I like her *enough*? She had been wearing blue jeans and a blue denim jacket, surely everyone knew that didn't go? At least girls knew. And her note, all the dialect, I hadn't really liked that.

We should get drunk together, then all the ambivalence would be gone. And if I was drunk enough, would I be able to see her naked without . . . well, without *that* happening?

I was asleep when she buzzed the next evening. I dashed into the hall and opened the door. She had her thumbs in her pockets and was smiling at me. Behind her a car was waiting with the engine idling.

"Feel like making a trip to Finnsnes?" she said.

"Definitely," I said.

The same friend who had been with her the first time, and whose name I had forgotten, was sitting next to the driver, a guy my age, maybe her boyfriend, maybe not. I got in beside Irene, and then we were off. Like everyone here, he drove fast. The music was loud, Creedence Clearwater Revival, obviously a local favorite, and by the bottom of the hill I had a bottle of beer pressed into my hand. All the way there I wanted her, she was so close to me, especially when she laid her arms on the seat in front and leaned forward to chat with the others. They asked me some questions, I answered and asked them some questions, and Irene filled the silences by chatting with the two in front. Occasionally she turned to me and explained the background to what they were talking about, her face constantly alternating between a smile and a great tremulous earnestness the times our eyes met.

After around an hour the driver parked in front of the discotheque in Finnsnes, we went in, found a table, and ordered some wine, which we shared. We danced, she pressed against me, I wanted her so much I didn't know where to start. Foolish small talk, what good was that? I knocked back the wine to fill the abyss in me, my pulse accelerated, soon we were dancing all the time. On the way home, at a hundred and twenty over the long flats, we sat in the back kissing. When "Stand by Your Man" came on, I leaned back and laughed, I would write about this in my letters, that's how redneck this place was, this was what my life was like now. She asked me what had made me laugh, nothing, I said, I'm just happy.

At the turnoff to Håfjord the car stopped.

"You'll have to walk from here," the driver said. "We're going on to Hellevika."

"Isn't that a hell of a distance?" I said.

"No, it'll take you an hour max," he said. "If you walk quickly, you'll make it in three-quarters of an hour."

I kissed Irene one last time, opened the door, and stepped out.

In the car they were laughing, I turned, she stuck her head out the window.

"We were just kidding. Jump in. Of course we'll drive you all the way home."

Through the tunnel, along the fjord. The sea and the mountains lay very still, wrapped in the gray, equally still, night air.

"Would you like to sleep here?" I whispered to Irene as we approached.

"I'd love to," she whispered back. "But I can't. I have to go home. But I can next weekend. Are you here then?"

"Yes," I said.

"Then I'll come," she said.

On Mondays I had gotten into the habit of walking up to the school an hour before classes started, I ran my eye over what had to be done that day, and when the bell rang, I was more often than not sitting at my desk waiting for the pupils to come in. I would talk to them about what they had done since I last saw them.

On this Monday something was brewing, I could sense it as soon as they entered the room. They sat down on their chairs in their usual clumsy way. Andrea looked at Vivian, who put her hand up.

"Is it true you're going out with Irene from Hellevika?" she said.

The other girls giggled. Kai Roald rolled his eyes, but he was grinning too.

"What I do when I'm not at school is none of your business," I said.

"But you normally ask us what we did over the weekend," Andrea said.

"Yes, I do," I said. "And you may ask me what I did. I'll tell you."

"What did you do?" Kai Roald said.

"On Saturday I was at home all day. In the evening I was in Finnsnes. On Sunday I was at home."

"Ooh!" said Vivian. "And who were you *with* in Finnsnes then?"

"That's got nothing to do with you," I said. "Shall we get started?"

"No!"

I raised my arms in mock frustration.

"Do you have something else to say then?"

"*Are* you going out with Irene?" Andrea said.

I smiled, didn't answer, put the box I had brought in on the desk, and handed out the books. We had Norwegian now, the novel they were going to read was *Poison* by Alexander Kielland, one of the few class sets we had. I had started on it the previous Monday, their reading was so bad, I had told the mentor about this in the session I had with her, she advised me to read a book with the class, and that was what we were doing.

"Oh no," they said when they saw the green 1970s cover. "Not that one! We don't understand a word!"

"It's in Norwegian," I said. "Don't you understand Norwegian?"

"But it's so old-fashioned! We really don't understand it."

"Kai Roald, you set the ball rolling."

Oh, how painful it was to listen to. First of all, he was a bad reader anyway, but Kielland's style and the dated language destroyed any flow there was and reduced everything to single syllables, hesitation, coughing, and stammering. None of them had any idea about the plot. I regretted having chosen this book, but it wouldn't look good if I just gave up, so I continued to torment them all the way through the lesson, and would do the same the following Monday.

I was on playground duty in the break, so I went to the vestibule in the staff room to get my coat while the pupils ran into the yard behind me.

"Your father phoned, Karl Ove," Hege said, coming toward me with a note in her hand. "He said to ring him back. Here's the number."

She passed me the note, I hesitated for a moment. The pupils shouldn't be outside unsupervised. On the other hand, Dad was a teacher himself, and if he rang during working hours, it was bound to be important.

Oh, of course. The baby must have been born.

I went in and dialed the number.

"Hello?" he said.

"Hi, Dad, this is Karl Ove. I was told you'd rung."

"Yes, you're a big brother now," he said.

"Oh great!" I said. "Boy or girl?"

"A little girl," he said.

Was he drunk or just very happy?

"Congratulations," I said. "That's wonderful."

"Yes, it's wonderful. We've just come home. I'd better look after them now."

"Everything OK with Unni?"

"Oh yes. We'll talk later. Bye."

"Bye. And congratulations once again!"

I put down the phone and went out, smiled at Hege, who sent me a look, buttoned up my coat, and hurried through the vestibule into the playground. I had hardly emerged before Reidar slunk up to me. He could be unbearably clingy and exploited every situation to make sure he was the center of attention. In the classroom he would answer everything, comment on everything, always know better, always want to be the best. With me and the other teachers he was always ingratiating. He was a particularly detestable boy. He reminded me of myself when I was younger. I took every opportunity to try to eradicate this behavior as it would make his life difficult later, but there was scant reward for my efforts, after every harsh word, there he was, right back like a steel spring.

When I found out that he was the brother of Andrea in my class, I felt slightly better disposed toward him, she was my favorite student, and their being siblings touched me in a way, although I didn't really understand why it should.

"Karl Ove, Karl Ove," he said, tugging at my coat.

"Yes, what is it?" I said. "And don't pull at my coat!"

"Can I go back into the classroom?"

"What do you want to do?"

"I forgot my Super Ball. I just want to get it. Please, please, please!"

"No," I said, walking toward the football field.

He followed me.

"If Torill had been on playground duty, she would have let me," he said.

"Do I look like Torill?" I said.

He laughed. "No!"

"Off you go," I said. "Scram!"

He ran off, slowed to a walk, and stopped near five other kids in his class, who were skipping just beyond the school wall.

A gust of wind blew across the field, whirled up sand and dust from the road, I blinked a few times to clear my eyes.

It was strange to think that Dad had become a father again.

I turned and looked toward the school building. Two ninth-grade girls came out the door and set off down the hill. Both wearing tight jeans, white sneakers, and big jackets. One with dark hair pinned up at the back, the other with light brown permed hair and big curls that kept falling in front of her eyes and making her toss her head. She had such an elegant neck, long and white and slender. And such a fantastic ass.

No, I couldn't walk around with such thoughts in my mind, I would end up going crazy or in prison.

I smiled, turned back, and looked toward the usual gang playing soccer, across at the kids skipping, who seemed to be fine.

Oh no, Fatty was making a beeline for me.

"Hi!" he said, fixing me with his sad and happy eyes.

"Hi," I said. "Have you been skipping?"

"Yes, but I was out right away."

"Life's like that," I said.

"Can I come to your flat today?" he said.

"My flat? Why?"

"A little visit would be nice, wouldn't it?" he said.

I smiled. "Yes, that's true. But today isn't so good. I have to work. But bring a friend along and drop by another day."

"OK," he said.

I took the watch from my pocket and checked the time.

"Two minutes to the bell," I said. "If we walk slowly, we'll be at the door by the time it rings."

He held my hand and we walked to the entrance together.

Andrea and Hildegunn were standing with their hands in their back pockets under Richard's window and watched us as we approached.

"*Poison*'s so boring," Andrea said. "Can we do something else?"

"It's a Norwegian literary classic," I said.

"We don't give a shit what it is," Hildegunn said.

I raised an admonitory finger to them.

They laughed and the bell rang.

On Saturday I played my first home game. Our jersey was green with thin white stripes, white shorts, and green socks. I played center back while Nils Erik, wearing tights under his shorts, shuffled up and down the touchline.

There were quite a lot of people watching, most of them on the touchlines, a few on the slope facing. Vivian and Andrea were there, I waved to them before the match started, and when someone shouted, "Come on, Karl Ove," a few minutes later I looked across and smiled. It was Vivian, while Andrea was yanking at her jacket to make her stop.

We won 1–0, the mood in the dressing room afterward was buoyant, everyone was going out for a drink, the majority to Finnsnes, as far as I could glean, and there was no shortage of invitations, but I couldn't go, Irene was coming.

On the way down to my place I popped into the staff room and called Yngve.

"How's it going?" I said.

"It's going fine," he said.

"Where's the letter you promised?"

"Oh that," he said. "I've had so much to think about recently."

"Like what?"

"Like breaking up with Kristin."

"Is it really over?"

"Yes."

"Why?"

"Your guess is as good as mine."

There was a silence.

"Karl Ove, I'm actually on my way out," he said. "I'm going to the film club tonight. We can talk later, can't we?"

"Yes," I said.

We hung up, I put on my jacket, locked the door, and left. The sky was gray and a strong wind was blowing off the sea. The tips of the waves in the middle of the fjord were white. I put a ready-made lasagna in the microwave when I returned home, ate it straight from the white plastic packaging, and drank a beer with it. I had just opened a second when a car pulled up outside.

That's probably for me, I thought, and got a hard-on. When the bell rang a second later, I stuffed one hand in my pocket to hide it and opened the door.

"Hi," said Irene.

The car hooted its horn and set off down the hill.

"Hi," I said.

She took a step forward and hugged me. I took my hand out of my pocket to reciprocate the hug and held back my groin so that she wouldn't notice.

"Nice to see you," she said. "I've been looking forward so much to coming here. I've almost been counting the hours!"

"Me too," I said. "Come in!"

"I have to go back tonight after all," she said. "But that's a long time away. Someone's going to pick me up at half past eleven. Is that OK?"

"Of course," I said.

I put the beer on the counter, opened a bottle of white wine, and filled two glasses. If this was going to work, I would have to drink, and drink something stronger than beer, that much was clear.

"*Skål*," I said, looking into her eyes.

"*Skål*," she said, smiling.

I put on a Chris Isaak record, I had worked all this out in advance, the muted, melancholic yet slightly wild mood fit perfectly.

She sat down on the sofa. I sat beside her, but not so close. She was wearing the same blouse she'd had on the first time she had been here. I couldn't see her full breasts underneath, but I sensed their presence as indeed I sensed her thighs under the tight blue jeans.

Oh.

"That was fun in Finnsnes," she said.

"Yes, it was," I said. "Are they an item, the two others who were with us?"

"Eilif and Hilde?"

"Yes."

She laughed. "No, they're brother and sister. They've always been good pals. *This* close," she said, holding two fingers entwined.

"Do you have any brothers or sisters?" I said.

"No," she said. "Do you?"

"Yes, a brother."

"Older or younger? No, let me guess. Older?"

"Yes, how did you know?"

"You're not the big brother type."

I smiled and refilled my glass. Knocked it back in one gulp.

"That's true," I said. "I've got a sister too. A half sister."

"Had you forgotten?"

"She's just a few days old!"

"Is she?"

"Yes, she is. A newborn baby. I haven't seen her yet. My father remarried."
Conversation flagged.

We looked at each other and smiled.

The silence continued.

It had to happen now. We had no time to lose. It had to happen now even though I couldn't feel the wine at all.

"What do your parents do?" I said, and cursed myself. A bigger turn off was hard to imagine.

But she answered politely. "Dad's a fisherman. Mom's a housewife. And yours?"

"My dad's a gymnas teacher, my mom's a teacher at a nursing college."

"And you're a teacher here!" she said. "Chip off the old block!"

"I'm not a teacher," I said. "And I'm not going to be one either."

"Don't you like it?"

"Yes, I do. But I don't want to spend my life teaching. I'm doing it for a year to earn money."

"How do you want to spend your life then?"

"I'm going to write. I'm going to be a writer."

"Are you? How exciting!"

"Yes, it is. But I'm not sure I'll make it."

"No," she said. "I mean, of course you will." She looked me in the eye.

"Would you like a bit more wine?" I said.

She nodded. I filled her glass. She took a sip. Then she got up and walked around the room. Stopped by the desk.

"So this is where you write," she said.

"Yes," I said.

She gazed out the window.

I emptied my glass and got up. Went over to her. Smelled the fragrance of her perfume, it was fresh, light, like a meadow.

"Nice view you've got from here," she said.

I swallowed and gently wrapped my arms around her. It was as though she had been waiting because she immediately leaned back, I rested my cheek against hers and stroked her stomach, she turned to me, I kissed her.

"Oh," she said, turning around and wrapping her arms around me. We kissed, long and lingering. I pressed against her. I kissed her neck, I kissed her cheek, I kissed her naked arm. My ears were rushing, my chest was pounding.

"Come on. Let's go to my bedroom," I said, took her hand and led her in. She got onto the bed and lay back, I clambered on top of her. With trembling hands I unbuttoned her blouse, underneath she was wearing a bra, I fumbled around trying to get it off, she laughed, sat up, reached behind her back and undid the hook, let the bra fall, and her breasts were freed. Oh God, how big and beautiful they were. I kissed them, my mind was running wild, first one, then the other, the nipples stiffened in my mouth and she said oh oh and I began to fumble with her trouser buttons, eventually managed to undo them, pulled them off, tore off my own, wrestled my sweater over my head and got on top of her again, felt her skin against mine, she was so wonderfully soft, I pressed against her, as hard as I'd ever done before, I rubbed against her, and then, oh no, for Christ's sake, it can't be true, not now! Not now!

But it was. A jerk, a spasm, and it was all over.

I lay quite still.

"What's up?" she said, looking at me. "Something happened?"

She half rose, supporting herself on her forearms.

"Nothing," I said, turning away. "I was just thirsty. Think I'll get something to drink. Do you want anything?"

If I could leave the bedroom without her seeing, I could "spill something" in the kitchen so that she wouldn't realize that the big wet patch on my underpants was sperm, she would think it was juice. And it worked. Standing in front of the fridge, I opened a carton of apple juice, poured some into a glass, some onto my underpants and my stomach.

"SHIT!" I shouted.

"What happened?" she said from the bedroom.

"Nothing," I said. "I've just spilt some juice. What did you say again? Did you want some?"

"No, thanks," she said.

When I went back in to her she covered her top half with the duvet, she clung to it. I sat on the edge of the bed with the glass in my hand. The moment was gone, the chance had slipped through my fingers, now I had to repair the situation.

"Ah, that's good," I said. "Shall we have a smoke? I haven't smoked since you arrived. You obviously exert a magnetic influence on me."

I smiled and got up, casually pulled on my trousers and sweater, went into the living room and put on a record, played the Housemartins this time. There was no need for Chris Isaak and his hypnotic moods anymore. Then I sat down on the sofa, filled my wineglass, and rolled a cigarette. After a while Irene appeared, also dressed.

How the hell could I get out of this?

Was it possible to raise this situation from zero to the heights we had previously scaled?

All the excitement was gone. Irene sat down at the other end of the sofa, straightened her rumpled hair with her hand, then reached out for her glass.

When she looked at me a smile was playing around her lips and there was a glint in her eye.

A pain shot through my chest.

Was she mocking me because I wasn't good enough?

"I think I'm seriously falling in love with you, Karl Ove Knausgaard," she said.

What?

Was she making fun of me?

But there was nothing of that detectable in her eyes, they were warm and happy and passionate.

What was she thinking? Did she imagine that I had refrained from taking her and all she had to offer out of chivalry? Could she not see that I couldn't do it? That I would never be able to do it? That a kind of freak, a monster, was lurking behind what she saw?

"Do you like me a little bit too?" she said.

"Of course!" I said. But the smile I sent her couldn't have been very convincing. "Irene," I said. "Why don't we go for a walk? It's still nice out."

"Yes," she said. "Good idea. Let's do that."

I regretted my suggestion the moment we were outside. Here there was only one walk, which was along the road between the houses and back again. We wouldn't be on our own for a meter of it, we would be seen everywhere.

Irene held my hand and smiled up at me. Perhaps it didn't matter, I thought, and smiled back.

We set off downhill. Neither of us said a word. The light pressure from her hand, which I felt now and then, and her presence only a few centimeters from me, were enough for my lust to return. Around us the countryside was at peace. The sea was perfectly calm. Some clouds hung motionless on the horizon and above the mountains on the other side, which in the gathering dusk were completely black. All I wanted to do was throw her to the ground and take her. But I couldn't. Not here, not anywhere, not at home, I had just tried that, I hadn't succeeded, it hadn't worked. I could have yelled, I could have screamed. I wanted her, I could have her, but I wasn't able to do it.

Darkness hovered above the sea, between the mountains, beneath the sky: floor, walls, and roof. The first stars had begun to burst through. There wasn't a soul around.

"Are you going to go back to Kristiansand after you've finished here?" Irene said.

I shook my head. "Definitely not," I said. "That's the last place on earth I want to live."

"Is it so awful?"

"Yes, you have no idea."

"I've been there. Dad's got some family there."

"Oh? Where?"

"I think it's called Vågsbygd," she said. "But I don't remember exactly."

"Yes, that's what it's called," I said.

We had reached the bend at the end of the village, by the chapel. She stopped and put her arms around me.

"We're going out now," she said. "Aren't we?"

"Yes," I said.

We kissed.

"My writer," she said with a smile.

This time it was obvious she was teasing me. But also that she liked the idea.

Oh Christ, when was this going to end? I could barely walk I was so excited by having her this close to me.

We went on, she told me a bit about what she was doing in Finnsnes, I told her a bit about what I had done in Kristiansand.

As we approached my flat and I saw the school standing there like a social-democratic fortress, it struck me that we could walk up there, I could unlock the pool and we could have a swim. Have a shower together, have a sauna together, swim together. But as I imagined it the certainty that I wouldn't be able to perform and that it would be impossible to conceal it sank its claws into my breast.

I unlocked the door, we chatted and drank some more wine. The silences became longer and more uncomfortable until it was half past eleven and I could finally accompany her to the door and kiss her good-bye.

She looked back once on her way to the car. Her eyes were gleaming. Then she got in, the door closed, and she was gone.

The next day I tried to write. It didn't go very well, and the evening's defeat cast a shadow over everything. Not only over my individual lessons and what I did in them but the whole of my accursed life. There was a reason for this, and I knew the reason, but it was somehow ill defined, surrounded by a fog-like vagueness, something deep, deep in the mists of my mind.

The fact was I had never masturbated. Had never beat off. Had never played with myself. I was eighteen years old now and it had never happened. Not once. I hadn't even tried. My lack of experience of this meant that I both knew and didn't know how to do it. And once I hadn't done it as a twelve- or thirteen-year-old, time passed and it slowly became unthinkable, not in the sense of unheard of, more in the sense of beyond my horizons. The direct result of this was that I had heavy nocturnal emissions. I dreamed about women, and in my sleep not even touching was required, it was enough just to lay my eyes on them, standing there, with their beautiful bodies, and I came. If I was close to them in my dreams, again I came. My whole body jerked and convulsed through the night, and my underpants were soaked with semen in the morning.

I had read porn magazines like everyone else when I was growing up, but it had always been with others around me, in the forest with Geir or Dag Lothar or some of the other boys, never alone, not once had I taken a magazine home, I wouldn't have dared. There were few things I found more stimulating and exciting than looking at a porn magazine, but the desire it aroused in me never led to masturbation as there were always others around. At most I would lie on my stomach and rub my groin against the ground while I read. When I was alone at home I sometimes flicked through the mail-order catalogs that existed then, staring at the lingerie or bikini models, and my throat constricted as I studied the cloth pressing against the soft arch between their thighs, or the nipples occasionally visible under their bras or bikini tops. But that was where it stopped, at the constricted throat, the throbbing heart. I didn't masturbate. This was never a conscious decision, it wasn't that I told myself, no, I'm not doing that. Everything was vague and unclear, unconscious and tenebrous. By the time I was in my teens it was too late. Reading porn magazines in the forest was over and not replaced by anything else. In my teens I didn't see a single pornographic film and didn't read a single pornographic magazine. Desire was never focused on one point, it broadened out, it was large and nebulous and hard to handle. Somewhere

I knew that my situation with regard to girls, or Irene, as she was the one in question now, would improve dramatically if I just started masturbating. Nevertheless, I didn't. Even though I knew this, at the same time I didn't, it belonged to the unthinkable, and that was where I was on this day, with the aroma of Irene still clinging to the sheets, I should have, I had to, I wanted to, but I didn't.

No, I played Led Zeppelin at full volume, summoned all the concentration I had, and tried to race ahead with a new short story. When darkness fell I let it enter the flat too, apart from on the desk, where a small lamp shone like an island in the night. There was me and my writing, an island of light in the darkness, that was how I imagined it. And then I went to bed and slept until the alarm clock woke me and another Monday at Håfjord School began.

The first thing the pupils did when I entered the classroom was to tease me about Irene.

I let them run on, then fixed them with a stare, said, now that's enough of that nonsense, we have to start work if anything is to become of you. They took out their books and started work, I walked around and helped them, I liked the way they went from being a small, chatty, giggly class to falling into step and just being themselves.

Sitting like this, without speaking, without looking at each other, fully occupied with their own work, it was as though their ages melted away. Not that I no longer saw them as children, it wasn't being children that defined them but their personalities, who they were in themselves and probably always would be.

I didn't think about Irene much at school, these thoughts came afterward, alone in my flat, like an adrenaline rush through my body. And then the despair. Never one without the other. She saw a purpose in us, she wanted something from me, and although I liked her I wasn't in love, to start with we had nothing to talk about. I wanted to have her, but that was all I wanted.

Was she in love with me?

I doubted it. It was probably more that I was different, not one of her classmates but a teacher, not a thirty- or a forty-year-old but still her age, not from here but from the south.

In a year I would be gone, and she would still be here in her last year at gymnas. That wasn't the best basis for a relationship, was it? Besides, I was going to write and I couldn't tie up all my weekends, which I would have to do if this became serious.

In my head the arguments raged back and forth. On Tuesday we had a soccer match, it took us an hour to get to the field, which was made of shale and became so dusty that the players looked like Bedouin shadows. We lost narrowly, but I scored a goal in the melee after a corner. On Wednesday I received my first copy of *Vinduet*, the new journal I had subscribed to, in the post. The theme was literature's relationship with other art forms, I couldn't grasp any of it, but the mere fact that I had a literary journal on my desk was good enough. In the evening Hege came by, she had gone up to the school to do some work and on her way back she had decided on an impulse to see how I was. On Thursday I went to Finnsnes with Nils Erik, we went to the liquor store and the library, I bought a bottle of vodka and took out two novels by Thomas Mann, *The Confessions of Felix Krull* and *Doctor Faustus*. On Friday I went to school to call Irene. There was no one in the staff room and I took my time, brewed up a pot of coffee, watched some TV, paced back and forth a good deal. In the end I went into the cubicle, put the note on which I had written her number on the machine, dialed the number, and put the receiver to my ear.

Her mother answered. I introduced myself, she called, "Irene, it's Karl Ove," I heard footsteps and some thumping.

"Hi!" she said.

"Hi," I said.

"How are you? Has something happened? You sound so serious."

Her slightly husky voice was more obvious on the phone, where there was nothing to distract my attention. It made her sound incredibly sexy.

"I don't know . . ." I said.

There was so much that created doubt as far as she was concerned. Wasn't I just the first best person to come along? We had seen each other on the *bus*, for God's sake. And she hadn't offered me any resistance at all, she had just got into bed, ready for anything.

"Tell me now," she said.

What was I doing? Should I end it over the phone? That was cowardly, it had to be done face-to-face.

"No, there's nothing," I said. "It's just . . . well, I'm not in the best frame of mind right now. But it's nothing serious. A bit down, that's all."

"Why? Has something happened? Are you homesick?"

"Maybe a little," I said. "I don't know. It'll be fine. Tomorrow it'll be gone."

"Oh, I wish I could be there to comfort you," she said. "I miss you!"

"I miss you, too," I said.

"Can we meet tomorrow?"

If she was being picked up at twelve, like the last time, it would be almost impossible to end the relationship. Because it would have to be done right away, you couldn't stay together with someone for four hours, as before, perhaps end up in bed together again, and then go your separate ways. If I did it at once, what would she do in the meantime, before her lift arrived?

"That won't work," I said. "I'm busy then. What about Sunday?"

"I have to go to Finnsnes again."

"Come here first! You can catch the bus from Håfjord. That would work."

"Maybe. Yes, I can do that."

"Good!" I said. "See you then."

"See you then. Take care!"

"Take care, Irene."

The next morning I was stopped by a group of boys standing outside the shop, they asked how I was getting on, fine, I said, did I want to go to a party later that day, they asked, where, I said, it's no big deal, they said, we'll just be sitting around drinking up at Edvald's, come up if you feel like it, no need to bring any booze, we've got enough.

Leaving them and walking up to my flat, I thought about how open people were here, inviting me to all sorts of events although I was not one of them, and I pondered why. What did they want from a Kristiansander with a black coat, a beret, and progressive musical tastes, why take him in tow in the evening? At home going out demanded planning, lots of obstacles had to be overcome, you didn't just turn up at someone's house or sit down at a table in a bar with someone you vaguely knew. Everyone had their own circle, and if you didn't, you were on the margins. Here there may have been similar circles, but if so they were open. In the few weeks I had lived here the most striking discovery was that everyone was accepted. Not necessarily liked, but always accepted. They didn't have to wave to me and invite me out, but they did, and not just a few people but everyone.

Perhaps the answer was they had to, it was as simple as that. There were so few of them that they couldn't afford to leave anyone out. Or else it was their attitude to life that was different, rawer, more casual. If you lived your life on a boat deck, if you did hard physical work every day and drank as soon as you were on shore, there was no reason to bother with petty clockwork-like social etiquette and distinctions. A more natural course of action was to proffer the hand of friendship, say join us, have a drink, have you heard about the time . . . ?

Vivian, Live, and Andrea came racing down the hill on their bikes. They waved and shouted to me as they passed, their hair flapping and their eyes squinting to meet the oncoming wind. I was smiling to myself long after they had passed. They were so funny, the way the immense seriousness they possessed was shattered internally by their equally immense childish glee.

I worked for a few hours on a short story about some boys who nailed a cat to a tree, then I heated a frozen meal in the microwave for dinner, lay down on the sofa, and read *Doctor Faustus* until it began to grow dark outside and I had to get ready to go out.

I hadn't read Thomas Mann before. I liked the elaborate, old-fashioned, formal style, and the scenes at the beginning when the protagonists are children and the father of one of them, Adrian, shows them experiments with dead material, which he brings to life, were fantastic, there was something eerie about them that at first forced itself to the front of your consciousness and then seemed to sink to the bottom. I was reminded of the open heart I had once seen on TV as a child, how it had throbbed in all that blood, like a small, blind animal. It was alive and belonged to a different category from Adrian's father's experiments, but the blindness was the same and also the way it was subject to laws, moving according to them, not independently.

I was unable to grasp the part about music and musical theory, but I was used to that in this kind of novel, there were always great expanses I just skimmed without understanding, more or less like the French dialogue that could suddenly crop up in some books.

I showered, changed, put a bottle of vodka in a bag, and walked up to Edvald's house, he was a fisherman, older than the others, around thirty-five, single, liked drinking, and I stayed there until five in the morning, when I strolled back through the village with a head as empty and desolate as an unfrequented tunnel. On waking up at two the next day, I remembered nothing apart from standing on the quay watching the seabirds bobbing on the water, wondering if they were asleep, and pissing against the shop wall. Everything else was gone. All the details and individual moments were lost. I had drunk a whole bottle of spirits, that was what you did here, and I was still drunk when I woke up. Writing was out of the question. Instead I lay in bed reading, but that didn't go very well either, my brain seemed to be soaking in a kind of yellow liquid, which I watched. If I stopped reading, the feeling went away, it was as though it were me in the liquid.

At a few minutes to five there was a ring at the door. I had been asleep and jumped off the bed, it was Irene.

I opened the door.

"Hi!" she said with a smile. There was a bag on the ground beside her. I took two big steps back so that she couldn't hug me.

"Hi," I said. "Do you want to come in?"

Her eyes questioned me.

"What is it, Karl Ove? *Is* there something up?"

"Yes, actually there is," I said. "We have to talk."

She stared at me.

"I haven't told you," I said. "But I was in a relationship before I came here. I received a letter from her after a few days. She broke it off with me. I haven't really gotten over that yet, actually. And now it's begun to get serious with us . . . But I don't have the mental space, it's too early, do you understand? I like you so much, but . . ."

"Are you finishing this?" she said. "Before it's even begun?"

I nodded. "I think so."

"What a shame," she said. "Just when I was starting to like you so much."

"Yes, I'm sorry. But it won't work. It doesn't feel right."

"Then maybe it's better we drop it," she said. "I wish you all the best for your life."

She came over and hugged me. Then she grabbed her bag, turned, and went to go.

"Are you going?" I said.

She turned her head.

"Well, we can't sit here, can we? What's the point of that?"

"But the bus won't be here for ages yet, will it?"

"I'll walk," she said. "I can get on the bus whenever it turns up."

Watching her walk down the hill, with the bag in her hand, toward the road that ran alongside the fjord, I was full of regret. An enormous opportunity had slipped away. At the same time I was relieved that it had been so painless. Now it was over. Now there was nothing to think about.

The days became shorter, and they became shorter quickly, as though they were racing toward the darkness. The first snow arrived in mid-October, went after a few days, but the next time it fell, at the beginning of November, it came with a vengeance, day after day it tumbled down, and soon everything was packed in thick white cushions of snow, apart from the sea, which with its dark, clean surface and terrible depths lay nearby like an alien and menacing presence, like a murderer who has moved into a neighboring house and whose unheeded knife glints on the kitchen table.

The snow and the darkness changed the area beyond all recognition. When I first came, the sky had been high and luminous, the sea vast, and the countryside open, nothing seemed to hold together the village with its random huddle of houses, it barely existed in its own right. Nothing stopped there, that was the feeling. Then came the snow and the darkness. The sky fell, it lay like a lid over the rooftops. The sea disappeared, its blackness merged with the blackness of the sky, no horizon was visible any longer. Even the mountains disappeared and with them the sensation of finding yourself in wide-open country. What remained were the houses, which were lit day and night, always surrounded by darkness, and now the houses and the lights were the focal point to which everything gravitated.

An avalanche blocked the road, a ferry service was started, and the fact that you were only able to leave twice a day increased the feeling that this village was the only village, these people the only people. I was still getting lots of letters, and spent a lot of time answering them, but the life they represented was no longer the one that counted, the one that did was this: up in the morning, out into the snow, up the hill to school and into class. Stay there all day, in a low-roofed, illuminated bunker, weighted down by the darkness, go home, go shopping, have dinner, and then in the evening train in the gym with the youngest fishermen, watch TV at school, swim in the pool or sit at home reading or writing until it was so late that I could go to bed and sleep off the dead hours before the next day started.

On weekends I drank. Someone always came over and asked if I wanted to go to Finnsnes or a village a few hours away, if the road was open. When it was closed it was up to someone's place or down to someone's, there were always people sitting around drinking and they always wanted company. I didn't say no, I joined in, and a bottle of spirits over the evening was no longer the exception but the rule, so I was invariably wandering around doing things which I had forgotten by the next day. Once, I fell out of the band bus, started walking away from the village instead of toward it, no one said anything until I had gone a hundred meters wearing only a shirt and a thin jacket, shivering and trembling, and then I heard their shouts, over here you idiot, over here! At another party I danced with a substitute teacher from Husøya, her name was Anne, she came from somewhere in Østland and was pretty in that cold blond way I was so attracted by, we stood kissing forever in a corner of the corridor where the coatroom was, I called her a few days later, invited her to dinner at my place with her girlfriend and Tor Einar and Nils Erik, I tried to kiss her then but she lowered her head, she had a boy-friend, she said, she had someone else, what happened at the party should never have happened, I wasn't her type at all, she had no explanation except that she had been drunk. And perhaps that it had been dark? I said, trying to make a joke out of it, but she didn't laugh, she wasn't the sort. Cold and sincere, that was Anne.

At other weekends people came home from schools or universities across Norway, and just the fact that they had different faces was a liberation. I traipsed after one of them like a dog, her name was Tone, she was Frank's sister and the daughter of the teacher who couldn't stand me, but I didn't care about that, I was drunk and had been watching her all evening.

Now she was about to leave, and I decided to follow her.

Snowflakes were whirling through the darkness. She walked fifty meters down the road with her head lowered, beneath the light of the street lamps. I wrapped my scarf around my mouth and set off. She went into her parents' house, banged the snow off her boots, then closed the door behind her.

I stood outside for a few minutes. I thought she would be happy to see me because she had wanted to sleep with me all evening.

The kitchen window was dark, the living-room window, too. But light streamed out from the narrow window at the end of the house.

I opened the door and went in. Didn't bother to remove my shoes, glanced around the living room, it was dark and empty, walked down the hall toward the open door at the end.

She was standing in the bathroom brushing her teeth in front of the mirror. Her mouth was full of foam.

"Hi," I said.

She must have heard me, yet didn't appear the slightest bit frightened when she turned toward me.

"Get out," she said.

I sat down on a chair by the wall and stared intensely at her. First at her face, then at her breasts under the green jumper.

She shook her head.

"You're wasting your time. You haven't got a hope with me," she said almost incomprehensibly as everyone does when cleaning their teeth and talking at the same time.

"Do you want me to go?" I said.

She nodded.

"Fine," I said, got up and went out. The wind formed a wall in front of the door filled with small, frozen-hard particles of snow. What a shame, I thought, looking up at the immense darkness above us. She is so classy. Yes, unbelievably classy! After wandering back and forth in the snow-blown road under the light from the street lamps, which with the snow and the darkness as background had a greenish glare and cast an underwater glow over the surroundings, I found my way back to the party, which was no longer a party but a table littered with glasses and bottles, empty cigarette packets and ashtrays in an otherwise empty room. All sense of time in me must have stopped – had I really been away that long? – and then my sense of space went too because the next thing I remember is waking up in my bed at home.

Actually *doing* things, not denying myself anything when I was drunk, in that intoxicating state of total freedom, had in the course of these months gradually begun to take its toll. At gymnas I was either hungover or not, there were no other consequences. If I felt any pangs of conscience at all, they were pinpricks, nothing a hearty breakfast and a walk to town couldn't cure. Up here in the north, however, it was different. Perhaps the gulf between the person I usually was and the one I became when I drank was too great. Perhaps it was impossible for a man to have such a wide gulf inside himself. For what happened was that the person I usually was began to draw in the person I became when I was drinking, the two halves slowly but surely became sewn together, and the thread that joined them was shame.

Oh hell, did I do *that*? the cries resounded inside me the next day as I lay in the darkness. Oh no, shit, did I say *that*? And *that*? And *that*?

I lay there, rigid with fear, as though someone were throwing bucket after bucket of my own excrement over me.

Look what an idiot he is. Look what a stupid fool he is.

But I got up, started a new day, and I always got through it.

The worst was probably the notion that others *saw* me, that I put on a show for them, and that the side of me I displayed then was reflected in the way they looked at me every day.

I pretended I was a young teacher who took the best possible care of his children, whom they watched on his way to and from the post office or the shop, while in reality I was a babbling idiot who sat drooling over all sorts of girls at night, who would cut off both his hands for one of them to take him home, but none wanted to, after all he was a babbling, drooling idiot.

At school too I occasionally felt like that, but not with the pupils, I had the situation fully under control there, nor with Nils Erik and Tor Einar, they of course knew what was what.

Yes, I had the situation under control, yet that didn't prevent me from feeling the pain and torment there too, opposite my pupils, sitting at my desk in the minutes before the new week officially started, with the disgraceful behavior of the weekend still fresh in my mind.

They had taken off their padded jackets, and were sitting there in their Icelandic sweaters, their skin still red from the cold, squirming restlessly on their chairs, wanting to go home and back to bed while the presence of the others drew them in the opposite direction, for they were exchanging glances, whispering little comments, sniggering, breathing, living.

The light glared from the ceiling, and against the deep darkness that always hovered above us the windows reflected back the other end of the whole classroom. There sat Kai Roald, there sat Vivian, there sat Hilde-gunn, there sat Live, there sat Andrea. Faded blue jeans, white boots, a white sweater with a high neck. And there I was, behind the desk, in a black shirt, black jeans, trembling inside with exhaustion. Even the slightest little transgression seemed monstruous to me, all I wanted and needed was security.

I opened the book at the chapter we were going to read. The room was full of the buzz of voices from other classes. My own pupils were sleepy, not interested.

"All right, take your books out! There's a limit to sleepiness!"

Andrea smiled as she bent forward and took the book from her satchel. It was bound in brown paper and covered with the names of pop stars and film stars in felt-tip pen. Kai Roald groaned, but when I met his eyes he smiled. Hildegunn already had her book ready of course. Live turned to the window. I looked in the same direction. A figure was on its way up the hill, though more like a ghost, for it was impossible to distinguish a body from the shadowy contours coming toward us, enveloped in swirling snow.

"Live! Take out your book!"

"OK, OK. What subject do we have now?"

"Are you serious? Don't you know?"

"No-oo!"

"Six months you've been here for the first lesson on Monday morning. We always have the same subject. And that is . . . ?"

Her eyes stared at me nervously.

"You don't remember?" I said.

Neither did I. Panic rose in me like water in a blocked toilet.

She shook her head.

"Does anyone know?"

Everyone looked at me. Did they understand?

No.

There. Kai Roald opened his mouth. "Christianity," he said.

"Oh yes, Christianity!" she said. "Of course. I knew that. I just went all blank for a moment."

"You're always all blank," Kai Roald said.

She looked daggers at him.

"And you aren't?" I said.

He laughed. "You're right, I guess I am."

"I've gone blank too for the moment," I said. "But it's no good. We have to get through the syllabus. And we can only do that by working hard."

"That's what you always say," Vivian said.

"But it's true. Do you think I stand here talking about Martin Luther for my sake? I know enough about him. But you don't know anything. You're a bunch of ignoramuses. But on the other hand all thirteen-year-olds are, so it's not your fault. By the way is there anyone who knows what an ignoramus is?"

Complete silence.

"Has it got something to do with ignorant?" Andrea said. A faint blush rose up her cheeks as she watched her hand doodling in her book.

"Yes," I said. "To ignore is to fail to notice or to show no interest. An ignorant person is someone who shows no interest in anything. And if you aren't interested in anything, you don't know anything about it either."

"Then I'm ignorant," Kai Roald said.

"No, you're not. You know lots of things."

"Like what?"

"You know a lot about cars, don't you? More than me anyway! And you know a lot about fishing. I know nothing about that."

"Why don't you have a driver's license, by the way? You're eighteen after all," Vivian said.

I shrugged. "I can manage fine without one."

"But you have to get a ride whenever you want to go anywhere!" Vivian said.

"I get around, don't I?" I said. "But that's enough now. Let's get on with our work."

I stood up.

"What do you know about Martin Luther?"

"Nothing," Hildegunn said.

"Nothing?" I said. "Absolutely nothing?"

"Yes," said Live.

"Was he Norwegian?" I said.

"No," said Hildegunn.

"What nationality was he then?"

Hildegunn shrugged. "Wasn't he German?"

"Is he alive now?"

"Of course not!"

"When did he live? When your parents were small? The sixties?" I said.

"He lived in the olden days," Vivian said.

"In the fifteen hundreds," Hildegunn said.

"What did he do? Was he a plumber? Fisherman? Driver?"

"No," Kai Roald said, and giggled.

"He was a priest," Andrea said in the casual way that was intended to show that this was one of many things she knew.

"You know *a lot*," I said. "Martin Luther was a priest who lived in Germany in the sixteenth century. Now why don't you find out ten things about Martin Luther and write them down. Then we'll go through them at the end of class."

"How will we find them out?" Vivian asked.

"Isn't it your job to tell us actually?" Hildegunn said. "Isn't that what you get paid for?"

"I get paid for teaching you," I said. "And there won't always be a teacher in front of you telling you what you need to know. So what do you do? You have to learn where you can find things out. Don't you? Look them up in a book. Find an encyclopedia. I don't mind what you do as long as you find out ten things. Off you go!"

With sighs and groans and grimaces they got up and made for the school's modest library, each armed with a pencil and a notebook. I sat down behind my desk and looked up at the clock on the wall. Half an hour left. Once this was over, there were five classes left. And Monday was crossed off. Then there were Tuesday, Wednesday, Thursday, and Friday left.

This weekend I would definitely have to write. No trip to Finnsnes during the day, no party in the evening, just sit in front of the typewriter from the moment I got up to the moment I went to bed.

I had five short stories now, apart from the two stories based on dreams. All of them had the same protagonist, Gabriel, and the same cast of characters. The action took place in Tybakken. What was strange was how close the place was to me. Sitting in front of the typewriter was like opening a door to it. The scene rose inside me in its entirety and repressed everything around me. There was the road outside the house, there was the tall spruce with the stream running past, there was the slope down to Ubekilen, the stone wall, the rocky outcrop, the boathouse, the crooked rickety pontoon, the island with all the seagulls. If anyone rang my doorbell now, and they did all the time, fourth graders, seventh graders, the tall ninth grader who for some reason gravitated toward me, some of the young fishermen, I would jump out of my skin. It didn't feel as though my childhood surroundings were intruding on the present but vice versa: I was really back in my childhood, and it was the present that was intruding. If I was interrupted, a whole hour or more could pass before Tybakken would rise again.

That was what I longed for. When the trees were trees, not "trees," cars not "cars," when Dad was Dad, not "Dad."

I got up and took a few steps into the common area so that I could see what they were doing. Everyone was sitting around the table in the library, apart from Andrea and Hildegunn, who were heading for their chairs.

"Did you find anything?" I said as they walked past.

"Of course," Hildegunn said. "We've finished. What should we do now?"

"Sit down and wait."

In the classroom beyond, separated from the library by a long stack of bookshelves, sat the third and fourth graders bent over their desks, some with their hands in the air, while Torill went around helping them. In the other corner of the room sat the first graders, on cushions, around Hege, she was reading from a book, they were staring ahead, their eyes dreamy, their faces sleepy. She caught my gaze, looked up without a pause in her reading, and smiled at me. I rolled my eyes, turned to my classroom, and met Andrea's look. She had been watching me. Now she looked down.

"What did you find out then?" I said.

"Do you want to hear now?" Hildegunn said.

"No," I said. "Not really. We'll wait until the others have finished."

"Then why did you ask?" said Andrea.

"Reflex action," I said.

Across the carpet came Kai Roald and Vivian. After they had sat down I walked over to the library corner, where Live was still busy writing.

"How's it going?" I said.

"I've got five," she said. "No, six."

"That's good," I said. "That'll do. You can write down the last four as we go through them."

She picked up her bits and pieces with that serious expression she put on when somebody told her to do something. But it was unable to conceal her great inner insecurity, at least not from me. What her peers saw when they looked at her was not easy to say.

We spent the last twenty minutes of the lesson going through their points. I talked and expanded while they watched me with vacant eyes. What good Martin Luther would ever do them I had no idea. For them it was probably more about being here and writing in their notebooks with their pencils. Sitting in their seats and listening to someone talking about something.

The bell rang. They asked if they could stay indoors during the break, the weather was so bad, I said absolutely not, off you go, waited while they put on their jackets and hats, went into the staff room, where everyone was busy with their own preoccupations, and sat down with a cup of coffee, which was already bitter after an hour in the machine.

Nils Erik, who was reading the local paper, glanced across at me.

"Coming up to the pool later today?" he said.

"OK," I said. "Drop by my place."

In front of us, Torill opened the fridge door, leaned forward, and took out a yogurt. She removed the lid and licked it before throwing it in the bin under the sink, found a spoon in the drawer, and started to eat. She looked at us and smiled with a streak of pink yogurt on her lower lip.

"I get so hungry at this time," she said.

"You don't have to apologize," I said. "We snack too."

Beside me Nils Erik folded the newspaper, got up, and went to the bathroom. I drank a mouthful of coffee and turned to Jane, who came out of the photocopy room at that moment with a pile of papers in her hand. The corners of her mouth drooped as always, her eyes were bored and introspective, leaving you with no real desire to find out what went on inside her.

"Did you make the coffee, Jane?" I said.

She scrutinized me. "Yes, I'm on kitchen duty today. Why?"

"Nothing," I said. "Except that this is the worst coffee I've ever tasted."

She grinned.

"You've been spoiled then," she said. "But I can put a fresh pot on if you like."

"Not at all. I was only joking! It's good enough for me."

She went to her desk, and I got up and stood by the window. A lamppost was encircled by light, thick with tiny white snowflakes whirring around like a swarm of insects. Some children were fighting in the snow below, four of them on top of one another in a drift, and my hand twitched when I saw them, so strong was my impulse to knock the top ones off, for I couldn't imagine anything more claustrophobic than lying underneath them, face down in the snow.

I stepped to the side and scanned the playground.

Where was the teacher?

Oh, when would I get it into my head? This was my playground duty!

I hurried toward the line of hooks in the vestibule.

"Three minutes left of the break," Sture said. "No point going out now. You can catch up after school."

He smirked at his own joke. I looked at him without smiling, pulled my hat down over my head, grabbed my gloves. Even though he was right that there was no point going out now, I had another reason: the impression of regret and energy I would leave behind me as I jogged out and came into the view of those standing behind the window. The last thing I wanted to give was an impression of slackness. The last thing I wanted was for people to think I was a shirker.

Out of the wet-weather shelter came a small, plump figure. I dashed over to the boys who had been wrestling in the snow and were now brushing it off their jeans. The denim material was almost black from where the snow had melted.

"Karl Ove!" he said from behind me, and tugged at my jacket.

He must have run after me.

I turned. "What's up, Jo?" I said.

He smiled.

"Can I throw a snowball at you?"

Last week I had given them permission to throw snowballs at me. It had been a big mistake because they thought it was so much fun, especially when they hit my thighs with a couple of stingers, that they refused to stop when I asked them to. They had reached a kind of amnesty, what had not been allowed was suddenly allowed, and they had a sense of how difficult it would be to punish them if all of a sudden it wasn't allowed any longer.

"No, not today," I said. "Besides, the bell's about to ring."

The four boys scowled up at me from under dark woolen hats pulled down over their faces.

"Is everything all right out here?" I said.

"Of course," Reidar said. "Why wouldn't everything be all right?"

"None of that," I said. "You should show respect for adults."

"You're not an adult," he said. "You don't even have a driver's license!"

"No, that's true," I said. "But at least I know my times tables. That's more than you can say. And I'm big enough to paddle your bottom three times a day if I have to."

"My dad would beat you up if you did," he said.

"Karl Ove, come on," Jo said, pulling at my jacket again.

"I've got a dad too, you know," I said. "He's much stronger and taller than me. And on top of that, he's got a driver's license."

I looked down at Jo. "Where do you want to go?"

"There's something I want to show you. It's something I've made."

"What is it?"

"It's a secret. No one else must know."

I looked across. The girls in the seventh grade were standing by the wall of the wet-weather shelter. Behind, on the fringes of the soccer field, a group of children were chasing after each other in the dark.

"The bell's about to ring, you know," I told him.

He took my hand. Didn't he understand how this looked to his classmates?

"It'll be quick," he said.

He'd hardly uttered the words before the bell rang.

"Next break then," he said. "Will you come with me?"

"OK," I said. "Now get going."

The kids on the soccer field had either not heard the bell or were ignoring it. I walked over to the field. Cupped my hands around my mouth and shouted that the bell had rung. They stopped and looked at me. The snow covering the field drew it into the surrounding terrain, it was a flat surface in the middle of a slope which, farther up, became a mountain, and in all this whiteness, which the sky's all-pervasive darkness muted to a blue, the pupils resembled tiny animals, rodents of some kind perhaps, it seemed to me, romping around outside the entrances to their ingenious networks of passageways and tunnels in the snow.

I waved to them. They set off at a lope toward me.

"Didn't you hear the bell?" I said.

They shook their heads.

"Didn't you think it was time for the bell to ring?"

They shook their heads again.

"Hurry up now," I said. "You're very late."

They ran past me. As I rounded the corner of the wet-weather shelter, the door slammed after the last straggler. I kicked the snow off my shoes against the wall and followed. Opened the door to the staff room, hung my coat and hat on the hook, and went for my books for the class. Behind me the toilet door opened. I turned around. It was Nils Erik.

"Have you been in there all this time?" I said.

"What kind of question is that?" he said.

"I was just surprised," I said, scanning the book spines. "You were in there a long time. I wasn't making any insinuations."

I looked at him and smiled. Picked out a natural science booklet.

"That's good to hear," he said. "Insinuations are such crap. No, it was Torill. She's so sexy it's unbelievable. And when she bent forward . . . I just had to go in and relieve the emergency that had arisen."

"Emergency?" I said.

"Yes," he laughed. "You know. Man sees woman. Man is attracted. Man runs to the john and whacks off."

"Oh, that emergency," I said, smiled, and went to the class.

In the next break Jo ran over to me the second I stepped into the playground.

"Come with me now!" he said, taking my hand and dragging me off.

"Take it easy," I said. "What are you going to show me?"

"Something I've made with Endre," he said.

"Where's Endre?"

"I think he's over there."

Endre was in the third grade, Jo was in the fourth. When they were together they usually kept away from the others.

"There," he said, pointing to a large snowdrift behind the building, out of sight of the rest of the school. "We've made a snow cave. It's really big. Do you want to have a look inside?"

Endre saw us coming, crawled in the entrance, and disappeared from sight.

"That's fantastic," I said, and stopped. "I think it's probably too small for me. But you go in."

He smiled up at me. Then he lay down on his stomach and wriggled in. I took a few steps back and looked across at the other children. Two fourth-grade boys came around the corner and headed toward us. Jo stuck his head out of the cave.

"There's room for you too, Karl Ove. It's really big."

"I have to keep an eye on everyone, you know," I said.

He spotted the two boys.

"This is our snow cave," he said, looking at me. "We made it."

"You sure did," I said.

"Have you ever made a cave?" Reidar shouted.

"It's ours," Jo said. "You can't come in."

They stopped by the entrance.

"Let's have a look," Stig said, trying to crawl past Jo.

"It's ours," Jo said, looking to me again. "Isn't it, Karl Ove?"

"You made it," I said. "But you can't refuse to let others in. You'd have to stand guard day and night if you did."

"But it's ours!" he said.

"It's on school premises," I said. "You can't stop anyone going in."

Reidar smiled and pushed past Jo. Soon the cave was full of kids. They immediately started planning how they could make it bigger and began to dig a tunnel from the end. Jo tried to take charge, but they ignored him, he had to find his place, which was and would always be at the bottom of the pecking order. I turned and went. I did have a bit of a bad conscience, Jo was as unhappy now as he had been happy a few minutes before, but there was nothing I could do about it, he would have to work out the social game for himself. He would have to learn he would get nowhere by whining or making up stories.

"Are you hanging around here again?" I said to the gum-chewing seventh-grade girls standing inside the wet-weather shelter.

"It's snowing and windy," Vivian said. "You don't really think that we should have to stand outside in this weather, do you?"

"You don't have to stand, do you?" I said. "You could run around like the other kids."

"We're not kids," Andrea said. "And it's not fair. The eighth and ninth graders can stay indoors."

"Only kids say something is unfair," I said. "Besides, the eighth and ninth graders have a double slot, so they're in class now."

"That's what we want. Working indoors is better than being out in this weather," Andrea said, and looked up at me. Her cheeks had reddened with the cold. Her eyes were narrow and beautiful.

I laughed.

"So all of a sudden you want to work, do you? That's a new tune," I said.

"You just laugh at us," Vivian said. "You don't have any respect for us at all."

"I treat you how you deserve to be treated," I said, eyeing the clock on the wall between the entrance to the main school building and the large wing where the swimming pool and gymnasium were. Four minutes left of the break.

I went to the other side to see how the fourth graders were doing. No sooner had I rounded the corner than I saw Jo and Endre trudging along, heads bowed into the wind, feet stamping on the snow.

"How's the cave?" I said.

"It's ruined!" Jo said. "Reidar put his head through the roof. The whole damned cave collapsed."

His eyes were moist.

"Don't curse," I said.

"Sorry," he said.

"It can happen," I said. "I'm sure you didn't mean to."

"But it was *our* cave! *We* built it! And now it's ruined."

"Build one with them next time," I said. "Then they won't ruin it."

"We don't want to," he said. "Come on, Endre."

They walked past me.

"I can help you make a new one, if you want," I said. "In the next break."

"Can you?"

"We can get started at least. But the others might join in."

"Yes, but then *you're* there," he said. "They won't dare smash it up."

It had been a stupid offer to make, I thought as I went back into the staff room a few minutes later. Now I would have to dig in the snow with the ten-year-olds for the rest of the breaks. On the other hand, Jo's face had lit up, I remembered, and I closed the toilet door behind me, unzipped, and began to pee. I aimed the jet at the porcelain so that the teachers who were still in the toilet wouldn't hear the splashing sound. While I washed my hands I stared at my reflection in the mirror. The singular feeling that arose when you looked at your own eyes, which so purely and unambiguously expressed your inner state, of being both inside and outside, filled me to the hilt for a few intense seconds, but was forgotten the moment I left the room, in the same way that a towel on a hook or a bar of soap in the small hollow in the sink also were, all these trivialities that have no existence beyond the moment, but hang or lie undisturbed in dark, empty rooms until the door is opened the next time and another person grasps the soap, dries his hands on the towel, and examines his soul in the mirror.

I was in the living room eating when Nils Erik rang at the door. Snow from the drift beside the porch swirled in the air around him. The gusting wind hung like an invisible cupola above the village.

"I'm eating," I said. "But I'll be done soon. Come in."

"But you won't want to go swimming after eating," he said.

"I'm eating fish," I said. "They're used to swimming."

"That's true," he said.

"Do you want some? Fish roe and potatoes?"

He shook his head, untied his boots, and came into the living room.

"Well?" he said. "How's it going?"

I shrugged, swallowed, and took a long drink of water.

"How's what going?" I said.

"Everything," he said. "Writing, for example."

"It's going fine."

"Teaching?"

"Fine."

"Sex life?"

"Hm . . . what shall I say? Not very good. What about you?"

"Well, you saw for yourself today," he said. "That's about all there is."

"Oh well," I said, scraping up the last roe, butter, and some crumbly potato with the knife, offloading it onto the fork and lifting it to my mouth. My lips became greasy with the fat.

"And my prospects in that direction are not particularly rosy either," he continued. "All the girls over sixteen have moved out. All that's left are schoolgirls and their mothers. The age ranges in between have been wiped out."

"Completely wiped out," I said, got up, put the cutlery on the plate, took them in one hand and the glass in the other and went to the kitchen. "But you make it sound as though they've been hunted to destruction or something."

"They have been! If they'd stayed here, we could have hunted them. But where they are, there are others chasing after them."

I put the plate and glass on the counter and went into the bedroom to get my swimming gear.

"Now I finally understand what's meant by the term 'happy hunting grounds,'" I said. "I've never understood what was supposed to be so fantastic about it. Running around in the forest until eternity. But obviously it was meant in a figurative sense."

"I don't know how fantastic it is," Nils Erik said in a loud voice so that I could hear him. "It's a lot of work and there's little to show for it at the end. At least for me. Much, much better to be in a relationship."

I put my trunks and a towel into a plastic bag, considered whether I needed anything else, no, that should do it.

"When was the last time you were in a relationship?" I said.

"Three years ago," he said, and moved toward the door when he saw me emerge with the bag in my hand.

"What about one of the other temporary teachers?" I said. He was bending down and tying his laces, and straightened up a touch redder in the face.

"If they'd be up for it, fine by me," he said.

We walked up the steep hill in silence, walking was as much as we could manage in the gale. Snow stung against the skin I hadn't covered. When we closed the school door behind us it was like leaving the top deck of a large ship and going inside. Nils Erik switched on the light, we bounded down the stairs in long strides, sat on opposite sides of the dressing room, and changed. Although the wind made the walls creak and the ventilation howl, it still seemed quiet indoors. Perhaps because of the lack of movement? All the rooms were empty, the pool was empty and smooth and still.

The smell of chlorine cast a spell over me. Childhood memories of when we used to go swimming every week in Stintahallen came flooding back: the conical bags of candy we bought at the little shop, the taste of the boiled sweets shaped like nuts and bolts, green and black, licorice and mint. The light displays around the pool, which were supposed to represent tropical waterfalls. The white bathing cap with the Norwegian flag on the side, the dark blue goggles.

I pulled on my trunks and went into the small swimming hall, the tiles were cold and rough on the soles of my feet, the snow eddied round in the light of the lamp outside, behind it the great black void.

The surface of the water was dark with a faint shimmer of blue from the bottom of the pool and as shiny as a mirror. Almost a shame to break it, I thought. I definitely wasn't going to dive in. No, instead I would climb down the metal ladder and try to make as few ripples as possible. All in vain, for along came Nils Erik: he ran to the edge and threw himself into the water with a splash. Swam underwater to the far side, where he broke the surface with a snort and a toss of the head.

"Wonderful!" he shouted. "What's up with you, you wimp?"

"Me, nothing!" I shouted back.

"You're getting into the water like an old woman!"

Suddenly I remembered how I had once tricked Dag Lothar. I had got into the pool a few minutes before him, turned my bathing cap inside out so that it was all white, pulled it away from my head so that it was wrinkled and looked like the caps old ladies wore, and started to swim in a studiously slow style with my head as far out of the water as I could manage. This mimicking of an old lady swimming was so good that Dag Lothar didn't see me, even though there were only four of us in the big pool. He glanced at me, categorized me wrongly, and thus I didn't exist. He called my name and when he received no answer went back into the changing room.

Chest first, I moved slowly out into the water, ducked my head beneath the surface and took a couple of powerful strokes that were almost enough for me to glide to the far edge. Nils Erik was plowing along on the other side, doing free-style. I swam as fast as I could for a few lengths, then stopped at the end by the window and gazed out into the snowstorm.

I turned, rested my elbows on the edge, and watched the white foam spraying up around Nils Erik's thrashing arms and legs, and was reminded of what Geir's father had once said, that you should lie as if on cotton when you swim the crawl, and behind Nils Erik I saw the open door to the empty rooms beyond.

Shit, I had forgotten. The sauna.

I dragged myself out of the water, went to the changing room, and switched on the stove. When I went back I dived in and swam back and forth for perhaps half an hour until we decided to give up.

We sat on the top bench in the sauna. I poured water on the stones in the stove, a wave of hot steam met my skin and drifted farther into the small, cube-shaped room.

"This is the biggest fringe benefit we get with the job," Nils Erik said, stroking the wet hair at the back of his head.

"It's also the only one," I said.

"Free coffee," he said. "And newspapers. And cake at the farewell party."

"Hurrah," I said.

There was a pause. He moved down to a lower bench.

"Have you had lots of other jobs?" I said at length, leaning back against the wall. The heat was making my head heavy, as though it was slowly being filled with lead or something similar.

"No. Just the health service. Oh, and the parks a couple of summers ago. And you?"

"Gardening, floor factory, newspaper, nuthouse. And radio. But it wasn't paid, so I suppose that doesn't count."

"No," he said lethargically. I looked at him. He had closed his eyes and was leaning back with his elbows on the step where I was sitting. There was an energy and vivacity about his personality that seemed to conflict with something else, an old-man-ish quality that was hard to define because it didn't manifest itself in anything specific, it was more an aura he had, I only noticed it in a negative way, when for example I was taken aback that he had heard of the Jesus and Mary Chain and liked them, because why in the world would he not have heard of them?

He sat up straight and turned to me.

"Karl Ove," he said. "Just had a thought. You know Hilda's cottage?"

"Hilda's cottage? What's that?"

"The yellow house on the bend. It used to belong to Hilda, Eva's mother-in-law. She died a few years ago, and now the house is empty. I've had a chat with them, and they'd be happy to rent it out. After all, it'll fall into disrepair faster if no one's living there. So they don't want much rent. Five hundred a month, that's all."

"And?" I said.

"Living in a whole house on my own is no good. I wondered perhaps if we could rent it? We'd save loads of money on accommodation, and food would be cheaper if there were two of us. What do you think?"

"Ye-es," I said. "Why not?"

"We can have a room each and share the rest."

"But everyone will think we're a couple of gay guys," I said. "Two young teachers have found each other, they'll say."

He laughed. "And here we are in the sauna all alone . . ."

"So the rumors have already started?"

"No, are you out of your mind? You've shown an unequivocal interest in the opposite sex up here. No one is in any doubt about your preferences. Well, are you in or out?"

"Yes. I mean no. I have to write and for that I need to be alone."

"There's a room next to the sitting room. You can have that. It's perfect."

"OK, why not then," I said.

After we had gotten dressed and were on our way upstairs, I asked him about something that had been occupying my mind for a long time but that my nakedness had prevented me from articulating.

"I've got a little problem in the area we touched on the other day," I said.

"What was that?" he said.

"About sex," I said.

"Come on. Out with it!" he said.

"It's not easy to talk about," I said. "But the thing is . . . well, I come too quickly. Put bluntly. That's the long and short of it."

"Ah, a classic," he said. "And?"

"No, there's nothing else. I was just wondering if you had any tips. When it happens it doesn't feel great, but I'm sure you understand."

"How quickly are we talking about here? A minute? Three minutes? Five?"

"Hm, it varies," I said, inserting the key into the lock of the large glass door and pushing it open. My skin was so hot after the sauna that the cold wind didn't bite, I watched it sweep between the buildings but barely noticed it. "Maybe three or four?"

"That's not bad, you know, Karl Ove," he said, winding his scarf around his neck, pulling his hat well down over his ears. "Four minutes, that's a pretty long time."

"How do you manage in this area?"

"Me? The opposite. I can hump away till eternity and nothing happens. In fact, that's a problem too. I can be at it for half an hour without getting near an orgasm. Sometimes I just have to give up."

We set off down the road.

"And when you beat the meat?" he said. "Is it the same?"

My cheeks went red, but he couldn't see that in the dark. He wasn't expecting a lie, so I was on safe ground.

"About the same," I said.

"Mhm," he said. "I've got problems there too. Well, you may have realized that today. I can keep at it forever."

"Do you think it's physiological?" I said. "Or is it a mental thing? I wish I could swap. The opposite problem would be a thousand times better."

"No idea," he said. "Probably physiological. I've always been like this anyway. Ever since the first time. So I don't know anything else. But I've heard it's supposed to help if you pinch the tip. Hard. Or pull at the scrotum. Then just keep pumping."

"I'll try that next time," I said, and smiled into the darkness.

"Yes, should an opportunity ever present itself," he said.

"At Christmas, for example? All the young women from the district will be back then."

"Do you reckon they'll be coming back here to get laid? I doubt it. I think they're getting it where they are now and they come back here for some R & R, ready to go again in January."

"Yes, you're probably right," I said, and came to a halt, we had reached the road to my flat. "If everything goes through with the house, when do we move in?"

"We have to give notice first and all that. After Christmas? If we shorten our holiday by a couple of days, we could do it then."

"Sounds good," I said. "See you!"

I raised my hand and waved, opened the door, and went in. Ate eight slices of bread and drank half a liter of milk, lay down on the sofa, and read the first pages of a new book I'd bought: *The Great Fairy Tale* by Jan Kjærstad. I had read *Mirrors* and *Homo Falsus* by him before and had just borrowed *The Earth Turns Quietly* from the library in Finnsnes. But this one was new, it had just been published, and the first thing I did when I held it in my hand was smell the fresh paper. Then I flipped backward and forward. Every chapter started with a big O. Some of the chapters were set in several columns – one column looked like notes and popped up here and there alongside another, which was the main story. Some chapters were letters. Some were printed in bold type, some in italics, some in normal font. Something called Hazar and something called Enigma cropped up at regular intervals. And definitions of k – that had to stand for *kjærlighet*, love.

I started reading the first page.

She was very young. Neck as fresh as dew. They stood a meter apart, in their own worlds. He had felt the tension, even with his back to her, he turned and stole a glance. An enormous kick. Made a few feints with his leg. She noticed, smiled. Sparks between kohl and mascara. She thrust her right shoulder in his direction, twice, a different beat, bit her lower lip, lowered her gaze. The percussion and bass set off a funky groove in his sensory receptors. Contrary to nature to stand still. He took a few steps on the carpet, toward her, away from her, inviting, teasing. She mimicked his steps, same rhythm, tiger wrinkles by her nose. Black curly hair, kerchief wound around her forehead, brazen makeup. What was she listening to? Cramps? Split Beaver? ViViVox? Kimono jacket with leaf pattern, baggy silk trousers, sandals with toe strap. Breathtaking. And around her: the covers' flickering kaleidoscope of figures, forms, and fancy calligraphy.

I read it over and over again. The style was so alien, and yet so cool with the short incomplete sentences, all the alliteration and the sprinkling of English words. And the foreign words. Kimono – that was Japanese. Tiger wrinkles – that was Indian and animalistic. Kohl – that sounded German, was it? Within the space of a few lines a whole world was opened up to me. And it was a different world, it had something futuristic about it, which attracted me. But I couldn't write like that, even if I wanted to, it would be impossible. When I read *Vinduet*, which Kjærstad edited, I knew as good as none of the names and the featured titles and only a few of the terms used. *About Burning the Aeneid*, one article was called, for some reason it rumbled around in my head, cropping up here, there, and everywhere, although I had no idea what an Aeneid was. All this was postmodernism, Kjærstad was the greatest Norwegian postmodernist writer, and although I liked it, or the whole world that I suspected lay behind what stood in the text, I didn't know what it was or where it actually existed. Toe strap, *tårem* in Norwegian, was there some echo there with *harem* and the Orient? Kjærstad's books were full of the Orient, a *Thousand and One Nights* atmosphere, narratives within narratives, and I imagined part of what he was doing was drawing that world into ours, along with a host of other worlds. What it meant, I had no idea, but intuitively I liked it, in the same way that intuitively I disliked Milan Kundera. Kundera was also a postmodernist writer, but he completely lacked this embracing of other worlds, with him the world was always the same, it was Prague and Czechoslovakia and the Soviets, who had either invaded or were on the verge of doing so, and that was fine, but he kept withdrawing his characters from the plot, intervening and going on about something or

other while the characters stood still, sort of waiting, by the window or wherever it was they happened to be, until he had finished his explanation and
they could move forward. Then you saw that the plot was only "a plot" and
that the characters were only "characters," something he had invented, you
knew they didn't exist, and so why should you read about them? Kundera's
polar opposite was Hamsun, no one went as far into his characters' worlds
as he did, and that was what I preferred, at least in a comparison of these
two, the physicality and the realism of *Hunger*, for example. There the world
had weight, there even the thoughts were captured, while with Kundera the
thoughts elevated themselves above the world and did as they liked with it.
Another difference I had noticed was that European novels often had only
one plot, everything followed one track, while South American novels had a
multiplicity of tracks and sidetracks, indeed, compared with European novels, they almost exploded with plots. One of my favorites was *One Hundred
Years of Solitude* by García Márquez, but I also loved *Love in the Time of Cholera*.
Kjærstad had a little of the same, but in a European way, and there was also
something of Kundera in him. I thought so anyway.

What about my own writing?

Writing in a postmodernist style like Kjærstad was way beyond my reach,
I couldn't do it even if I wanted to, I didn't have it in me. I had only one
world, so that was the one I had to write about. At least for the time being.
But I tried to include the exuberance that García Márquez possessed. The
multiplicity of stories too. And Hamsun's being present in the moment.

I read on. I had seen in the reviews that in this novel Oslo was situated
somewhere in the southern hemisphere. That was a fantastic idea, it meant
Oslo became everything it wasn't in reality. But the way this world was
evoked was more important. There was something Márquezian about the
exuberance and the density and the multiplicity in this passage.

I laid aside the book and went to the desk, sat down and started to flip
through the little pile of texts I had written. It was so thin! So unbelievably
thin! I only included the bare essentials – the forest, the road, the house – I
let everything else go. But what if I let all the rest explode?

I took a fresh piece of paper and wound it into the typewriter, glanced at my reflection in the window as the typewriter carriage buzzed into position.

Where was there a subject with more breadth and depth and an abundance of detail?

I imagined the road outside the house in Tybakken.

I went onto the road. It was black and beside it the green spruce trees swayed in the wind. A car drove past. It was a BMW. On the pavement Erling and Harald stood by their bikes. Erling had an Apache, Harald a DBS. Behind them the hill was lined with houses. In the gardens there were chairs and tables, kennels, barbecues, tricycles, small plastic pools, hoses, and an abandoned rake. In the sky above, a plane flew past, so far up that only the white vapor trail was visible.

I tore the sheet out of the roller, crumpled it up, and threw it on the floor. Inserted another. Stared straight ahead for a while. Two years ago I had visited Yngve and Mom in Bergen. The fish market there had swarmed with life: people, stalls, fishermen, and crabs, cars and boats, flags and pennants, birds and water and mountains and houses. That would be a perfect place to get the density!

I started writing again.

The fish were lined up side by side on a bed of ice. They glistened in the sunlight. Women with money to spend and bulging bags walked back and forth between the stalls. A little boy was holding a balloon in one hand and clasping the stroller his mother was pushing with the other. Suddenly he let go and ran over to the tank full of cod. "Look, Mom," he shouted. An old man in a black suit and hat was staggering along, supporting himself on a stick. A fat woman in a coat was examining some mackerel. A sparkling jewel hung from her neck. The two assistants had fish blood smeared over their white aprons. One was laughing at something the other had said. On the road behind them cars raced by. A girl with dark shoulder-length hair, a white T-shirt, her breasts visible beneath, and a blue Levi's 501-clad bottom stood gazing across the harbor. I glanced at her as I hurried past. She looked at me and smiled. I thought how wonderful it would be to fuck her.

I leaned back, took out my watch, it was already a few minutes to nine. I was content, that was a good start, he could meet her again later, anything could happen then. I switched off the typewriter, put a pan of water on the stove, sprinkled some tea leaves into the bottom of the teapot, and suddenly realized that this was the first time I had written without any music in the background. While waiting for the water to boil, I reread the passage. The sentences should be broken up a bit and made more abrupt. There should be something about the various smells and the sounds. Maybe even more detail. And some alliteration.

I switched on the typewriter again, took out the sheet, and inserted another.

The fish were lined up side by side on a bed of ice, everything glinted and glistened in the sunlight. The air smelled of salt, exhaust fumes, and perfume. Voluminous women with bulging bags and money to spend walked back and forth between the respective stalls, pointing authoritatively at what they wanted. Prawns, crabs, lobsters, mackerel, pollock, cod, haddock, eels, and plaice. The sounds of mumbling and laughing filled the air. Some children were shouting. A bus let out a deep sigh as it stopped at the bus stop across the street. The pennants along the quay were flapping in the wind. Flap! Flap! Flap! A little boy, pallid and puny, was holding a Winnie-the-Pooh balloon in one hand and clutching the stroller his mother was pushing with the other.

The steam from the boiling pan wafted in through the door. I switched off the typewriter again, poured the water over the tea leaves, took the teapot with a cup, a carton of milk, and a bowl of sugar into the sitting room, sat down, rolled a cigarette, and with it hanging from my lips continued to read *The Great Fairy Tale*, this time without an eye for the detail or a thought about the style, within a few minutes I was totally absorbed. So when the doorbell shrieked through the flat a little later there was something brutal about the way it jerked me back into reality.

It was Hege.

"Hi," she said, pulling the scarf down from her mouth. "You haven't gone to bed?"

"Gone to bed? No. It's only half past nine."

"It's ten actually," she said. "Can I come in?"

"Of course, sorry," I said. "Has something happened or what?"

She came into the hall, unwound the huge scarf, unzipped her down jacket.

"No, but that's the problem. Nothing is happening. Vidar's at sea and I was hanging around getting bored. And then I thought you were probably up."

"Good timing," I said. "I've even got some tea going."

We went into the living room, she sat down on the sofa, picked up the book and looked at the title.

"It's Kjærstad's latest," I said. "Have you read it?"

"Me? No. You're talking to an illiterate. Am I going to get some tea or was that just polite conversation?"

I got a cup, placed it in front of her, and sat down in the chair on the opposite side of the table. She tucked her legs beneath her and poured.

She was thin, long-limbed, with an almost boyish body. Her facial features were pronounced, long nose, full lips, hair big and curly. There was a hardness about her, but in her eyes, which were vivacious and sparkling, often something else would appear, something softer and warmer. She was sharp, had a ready answer for everything, and treated the fishermen around her with a characteristic unflinching aloofness.

I liked her a lot, but I wasn't attracted to her at all, and that was what I realized allowed us to be friends. If I had been attracted to her I would have been sitting there paralyzed, thinking about what I should say and the impression I was making. Since I wasn't, I could be who I was, without a further thought, just chat away. The same applied to her. And as was so often the case when I talked to girls I liked but wasn't attracted to, the conversations tended toward emotional, intimate matters.

"Anything new?" she said.

I shook my head.

"Not really. Oh yes, Nils Erik has suggested we move into the yellow house on the bend."

"And what did you say?"

"I thought it was a good idea. So we're going to move after Christmas."

"I can't imagine two more different men than you and Nils Erik," she said.

"I'm a man now all of a sudden?"

She looked at me and laughed. "Aren't you?"

"I don't feel like one."

"What do you feel like then?"

"A boy. An eighteen-year-old."

"Yes, I can understand that. You aren't a man like the others here in the village."

"What do you mean?"

"Have you ever had a look at your arms? They're as thin as mine! You can't say you're broad-shouldered either."

"So?" I said. "I'm not a fisherman."

"Oh, moody now, huh?"

"No."

"No," she said with the same intonation and laughed. "You're right though. All you have to do is sit still and write for the rest of your life. You don't need big muscles to do that."

"No, you don't," I said.

"Come on, Karl Ove," she said. "You don't take yourself that seriously, do you?"

"It's got nothing to do with how seriously I take myself," I said. "What you say is true. I'm very different from Vidar, for example. But that doesn't mean you can walk all over me."

"Oooh, I obviously touched a sore spot there!"

"Give it up now."

"Oh dear!"

"Do you want me to throw you out?"

I raised my cup in a threatening manner.

She laughed again.

I leaned back, took my tobacco pouch, and started to roll a cigarette.

"I know you want men to be men," I said. "In fact, you've said that many times. The strong silent type. But what does Vidar do to get on your nerves? What do you usually complain about? He never says anything, he never talks about himself or the two of you, there isn't a scrap of romanticism in him."

She eyed me. "Is there anything more romantic than being fucked hard by a strong man?"

I could feel my cheeks glowing, made a grab for the lighter and lit the rollie.

Then I laughed.

"Actually, I don't know anything about that. I can't even imagine what it's like."

"Have you never fucked a girl hard?"

I sensed she was watching me and our eyes met.

"Yes, yes, of course," I said, averting my gaze. "I was thinking the other way round. Of your role in all of this."

I got up and went over to my record collection.

"Any requests?" I said, turning to her.

"You choose," she said. "I have to go soon anyway."

I put on the latest deLillos record: *Før var det morsomt med sne*.

"The biggest argument in favor of moving is that I won't have to listen to the two upstairs any longer," I said, and pointed to the ceiling.

"Torill and Georg?"

I nodded.

"The walls are incredibly thin here. Especially between bedrooms. And there's lots of romanticism, to use your definition of the term."

"How nice for Torill."

"And him by the sound of it."

I sat down again. "You don't like Torill much, do you?" I said.

"No, I can't say I do."

A false smile slid across her mouth, she raised her face and chirruped some words. "She's so good and sincere it hurts to watch and at the same time she offers herself to everyone who wants to look."

"Offers herself?"

"Yes, you don't think she walks around like that when she's on her own, do you?"

She pushed out her bosom, wiggled her hips on the sofa, and coquettishly stroked her hair from her forehead.

I smiled.

"It had never struck me," I said. "But now that you say that I believe it has struck Nils Erik. And pretty hard. He hurried into the john immediately after she had bent forward in front of the fridge today."

"You see. She knows what she's doing. And you?"

"Torill?" I said with a snort. "She's twelve years older than me."

"Yes, of course, but do you like her?"

"I don't dislike her. She's pleasant enough."

There was a pause. The windows reflected the light from the lamps and between them the vague outlines of the furniture in a room that seemed to be underwater.

"Do you have any plans for this Friday?" Hege said.

"No," I said. "Not as far as I know."

"I was thinking of inviting some of the temps over. Making a pizza and drinking some beer. Are you up for it?"

"Of course."

She got up.

"Time to wend my way home. Sleep tight, you writer wuss."

"If you're not careful, I'll start calling you names," I said.

"I'm a woman, you know. That's not done. For you I'm Frøken or Hege. And you're overwatering your flowers. You're drowning them."

"Is that what's wrong? I thought it was imperative they shouldn't get too dry."

"No, it's almost always the opposite. Poor flowers. They've ended up with a murderer. The worst kind, in fact, one who doesn't know he's a murderer."

"Well, actually I am sorry when they die," I said.

"What about fish?" she said.

"What about them?"

"Are you sorry when they die too?"

"Yes, I am. I hate it when they're pulled up from the sea, wriggling and squirming, and I have to kill them."

She laughed.

"I don't think I've ever heard that said here before. I can't imagine it. It must be the very first time."

"There's one fisherman who's been seasick all his life," I said. "That's almost the same."

"No, it isn't," she said. "But now I do have to go."

I followed her into the hall.

"OK, Frøken, I wish you goodnight," I said. I stood waiting in silence while she put on her outdoor gear. Smiled when she had finished. Only her nose was protruding from between her scarf and hat. She said good-bye and went out into the darkness.

The next morning I had the third and fourth graders for the first two lessons. I got up ten minutes before the bell was due to ring, threw on my clothes, and dashed up the hill under a sky that was as black and wild as it had been when Hege left ten hours earlier.

When the children ambled across the floor in their stockinged feet, wearing their sweaters, with their hair rumpled after removing their woolen hats, eyes narrow, I saw them as they were, tiny and vulnerable. It was barely comprehensible that I could on occasion get so irritated and angry with some of them. But there was something in them that rose and sank during the day, a vortex of shouting and screaming, pestering and fighting, games and excitement, which meant that I no longer saw them as small people, only whatever was coursing through their veins.

Sitting in his chair, Jo raised his hand.

"What is it, Jo?" I said.

He smiled. "What are we going to do in the first lesson?"

"You'll have to wait and see," I said.

"Are you going to read to us at the end of the second lesson, like you usually do?"

"All things come to those who wait. Have you heard that saying?"

He nodded.

"Well, there you have it."

The door at the end of the building kept opening and shutting as pupils trickled in. Every time it did, I automatically looked up and across. To the right of the door was the part of the block my class used. Nils Erik was teaching them, he sat behind the desk staring into the air waiting for them to quiet down.

In came Reidar and Andrea. They were brother and sister, they walked to school together, arrived late together, what was so touching about that?

Reidar set off at a run across the floor, must have remembered they weren't allowed to run, then stopped with a jolt and looked at me, and walked quickly to his place. From the other side Andrea watched us. I met her stare. She immediately turned her head away, to where the seventh grade was, and she joined them a moment later.

This little interlude ought to have been perfectly natural, but it wasn't, there was a woodenness about Andrea's movements, as though she was forcing herself to perform them.

"Hi, Karl Ove," Reidar said with a smile. He used my name as a kind of buffer, to make a reprimand for lateness harder because of the friendly interaction. He was a crafty little devil.

"Hi, Reidar," I said. "Sit down. You've held up the whole class now."

Andrea was in love with me.

Of course.

That explained her behavior. All the looks, all the evasiveness, all the blushes.

A warm feeling spread through me. I got up and went to the board.

"What does it mean to have a profession?" I said. "What is a profession?" Poor little girl.

"A job," Reidar said.

"Put your hand up if you know," I said.

He put up his hand. Fortunately some others did too. I pointed to Lovisa.

"It means having a job," she said.

"That's what I said!" Reidar said.

"Could you give me some examples of professions, Lovisa?" I said.

She nodded. "Fisherman."

"Good," I said, and wrote it down. "Any others?"

"Working in the fish hall?"

"Yes! Any more professions? Hands up!"

Suggestions poured in. Bus driver, truck driver, shop assistant, ship's captain, cleaner, policeman, fireman. Of course "teacher" never occurred to them, even though one was standing right in front of them. For them it wasn't a real job. Chatting with children day in, day out.

"What about me?" I said eventually. "Don't I have a profession?"

"You're a teacher! Teacher! Teacher! Teacher!" they called out.

"And if you're sick?"

"Nurse! Doctor! Ambulance driver!"

When the board was full I asked them to write down the job they would like to have, say why, describe what it involved, and draw a picture. While they were doing that I walked around monitoring, talking to them individually and standing by the window with my hands on my hips staring into the darkness. The thought that she was in love with me was touching, both heartening and sad.

I went up to the desk, we began to go through what they had written and we covered a little more than half before the bell rang. In the following lesson we continued where we had left off, changed to reading from the textbook, they answered the questions in it, and then in the last twenty minutes I read an excerpt from *One Thousand and One Nights*. When I took out the book and started reading they left their chairs and sat in a semicircle on the carpet in front of me, they always did that, it must have been what they were used to from the first or second grade, and I liked it, I felt as if I was giving them something warm and secure. Or rather that they turned a normal situation into something warm and secure. Blank-eyed, they sat listening to the oriental tales, somehow turned in on themselves, as though they were sitting before the fount of their soul, in the midst of the desert of their minds, and saw all the camels, all the silk, all the flying carpets, all the spirits and robbers, mosques and bazaars, all the burning love and sudden death, the billowing mirages across the empty blue sky of consciousness. To them it made no difference that a world more different from theirs, from where they sat on the edge of the world in complete darkness and freezing temperatures, could hardly be imagined; the story took place in their minds, where everything was possible, where everything was permitted.

In the lesson afterward I had the fifth, sixth, and seventh graders for Norwegian.

"OK, let's get cracking," I said as I entered. "Sit down and take out your books!"

"Are you in a bad mood today?" Hildegunn said.

"Don't you try any red herrings," I said. "Come on, books out. We're going to do a bit of group work today. By which I mean you're going to work in pairs. Hildegunn and Andrea, put your desks together. Jørn and Live. Kai Roald and Vivian. Come on. Do you always have to dillydally?"

They placed their desks together in the way I had explained. Apart from Kai Roald. He sat with his elbows on his desk and his cheeks in his hands.

"You too, Kai Roald," I said. "Move your desk next to Vivian's. You'll be working together."

He looked up at me and shook his head. Stared into space again.

"There's no choice," I said. "You have to. Come on now."

"I'm not doing it," he said.

I went over to him.

"Didn't you hear what I said? Come on now, move your desk over."

"I don't want to," he said. "I'm not doing it."

"Why not?" I said.

The others, who had finished their maneuvers, sat watching us.

"I don't want to," he said.

"Shall I do it for you?" I said.

He shook his head. "Didn't you hear what I said? I'm not doing it."

"But you HAVE TO," I said.

He shook his head.

I grabbed the desk on both sides and lifted it. He pressed his forearms down on the top with all his might. I pulled harder, he grabbed it with his hands and held on, red-faced now. My heart was beating faster.

"Now you do as I say!" I said.

"No!" he said.

I snatched at the desk and took it from his grasp, carried it over to Vivian and put it down. He didn't move from his chair.

"I'm not budging," he said.

I held his arm, he wrenched it away.

"Now you go and sit over there!" I said in a loud voice. "Do you want me to carry you? Is that what you want?"

From the corner of my eye I sensed Hege watching us from the other side of the room.

He didn't answer.

I went behind him and grabbed the seat of his chair, intending to lift it with him in it. He stood up, went behind his desk and grasped it with both hands, presumably to move it back.

"Put the desk down!" I said.

His face was scarlet, his eyes rigid and inaccessible. When he started moving the desk I seized it and tore it out of his hands.

"You horse prick!" he shouted.

I put down the desk. Anger throbbed in my veins. My eyes were white with fury.

I took a deep breath to calm myself down, but it didn't help, my entire body was shaking.

"You can go home," I said. "I don't want to see you here any more today."

"What?" he said.

"Go," I said.

He suddenly fought back tears and looked down. "But I haven't done anything," he said.

"Go," I said. "I don't want to see you. Come on. Out. Out."

He lifted his head, sent me a wild, defiant glare, slowly turned and left.

"All right, let's get going," I said with as much composure as I could muster. "Open the exercise book to page forty-six."

They did as I said. Outside the windows Kai Roald walked past, swinging his arms, apparently unconcerned, staring ahead. I explained to them what they had to do. Glanced out the window, he was walking beneath the light from the last lamp on the school premises, neck bent, head down. But I had behaved correctly, no one should be allowed to call a teacher a horse prick and go unpunished.

I sat down behind the desk. For the rest of the class I was completely out of myself, concerned only that the pupils shouldn't notice anything.

In the staff room Hege came over and asked what the scuffle had been about. I shrugged and said I'd had a difference of opinion with Kai Roald and he had called me a horse prick.

"So I sent him home for the rest of the day. Unbelievable . . ."

"Things are different up here, you know," she said. "Swearing's nowhere near as serious."

"It is for me," I said. "And I'm the homeroom teacher."

"Yeah, yeah," she said.

I went over and got a cup of coffee, sat down on my chair, leafed through a book. Then, in a flash, it came to me.

He didn't want to sit next to Vivian because he was in love with her.

This sudden insight made me flush with embarrassment. Oh, what an idiot I had been! How stupid could you be? Sending a pupil home was serious, he would have to explain himself, and his parents wouldn't believe it was the teacher's fault. But it was.

I liked Kai Roald.

So he was in love, that was all!

But it was too late, I couldn't undo anything now.

I went back into the staff room, picked up the newspaper from the table, sat down, and started reading. At the end of the small vestibule the door opened. It was Richard. He spotted me.

"Karl Ove," he said, and beckoned. "Can I have a word with you? Why don't we go to my office?" he said.

I followed him in silence. He closed the door behind us and turned to me.

"Kai Roald's mother just called," he said. "She said he'd been sent home. What happened?"

"He refused to do what I asked him to do," I said. "We had a little altercation. He called me a horse prick, and so I told him to leave. That's where I draw the line."

Richard studied me for a while. Then he lowered himself onto the chair behind his broad desk.

"Sending someone home is a serious measure," he said. "It's the most severe punishment we have. A lot has to happen before we do that. But you know that. Kai Roald is a fine fellow. Do we agree on that?"

"Yes, no question. But that isn't what this is about."

"Hang on a moment. This is Northern Norway. It's a bit rougher up here than down south. We don't take swearing seriously, for example. Calling you what he called you isn't good, but nor is it as serious a crime as you seem to believe. The boy's got a temper. Surely he's allowed to have that?"

"I will not put up with being called a horse prick by a pupil. Regardless of where in the world it happens," I said.

"No, no, of course not," he said. "I appreciate that. But there are always

ways of resolving conflict. There has to be a bit of give and take. Sending a pupil home is absolutely the last resort. I have a feeling that your disagreement hadn't really got that far. Am I right?"

I didn't answer.

"You haven't been a teacher for long, Karl Ove," he said. "And even the most experienced of us make the wrong calls on a regular basis. But next time, if you can't resolve a situation yourself, come and get me. Or bring the pupil to see me."

In your dreams.

"I'll consider that if it happens again," I said.

"It will happen again," he said. "You'll have to sort this one out anyway. You'd better ring Kai Roald's mother and explain why he was sent home."

"Isn't it enough if I give him a message tomorrow?" I said.

"She rang here and was very worried. So I think it would be best if you spoke to her."

"OK," I said. "Then I will."

He held out an open palm to indicate the gray telephone on his desk. "You can use this one."

"But the bell's about to ring," I said. "I'll do it in the next break."

"I'll take your lesson for the first few minutes. Who do you have?"

"Fifth, sixth, and seventh graders."

He nodded, got up, and stood beside his desk.

Was he going to stand there while I made the call? Was he going to listen to the conversation? Was he a total control freak?

I looked up the number in the phone book, found it, and glanced at Richard, who didn't bat an eyelid.

What a sack of shit he was.

I dialed the number.

"Hello," said a woman's voice.

"Oh, hello, this is Karl Ove Knausgaard, Kai Roald's homeroom teacher."

"Oh, hi," she said.

"Kai Roald and I had a disagreement this morning. He refused to do what

I asked him to do and then he called me – well, he swore at me to my face. So I sent him home."

"I see," she said. "Kai Roald can sometimes be a bit unruly."

"Yes, he can," I said. "But he's a good kid. It wasn't that serious and there won't be any consequences for him. He had to be taught a lesson though. Tomorrow everything will be back to normal. Is that all right?"

"Yes. Thank you for your call."

"No problem. Good-bye."

"Good-bye."

The moment I put down the phone the bell rang. Richard nodded to me, I left his office without a word and went straight to the teaching block, where I would have math with the fifth, sixth, and seventh graders. This was my weakest subject, I had nothing to say about it, there was nothing there that I could develop or make interesting, they did the problems in their exercise books and every now and then we went through new material on the board. They knew this and seemed to try even harder at the beginning of class to distract me.

"Who were you calling?" Vivian said after they had sat down.

"How do you know I called anyone?" I said.

"We saw you through the window," Andrea said. "You used the head teacher's phone."

"Did you call Kai Roald's parents?" Hildegunn said.

"Is he coming back today?" Vivian said.

"It's none of your business who I call, as you know," I said. "The fact is if you don't quiet down soon, I'll phone *your* parents."

"But they're at work," Vivian said.

"Vivian!" I said.

"Yes?" she said.

"That's enough now. Come on, get to work! That means you too, Jørn."

Andrea had stretched her legs out under the desk and was rubbing her feet against each other while reading through the passage in the book with a pencil in her hand. Live was looking around as she always did when she was stuck and didn't want to show it. I watched Jørn doing the mental calculations at breakneck speed with his tongue sticking out of the corner of his mouth. Then I met Live's gaze and she raised her hand.

I leaned over her desk.

"I can't do this one," she said.

She pointed to a problem with her pencil. Her eyes darted back and forth behind her glasses. I explained it to her, she sighed and groaned, which was her way of playing down her ignorance in front of friends.

"Are you with me?" I said.

"Yes, I am," she said, and waved me away.

"Teacher." Vivian giggled. "Teacher, I can't do this one, teacher!"

When I leaned over her it was as if she was completely at sea. Her face was blank and expressionless, her eyes were blank and expressionless. The receptivity I sensed in her was a little eerie.

"Why have you gotten stuck on this one?" I said. "You've cracked fifteen of them in exactly the same way before!"

She rolled her shoulders.

"Give it another try," I said. "Look at the other ones. If you still can't do it, I'll come and help. OK?"

"OK, teacher," she said, glancing around with a giggle.

As I straightened up, I looked straight into Andrea's eyes.

There was a longing in them, and my cheeks burned.

"Everything OK?" I said.

"Not really," she said. "I need some help."

My heart beat faster as I stopped beside her. Oh, it was ridiculous, but the awareness that she might be in love with me made it suddenly impossible to behave normally.

I leaned over and she seemed to shrink back. Her breathing changed. Her eyes were locked on to the book. I could smell the fragrance of her shampoo, I studiously avoided any form of contact, placed my finger on the first number she had written. She stroked her hair to the side, rested one elbow on the table. It was as if everything we did had become conscious: every detail became visible, it was no longer unthinking and natural but considered and artificial.

"There's the slip," I said. "Can you see it?"

She blushed, said yes in a soft voice, pointed to the next problem, what about this one, said yes again after a few seconds in a soft, low voice, and her breathing was shaky.

I stood up and walked on, surveyed the whole class and the whole teaching area, but I had not been left unmoved, the tiny moment lived on, and to release myself from it I collected all the books on the desk, piled them high with a bang, and addressed the whole class. The moment had to be destroyed by a new, a greater moment. And I had to make the class a place for everyone, a unit, a class that would learn.

"It looks as if some of you are having the same problem," I said. "Let's go through it on the board. Fifth and sixth graders, close your ears."

Once it was done, the lesson proceeded as before. Even before I realized that Andrea had feelings for me, I had been careful to keep my distance from them. I never put my arm around them, indeed I never touched them at all, and if the conversation or jokes went too far, into vaguely sexual areas, I always stopped them. The other teachers didn't need to do this, for them distance was a fact of life that nothing could break. For me it was something I had to create.

In the afternoon, I called Dad. His voice was somber and cold and sober. He asked me how things were, I said fine but I was looking forward to Christmas vacation.

"Are you going to celebrate Christmas with your mother?" he said.

"Yes," I said.

"We thought you would. Fredrik isn't coming either. So we're off down south again this year. You've got a sister here, Karl Ove. Don't forget that."

Did he really think I would fall for that? If I had said I wanted to celebrate

Christmas with them, they would have come up with a thousand and one excuses. He didn't want me there. So why pretend that we were letting him down?

"But I could maybe come up during the winter break," I said. "Is that convenient? You won't be heading for the sun?"

"We haven't planned that far ahead," he said. "We'll have to see when the time comes."

"I could catch the express boat or something," I said.

"Yes, that's a possibility. Have you heard from Yngve recently?"

"No, it's been a while ago now," I said. "I think he's very busy."

Throughout the short telephone conversation it was as if he was trying to find a way out. We hung up after about two minutes. I was glad it was like this. Whenever it happened I became aware that he wasn't someone I needed.

Wasn't it like this with everyone?

Walking downhill, with the snow arrowing in off the black sea, I wondered whether there was anyone I needed. Whether there was anyone I couldn't manage without.

If so, it had to be Mom and Yngve.

But they weren't indispensable either, were they?

I tried to imagine what it would have been like if they didn't exist.

Roughly like now, minus the phone calls and the get-togethers at Christmas and over the summer.

Weren't they indispensable?

But when I made my breakthrough as a writer, Mom would have to be there.

I kicked away the snow in front of the door and went in. And maybe if I had children?

But I wasn't going to. It was unthinkable.

And, the way things were going, unfeasible anyway.

I smiled to myself as I removed my jacket. Then I was depressed. Everything connected with it lay like a shadow over my life. I couldn't do it. I'd tried, I'd failed, it didn't work.

Oh, fuck, fuck, fuck, shit.

I threw myself onto the sofa and closed my eyes. How unpleasant it was, it was as though someone could appear outside at any moment and look in at me, indeed as if someone was standing there right now.

On Friday evening all the temporary teachers went to Hege's, ate pizza, and drank beer. Hege was the driving force and the center of attention, as high-spirited as she was fast-talking, telling one story after the other. Nils Erik liked her and tried to impress her with his imitations and caricatures. I didn't get a glance, and that was strange as she had been at my place quite a bit over the past few weeks talking on and on about matters that were close to her hard heart.

After the food had been cleared from the table, she got a bottle of vodka from the freezer. The cold shiny drink elevated me into a cold happy world while Hege gradually began to lose control of her facial muscles and physical coordination. When she stood up to go to the toilet she hurried over to the wall, supported herself on it, swayed and focused on the hall, laughed and set off again across the large open living-room floor, with more luck this time, for apart from the exaggeratedly straight line and a couple of staggers she reached the toilet door without further mishap. Half an hour later she was dozing off in a chair. I stroked her cheek, she opened her eyes and looked at me, I said she should go for a walk with me, the cold air would do her good. She nodded, I helped her to her feet and half carried her downstairs, she grinned, put her arms into the sleeves of the jacket I held out for her, pulled her hat over her head, and slowly wound her scarf around her neck.

Outside, it was dark and still. The temperature had taken a nosedive over the past few hours, and the cloud cover that had hung over the area like a tarpaulin all week was now drawn to one side: the stars twinkled above us. I hooked her arm in mine and we began to walk. She stared straight ahead as we walked, her eyes were glazed and vacant, now and then she burst into laughter for no reason. We went down to the chapel and back, on to the school and back. Just above the mountain to the west a wave of green rippled across the sky, leaving a yellow and green veil after it was gone.

"Look at the Northern Lights," I said. "Did you see them?"

"The Northern Lights, yes," she said.

We walked down to the chapel once again. Our shoes creaked in the dry snow. The mountains across the fjord stood silent and wild, a touch lighter than the night around them because of the snow. The cold lay around my face like a mask.

"Are you feeling better?" I said as we turned again.

"M-hm," she said.

If this didn't clear her head, nothing would.

"Shall we go in then?" I said by her driveway. She looked up at me and smiled what I interpreted as a devilish smile. Then she wrapped her arms around my neck, pulled me in, and kissed me.

I didn't want to offend her, and let her continue for a moment, then straightened up and freed myself.

"We can't do this," I said.

"No," she said, and laughed.

"Shall we go back to the others?" I said.

"Yes, let's."

The clarity of mind she had gained dissolved quickly once she was back in the warm, soon she repaired to her bedroom, where she stayed for so long that we, without our hostess, cleared the bottles and glasses from the table, glanced in to see her, she was lying on her back in a large double bed, fully clothed and snoring, and then we all went our separate ways.

I wrote for the rest of the weekend. On Sunday afternoon Hildegunn, Vivian, Andrea, and Live came by, they were bored as usual, I chatted with them for half an hour, avoided looking at Andrea, didn't look at her, apart from once, and it was as though my eyes were magnets and hers were made of iron because a quarter of a second later she glanced toward me and blushed.

No, no, no, little Andrea.

But she wasn't little, her hips were a woman's, her breasts as big as apples, and it wasn't just a child's happiness that shone in her green eyes.

I said they had to go, I had other things to do than entertain kids all evening, they snorted and groaned and left, Andrea last, she leaned forward and pulled on her high boots, flashed me a look before leaving to join the others, who were already outside waiting, surrounded by driving snow, motionless for an instant. Then life flooded back into them, and they walked down the hill laughing while I slammed the door and turned the key.

On my own at last.

I turned the music up as loud as I could without speaker distortion, and sat down to try to finish the short story I'd started the day before.

It was about some seventeen-year-olds who were on their way home from a party and saw a car that had been driven into a cliff. They were drunk, it was early one Sunday morning, the road they were on was empty, thick wet mist hung over the countryside. They came around a bend and saw the car, the front was smashed in, the windshield shattered. At first they thought it had happened a long time ago, that it was just an old wreck lying there, but then they spotted someone in the car, a man, he was sitting in the driver's seat, which had been shunted back, his face was covered in blood, and they realized the accident must have only just happened, perhaps no more than ten or fifteen minutes before. Are you all right? they said to him, he stared at them and slowly opened his mouth, but not a sound emerged. What shall we do? they said, looking at one another. There was something dreamlike about the whole scenario because the surroundings were so quiet and the mist so thick and because they were so drunk. We have to call for an ambulance, Gabriel said. But where from? The nearest house was on an estate a kilometer away. They decided that one of them should run there and call, and that the other two should stay by the wrecked car and keep an eye on it.

Moving the man was out of the question, he was trapped and probably also had internal injuries.

That was as far as I'd gotten. What would happen next I had no idea, other than that the man would die while they were standing there watching. Perhaps he would say something, anything from a different context, incomprehensible to them yet still clear. I also toyed with the idea of the man coming from a place where another story was being enacted. He had locked his father in a room, for example, where he had subjected him to brutal treatment, a secret that he was now taking with him to the grave. Or this was all there was, a car accident early in the morning, a man who died.

Immersed totally in this image – the gleaming asphalt, the motionless spruce trees, the glass splinters and the contorted metal, the smell of burned rubber and the rain-wet forest, perhaps the pillars of a bridge just visible thanks to flashing red lights deep in the mist – I jumped up from my chair like a lunatic when someone knocked on the window in front of me.

It was Hege.

My heart seemed to stampede, for even when I saw that it was her and realized that she must have been ringing the bell for some time without any success, my chest was still pounding. She laughed, I smiled and pointed to the door, she nodded, I went to it and opened up.

"Hi," she said. "I didn't realize you were so jumpy!"

"I was writing," I said. "My head was somewhere else entirely. Would you like to come in?"

She shook her head.

"I told Vidar I was going down to the kiosk. So I thought I'd pop by and apologize for Friday."

"There's nothing to apologize for," I said.

"Maybe not," she said. "But I'm doing it anyway. Sorry."

"Apology accepted."

"Don't you go getting any ideas, by the way," she said. "I'm always like that when I'm drunk. Completely lose control of my emotions and launch myself at the first person I see. It doesn't mean anything. You do understand, don't you?"

I nodded.

"I'm the same," I said.

She smiled.

"Good! So everything's back to how it was. See you on Monday!"

"Yes," I said. "Bye."

"Bye," she said, and walked back to the road.

I closed the door and noticed that I was angry, it would take me at least an hour to get back into the text, and it was already eight o'clock. Might as well go up to the school and watch *Sportsrevyen*, I thought, standing by my desk and staring at the last sentences I had written.

No. If this was going to be any good, I had to invest everything I had into it.

I continued writing.

Then there was someone at the door again.

I switched off the music and went to answer it.

It was three of the young fishermen. None of them was on the soccer team, two of them I had barely exchanged a word with, despite being at the same table three or four times. The third was Henning. He was a year older than me, had been to gymnas and set great store on showing himself to be different in minor details, like the pointed shoes he wore, his black Levi's, the music he played on his car stereo, which had more in common with what I liked than anything anyone else here listened to.

"Can we come in?" he said.

"Course," I said, and stepped aside. They hung up their jackets, with snow on the shoulders, kicked off their shoes, dark from the slush, went into the sitting room and sat down.

The wind had picked up. Down by the sea, waves were hurling themselves at the shore like furious beasts. The wash that was always present had a darker undertone when there was a storm, a kind of boom or a muted rumble.

They each put a bottle of Absolut on the table.

"I don't have any mixers, I'm afraid," I said.

"We stick them in the freezer and drink it neat," Henning said. "That's what the Russians do. That's how it's supposed to be drunk. If you add a bit of pepper, it tastes great."

"OK," I said, and went for some glasses. After they had filled theirs, and also mine, to the brim, I put on one of the two U2 mini LPs I had, which not many people had heard. Henning, who liked U2, actually asked me what the music was, and I was able to bask in the sun for a while.

The music evoked at once the atmospheres of my ninth grade and the first at gymnas. The enormous, bare, beautiful but also lonely space for music that I had loved, and now discovered that I still loved, as well as everything else around it, everything that had been going on in my life then, condensed into this unbelievably vibrant concentrated moment that only feelings can produce. A year relived in a second.

"Just fantastic!" I said.

"*Skål*," said Kåre.

"*Skål*," said Johnny.

"*Skål*," said Henning.

"*Skål*," I said, and drained my glass with a shiver. Turned up the music. With the darkness so dense outside and the lights so bright inside, it was as if you were being transported. In a shuttle of some kind. Way out into space.

And it was true too. We *were* hovering out in space. I had always known that, but it was only when I came here that I understood. Darkness did something to your perception of the world. The Northern Lights, this cold burning in the sky. And the isolation.

I cursed myself for not having been able to keep my eyes off Andrea. Whatever I do I must not encourage her feelings.

I must not look at her again.

Or at least only in a teaching context.

I didn't need it. Liking her had nothing to do with it, I liked lots of the others as well. Fourth graders as much as seventh graders. The exception was Vivian's sister Liv, but for Christ's sake she was sixteen, only two years younger than me, no one could object to my looking at *her*.

"Did you get back today?" I said, looking at Henning.

He nodded.

"Did you catch anything?"

He shook his head.

"Black sea."

They didn't leave until five. By then I had drunk almost a whole bottle of vodka. I had enough presence of mind to set the alarm clock, but when it rang at a quarter past eight I must have been dead to the world because it was still beeping in its devilish way when I was brought to by other sounds that had merged with it, namely, someone ringing the doorbell and knocking on the door.

I tumbled out of bed, threw some cold water over my face, and opened up. It was Richard.

"You're awake, are you?" he said. "Come on then. Your class is waiting. It's a quarter past nine."

"I'm sick," I said. "I'll have to stay at home today."

"Nonsense," he said. "Come on. Have a shower and get your clothes on. I'll be waiting here."

I looked at him. I was still drunk, my brain was in a corridor with glass walls. I saw Richard from far off although he was a meter from me.

"What are you waiting for?" he said.

"I'm sick," I said.

"You've got one chance," he said. "I suggest you take it."

I met his eyes. Then I backed away and went into the bathroom, turned on the shower, and stood under it for a few seconds. I was furious. I was an employee, a teacher, and if one of the others didn't appear for work one day and said they were ill, Richard wouldn't dream of going to get them. Not a chance. The fact that he was right – after all I wasn't sick – was irrelevant. I was an adult, not a child, a teacher, not a student; if I said I wasn't well, I wasn't well.

I turned off the shower, dried myself, rolled deodorant under my arms, got dressed in the bedroom, put on a coat, shoes, and a scarf in the hall, and opened the door again.

"Good," he said. "Let's head up then."

He had humiliated me, but there was nothing I could do about it. Right and power were on his side.

I had always liked darkness. When I was small I was afraid of it if I was alone, but when I was with others I loved it and the change to the world it brought. Running around in the forest or between houses was different in the darkness, the world was enchanted, and we, we were breathless adventurers with blinking eyes and pounding hearts.

When I was older there was little I liked better than to stay up at night, the silence and the darkness had an allure, they carried a promise of something immense. And autumn was my favorite season, wandering along the road by the river in the dark and the rain, not much could beat that.

But this darkness was different. This darkness rendered everything lifeless. It was static, it was the same whether you were awake or asleep, and it became harder and harder to motivate yourself to get up in the morning. I succeeded, and five minutes later I was standing in front of my desk again, but what happened there was also rendered lifeless. It felt as though I was getting nothing back from what I was doing. However much effort I put in, nothing came back. Everything vanished, everything dissolved into the great darkness in which we lived. I might as well say this as that, do this as that, nothing made any difference.

At the same time there was the weight of being under constant observation, of everyone always knowing who I was, by never being allowed to have any peace. Especially at school, where Richard hovered over me like some damn bird of prey, ready to pounce on me the second I did something he didn't like.

All the drinking reinforced my unease, and since nothing of what I did gave me anything back, I became more and more worn down, it was as though I was being drained, I became emptier and emptier, and soon I would be walking around like a shadow, a ghost, as empty and dark as the sky and the sea around me.

I would drink several times in the middle of the week after the day Richard came to get me, but I always managed to stagger out of bed and get myself to school punctually. The next occasion he had reason to find fault with me was different. I had been to a party in Tromsø over the weekend, Jøgge was on leave and wanted to meet me, and on Sunday evening I missed the boat to Finnsnes, had to stay overnight in Tromsø, and then when I finally returned to the village it was too late in the morning for it to be worth going to school.

The next day Richard called me into his office. He said he had confidence in me, I was an important part of the school, but things had to function smoothly, things had to function smoothly every day, and if I didn't turn up for work this created big problems for everyone. Also for the pupils. It was my responsibility, no one else's, and this must not happen again under any circumstances.

As I stood there, with pupils running in all directions outside the window and him sitting behind his desk and telling me this in a loud, harsh voice, I was raging inside. But his voice paralyzed my fury, it could not find a vent, except in the old despised way that it used to, as tears.

He humiliated me, although he was right, it was my responsibility, I couldn't skip work the way I had ditched classes in gymnas.

All my strength had ebbed away, and all my resolve.

I closed the door behind me, washed my face in the staff bathroom, sat down on the sofa without even the energy to pour myself a cup of coffee.

Torill was sitting at the table making some Christmas decorations. She noticed me looking at her.

"Just have to make sure I can do this before I ask the kids to do it," she said.

"Don't they teach you that kind of thing at training college?" I said.

"That wasn't the main priority, no. Pedagogics and that kind of useless stuff was more the style," she said with a grin.

I sat up.

I could just stop teaching.

Who said I couldn't?

Who said so?

Everyone said so, but who said I had to listen to them?

No one could stop me handing in my notice, could they? I didn't even need to hand it in, all I had to do was stay down south after Christmas, just not return. I would be putting the school in a predicament, but who said I couldn't do that?

The teacher my class had had the year before turned up drunk for classes, was always taking days off, and finally had just taken off and never returned.

Oh, how they had moaned and groaned about him in the months I had been up here.

I got up, the bell rang the next moment, so deeply were the routines ingrained in my body. But the thought of stopping glowed in me. I wanted to be free, and freedom existed everywhere but here.

After the last lesson that day I called Mom. Caught her as she was about to leave work.

"Hi, Mom," I said. "Do you have time for a little talk?"

"Yes, of course. Has something happened?"

"No. Nothing has changed here, but the job's beginning to weigh me down. I can only get out of bed in the morning with the greatest of difficulty. And it struck me today that I could just hand in my notice. I'm really not enjoying it at all. I haven't been trained for this either. So I wondered about studying after Christmas instead. Doing the foundation year."

"I can understand you being frustrated and that it's tough going," she said. "But I think you should sleep on it before you decide. Christmas is around the corner, and you'll be able to unwind and relax lying on the sofa here if you like. I think everything will look different then, when you go back up."

"But that's exactly what I don't want!"

"Work goes through patches. There was a time when you thought it was a lot of fun. It's quite normal for you to have a down period now. I'm not saying you shouldn't quit. That's up to you to decide. But you don't need to make up your mind right now, that's all I'm saying."

"I don't think you understand what I'm telling you. It won't get any better. It's just a huge drag. And for what?"

"Life is a drag at times," she said.

"That's what you always say. Your life may be a drag, but does mine have to be?"

"I was only trying to give you some advice. In my opinion, it's good advice."

"OK," I said. "The odds are I'll give up the job, but you're right, I don't need to make a decision now."

Usually I took care to make sure the staff room was empty when I phoned, or that only Nils Erik was there, but this time I had been so upset and desperate that I hadn't given it a thought. When I opened the door to leave, Richard was in the kitchen.

"Hi, Karl Ove," he said. "I'm just doing the washing up. Are you on your way home?"

"Yes," I said, turned and left.

Had he heard? Had he been standing there and listening *too*?

I couldn't believe it.

But then came the last day of school before the break, report cards were handed out, coffee was drunk, and cakes were eaten, in an hour I would be getting on the bus to Finnsnes and setting off on the long journey down to Mom in Førde, where we would stay for a few days before going to Sørbøvåg for Christmas Eve. Richard stopped in front of me.

"You should know that I consider you've done a fantastic job here this term. You've been an invaluable member of staff. And you managed the occasional difficulty with grace. Now you have to promise me you'll be back after the Christmas holidays!"

He smiled to soften the impact, to make it seem like a pleasantry.

"Why would you think I wasn't coming back?" I said.

"You *must* come back, you know," he said. "It's not easy up here in the north, but it is still extraordinary. We need you here."

This was unadulterated flattery, as transparent as glass, but that didn't stop me puffing out my chest with pride. Because he was right. I *had* done a good job.

"Of course I'll be back," I said. "Merry Christmas! See you in 1988!"

The next day, in the evening, Mom was waiting on the quay as the *hurtigrute* boat from Bergen docked in Lavik. It was half past eight, pitch black, the crew lowered the gangplank while the roaring propellers churned up the sea. The light from the lamp above the tiny waiting room glimmered in the film of water that lay over the asphalt. I stepped ashore, leaned forward and gave Mom a hug, we walked together to the car. Around us doors were being opened and closed, engines started and the express boat was already speeding off down the fjord. The weather was mild, the countryside snowless, the car windshield dotted with small raindrops that were intermittently swept away by the wipers. The cones of light from the headlights roamed like two frightened animals in front of us. Trees, houses, gas stations, rivers, mountains, fjords, whole forests appeared in them. I leaned back in my seat staring. I'd had no idea that I had missed trees until I was back there and saw them.

Mom had made a casserole before she left, we ate it, chatted for an hour, then she went to bed. I stayed up to write but didn't get much done beyond a couple of lines. She had rented a furnished flat, and I felt like a stranger there.

The next day we drove to town to do our final Christmas shopping. The sky was overcast, but the clouds hiding the sun were thin and straggly, my back was cold as I opened the door, stepped out of the building, and for the first time in several months saw the burning globe hanging behind the clouds. Even if the colors of our surroundings were reduced to a minimum in which only the pale yellow of the grass and the wan green of the hedges stood out from the gray, to me they seemed to glow. There was no sharpness, there were no marked contrasts, no steep mountain peaks, there was no endless sea. Only lawns, hedges, housing blocks, and behind them gentle friendly mountains, all muted by moisture and gray winter light.

In the evening, Yngve came. It was his birthday, he was twenty-three, after dinner we ate cake, drank coffee, and had a glass of brandy. I gave him a record, Mom gave him a book. After Mom had gone to bed, we sat up and had a couple more glasses of brandy. I asked him to read the latest short story I had written. I stood outside on the veranda in the drizzle gazing into the distance, I was overjoyed to be home, although the few signs of Mom and her life that existed in the flat didn't make the alienness any more homey, as one might imagine, more the contrary, they made the homeyness more alien. Seeing her things there was like seeing them in a museum. But then home was no longer a place. It was Mom and Yngve. *They* were my home.

I craned my neck and looked into the living room. He was still reading.

Was that the last page?

It looked like it.

I forced myself to wait a little longer.

Then I pushed up the long handle and slid open the glass door. Closed it behind me, sat down on the sofa across the table from him. He had placed the sheets of paper in a pile. He was busy rolling a cigarette, oblivious of my presence.

"Well?" I said.

He smiled. "Well, it's good."

"Sure?"

"Ye-es. It's similar to the other ones I've read."

"Good," I said. "I've done six now. If I can speed up, I could have fifteen ready by the time I finish at the school."

"What are you going to do then?" Yngve asked, putting the somewhat crooked rollie between his lips and lighting up.

"Send it to a publishing house, of course," I said. "What do you think?"

He looked at me.

"You don't think anyone's going to publish it, do you? In all seriousness? Do you think they will?"

Chilled to the depths of my soul, I met his gaze. All the blood had drained from my face.

He smiled. "You did, didn't you," he said.

My eyes glazed over and I had to turn away.

"You can send them anyway," he said. "And see what they say. They might go for them, you never know."

"But you said you liked them," I protested, getting up. "Didn't you mean what you said?"

"Yes, I did. But everything is relative. I read it as a story written by my nineteen-year-old brother. And it is good. But I don't think it's good enough to be published."

"OK," I said, going back out onto the veranda. I watched him go back to reading the Fløgstad book Mom had given him. The brandy glass resting in his hand. As though what he had said had no special significance.

To hell with him.

What did he know, really? Why should I listen to *him*? Kjartan liked it, he was a writer. Or did he also say that based on who I was, his nineteen-year-old nephew, I wrote well considering who I was?

Mom had said she considered me a writer after reading it. You're a writer, she had said. As though that surprised her, as though she hadn't known, and she couldn't have put that on. She meant it.

But for Christ's sake I was her son.

You don't think anyone's going to publish it do you? In all seriousness?

I'll damn well show him. I'll damn well show the whole fucking world who I am and what I am made of. I'll crush every single one of them. I'll render every single one of them speechless. I will. I will. I damn well will.

I'll be so big no one is even close. No one. No. One. Never. Not a chance. I will be the greatest ever. The fucking idiots. I'll damn well crush every single one of them.

I *had* to be big. I *had* to be.

If not, I might as well end it all.

The sight of the pallid winter sun in the damp, muted countryside continued to keep me enchanted throughout Christmas, it was as though I hadn't seen the sun before it was gone again, what energy it brought, how rich the play of light on nature when its rays were filtered through the clouds or the mist or just flooded down from a blue sky, and all the endless nuances that appeared when nature reflected the light back.

Nothing had changed in Sørbøvåg. Grandma's state hadn't noticeably worsened, Grandpa hadn't noticeably aged, and the fervor in Kjartan's eyes wasn't noticeably diminished. Since last Christmas he had passed a philosophy exam in Førde, and now it was his lecturer's name, rather than Heidegger's and Nietzsche's, that was mentioned, at least they were not referred to as often as before, in that casual, confidential way of his. I might have imagined we could talk about literature, but apart from him showing me some poems, hardly a word of which I understood, nothing came of this. He had also acquired an astronomical telescope, it stood there on the living-room floor, beside the ceiling-high window, from where he studied the universe at night. He had also developed an interest in ancient Egypt, ensconced in his old leather chair reading about that mysterious culture, which was so far removed from ours it seemed almost nonhuman to me, as if they actually had been gods. But then I knew nothing about it, and just flipped through his books when he wasn't there and examined the pictures.

On December 28 I went down to Kristiansand, celebrated New Year's Eve there, Espen had hired a room with some others at the Hotel Caledonien, which had just reopened after the fire, it was heaving with people, everyone was smoking and drinking, and it wasn't long before two firemen came dashing along the corridor in full uniform. I laughed myself silly when I saw them. I had been on my way up to the rooftop with some others, I sat on the edge and dangled my feet over, with the town beneath me and the sky lit up with fireworks. We talked about a crowd of us going to the Roskilde Music Festival in the summer, and with Lars I semiplanned a hitchhiking trip down to Greece afterward. I managed to include a visit to Grandma and Grandad as well, nothing had changed there either, with them, the house, everything inside and its smells. It was me who had changed, it was my life that was on a wild trajectory.

On the third of January I caught the plane up to Tromsø, shortly after halfway we flew into a tunnel of darkness, and I knew it wouldn't end, this was how it would be, pitch black all day for some weeks yet. Then everything would slowly change, soon the darkness would be gone and the light would fill every hour of the day. This was just as wild, I thought, smoking in the narrow seat.

But first came the darkness. Dense and heavy, it lay over the village when I arrived by bus the next morning, not open, as it could be when the sky was cloud-free and the stars were shining out in space, but dense and heavy like at the bottom of an abandoned well.

I unlocked the door to my flat, went in, unhitched my rucksack, and switched on the light. It was like coming home.

There was my *Betty Blue* poster, there was the Liverpool FC poster, there was the new landscape poster I had bought in Finnsnes on one of my first days here.

I turned the coffee machine on, crouched down by my record collection and began flicking through it. After that I surveyed the tiny library of books I had bought. It all filled me with pleasure.

I went into the kitchen and poured some coffee into a cup. Through the window I saw a little group of kids coming up the hill. In case they were coming to see me I put on Mozart's Requiem, one of the two classical LPs I possessed, and turned the volume up to full.

There was a ring at the door.

Andrea, Vivian, Live, Stian, and Ivar, the tall ninth-grade boy, stood outside.

"Happy new year," I said. "Come in."

From the hall, where they were hanging up their coats, I heard Vivian say: *He likes opera!*

I smiled to myself, standing with a steaming cup of coffee in my hand as they came in. Stian had been here only once before, right at the start, with Ivar, he had gone through my record collection and asked whether I had any heavy metal. In the few lessons I had with him at school I ignored him as far as I was able, trying not to rise to all the provocation he dished out. I placed no demands on him, he had made up his mind anyway. Tor Einar had them much more than me and had made a stand against them, which didn't go too well, once he had returned to the staff room trembling all over, two of them, Stian and Ivar, had knocked him to the ground, Ivar had gotten him in a stranglehold. They were sent home for a few days because of the incident, but the school was so small, the place so transparent that what would have been a serious matter elsewhere wasn't so serious here. We were expected to deal with the likes of Stian and Ivar. When they went fishing or hung out with some of the younger men, they were young kids, pests no one bothered about. So Tor Einar could hardly say they had held him by the throat. Not if he wanted to elicit any sympathy or understanding at any rate.

Stian sat down brazenly on the sofa with his legs wide apart. He was the only one not to have taken off his coat. The three girls hung on his lips, I could see, as though ready to obey his every command. If he spoke, they watched him with rapt reverence. If he addressed one of them directly, they cast down their eyes and squirmed uncomfortably on the sofa.

"Get anything nice for Christmas?" I asked.

Vivian giggled.

I went over and sat in the chair opposite them.

"What about you, Stian?" I said. "Did you get anything good?"

He blew out his cheeks.

"I went fishin' over Christmas. Didn't do too bad. Gonna buy a moped as soon as the snow's gone."

"He'll be sixteen in March," Andrea said.

Why did she say that?

"Then you're only three years younger than me," I said. "It won't be long before you can have my job. That's what you have in mind, isn't it, to become a teacher?"

He blew out his cheeks again, but a tiny smile crept into the corners of his mouth.

"No, no," he said. "The only book I'm going to open after I've left school will be a bankbook."

They laughed.

"What about you, Ivar?" I said.

"Goin' fishin'."

He was only sixteen but already the tallest person in the village. His height was so conspicuous that he probably never thought about anything else. Seeing him beside the three seventh-grade girls was painful, anything that was small and delicate caused him difficulty: letters, numbers, conversation, ball games, girls. In most ways he was a child, he burst into loud guffaws at the most basic, the most stupid things, blushed to the roots when he was corrected, and only really felt at ease with Stian, who controlled him as you would a dog. He had lost his father when he was small, and on the few occasions he had come to talk to me that had been the topic. It had all happened in the 1970s, a fishing boat sank without trace, the whole of Norway talked about it for some days, but then it faded into oblivion except for Ivar, his mother, and the rest of the family. Barely a year after the accident they had moved up to Håfjord, where his mother had relatives. That was his story, his fate, the father who died when he was small.

"What about you?" I said, looking at the three girls.

They shrugged. Usually they had a certain confidence when they were here, I teased them, they laughed and talked back, had a good time being cheeky. But now they were more reserved. They didn't want to give anything away in front of Stian, this was a different game, the stakes were higher.

"Vivian's got a boyfriend," Live announced.

Vivian gave her a dirty look. Punched her hard on the shoulder.

"Ow!" Live exclaimed.

"Have you?" I said.

"Yes," Live said, rubbing her shoulder. "She's going out with Steve."

"Steve?" I said. "Who's he?"

"A guy who moved here at Christmas," Stian said. "He's from Finnsnes and is going to start fishing this spring. He's completely useless, they say."

"He is not," Vivian said. She blushed.

"He's twenty," Live said.

"Twenty?" I said. "Really? You're thirteen, aren't you?"

"Yes!" Vivian said. "And?"

"They're crazy up north," I said, and laughed.

I got to my feet.

"I'm afraid you'll have to hop it now. I've just come in the door. I have to unpack and so on. Prepare some lessons. I've got such a terrible class, you know. They don't know anything."

"Ha ha," Andrea said, levered herself off the sofa, walked toward the hall, where she had hung her white jacket. The others followed, for a few seconds everything was jackets and arms, hats and gloves, and then they went out into the darkness, laughing and poking each other. I unpacked my clothes, ate some supper, read in bed for a couple of hours before switching off the light and going to sleep. Once I was woken by sounds from the room above, it was Torill and her husband, the floor shook, she shouted and screamed, he groaned, I took the duvet with me to the sofa and slept there for the rest of the night.

Nils Erik and I moved into the house the following weekend. Apart from the bedrooms and the little room leading off the sitting room, where I would do my writing, we shared everything. We took turns cooking and doing the dishes. There was hardly an evening when we didn't have visitors, either pupils or the other teachers, especially Tor Einar, he dropped by almost every day, but Hege also came a lot. On weekends Nils Erik went on walks, he always asked me if I wanted to join him, I always said no, nature was not the place for me, besides, more often than not there was a party somewhere, and if I didn't go I stayed home writing, no more short stories but a novel called *Vann over/Vann under – Water Above/Water Below*. I'd gotten the title from a song Yngve and his friend from Arendal, Øyvind, had written. The novel was about a young man, Gabriel, who went to gymnas in Kristiansand, and would consist of a mysterious frame narrative with short, report-like sequences and a present-tense plotline about drinking and girls, punctuated at regular intervals by little episodes from his childhood. It all culminated in him being bound up at a party in a cabin in Agder Province, having a nervous breakdown, and being admitted to a psychiatric clinic, where the circle was closed, since this is where the short objective reports that had introduced every chapter stemmed from.

To ensure I had more time to write, I completely altered my daily routine, it made no difference when you slept and when you were awake, morning and evening, night and day, in practice everything was the same. I started getting up at eleven at night, I worked through until eight in the morning, had a shower, went to school, and took a nap after I finished at around three in the afternoon.

If I couldn't write, I would sometimes put on my coat and go out, wander around the silent village, listen to the roar of the waves beating against the shore, gaze up at the mountainsides, which at first, because of the snow, seemed to be floating in the darkness and then became totally swallowed up by it. Sometimes I went to school. It might have been three or four in the morning, I saw my reflection in the windows I passed, my vacant expression, my vacant eyes. Occasionally I stayed there, read a book on the sofa in the staff room or watched a film on the TV, or simply slept for a few hours, until the sound of a door being opened suddenly woke me, and Richard came in, he was usually the first to appear in the morning. This was all that was needed for a feeling of chaos to come over me, a feeling of not having anything under control, of finding myself on the edge of . . . well, of what?

I did my job. Did it make any difference that I worked at the end of my day rather than the beginning?

But there was something about the darkness. There was something about this small, enclosed place. There was something about seeing the same faces every day. My class. My colleagues. The assistant at the shop. The occasional mother, the occasional father. Now and then the young fishermen. But always the same people, always the same atmosphere. The snow, the darkness, the harsh light inside the school.

One night I was out walking, on my way to the school, when a bulldozer drove up behind me. It had a snowplow mounted on the front, the snow flew alongside into mounds by the road, an orange light flashed from the roof, thick black smoke belched from an exhaust pipe at the front. The man driving didn't look at me as he passed. Some way up the hill he stopped, with the engine still running. As I came alongside he set off again. He drove at the same speed as I walked. I watched him, he was staring straight ahead, and I shivered with unease, the vibrating, roaring, scraping, flashing vehicle shook my soul. I walked faster. He drove faster. I turned right, he turned right. I turned around, he drove straight on, and I'll be damned if he didn't turn around as well, and as I reached the hill leading to the school he was right behind me again. I set off at a run, this was scary, because around us everything was lifeless and black, the village was asleep, it was just us two outside, me and some mad snowplow man chasing me. I ran, but I was no match for him, he accelerated and followed me right into the school playground. I unlocked the door, my heart pounding in my chest, would he follow me in here too?

From the staff room I watched him steadily and methodically clearing the playground of snow, it took him perhaps a quarter of an hour, before he turned and drove back down to the village.

On my way home from school the following afternoon I caught a glimpse of Vivian's twenty-year-old boyfriend. She was in his car, so overcome by her triumph that she didn't know where to look as they drove past and our eyes met. He was a puny-looking blond-haired guy who – I could see when I met them by the shop shortly afterward – laughed a lot. He had been unemployed and had moved here when he was offered a job as a crewman on one of the boats. Nothing of the Vivian we saw in the lessons, her childish questions, the teasing and giggling, was on show here, it had to be stowed away, and it was strange to see, she had sat in the front seat of the car like royalty, with a hard-won stateliness that threatened to crack at any moment, held together only by the fragile bonds of vanity, such that the child she also was could reappear at any moment or even take total control. One giggle, one gesture, one blush, and it was over. Her boyfriend was not the world's brightest, to put it mildly, so in this way they were well matched. In class her behavior changed, she became more self-important, she no longer liked all the childishness the others exhibited. But she was easily led, it didn't take many comments before she lost the stateliness she'd worn like a cloak only a few minutes earlier. That didn't mean that she was really unchanged, really untouched by what was going on around her, only that everything in her was still fluid. She might refuse to laugh at my jokes and say I was stupid, then burst into laughter anyway, and after that she might look at me with a different nuance in her eyes, and this nuance, which was quite new and also present in Andrea's eyes, although not so clearly, I had to protect myself against, for what it did, insidiously, was to draw me closer to them. Through this look the distance between me and them narrowed, and it wasn't because I had approached them, quite the contrary, I saw that in this look, which was completely open, half knowing, half unknowing.

Or was I imagining all of this? For when I had seen them in other contexts, such as in Torill's or Nils Erik's lessons, or in the shop with their mothers, it was as if this side of them had never existed. They toed the line, and if they didn't, they tried to rebel with defiance, sulks, or protests, and not, as they occasionally did in my classes, with charged looks.

This wasn't something I spent tracts of time mulling over, more impressions that blew through me, tiny gusts of pleasure and fear while I was writing during the January and February nights. Nor did I have any concrete basis for these impressions, nothing had been said or done, it was all about moods and feelings triggered by something as intangible as a gaze or a certain way of moving.

As I plodded through the village on my way to the first class, my feelings were ambivalent – I liked being at school yet I didn't. Now and then I felt a slight flutter in my chest at the thought that I would be seeing her again the following day.

No one knew, and I hardly knew myself.

One Friday at the beginning of February, all these small impressions, which in themselves were insignificant and vague, and as such unexacting, were suddenly intensified. I had as usual got up late in the evening, written through the night, and as the clock passed five in the morning I'd had enough and went out into the darkness. Through the still sleeping village, up to the school, where after a stroll through the teaching block I sat down on the sofa with a book until tiredness overcame me and I leaned back with eyes closed and the book resting on my chest.

The door opened. I sat up with a start, ran a hand through my hair while staring straight into Richard's eyes with what must have been a guilty expression on my face.

"Have you spent the night here?" he said.

"No," I said. "I came here early to do some preparation. And then I dozed off."

He scrutinized me carefully.

"I'll make some extra strong coffee," he said at length. "That'll wake you up."

"Make it strong enough for a horseshoe to stand upright in," I said, and got to my feet.

"What?" he said. "Who said that?"

"Lucky Luke, I think."

He laughed and poured water into the machine while I sat down at my desk. It had been several months since I'd prepared a lesson in any other way than with a quick glance at a textbook shortly before I walked into the class. I had ditched most of my alternative teaching methods, now the majority of my lessons consisted of going through whatever topic had to be dealt with, after which I gave them some exercises. The aim was to get through the syllabus in all subjects. Whether they absorbed everything or not no longer bothered me. The main thing was the framework this approach gave and, with it, the distance.

"Coffee's ready if you want any," Richard said, heading for the hall with a cup in his hand, probably on the way to his office.

"Thank you very much," I said.

When the bell rang half an hour later, I was standing by the window in the classroom watching the pupils coming up the hill. Tiredness lay in me like stagnant water. We had math for the first two lessons, incomparably the most boring subject. It was February, incomparably the most boring month.

"Open your books and get started," I said after they had trickled into the room and found their places. For math we were joined by the fifth and sixth graders, so there were eight pupils in all.

"Same as always then. You work on the problems, and if you run into any problems, I'll come and help. Then we'll go through the new material on the board at the beginning of the next lesson."

No one objected, they slipped acquiescently from the state they arrived in at school to the state the solving of the math problems demanded. Live put her hand up before she had even glanced at the book.

I went over to her and leaned forward.

"Try on your own first," I said. "Have a shot."

"But I can't do this, I know. It's so difficult."

"Maybe it'll be easy. You don't know until you've tried. Give it ten minutes, then I'll come back and see how you're doing. OK?"

"OK," she said.

Jørn, the sharp little sixth grader, waved me over.

"I did some of the exercises at home," he said when I was by his desk. "But then I got stuck. Can you help me?"

"Possibly," I said. "I'm not that great at math myself."

He looked up at me and smiled. He thought I was joking, but I wasn't; after the syllabus for the seventh grade I started having problems. I could even get into difficulties before then too, suddenly forgetting how to divide two big numbers, and I had to wriggle my way out by asking pupils how to do it. Not that I didn't know of course, it was just that I couldn't remember.

"But this one doesn't look too bad," I said.

He followed carefully while I explained it to him. Then he took over, I left him and went to the window.

He was a determined character, but his attitude to school was either-or, on or off. Math he liked, so there was no problem. In some subjects though he switched off completely.

Live put up her hand again.

"I can't do it," she said. "And I mean it."

I showed her. She nodded, but her eyes were vacant.

"Can you do the rest yourself now?" I said.

She nodded.

I felt sorry for her, almost every lesson held a humiliation of some kind, but what could I do?

I sat down behind my desk, scanned the class and looked up at the clock, which had barely moved. After a while Andrea put up her hand. I met her eyes, smiled, and stood up.

"Karl Ove's in love with Andrea!" Jørn said loud enough for everyone to hear.

I gave a start. Red-faced, I pretended I hadn't heard, leaned over her desk, and tried to concentrate on the little math problem.

"Karl Ove's in love with Andrea!" Jørn repeated.

Some of the pupils giggled.

I straightened up and eyed him. "Do you know what that's called?" I said.

"What what's called?" he said with a grin.

"When you say that other people feel what you feel? It's called transference. For example, if you, a sixth grader, were in love with one of the girls in the seventh grade. Instead of admitting it, you say your teacher is."

"I'm not in love with *anyone*," he said.

"Me either," I said. "So shall we do some problem-solving now?"

I leaned forward again. Andrea whisked her hair away from her forehead with one hand.

"Don't take any notice of him," she whispered.

I ignored her remark, stared at the column of figures she had written and pointed to where she had slipped up.

"There," I said. "That's wrong. Can you see?"

"Yes," she said. "But what's it supposed to be?"

"I can't tell you that!" I said. "You have to do the problem. Try again. I'll be at my desk if you can't do it."

"OK," she said, looked up at me, and gave a fleeting smile.

My insides trembled.

Was I in love with Andrea?

Was I *in love*?

No, no, no.

But I was drawn to her in my thoughts. I was.

When I was at the school during the night, when I stood by the dark, motionless water in the swimming pool, I imagined she was in the changing room, alone, and that soon I would go in. She covered herself, looked up, I knelt down in front of her, she looked at me, at first with apprehension, then tenderness and openness.

I imagined this and at the same time thought the opposite, that she wasn't in the changing room, how could I think like that, no one must find out how my mind worked.

My insides trembled, but no one knew because my movements were controlled, what I said was thought through, nothing of what others saw could betray my inner thoughts.

I hardly knew I had these thoughts, they lived in a kind of no-man's-land, and when they came, in an explosion, I didn't hold on to them, I let them fall back to where they'd come from, and so it was as though they didn't exist.

But what Jørn had said, that changed everything, because that came from the outside.

Everything that came from the outside was dangerous.

There was something almost morbid about writing alone at night while everyone else was asleep and then teaching the children with the dregs of my strength, and I was becoming more and more worn down, so at the end of February, I switched back as the tiny pulse of light in the middle of the day slowly began to widen. It was as if the world was returning. And living together with Nils Erik was good: when the pupils came visiting, from the fourth graders to the seventh graders, the meetings weren't so charged – if I didn't play such a dominant role, it didn't make much difference. It was different with Hege, she invariably came when Nils Erik was out, how she knew I had no idea, nor why she did it. But she liked talking to me, and I liked talking to her, we could sit for hours in the evening despite our being so different.

The writing on the other hand was going badly, I had reached a point where I kept repeating myself, all of a sudden I was unsure why I was writing at all.

Aschehoug Publishing House had put an advert in *Dagbladet*, announcing a short-story competition, my enthusiasm was rekindled and I sent in two of my best stories: the one about the garbage dump and the one about the funeral pyres on the plain.

Various community centers on the island took turns organizing parties, and at the beginning of March it was Håfjord's turn. We had pre-drinks in our house, almost all the temporary teachers were there, and after only a few drinks I was floating on air, they made me so happy, these people, and I told them so too, on the way up to the community center, swinging the bag with the bottle of vodka and the extra pouch of tobacco.

What was special about these parties was that they weren't restricted to or arranged for particular age groups – desperate twenty-year-olds here, resigned forty-year-olds there – no, *everyone* came to these community center parties. Seventy-year-olds sat at the same table as teenagers, fish-processing workers at the same table as school inspectors, and the fact that they had known one another all their lives did not prevent them from letting their hair down, normal social relationships were set aside, you could see a

thirteen-year-old necking with a twenty-year-old, a juiced-up old lady dancing and shaking her dress cancan style while grinning a toothless grin. I loved
it, couldn't help myself, there was a freedom in this I had never encountered
anywhere else. Yet you could only love it if you were there, part of the untram-
meled euphoria, for with even the tiniest hint of criticism or good taste everything would collapse and become a wild parody or perhaps even a travesty
of the human condition. The young men who lit their coffee so it burned
with a low blue flame, the very elderly women who looked at you with mis-
chievous, flirty eyes, the bald men dressed in formal suits and ties who one
minute were making passes at fifteen-year-olds and the next were hunched
over a ditch beneath the glittering community center spewing, women staggering and men crying, all wrapped up as it were, packaged in a long stream
of badly performed 1960s and '70s hits by bands that no one but people up
here cared about any longer, and a cloud of smoke that was so dense that if
you hadn't known better, you might have assumed came from a blaze in the
cellar.

For me this was alien and exotic. I had grown up where almost no one
drank or at least was ever visibly the worse for wear. There was a neighbor
who drank himself silly once or twice every six months, this was a sensation
and caused quite a stir. There was an old alcoholic who cycled to the shop
every day to buy his brown bottles of beer. And that was it. Mom and Dad
never drank, apart from a couple of bottles of beer or a glass of red wine with
their food. Grandma and Grandpa in Sørbøvåg didn't drink, Grandma and
Grandad in Kristiansand didn't drink, none of my uncles and aunts drank,
and if they did, never in front of me. It was only two and a half years ago that
I had seen my father drunk for the first time.

Why didn't they drink? Why didn't everyone drink? Alcohol makes everything big, it is a wind blowing through your consciousness, it is crashing
waves and swaying forests, and the light it transmits gilds everything you
see, even the ugliest and most revolting person becomes attractive in some
way, it is as if all objections and all judgments are cast aside in a wide sweep
of the hand, in an act of supreme generosity, here everything, and I do mean
everything, is beautiful.

Why say no to this?

I plunged into the party on this March evening, I was in my element, I even went over to Richard, who was sitting in a late '70s suit a size too small for him, with his wife, to say how much I liked him, he had kept a tight rein on me, he was right to do so, and everything had gone well, hadn't it? It was going well, wasn't it?

Yes, I was doing fine.

He didn't like me, but he couldn't say that, all he could do was force a goatish smile. I was in the ascendancy, I was the shining star, he was just the head teacher at a small school, of course I could spare a moment for a little chat with him.

I saw Vivian and Andrea's mothers, they were friends and were sitting at a table smoking, I sat down beside them wanting to have a chat about their daughters, they had such fantastic girls, they were so lively and pretty and would do well in life, I was sure of that.

I had never spoken to them before, apart from at parents' evenings, but those had been formal occasions, I had discussed the girls' behavior and performance in various subjects then, they had listened carefully to what I said and asked a few questions, no doubt prepared, before disappearing into the darkness, on their way home to their children, who had been nervously waiting to hear what the meeting might bring, or reveal. Now the situation was different, we each had a glass in front of us, people were staggering past on all sides, the music was loud, the air close and warm, I was drunk and so eager to say something nice that I was leaning over the table towards them with a huge smile on my face. They said their children talked so much about me, there was no end to it, in fact it was almost as though they were in love with me! They laughed, I said yes, that can be difficult, a teacher who is only eighteen years old, nevertheless they are incredibly nice girls!

For a moment I wondered whether to ask one of them to dance, but rejected the idea, they were at least thirty-five, so even though they had a twinkle in their eyes when I appeared, I got up and wandered around the room, sat down first here and then there, went outside and saw Håfjord gleaming beneath me, the black sea straight ahead, and when I went back in

I searched for Nils Erik to tell him what a good friend he was and how much I liked sharing the house with him.

Having done that, I went outside again, I wanted to take in the view one more time. At the bottom of the hill were my girls, I went down, Vivian was with Steve, Andrea with Hildegunn, I asked them if they were having a good time, they were, and they laughed at me, perhaps because I was drunk, who knows, but it made no difference, I moved on, into the thick, smoke-filled atmosphere, bounded up the steps in two strides, plowed my way into the room, and there in front of me, like a revelation, stood a girl.

I stopped in my tracks.

Everything in me stopped. She was beautiful, but there were many who were, that wasn't the point, it was the eyes she looked at me with, they were dark and brimful with a life I wanted to share. I had never seen her before. But she was from here. She came from the village, I could see that the moment I clapped my eyes on her, for she was wearing a soccer uniform, the whole deal, shirt, shorts, socks and cleats, everyone who was working there tonight was, the event had been organized by the soccer team, and would anyone not from the area volunteer to work at a party for Håfjord Soccer Club?

She was holding a tray of empty glasses.

Seeing her, so beautiful and so shapely, in football garb and cleats, made my senses reel. I glanced at her bare thighs and calves, and I knew I was doing it, so to disguise this fact I looked slightly to one side, and then the other, as though I was inspecting this clubhouse and everything in it very thoroughly.

"Hi," she said with a smile.

"Hi," I said. "Who are you? I've never seen you before, I'm sure of that, you're so beautiful I would have remembered if I had."

"My name's Ine."

"You live here, but you never go out, is that right?"

"No," she laughed. "I live in Finnsnes, but this is where I come from."

"I live here," I said.

"I know," she said. "You work with my sister."

"Do I? Who's that?"

"Hege."

"Are you Hege's sister? Why didn't she say she had such a pretty sister? Because you are younger than her, aren't you?"

"Yes. Yes, why didn't she tell you? Perhaps she wants to protect me?"

"From me? I'm the most harmless person out here."

"Yes, I'm sure you are. But I have to go in with this. I'm working here tonight, as you can see."

"Yes," I said. "But can we meet again? When you finish? There must be some get-together afterward somewhere. Why don't you come along? Then we can talk a bit more."

"Well, we'll have to see," she said, turned and made for the little room beside the stage, where the kitchen was.

After that, the party was over as far as I was concerned. Nothing going on there interested me anymore. All I had in my head was the beautiful waitress in her soccer uniform, and I spent the rest of the evening looking longingly at her.

Hege's sister!

She told me everything, why hadn't she told me about her?

I searched for Nils Erik and said we should organize some drinks at home. He hesitated, he was already exhausted, but I was determined, we were going to do this. As long as he didn't have to join in, it was fine with him, he said. You have to stay up for a while, I said. And you don't need to invite anyone else. What are you up to? he said. Have you got your beady eye on someone? You bet, I said, filling my glass to keep myself on the boil while doing what I could to kill time. I caught fleeting glimpses of her as she went in and out of the kitchen, for a while she served in the snack bar as well, but I didn't go over, although I would have loved to buy a hot dog from her, just to watch her squeezing the ketchup and mustard from the plastic bottles over the sausage, but I didn't want to waste the little time I had on anything that wasn't to do with my plan for her and me at our place. I didn't want to be a nuisance or force myself on her. When she smiled at me I said there would be drinks at our place afterward, we were staying in the yellow house on the bend and it would be an enormous boost for everyone there if she came along.

"We'll see," she said again, but not without a smile, not without a glint in her dark eyes.

Oh, dear God, please let her say yes! Please let her come along!

The band started up again. Eric Clapton's "Cocaine."

I applauded when they had finished, couldn't take much more, staggered out into the cold, saw Tor Einar chatting with two girls in the ninth grade with a big smile on his face, a couple farther away making out in a car, the school at the other end of the soccer field looking like an embankment in the darkness, lit a cigarette, drained the vodka, turned and glimpsed Hege on her way over. My intuition told me I shouldn't say anything about Ine to her, otherwise she would be sure to come along too and the situation would be impossible.

"How are you?" she said.

"Can't complain," I said.

"So you've been talking to my sister?"

"Yes, you kept her well hidden. I didn't even know you had a sister."

"We're only half sisters. Same dad, but we didn't grow up together. She lives her own life."

"Does she live in Finnsnes?"

"Yes. She opted for the motor mechanics course. She likes motorbikes. And motorbike riders!"

"Oh."

Vidar appeared in the doorway. His eyes scoured the people standing outside. And stopped at us. Held us in his gaze, then he came in our direction. He was drunk, I could see that by the way he was concentrating on walking properly and in a straight line. Broad and powerfully built, his shirt open at the chest, a gold chain visible, he stopped in front of us.

"So this is where you are," he said.

She didn't answer.

He looked at me. "We don't see much of you anymore. You should drop in. Or perhaps that's what you do when I'm away?"

"It has happened," I said. "We had a little get-together there for the teachers a couple of weeks ago, for instance. But mostly I stay at home and work in the evenings."

"What do you think about Håfjord actually?"

"It's great here," I said.

"Are you happy?"

"Yes, I am."

"Good," he said. "It's important that teachers are happy."

"Shall we go in?" Hege said. "It's beginning to get cold."

"I'll stay here for a bit," I said. "Have to clear my head."

They went in side by side, next to him she was extremely slight. But she was tough, I thought, and looked out over the village again, it was so quiet and peaceful compared to the hubbub of vying personalities and wills in the clubhouse behind me.

Some time after the band stopped playing, the music was also switched off, and as people began to drift away the lights came on, harsh and quivering, and the magic veil in which the darkness had wrapped everything was torn aside. The dance floor, which moments before had been the scene for the sweetest and hottest dreams, was now bare and empty and covered with dirt and gravel from all the boots that had stomped around on it during the course of the evening. The space beneath the ceiling, which as if underwater had pulsated in hues of red, green, and blue except when it had sparkled like a starry sky, was empty apart from a light rig with some light cannons and an idiotic cheap shiny disco ball hanging from the middle. The tables, where people had been sitting and enjoying themselves in what resembled a wall of human warmth, were strewn around, beneath them a sea of empty bottles and scrunched-up cigarette packets, here and there shards of broken glass, and the odd trail of toilet paper someone had unwittingly brought with them. The tabletops were stained with all sorts of sticky mess and covered with small burn marks from forgotten cigarettes, there were overflowing ashtrays, piles of cups and glasses, empty bottles of all descriptions, cheap Thermos flasks with long rivulets of coffee under the spouts. The faces of those who had not yet gone home were tired and lifeless, bone structures covered with skin, white and creased, eyes two lumps of jelly, bodies either rippling with fat and folds of skin or so bony and lean that your thoughts were led to the skeletons beneath, which would soon be lying picked nice and clean under the ground in some windblown graveyard with saline soil somewhere by the sea.

No, under the lights this room was nothing special. But then in came six girls wearing soccer uniforms to clean up, they scurried around with their trays and cloths and it was as though life had come to chase away death. I would have loved to stand watching them, but now it was important to give the right impression, not to be a pest and stare and harass, so I went for a walk outside, chatted to people and tried to plan the next phase of the evening, that is, to discover where people were going to drink in case she didn't want to join me.

A quarter of an hour later the crowd outside the community center had thinned and I ventured in. With another girl she was carrying a table across the floor to the corner below the stage. After they had put it down she ran one hand across her forehead, rested the other on her hip, and looked across at me.

"After all this hard work you deserve a break," I said. "I know a house with a great location by the water. You can relax and recover there."

"And no one will come and bother me?" she said.

"No," I said with a smile.

She held her index finger against her cheek, supported her chin on her thumb and regarded me with raised eyebrows. God, she was so attractive.

Five seconds passed. Ten.

"OK," she said. "I'll come with you. We've finished here anyway. I just need to change first."

"I'll wait outside," I said, and turned so that she couldn't see I was smiling so much my mouth was in danger of splitting open.

———

A few minutes later she came down the steps zipping up her dark blue down jacket and straightening her white woolen hat in a way that was making my heart thump as I waited in the darkness.

She stopped in front of me and put on her gloves, also white, and shifted the bag she was carrying from one hand to the other.

"Shall we go then?" she said, as though we had known each other for years. I nodded.

All the light-headedness vanished as we set off down the hill. Now it was just her and me. And oh, how aware I was of her movements and facial expressions as we walked down the snow-covered road.

She was tall, slim, her nose was small like a child's, her hips were beautifully rounded, her feet small, yet there was nothing of that dainty grace about her, she wasn't someone you wanted to protect, someone you wanted to take care of, and her strength, which was also a coldness, was what perhaps I found most irresistible about her.

When her eyes didn't flash with life they were dark and calm.

This had been my initiative, she had waited for me, I had set this in motion. We had already reached my old flat.

"Where do you stay when you come here?" I asked.

"At Mom's," she said, pointing down to the right. "She lives down there."

"Did you go to school here?"

"No, I grew up in Finnsnes."

"And now you're at the tech?"

"Have you been talking to Hege?" she said, looking at me.

"No, no," I said. "It was a wild guess."

Then there was silence. I was uneasy and tried to think of something else so that she wouldn't notice my nerves. If dogs can smell fear, girls can smell nervousness, that was my experience.

From a distance I could see lights in the sitting room. When we went in Nils Erik, Tor Einar and Henning were there. They were playing Nick Cave and drinking what looked like red wine. We sat down on the sofa. It felt as if the party was over, there was no energy in the room, only lifeless eyes and some sipping of wine. Tor Einar tried a couple of times to whip up some atmosphere, but no one was biting, his laughter was met with polite smiles and weary looks.

"Would you like something to drink?" I asked Ine. "A glass of red wine? Some vodka?"

"Do you have any beer?"

"No."

"A little vodka then."

I went into the kitchen, which was freezing cold as usual, and took two glasses from the cupboard, poured a dash of vodka in each and mixed it with 7UP as I wondered what to do. Perhaps best to wait? They would soon go, and then we would be alone. But if they didn't, if this dragged on for another half an hour, there would be a good chance she would leave. There was nothing of interest for her here. Could I simply suggest we go up to my bedroom?

No, no, that was the last thing I should do. Then they would be sitting underneath us listening to every movement upstairs, she would know that and refuse, that wouldn't work.

But I had to get her on her own.

Could we go into my study?

With a glass in each hand I went into the sitting room. Put one on the table by Ine, who looked up at me and gave a weak smile.

"This music is depressing me," I said. "Can I put something else on?"

"Be my guest," Nils Erik said.

What might she like?

Or should I choose a record I liked, one which might give her a sense of who I was? Hüsker Dü, for example? Or *Psychocandy* by the Jesus and Mary Chain?

"Any requests?" I said, crouching by the LPs.

No one answered.

The Smiths maybe?

No, that was too whiny. And something told me she hated whining.

Something hard and masculine. But what?

Did I really not have anything? Was all the music I had feminine and whiny?

It would have to be Led Zeppelin.

As the stylus crackled on the first groove I stood up. It was important to keep on the move because if I sat down, the inertia in the room would make everything I did from then on conspicuous.

"*Skål!*" I said, reaching out my glass and clinking it against the others, Ine's last.

"Come with me," I said. "I'm going to show you something."

"Oh, what?" she said.

"It's in there," I said, motioning toward the other end of the sitting room. "It's something I talked about before. Come on!"

She got up, we crossed the floor, I closed the door behind us and there we were, each holding a glass and standing between the towers of books and piles of paper and cardboard boxes.

She looked around. I sat down on the chair.

"What were you going to show me?" she said.

"Nothing," I said. "It was just so boring in there. Come and sit over here."

I held her hand, she sat down on my lap. Then she took the initiative, picked up my hand and studied it. Ran her thumb over my palm.

"Wow, they're so soft," she said. "You've never done any manual work in your life, have you?"

"Not a lot," I said.

"Never used a spade? Or a wrench?"

"No."

She shook her head.

"That's not good," she said. "And you bite your nails, I can see. Are you the nervous type?"

"Yes, I guess so."

"And why was I to go home with you, did you say?"

I sat there with a hard-on, not knowing what to say.

She leaned forward and opened her mouth. We kissed. I stroked her back, then I held her tight and pulled her to me, hard, she was so *lovely*, and she moved her head away.

She stroked my cheek.

"You're nice," she said.

Her dark eyes lit up as she smiled.

We kissed again.

Then she got up.

"I have to go," she said.

"No. You can't," I said. "Not now."

"Yes, I can. But I'm here tomorrow too. Come by if you like. I'll be at Mom's."

She opened the door, I accompanied her to the hall, she put on her jacket and went out, turned briefly and said good-bye, disappeared down the road.

Leaving her bag behind.

The next day, well, what was on my mind the next day?

Ine.

A miracle had taken place. In my room, last night, a miracle.

Ine, Ine, Ine.

But I put off the visit. The night before I had been drunk, everything took its own course. Now I was sober and could lose everything.

It was three o'clock before I dared venture out and set off on the long road there.

Her mother, an elderly woman with white hair, opened the door.

"Is Ine at home?" I asked.

"Yes, she is," she said. "She's in the living room. Come in."

Ine in the living room, that was quite different from Ine at a party. She was wearing gray jogging pants and a white T-shirt with a picture of a motorbike on it. Her hair was pinned up. She smiled when she saw me, jumped to her feet, and asked if I wanted some coffee.

"Yes, please."

She found a cup and placed a white Thermos on the table next to me.

I grabbed it and tried to unscrew the top. But my palms were too sweaty. My hand slipped around without gaining any purchase. When I applied all my strength it budged a little, but by then I had used all my strength and had none left to turn it.

She watched me.

I blushed.

"Shall I give you a hand?" she said.

I nodded.

"My hands are so slippery," I said.

She came over and unscrewed the top with ease.

"There you go," she said, and sat back down.

I poured the coffee, took a sip.

So far I hadn't said a word.

"When are you going back? Tonight?"

She nodded. Her mother came in behind me.

"You work with Hege, don't you?" her mother said.

"Yes."

"Hege really likes you," Ine said. "She talks about you a lot anyway."

"Is that right?" I said.

"Yeah," she said.

What was this? What was I doing here? Were we going to make *small talk*? How wrong was that? Wrong, wrong, wrong!

"Where do you live in Finnsnes?" I said.

"Right behind the bank."

"Renting somewhere?"

She nodded.

"Do you like Håfjord?" her mother asked.

"Yes, I like it a lot," I said. "I'm having a great time here."

"Yes, it's a fine little place," her mother said.

"Mom!" Ine said. "You're boring him."

Her mother smiled and got up.

"OK, OK," she said. "I'll leave you two in peace."

She left the room. Ine drummed her fingers on the table.

"Can I meet you again?" I said.

"You're meeting me now," she said.

"That's true," I said. "But I meant in a different way. We could have dinner together or something like that. What do you think?"

"Maybe," she said.

She looked beautiful sitting there. A red-faced sweaty boy was the last thing she needed in her life.

"Actually I dropped by on my way to the school," I said. "I've got to do some work and prepare for tomorrow."

I got up.

She got up.

I went into the hall, she followed and watched me put on my coat.

"Bye then," she said.

"Bye," I said, and hurried up the hill toward the school, where I had nothing to do, but I unlocked the door anyway, in case she was watching me from her house. I was fairly sure she had forgotten I existed the moment she closed the door behind me, nevertheless, I didn't want to be caught out telling such a cowardly lie, and now that I was at the school I might just as well watch some TV, it was Sunday, there were always sports on then.

Ine, Ine, Ine, all the girls tittered when I went into the classroom for the first lesson the following day.

So everyone knew.

I ignored them but thought of nothing else.

Ine, Ine, Ine.

At night I lay awake musing on my next move. She had left her bag at my place, she would have to come and get it, wouldn't she? Or should I take it to Finnsnes?

I had already put the nightmare visit to her house behind me, I hadn't even been able to open the Thermos, so what could I expect of another visit? That she would she throw herself into my arms?

I would have to meet her when I was drunk, that was my only chance.

Ine, Ine, Ine.

The brief memory of her burned inside me, I had never experienced anything similar, it was so unassailable, it was the focal point of everything, suddenly she was all that counted.

I walked back and forth between the house and the school during the day, went for long runs in the evenings to sweat out any thoughts of her, and then the following Sunday she appeared.

There was a knock at the door, I opened up, there she stood.

Beautiful Ine.

"I left a bag here, I believe. Just came by to pick it up."

"Is it this one?" I said, holding it up.

"Yes," she said. "Thank you."

She turned to go.

"Wouldn't you like to come in for a while?" I said.

She shook her head, but not from side to side, the movement seemed to stop halfway, and I loved it.

"I have to go back to Finnsnes," she said, starting to walk up the little slope to the road. It was slippery, she took small steps.

"Did you come all this way just to get the bag?" I said.

"No. I've been here all weekend," she said. She had reached the top now and was striding out.

I knew nothing about her except that she was sixteen, liked motorbikes, and went to a technical school.

Not much to base a relationship on.

But she was a miracle of nature, and she was tough.

Her breasts were big, her legs long.

What more could I want?

Nothing, that covered everything.

So what should I do?

Nothing, I meant nothing to her, that had taken her under five minutes to figure out.

I told Hege everything. We sat nursing cups of tea.

"Ine's no good for you," she said. "You have no idea. So you'll just have to forget it."

"I can't," I said.

She looked at me. "You're not *in love* with my little sister, are you?"

"Yes, I am. That's exactly what I am."

She sipped her tea, stroked a long strand of hair away from her eyes.

"Oh, Karl Ove, you are something," she said.

"It's a terrible cliché, but I can't stop thinking about her."

"You'll never make it with her. It just won't work. In fact, it's inconceivable."

"Saying that is not helpful," I said. "I have got to try."

"OK," she said. "Let's go to Finnsnes, go to the disco, miss the bus home, and crash at her place."

"Why can't she come with us to the disco?"

"She doesn't like discos."

It was a plan, and we followed it to the letter.

On Friday night we stood outside a house behind a bank, not far from a disco, Hege rang the bell and Ine came down.

If she was angry that her sister had tricked her, she didn't show it.

They hugged, I looked down and tried to be as unassuming as possible, followed them up the stairs, sat down on a chair rather than the sofa so that she wouldn't feel compelled to sit next to me.

She was just as casually dressed this time as last. Shiny tracksuit bottoms tight around her thighs and a plain white T-shirt.

She made some tea and they did the talking, I sat listening and offering the occasional comment.

The place consisted of a single room with a little kitchenette at one end. The room was quite big, though by no means immense, and while I sat there I kept wondering what Hege had imagined. How could anything possibly happen here?

Ine made up a bed on a mattress on the floor, it was positioned right next to the door and that was where I was to sleep. Hege would be sharing the double bed with her.

Oh well.

The light was switched off, the two of them whispered for a while, then all went quiet.

I lay on my back staring at the ceiling.

How strange my life had become.

As if in a dream a figure rose from the bed. It was Ine, she came over and slipped in beside me.

Jesus, she was naked.

She snuggled up to me, breathing hard.

We kissed, I caressed her whole body, her wonderfully large dark breasts, oh, I devoured them, and I felt her smooth hair against my thigh, and she was breathing heavily and I was breathing heavily, was it going to happen now, I caught myself thinking, with this stupendous motorbike girl?

She rubbed herself against me, and I came.

I twisted away and pressed myself against the mattress.

Shit. Shit. Shit.

"Did you come?" she said.

"Mhm," I said.

She got up, crept back into bed, and slid back into the dream from which she had so enticingly risen only a few minutes earlier.

And thet was thet, as Fleksnes used to say.

For the next few days my love grappled with the remainder of my pride. I *couldn't* go to see her again. I *couldn't* ring, *couldn't* write a letter, *couldn't* look her in the eyes again.

She was still all I thought about, but the incident at her place had been so definitive and so humiliating that not even the most enamored thoughts could withstand the pressure and slowly but surely they disappeared from my system.

Then it was just school again. School and writing and drinking.

But the days lengthened, the snow melted, spring was on its way. One day there was an envelope marked H. Aschehoug & Co. in my mailbox. I took it with me outside with the other letters, lit a cigarette, gazed at the jagged white mountains across the fjord gilded by the sun, which with every day that passed came closer to the village with its retinue of rays. The sight was invigorating, there was in fact a light that burned for us out in space.

A car drove past. I didn't see who it was but waved all the same. Some gulls screeched over by the fish-processing factory, I glanced across, they were circling in the air above the quay. The waves lapped against the stones on the shore. I opened the envelope. There were my two short stories. So they had been rejected. There was a letter attached, I read it. No contributions had been selected, it said. The general standard had been too poor, the anthology would not be published.

So at least I hadn't been rejected!

I walked up to the road and ambled toward our yellow house. Tor Einar's old blue Peugeot was parked outside. Tor Einar was chatting with Nils Erik in the sitting room, along with his cousin, Even, a boy in the eighth class, it was Saturday, we were going to Finnsnes. As I turned on to the little path down to the door, they came out.

"Are you ready?" he said.

"Yes," I answered. "Are we going now?"

"That was the idea."

I went back up, opened the passenger door, and got in. On the rear seat Even leaned forward and spread his arms across the front seats. He had kind blue eyes, dark hair, a small wispy moustache above his upper lip. His voice rose and sank in ways even he could not predict. Tor Einar started the car and drove slowly through the village, waving to the right and left to people on their way to or from the shop. I set about opening the pile of letters I had taken from the mailbox. The original twenty people I corresponded with had shrunk to twelve, still enough to ensure the mailbox was seldom empty. One of the letters was from Anne. She had worked as a technician on the radio programs I had done in Kristiansand. She lived in Molde now, went to the university there or whatever it was, I wasn't very interested, she *was* though, the letters I received were rarely less than twenty pages.

I opened it and took out the thick wad of paper. A small brownish lump came with it and fell onto my thigh.

"What was that?" Even said.

Christ! It was hashish.

"What was what?" I said, placing my hand over it.

"What fell out. What did you get?"

"Oh that?" I said. "It was nothing. A friend of mine's studying horticulture. She's interested in trees. So she's sent me a piece of bark from a rare specimen."

"Can I see?" he said.

I stared ahead at the tunnel opening a few meters in front of us. What would he do if he knew what it was? Tell someone? There would be a hell of a fuss then. DRUGS SEIZED ON HÅFJORD TEACHER. They drank like fiends, but they didn't have anything to do with hashish, marijuana, amphetamines, or that sort of thing.

"Let me see then!" he said.

"There's nothing to see," I said. "Just a rare specimen of bark."

"Why did she send it to you then?"

I shrugged. "We had a relationship."

Tor Einar glanced at me. "Tell us about it," he said.

"Nothing to tell," I said, putting the lump in my pocket with one hand while grabbing the handle above the door with the other. Not that it was necessary, Tor Einar was driving carefully as always. He and Nils Erik had to be the only drivers in the village who kept to the speed limits.

"Am I going to see it or not?" Even said.

Strange how persistent he was.

I turned. "Give me a break," I said. "I've put it in my pocket now. It's just a bit of bark."

"But it was rare," he said.

"Are you interested in *bark*?" I said.

"No," he said, and laughed.

"Well, there you are. Now I want some peace and quiet to read if that's all right with you," I said, skimming through Anne's pages.

When we returned a few hours later Tor Einar and Nils Erik were going to go skiing. They asked me if I wanted to join them, as usual I said no, I was going to write. The moment they were out the door I took out the lump of hashish, warmed it up, mixed it with tobacco and rolled a joint. I drew the curtains, locked the door, sat down on the sofa and smoked it.

On the wall next to my *Betty Blue* poster Nils Erik had hung one of Charlie Chaplin. Sitting there, I imagined I was him and then I mimicked his walk. With my feet at a quarter to three and a stick happily whirring around in one hand I walked back and forth across the floor. It was a perfect imitation and I didn't want to stop, I waddled up the stairs into my bedroom, which was bare except for a pile of clothes and a mattress against the wall, down again, did a circuit of the kitchen, back into the sitting room. I laughed several times, not because it was funny but because it felt so good. I was the tramp, I swung my stick and staggered around taking tiny footsteps, sometimes I lifted my hat and made a little pirouette to greet everyone. I could do no wrong. And my insides were lubricated to perfection, every movement rippled through my body, soon I was lying on the sofa and lifting first one shoulder, then the other, tensing my calf muscles, knees, abs, biceps, and it was as if I were both floating in the sea and the waves therein.

I woke up to someone knocking on the door. Outside, it was pitch black. I looked at my watch. It was half past five. I sat up, rubbed my hands over my face several times. There was another knock. The smell of hashish still hung in the air. I considered not answering, but when the third bout of knocking started I thought the person knocking must be sure I was here, I let some air in through a window, closed the sitting-room door behind me, went to the hall and opened up.

A man in his forties was standing outside. He was the father of one of my pupils although offhand I couldn't say which. I had a faint rushing sound in my ears.

"Hello," I said.

"Hello," he said. "I'm Jo's father. I wanted to have a little talk with you. It's nothing serious, but I'd like to speak about Jo. It's been on my mind for a while to drop by, but it hasn't been convenient until now. Is this a good time for you? I know this is not exactly school hours but . . ." He laughed.

"No problem at all," I said. "Come in. Would you like some coffee?"

"Please, if it's on. But don't make any especially for me."

He walked past me into the kitchen.

"I was just about to make some," I said. "I've been having a nap. It's been a long week."

He sat down at the kitchen table. Hadn't taken off either his jacket or his boots. I filled the coffee pot with water.

It was always women who took care of everything to do with children and school. They were the ones who went to parents' evenings, they were the ones who signed the slips children took home, they were the ones who did volunteer work and made sure school trips and such things were paid for.

I switched on the stove and sat down opposite him at the table.

"Yes, our Jo," he said. "He's not happy at school at the moment."

"Oh?" I said.

"No, he isn't. He says he doesn't want to go to school anymore, he wants to stay at home. Sometimes he cries. If I ask him why, he won't tell me. Or else he says it's nothing. But we can see there's something wrong. He really doesn't want to go. Well, he is . . . he always got along fine before, when he was younger. He liked school then. But now . . . no . . ."

He looked at me.

"I've come to you . . . I know you aren't his homeroom teacher . . . perhaps it would have made more sense to go and see her . . . but he talks very warmly about you. He likes you so much. It's Karl Ove said this and Karl Ove did that all the time. And so I thought I could talk to you about this. After all you know him."

I was so upset when he said that, I hadn't been so touched for many years. The trust he showed in me I had already betrayed. Not through anything I had done, but through what I had thought. Now, with him sitting opposite me, his face grave and tormented, it was obvious he loved his son, that for him Jo was unique and precious. I realized that what for me had been a minor matter, a maladjusted boy who cried over nothing, for him was major, it filled his life, indeed it *was* his life, everything he had.

My guilt burned in me like a forest fire.

I would have to make amends. I would have to make amends now, to the father, who fortunately, oh how fortunately, had no idea what I had been thinking. And then I would have to make amends to Jo. As soon as I saw him I would do that.

"Well," I said. "He's a fine boy."

"Have you noticed anything at school? Have there been any incidents?"

"No, nothing specific. But I've noticed he doesn't fit in. And that sometimes the others don't want him along, or they make fun of him. Nothing serious though, if you know what I mean. That is, no violence or systematic bullying. I haven't seen anything like that. I don't think it happens either."

"No," he said, rubbing his chin as he looked at me.

"But he's a . . . well, chubby kid. Other kids tell him that. And maybe he's not as good at ball games as some of the others. So he avoids them. And that means he's sometimes left to his own devices. He goes around on his own."

"Yes."

"I don't know what we should do," I said. "But it's a small school. We're not talking about a lot of pupils. Everything's quite open. Everyone knows everyone else inside out. So if he was being bullied it would be easy to do something about it. I mean, these are not children we don't know, big gangs or anything like that. This is Stig, Reidar, Endre. Do you understand what I'm trying to say? It shouldn't be impossible to talk to them about it."

"No," he said.

Oh, he did trust me, he was thinking through what I had said, and it hurt, it hurt him, he was a father in his forties, I was a boy of eighteen, so should he listen to me?

"It's all fine in the classroom," I went on. "There may be a comment now and then, but there is about everyone, more or less, and if anything more serious crops up, of course it's dealt with at once, so what we're really talking about is the breaks. Maybe we can try to set up some activities he likes and can do, and get others to join in? I can talk to Hege about it, and then we can draw up a little plan. It might be as simple as talking to the other boys and explaining the situation to them. I don't think they know how he feels."

"I think they do," he said. "I think they know all too well. They never come back to play with him anymore, and they exclude him from their games."

"OK," I said. "But I don't have the impression there's anything malicious in it or that it means much to them. It's more that it's just happened that way."

"Won't it get worse if you talk to them about it?"

"It's a risk we have to take. It has to be handled sensitively. And they're good kids, all of them. I think it'll be fine."

"Do you think so?" he asked.

I nodded.

"I'll have a word with Hege on Monday. Then we'll put together a plan of action."

He got up. "Then I won't take up any more of your time."

"It's not a problem," I said.

"Thank you very much!" he said, and shook my hand.

"Everything will be fine," I said.

After he had gone I flopped down on the sofa. The sitting room was freezing cold, the window was still open. Noises filtered in from outside and filled the room, which in the atmospheric conditions became distorted, everything seemed to be close. It sounded as if the waves on the shore were beating against the house wall. Footsteps on the road, the crunch of the snow, seemed to come from out of thin air, as though a ghost were walking past, on its way to the sea. A car passed, the drone of the engine rebounded off the wall I was lying next to. Someone laughed somewhere, how eerie, I thought, the devils are out tonight. The state of disquiet Jo's father had produced in me, the chasm between his trust and my betrayal, was like an ache in my chest. I got up, put on a record, the one I had been playing most of that year, Lloyd Cole and the Commotions' latest, which I sensed would always remind me of the moods up here, lit a cigarette, closed the window, pressed my forehead against the chilly glass. After a while I went into the little study adjoining the sitting room, full of piles of books and papers, switched on the light, and sat down at the desk.

The second I laid eyes on the sheet in the typewriter I saw someone had written something on it. I went cold. The first half of the page was mine, and then came five lines that weren't. I read them.

Gabriel stuck his fingers up her wet cunt. Oh my God, Lisa groaned. Gabriel took his fingers out and smelled them. Cunt, he thought. Lisa was squirming underneath him. Gabriel knocked back a slug of vodka. Then he grinned and unzipped his fly and stuffed his hard dick up her wrinkly cunt. She screamed with delight. Gabriel, that's my boy!

Shaken to the core, close to tears, I sat there staring at the five lines. It was a well-observed parody of the way I wrote. A good imitation. I knew who had done it, it was Tor Einar, and I recognized the spirit in which it had been done, the spirit of the good-natured joke, he'd "had a good laugh" while he was doing it, read it aloud to Nils Erik, who had laughed his Østland laugh.

It wasn't meant nastily, but I couldn't forgive them for this. I wanted nothing more to do with them, didn't want to speak to them beyond what was absolutely necessary: work and practical arrangements.

I tore the sheet out of the typewriter, crumpled it up and threw it on the floor. Then I got dressed and went out into the night. No point going to the village, along the illuminated road, I would be seen and might have to talk to people. Instead I followed the dead-end road after the bend, it ran along the gentle mountainside, it was dotted with houses. At the end there was a huge pile of snow. Behind it there was nothing, just snow, low trees, and a rock face that after about fifty meters rose sharply in the darkness. The snow reached to above my knees, it was futile going any farther, so I turned and waded through the snow down to the sea, stood gazing at the black water and the waves that rolled into the shore again and again, without much power, they were more like thoughtless little slaps.

Fuck.

It wasn't just a text he had tampered with, that wouldn't have offended me in the slightest, it was something else, much more than that, there was a soul in it, my soul. And when he tampered with that, I could feel it. It looked different from the outside than from the inside, and it was perhaps that which lay at the heart of my despair. What I wrote was worthless. So that meant I was worthless too.

I retraced my steps. At the crossroads I stood not knowing what to do. I could walk five hundred meters along one road, ending up at the school, or five hundred meters along the other, also ending up at the school. There were no other options. The shop was closed, the snack bar was closed, and if anyone was drinking somewhere, I didn't know about it. There was no one I knew well enough to drop in on. The sole exceptions were Nils Erik and Tor Einar, whom I no longer wanted anything to do with, and Hege, whom I didn't feel like visiting now, and nor could I, as her husband, who was always exceptionally open toward me but evidently also had a heart darkened with jealousy, was at home. Sitting at home reading and playing records wasn't an option either, I saw, a light had come on in the sitting room, which meant that Nils Erik was there.

I couldn't stay standing under the lamppost much longer either, someone somewhere would be watching me and wondering what I was doing.

Slowly I moved off. On reaching the house I warily opened the door, carefully removed my coat, and was about to creep upstairs as quietly as I could when the hall door opened and Nils Erik stood looking at me.

"Hi!" he said. "We got *mølje* at Tor Einar's grandmother's. Shame you weren't with us! It's something of a delicacy – cod with liver and roe and onions!"

"I'm going to bed," I said, avoiding his eyes. "Goodnight."

"Already?" he said.

I didn't answer, opened the door to my room, slipped in, and lay on the mattress in the dark, fully clothed. Staring at the ceiling. Heard Nils Erik washing up in the kitchen. He had the radio on. Now and then his humming, which I couldn't hear, but after two months of living in the house with him I knew he was humming, developed slowly into loud, hearty singing. A car with its stereo on full blast drove by. The throb of the drums became fainter and fainter as it went up the hill and followed the road to the other end, then the drums grew louder until they were again pounding outside the wall next to which I was lying.

I looked at my watch. It was a few minutes to eight.

What the hell should I do?

All the roads out of here were closed.

I was stuck.

For an hour I lay there in the darkness without moving. Then I swallowed my pride and went downstairs to the sitting room, where Nils Erik was reading.

"Didn't you have a bottle of red wine?" I said.

"Yes," he said, looking up. "Why?"

"Can I have it?" I said. "I'll buy you a bottle in the week."

"Yes, no problem," he said. "Are you going out or what?"

I shook my head, fetched the bottle, opened it, and went back up to my room. And glimpsed happiness as I started to drink. They had betrayed me, I was despondent, yes, there was black depression inside me, but I was alone and drinking, I was a writer.

They couldn't say that. They were nothing.

I finished off the bottle in ten minutes. My mind befuddled, as though mist had seeped into my skull, I went downstairs, ignored Nils Erik, opened the door to my study, locked it behind me, switched on the typewriter, sat down at the desk, and got started. A few minutes later it was as if my stomach was being torn apart. I launched myself at the door, but of course it was locked, vomit was pressing up my throat, I cast around, a box, a bucket, a corner, anything, found nothing though, my mouth opened and a cascade of purple spew arced and fell into the room.

I collapsed, my stomach churned, another torrent of wine and sausage was expelled, I groaned, my stomach churned again, but now there was nothing left, only the pain as it writhed and twisted and some thick mucus that I coughed up.

Oooh.

I sat on the floor for several minutes enjoying the peace that had descended on my innards. I didn't care that my books and papers were covered with vomit.

There was a knock at the door. The handle went up and down a few times.

"What are you doing in there?" Nils Erik said.

"Nothing much," I said.

"What did you say? Are you ill? Do you need help?"

"Not from you anyway, you idiot."

"What was that?"

"NOTHING! THERE'S NOTHING WRONG!"

"OK, OK."

I could imagine him holding up his palms to the locked door, then going back to the sofa. The stench of puke had filled the room, and for a moment I speculated on why the smell of your inner juices should be repugnant while that of your excrement was not. Could it have something to do with some kind of Neanderthal custom, shitting in the forest to mark your territory, whereas vomit had no such function to fulfill, it was no more than a reflex action to dispose of tainted food and therefore had to stink?

I staggered to my feet, opened the window and fastened it with the clasp. I couldn't bring myself to clean up the vomit, that would have to wait until the following day, I thought, unlocked the door and went to the hall without so much as a glance at Nils Erik, up the stairs and into my room, where I undressed, crept under the duvet, and slept like a log.

I stayed away from them all the next day, and the day after that too, but then I relented, they were going to the school in the evening for a swim, I joined them, not overjoyed, though not furious either. I didn't say much as we swam up and down, and I let them go into the sauna first, left them on their own, before I climbed out of the pool and stood by the door to try to catch what they were saying. I knew they were talking about me, and I knew they were laughing at me. That was obvious, they spent a lot of time together, and they ridiculed what I did and invested so much energy in.

But inside it was silent, so eventually I opened the door and joined them, sat in the corner at the top, supported my back against the wall, looked down at their two white bodies, which glistened with sweat, Nils Erik bent forward, Tor Einar was resting against the bench behind. Nils Erik's face was always in motion, either he was talking, smiling, laughing, or making faces, but now it was completely still, and it appeared wooden, as though he really *was* Pinocchio, a carved stump of wood into which a magician had breathed life.

He must have noticed I was staring at him because he smiled and turned toward me.

"I saw something today that might interest you, Karl Ove. There was an ad in *Dagbladet* for some kind of writing school. In Bergen."

"Oh yeah," I said in as bored a tone as I could manage. Surely he didn't believe I would fall for such an obvious gesture of appeasement?

At school it was decided that I should have the two school-weary disruptive ninth graders, Stian and Ivar, a few times a week. I was to teach them to play an instrument, we borrowed some equipment from the band in the village, Autopilot, so every Tuesday we trudged up to the community center, switched on the amps, and went through the few songs I knew, instrument by instrument. Ivar played bass, he was absolutely hopeless, but I told him to play the same note while watching me, then when I nodded he should change to a sequence he had been practicing. Stian played the drums, he was better but wouldn't listen to instructions, he was too proud for that, while I played the guitar. We could play three songs: "Smoke on the Water," "Paranoid," and "Black Magic Woman." I was used to playing them as instrumentals, I had done that with Jan Vidar, it was second nature to me, a voice on top of this jangling, inept, talentless performance would only sink it further. We stood on the stage and played with the whole of the spacious but empty community center before us. Stian and Ivar did as much posing with their instruments as playing. Toward the end of one lesson a fourth grader opened the door and stood watching us, wide eyed. Stian and Ivar tried to conceal the pride they felt by spitting and pretending this was no big deal for them.

At a planning meeting some days later Eva went berserk. We had been given permission to use equipment belonging to the band her son played in, but we had treated it carelessly, a string had been broken and not replaced, a drumstick had snapped and not been replaced, the band had had enough, she said, and moved without pause on to the next item on the agenda, which was the seventh grade's attitude to work, you couldn't talk to them anymore, they didn't listen to her, they informed her Karl Ove had said something very different, and when she told me to reprimand them I said I would, but I never did, at least not as far as she could see.

I said I didn't have any discipline problems in my lessons, but I would take the matter up with them. She said this was precisely the problem, I would "take it up with them" but I didn't treat the matter seriously, and they noticed. There had never been any problems with the seventh grade before, they had always been hardworking and bright, now they were smart-alecky and lazy.

"Not in my lessons," I said, looking at her.

She was so angry her head was trembling.

Richard intervened, he said both of us were right, but I needed to make it abundantly clear to them that this behavior would not be tolerated and there would be consequences for them if it continued. OK, I said, I'll do that. When the meeting was over and I was in the hall putting on my coat, Eva said Grete was wondering what had happened to the bed linen they had lent me in August, did I perhaps imagine I had been given it in perpetuity?

Oh, for Christ's sake, was she never going to let up?

"Not at all," I said. "It's not gone anywhere. I can return it tomorrow. It's not a problem."

People were so preoccupied with trivialities, they kept searching until they found something and then they went for the jugular instead of keeping sight of the bigger picture, here we all are, humans on one earth, we're only here for the short term, in the midst of all this wondrous creation, grass and trees, badgers and cats, fish and sea, beneath a star-strewn sky, and you get worked up over a broken guitar string? A snapped drumstick? Some silly bed linen that hasn't been returned? Come on, what's the matter with all of you?

The broken drumstick was the height of pettiness for me. So this was what we were going to discuss, not the results I had achieved with Stian and Ivar?

Why choose the little picture when the bigger one existed?

I hated the little picture, and I wasn't much good at dealing with trivialities, I had to confess. The installments on the stereo had been passed on to a debt-recovery firm, and the case of the dinner suit I had rented a year before and had not returned because it was ruined – a rocket had torn the trouser leg to ribbons – had gone to court, I had been ordered to pay for it and in addition there had been a hefty fine for not appearing in court! A fine for not appearing! What did they imagine? That I would hop on a plane to Southern Norway for the sake of a dinner suit?

But that was how it was, everyday life with its endless round of petty demands and obligations, petty conversations and arrangements, surrounded us like a fence. I lived this life, but not when I was drinking, then it was all open spaces and grand gestures, and even though the price was high, the fear afterward great, I always paid, and only a day or two later again I would feel the itch to cast myself out into it, and to hell with what people said.

One night when I had been out drinking at a community center at the other end of the island, Nils Erik was sitting up at home waiting for me.

"You've got an enemy," he said.

"Oh yeah?" I said from the doorway, drunk and weary.

"I went to bed after you left. Then I was woken up by someone sitting on my bed. It was Vidar. He wanted to know where you were. He had a gun in his lap."

"You're joking!" I said. "Don't fuck with me."

"It's true. If I were you, I'd lock the door. And then I'd get hold of Hege and tell her."

"But there's never been anything between us!"

"He doesn't know that. She's here two nights a week, minimum. That's a lot of time to spend with someone."

"But for God's sake I'm not even the slightest bit interested!"

"This is serious. He had a gun. I'm not kidding."

I wasn't frightened until the day after. I could bump into him at any moment, that was how it felt. That night I locked the door. And the following morning the first thing I did was visit Hege to tell her what had happened.

"He lost it," she said. "He won't do it again. Were you scared?"

"Me? No. I wasn't even there. But Nils Erik was."

"It's just nonsense really. He would never have used it, you know. He just wanted to frighten the living shit out of you."

"For what? For talking to you?"

She nodded.

I was already looking forward to describing what had happened in the letters I wrote. It was as crazy as it was flattering; I lived in a place where people broke in brandishing a gun, and I was important enough for it to be me the madman was after.

For the next few days I was nervous, not perhaps of being shot at, it was unpleasant enough imagining that he would probably beat me up if he got half a chance.

Did he really have a gun?

That is what I remember. But could it have been true?

Unlikely things happened in the north, things that only a year earlier would have seemed deeply alien, perhaps even impossible, and only a year later had that same deeply alien, impossible quality although they seemed absolutely normal, a matter of course, when I lived there.

Nils Erik, who had brought back his diving equipment from home at Christmas and in the spring would go down to the harbor wearing a wetsuit, put on a mask, flippers, and an oxygen cylinder, sit on the edge holding a harpoon, and slip down into the transparent water, a shimmering figure who became fainter and fainter until he disappeared, only to reappear ten minutes later with a fish speared on the harpoon, which he cooked for dinner.

Did that happen?

Did he have any diving equipment?

Did he harpoon fish for dinner after school?

I have never been back, but I do sometimes have nightmares about it, really terrible nightmares that consist of me driving into the village again after all these years, nothing else. That is obviously bad enough.

Why?

Did terrible things happen there? Did I do something I shouldn't have done? Something awful? I mean beyond staggering around drunk and out of control at night?

I once wrote a novel that took place there. I wrote it without a second thought. I paid no regard to the relationship between fiction and reality, for a world opened up when I wrote, it meant everything to me for a while, and it consisted partly of descriptions of real buildings and people, for the school in the book is the school as it was when I worked there, and partly of fictional ones, and it was only when the novel had been written and published that I began to wonder how it would be received up there in the north, by those who knew the world I described and who could see what was reality and what wasn't. I used to lie awake at night in fear. The story had not been plucked out of the air. On the contrary, it had been *in* the air. I worked as a teacher for a year in the north, and when occasionally I was able to relish the thought of going to work in the morning, it was because she was there.

She: Andrea.

A gaze, a hand cupping her forehead, a little foot bobbing up and down, a child who was a woman who was a child who I liked to be in the same room with so much.

That was how it was during the months where day was night, and that was how it was when the light unveiled the room in the mornings, at first cold and shimmery, then, slowly and imperceptibly, full of warmth. The snow on the road disappeared, the enormous piles of snow dwindled, patches of shale began to peep through on the soccer field, and from all the roofs and raised surfaces water dripped and gurgled.

It was as though the light rose in the people living there too. Everywhere there was a mood of gaiety and expectation.

In one class, Andrea and Vivian presented me with a diploma. They had chosen me as the school's sexiest teacher.

I hung the diploma on the classroom wall and said that the competition might not have been that fierce.

They laughed.

A few days later, with the sun shining from the middle of the endlessly blue sky, I told them to go outside and write down what they saw. They could go wherever they wanted, write whatever they wanted, the sole conditions I set were that they should write down what they saw and it had to be at least two pages.

Some went down to the shop, others sat against the wall outside the school in the sun. I went behind the school building and smoked a cigarette, gazed across the soccer field, which was now almost completely free of snow, and at the glittering fjord beyond. Made the rounds of the pupils and asked how it was going. They squinted up at me.

"It's going fine," Andrea said.

"Here comes Karl Ove," Vivian said slowly, to show me that this was what she was writing as her pen moved across the page of her notebook. "He's really sexy."

Andrea looked away when she said that.

"That's what Andrea thinks anyway!" Vivian said.

"Don't be so stupid," Andrea said.

Both looked up at me and smiled. They had tied their jackets around their waists and were sitting there in T-shirts with their arms bare.

I was overcome by the same feelings that had filled me in the spring I was in the seventh grade myself. When we ran after girls, held them tight, pulled up their T-shirts and fondled their breasts. The girls had screamed but never loud enough for a teacher to hear.

I was overcome by the same feelings, but everything else was different: I wasn't thirteen, I was eighteen and not their classmate but their teacher.

They couldn't see my feelings. They couldn't know anything about what stirred inside me. I was their young teacher, and I smiled at them.

"I'm going to read out what you've written in the class," I said. "So you might want to choose your material with a little more prudence?"

"Prudence?" Vivian said. "What does that mean?"

"Look it up when you get inside," I said.

"That's just like you," Andrea said. "We always have to look words up. Look it up, look it up! Can't you just tell us?"

"He doesn't know himself," Vivian said.

"Five more minutes," I said. "Then you have to go back inside."

I walked toward the entrance, heard them laughing behind me, I felt such warmth for them, not only for them though, for all the pupils and all the people in the village, in fact, for everyone in the world.

It was that kind of day.

Eleven years later I was sitting in the study of our first flat in Bergen answering e-mails when the phone rang.

"Hello, Karl Ove speaking," I said.

"Hi, this is Vivian."

"Vivian?"

The moment she said her name everything went cold and black inside me.

"Yes. Don't you remember me? You were our teacher."

There wasn't a hint of accusation in her voice. I rubbed my hand, which was clammy, on my thigh.

"Of course I remember you!" I said. "How are things?"

"Wonderful! I'm here with Andrea. We read about you in the paper, and then we saw you were going to give a reading in Tromsø. And so we thought perhaps we could see you."

"Of course," I said. "That would be nice."

"We've read your book. It was great!"

"Do you think so?"

"Yes! Andrea does too."

To avoid going into detail about what was actually in the book, to nip that discussion in the bud, I asked what they were doing now.

"I'm working at the fish-processing factory. No big surprise there. And Andrea's studying in Tromsø."

"Good," I said. "It'll be fun to meet you again. Should we arrange a time and place now?"

She suggested a café close to where I was going to read, some hours before. I said OK, see you then, and we hung up. A few weeks later I opened the café door and saw them sitting at the back of the room, they laughed when they spotted me, said I hadn't changed at all. But you have, I said, and indeed they had, for although their faces were the same, and the way they behaved, they were adults now, and the zone of ambivalence they had lived in then was completely gone. The woman in them held undisputed sway now.

I took off my coat, went over to the counter, and ordered a coffee. I was nervous, they had both read the novel and would probably have recognized themselves in it. I decided to take the bull by the horns. Sat down, lit a cigarette, so you've read the novel, I said. Yes, they both replied, and nodded. It's not you I was writing about, you know, although I'm sure there are similarities, I said. Enormous similarities, Andrea added. But don't worry about it, it's just funny, that's all.

They told me about everything that had happened in the village since I was there, and it was not so little. The biggest sensation was a sex scandal at the school, which had led to a conviction and prison, and the village had been split into two camps. Otherwise lots of the same teachers were still at the school. Vivian often met the people she had known then, as well as the fishermen who had been my age at the time, of course. Andrea lived in Tromsø, where she was a student, and went home during the holidays and for the odd weekend.

I treated them as if they were still thirteen years old, the mold was already set, I couldn't change that, and when I left an hour later it struck me how stupid that was, especially with regard to Andrea.

They went and listened to the reading and subsequent discussion, came over when it was finished and said their good-byes, I left with Tore, whom I had done my reading with, and a couple of others, and drank all evening. Later that night I saw Andrea again, she was standing with a guy in a taxi queue, he was behind her and she stretched her hands back while he kissed her neck and then stroked her breasts. An almost desperate feeling of failure came over me then, I crossed the street, she didn't see me or pretended she hadn't seen me, and I thought, I could be with her now if I had played my cards right. But I was married, and I wasn't playing a game, so I never got further than the thought, which pursued me across the ensuing months and years: I should at least have *tried* to get her out of my mind.

Two weeks after Vidar had sat down on the edge of Nils Erik's bed and asked where I was, I went south for the Easter holiday.

Mom, who was standing on the quay in Lavik when I arrived, seemed tired, she had worked a lot that year and when she wasn't working was looking after her parents in Sørbøvåg.

During the day we chatted, she did all the cooking and I lay on the sofa reading or walked down to the mall in Førde to do the shopping, in the evening we watched TV.

She told me that Jon Olav was also home, I called him, we arranged to meet in Førde the next night. He had grown up in Dale, an hour's drive away, and the disco where we went was full of people he knew.

I drank beer and talked to him, and away from the reservation, which was how I had come to consider Håfjord, everything felt much simpler and easier. I said I was thinking of applying for a writing course at the Skrive-kunstakademi in Hordaland. He had never heard of it even though it was in Bergen, the town where he was studying. But it was a new course, this year's intake was the first.

"Who are the teachers?" he said.

"I've never heard of them. I think they're some obscure Vestland writers. Ragnar Hovland, Jon Fosse, and Rolf Sagen. You heard of them?"

Jon Olav shook his head.

"It's sort of too bad that it's such a local affair," I said. "But it's one year and you can get a study loan. So at least I'd be able to write full time."

"In your last letter you were going to Goldsmiths in London," he said.

I nodded. "I'll apply there too. Yngve got me the address, and I've just written off for application forms."

Jon Olav was scanning the back of the disco, which was packed, it was the first day it had been open since the weekend.

"I'll just be a minute," he said.

"I'm not going anywhere," I said.

Oh, the pleasure of being in a place where no one knew me!

Felt the alcohol going to my head. Smoked a few cigarettes, eyed up some of the girls, relaxed completely for a change.

When he came back an hour later I was sitting on the same stool, in the same posture even, elbow on the bar, chin resting on my hand.

"I met some gymnas friends," he said. "We're over there. Come and join us."

I slid off the stool and followed him. He stopped by a table at the other end of the room, near the exit.

"This is my cousin, Karl Ove," he said.

Those sitting round the table looked at me without interest and nodded.

In the midst of them was a girl. She was talking to someone on the opposite side of the table and didn't see me. She laughed and leaned forward with both palms on the table. Her skin was pale, her dark bangs hung over her eyes, but that wasn't what made me stare at her, it was her eyes, they were blue and at first joyous, only to turn serious and gentle the next second.

There was something French about her, I thought, slipping down onto the chair next to Jon Olav. Her features were beautiful, but it was only when she laughed again that a shiver ran through me.

She had an aura around her.

"Do you want a beer?" Jon Olav said. "They're closing soon."

Two minutes earlier I would have been glad they were closing soon, now the thought made me desperate in the same senseless way that I was sad whenever anyone left a drinks party, as though with every person who left I came a step closer to death or some other calamity.

"I'll come with you," I said, and followed him to the bar.

"I can carry two beers," Jon Olav said.

"Who's she?" I said.

"Who?"

"The girl at the table."

Jon Olav turned. Hadn't he even noticed there was a girl sitting at our table?

"Oh her," he said. "That's Ingvild."

"Do you know her well?"

"No, hardly at all. She lives in Kaupanger. But I know her boyfriend. Tord. Sleeping in the chair over there. Can you see him?"

Typical.

As though I could have had a chance if she hadn't been with him.

I was on vacation, at my mother's, leaving in two days, what was I dreaming of? One look at a beautiful stranger, was that supposed to be the future? Me and her, yes?

Why?

She had an aura around her.

I drank half the glass at the bar while Jon Olav was paying, then I ordered another and took both glasses with me to the table.

Four of Jon Olav's friends at the table got up and left immediately afterward. They had come in the same car and were going home, I gathered.

Around the table now were only Jon Olav, someone he was talking to, Ingvild, and me. As well as her boyfriend, that is, but he was asleep and so didn't count.

I took a couple of long swigs.

She was staring over her shoulder.

"Do you want this beer?" I said when she finally turned her eyes back to the table. "It's untouched. I haven't had a sip."

"If anything was likely to make me suspicious it would be a total stranger offering me a beer he's had standing in front of him for a while. But you look harmless enough."

She spoke in the Sogne dialect, and her eyes narrowed when she smiled.

"I am," I said.

"But no thanks. I have to drive."

She motioned toward the guy sleeping at the table.

"I have to drive him home among other things."

"I'm a good driver," I said. "I can give you a few tips if you like."

"Oh please! I'm a terrible driver."

"First of all, it's important to drive fast," I said.

"Oh yeah?"

"There are those who claim it's best to drive slowly, but I think they're mistaken. It's better to drive fast."

"OK, fast. Anything else?"

"Well, let me see . . . Yep, I was driving along the road once. The car in front of me was going slowly. I think it's important to drive fast, so I simply overtook him. It was on a bend, I crossed into the opposite lane, stamped my foot down on the accelerator, and then I was past him."

"Yes?"

"That was all. I just carried on."

"You don't have a license, do you?"

"No. I really admire those who do. Actually it's incredible that I dare talk to you. Usually I would have just sat staring at the table. But I've had a bit to drink and I love talking about driving. The theory, that is. I think a lot about how best to change gear to get the smoothest drive, for example. The whole interaction between clutch and gear and accelerator and brakes. But not everyone likes to talk about it."

I looked at her. "Does your boyfriend have a license?"

"How do you know he's my boyfriend?"

"He who?"

"He on the chair."

"Is *he* your boyfriend?"

She laughed. "Yes, he is. And he has a license."

"That's what I thought," I said. "Was it driving cars that brought you together?"

She shook her head.

"But tonight it seems to be forcing us apart. I could have done with a few beers as well. Especially if he's asleep. He might have had the decency to fall asleep without drinking. Then I could have had one."

She looked at me.

"Are you interested in anything else apart from driving cars?"

"No," I said, and took a swig of beer. "What are you interested in?"

"Politics," she said. "I'm passionately interested in politics."

"What kind? Local politics? Foreign affairs?"

"Just politics. Politics in general."

"Are you flirting with my cousin while your boyfriend is asleep?" Jon Olav said.

"I'm not flirting," she said. "We're talking about politics. And then perhaps we'll end up talking about emotions, if I know me."

"I'm sure you do," I said.

"I have an abysmal emotional life. What about you?"

"It's not great, actually. Yes, if I'm honest. I never usually talk about it. But there's something about you that gives me the courage."

"Ironic girls tend to have that effect. That's my experience. Eventually people get so sick of irony they'll do anything to stop it. Since I started being ironic I've been told quite a few intimate details."

The music in the room was switched off.

Jon Olav turned to me.

"Shall we go?"

"OK," I said, and looked at her as I got up. "Drive home fast!"

"I'll drive like a bat out of hell," she said.

When I woke up the next morning she was on my mind. Jon Olav, who had slept at our place, went home to Dale in the morning. He was the only connection I had with her, and before he left I made him promise to send me her address when he got home, even though something told me he would only do so with a heavy heart, after all she was going out with someone he knew.

It felt completely meaningless going back to Håfjord, but on the other hand there were only three more months until it finished for good and I could spend the entire rest of my life in familiar surroundings, if that was what I wanted.

The letter from Jon Olav lay in my postbox a few days after I returned. She lived in Kaupanger, he wrote, and was in her final year at gymnas in Sogndal.

Kaupanger, I thought, that must be a fantastic place.

I spent more than a week on the letter to her. She knew nothing about me, had no idea what my name was, and had no doubt forgotten me the moment she left the disco that night. So I didn't immediately reveal my identity, I touched on driving a couple of times so that she could, if she remembered, figure out who I was. I didn't give an address; if she wanted to answer the letter she would have to make an effort to get hold of it, and in that way, I thought, I would have a deeper impact on her consciousness.

That same week I prepared my application for the writing course at the *akademi* in Bergen. They wanted twenty pages of prose or poetry and I enclosed the first twenty pages of my novel in the envelope, wrote a short letter of introduction, and sent it off.

Now the mornings were light when I woke and went downstairs for a shower and breakfast, outside the house, gulls were screaming, and if we opened the kitchen window, we could also hear the waves lapping and gurgling over the pebbles beneath. At school the younger children were running around in sweaters and sneakers during the breaks, the older ones sat on the ground leaning back against the wall with their faces to the sun. Everything that had happened in the darkness, when life had closed itself around me and even the tiniest details had become charged with tension and destiny, seemed incredible now, for out in the open, beneath this slow deluge of light, I saw it as it was.

How was it?

It was nothing special. It was how it was.

Oh, I still cast glances at Liv when I had the opportunity and could do so unobserved, and in English classes a shiver could still go through me when I saw Camilla's shapely body sitting there, but the mounds and curves, all the softness and grace they possessed, no longer had a disorientating effect, I was no longer fascinated. I saw, and I liked what I saw, but it wasn't part of me. With Andrea it was different, she was special, but if I was happy when she looked up at me from the corner of her eyes in the way she did, I didn't let it show, no one could see what I felt, not even her.

What was it I felt?

Well, it was nothing. A tenderness, that was all, something light and sparkling that whistled past and was gone, it had no right to exist.

One day a letter from Kaupanger arrived.

I couldn't read it standing in the post office or sitting at home or lying in bed, the conditions had to be perfect, so I put it aside, ate with Nils Erik, had a smoke, drank a cup of coffee, then I took the letter with me to the beach, sat on a rock, and opened it.

A strong smell of salt and decay rose from around me. The air was still and warmed by the sun, but every so often a gust swept in from the fjord taking everything with it, which then had to be painstakingly built up again. The mountaintops on the other side of the fjord were still white, but if I turned and looked toward the village, there was a faint green glimmer on the ground, and although all the low trees and bushes were still leafless, they didn't appear to be dead, as in winter, they stood as though they could sense life was on its way back.

I opened the letter and began to read.

She wrote nothing about herself. Nonetheless she began to take shape within me, I could sense who she was, this is different, I thought. This is quite, quite different.

When I folded the letter and replaced it in the envelope it was as though I was a new person. I walked slowly back to the house. She had an aura around her, and every sentence, no matter how tentative and probing, was testimony to that.

I considered getting on a bus the next morning, catching the boat to Tromsø, flying to Bergen, taking the boat to Sogndal, and then simply standing in front of her and declaring that the two of us belonged together.

I couldn't of course, that would have ruined everything, but that was what I wanted to do.

Instead I sat down and wrote another letter. Any hint of emotion or openness was stifled at birth, this was going to be an eloquent, calculating letter that would press all the buttons I had at my disposal, make her laugh, make her reflect, arouse a desire in her to want to know me.

Writing was, after all, something I could do.

On May 17 I stayed home reading the whole day. There was an expectation that teachers would take part in the Constitution Day procession and the subsequent activities, but it was not compulsory, so when the meager procession passed by on the road outside I was sitting on the sofa and watched it through the window, heard the pathetic flutes and the scattered cheers, lay back and continued reading *The Lord of the Rings*, which I had read only two years before but had already completely forgotten. I couldn't get enough of the battle between light and darkness, good and evil, and when the little man not only resisted the superior powers but also showed himself to be the greatest hero of them all, there were tears in my eyes. Oh, how good it

was. I had a shower, put on a white shirt and black trousers, tossed a bottle
of vodka into a bag, and walked up to Henning's, where there was a whole
gang of people drinking. There was a party on Fugløya, we drove there a few
hours later, one minute I was standing in the parking lot talking, the next
I was on the dance floor rubbing up against someone or other, or up on an
embankment fighting with Hugo, trying to prove that I wasn't the weakling
everyone took me for. He laughed and threw me to the ground, I jumped up
and he threw me to the ground again. He was much smaller than me, so it
was humiliating, I ran after him and said he wouldn't be able to do it again,
but he'd had enough and came over, wrapped his arms around me and threw
me to the ground with such force that he knocked the air out of my lungs.
And that was how they left me, gasping for air like a fish. I took the nearly
empty vodka bottle with me and sat on a little mound beside the parking lot.
The light hovered above the countryside. There was something sickly about
it, it seemed to me, and I don't remember anything until I was trying to prize
open a door surrounded by young fishermen, I must have told them I had
some experience in such matters, presumably I had given the impression
that a locked door was no problem for me, I could do a bit of everything,
had done a bit of everything, but now, trying all the keys I had found in the
drawer downstairs, and then a screwdriver and various other tools, it began
to dawn on them that we were not going to get into the locked studio in the
house Nils Erik and I were renting, and one after the other they trooped back
down to the sitting room, which was already bathed in sunlight.

When I woke up I couldn't remember a thing at first. I didn't know where I
was or what time of day it was. Fear pumped through me.

The light outside told me nothing, it could equally well have been morning as night.

But nothing had happened, had it?

Oh yes, it had. I had run after Hugo and had been thrown to the ground
time after time.

I had tried to kiss Vibeke when we were dancing and she had turned away.

And the girl standing by the entrance, the one with the sassy expression, I had stopped and exchanged a few words with her, and then I'd kissed her.

How old would she have been?

She had told me. She was in the seventh grade.

Oh God, was that possible?

Please be kind to me.

Oh no, oh no.

I was a teacher, for goodness' sake. What if this got out? Teacher kisses thirteen-year-old at party?

God almighty.

I covered my face with my hands. Heard music downstairs, scrambled out of bed, couldn't stay there being tortured by the awfulness of my deeds. No, I had to be active, move on, talk to someone who would say it didn't matter, that kind of thing happened.

But it didn't.

It happened only to me.

Why did I have to kiss her? It had just been a spontaneous move, something I did on impulse, it meant nothing.

Who would believe that?

As I left my bedroom I had to support myself on the wall, I was still drunk. Downstairs, Nils Erik was at the stove frying fish tongues. He turned when I entered the room. He was wearing a plaid shirt and a pair of those green hiking pants with loads of pockets.

"So you're honoring me with your presence?" he said with a smile.

"I'm still drunk," I said.

"I can believe that," he said.

I sat down at the kitchen table, rested my head on my hands.

"Richard was not best pleased today," he said. He slipped the spatula under the fried tongues and transferred them to a plate, filled the pan with more tongues coated in white flour. They hissed.

"What did you tell him?"

"I said you weren't feeling well."

"Which was true."

"Yes, but he was pretty angry."

"I don't give a shit about him. There's only a month left now. What's he going to do? Give me the boot? Besides, I haven't been ill once all damn year. So it's no big deal."

"A few cod tongues?"

I shook my head and got up.

"Think I'll have a bath."

But it was unbearable lying in hot water staring at the ceiling, it didn't fill me with peace, it just gave all my painful thoughts ample room to spread, so I got out after a few minutes, dried myself, put on my tracksuit, which was the only thing clean I could find, and lay down on the sofa with *Felix Krull* instead.

For a few minutes at a time I succeeded in engrossing myself totally in the book. Then the dreadful thoughts returned like an electric shock and everything became distorted. Again I had to force myself back into the confidence trickster's world, where I could stay for several minutes until another shock reopened the sores.

Nils Erik came in and put on a record. It was half past five. He stood for a moment gazing across the fjord, then he sat down with a newspaper. His presence helped, what I had done didn't seem so terrible when there was a friendly person in the room.

I read aloud a passage describing Krull's view of the Jews.

"He wasn't so high-minded, this Thomas Mann," I said. "That's pure anti-Semitism!"

Nils Erik looked at me.

"You don't think it's ironic then?"

"Ironic? No, do you?"

"He's famous for being ironic."

"So he doesn't really mean it. Is that what you're saying?"

"Yes."

"I don't think so," I said, because I hated it when Nils Erik thought he knew better than me. Which he often did.

The image of the seventh grader with her tousled hair and sassy expression was clear in my mind's eye again. And my lips closing on hers.

Why had I done it? Oh why, oh why!

"What's up?" Nils Erik said.

"What?" I said.

"You went like this," he said, and raised his head, narrowed his eyes and pinched his lips together hard.

"Nothing in particular," I said. "I was just thinking about something."

But nothing happened. I went to school the next day and no one there said anything about what had happened, everyone behaved as they normally did, even my pupils, who I thought might have heard about it, some of them probably knew her.

But no.

Could it simply pass, just like that?

The only place it existed was in me. And if I let it stay where it was, there was no problem, it would slowly lose its power and in the end vanish, as sooner or later all the other shameful things I had done had vanished.

Toward the end of May a letter from the *akademi* arrived in my postbox, I tore open the envelope and read it standing outside the post office. I had been accepted. I lit a cigarette and started to walk back toward the school, I would call Mom and tell her, she would be pleased. And then I would call Yngve because it meant I would be moving to Bergen that autumn. In a strange way I had expected to be accepted because although I knew what I had written might not have been that good and consequently they ought to have rejected me, it was me, however, who had done the writing and that, I felt, they would not be able to ignore.

May passed, June began, and it was as though everything was dissolving into light. The sun no longer set, it wandered across the sky all day and night, and I had never seen anything like the light it cast over the wild terrain then. The light was reddish and full, it was as if it belonged to the ground and the mountains, it was them that were glowing, as if after a catastrophe. On a couple of nights Nils Erik and I drove along the deserted coastal roads, and we seemed to be on a different planet, so alien was everything. Through sleeping villages, everywhere the reddish gleam and the strange shadows. The people were transformed too, out at night, couples walking, cars driving past, whole flocks of young people rowing out to the islands for picnics.

I received another letter from Ingvild. She said she had rolled up her trousers to her knees and was sitting with her feet in Sogne Fjord as she was writing. I loved Sogne Fjord, the feeling the surface gave of the enormous depth, the immense chains of mountains with the snowy peaks towering above it. All clear and still, green and cool. Ingvild, who was moving in these surroundings and who affected me in so many ways, wrote more about herself this time. But it wasn't much. The tone approached self-irony, she was in defensive mode. Against what? She wrote that she had been an exchange student in the United States for a year, that was why she was still a senior. So we were the same age, I reflected. She was going back there in the summer for a holiday with her host family, they were going to cross the country in a camper van. She would write more from the States. In the autumn she would be going to Bergen to study.

The last day of school came. I wrote HAVE A GOOD SUMMER! on the board, handed out the report cards to my pupils, wished them luck with the rest of their lives, ate cake with the teachers in the staff room, shook everyone's hand and thanked them for the past year. As I walked downhill on my way home I was, as I had expected, neither happy nor relieved because I had been waiting for this day for more than six months, just empty inside.

In the afternoon Tor Einar stopped by. He had brought with him some gull eggs and a crate of Mack beer.

"It's a scandal you haven't eaten seagull eggs before," he said. "There are two dishes which are the *essence* of Northern Norway. *Mølje* and seagull eggs. You can't leave before you have tried them."

Nils Erik had a temperature and was on the sofa, there was no question of him having beer or eggs, so it was left to Tor Einar and me to do them justice.

"Why don't we go down to the beach?" Tor Einar said, eyeing me with that knowing grin of his. "It's such fantastic weather."

"Why not," I said.

I had never quite found the right tone with Tor Einar. We were the same age and had a lot in common, much more than I and Nils Erik had, but it didn't help, it was irrelevant. I always played a role when I was with Tor Einar, which wasn't the case with Nils Erik, and I didn't like myself when I did, when there was a distance between the person I was and what I said, a kind of delay that allowed space for calculations, as if I wanted to say what he preferred to hear rather than what I had to say or talk about.

On the other hand, that is how I was with almost everyone, in fact it had even become like that with Jan Vidar, who was the closest friend I'd had for the past five years.

It wasn't a problem, just a little uncomfortable, and the only consequence was that by and large I tried to avoid being on my own with Tor Einar for any period of time.

Now this wasn't possible. Luckily, though, we had beer with us as we trudged down to the beach, it would only take a couple of bottles before such problems disappeared like chalk beneath a wet sponge.

Under the deep blue sky, beside the water, with the sun playing on it, we both sat down on a rock. Tor Einar opened a beer and passed it to me, opened one for himself, winked and said *skål*.

"Now we're laughing, eh!" he said. "Last day of school, the sun's shining, and we have enough beer for a long night."

"That's right," I said.

Some fishing boats were chugging shoreward, bobbing up and down on the waves in the middle of the fjord, with a trail of gulls behind them.

What a scene.

"How about if we sum things up," said Tor Einar.

"Regarding the school year?" I said, producing a pouch of tobacco.

"Yes," he said. "Has it fulfilled our expectations?"

"I didn't have any, I don't think," I said. "I just came up here and hoped for the best. But you? Are you happy with how things went?"

He hesitated.

"Every year without a girlfriend is a bad year," he said, squinting into the sunlight. Then he turned to me.

"You had a couple of adventures anyway. Ine and Irene? And that temp on Fugleøya, what was her name? Anne?"

"Yes," I said. "But it didn't work out. Actually nothing worked out."

"Didn't you have them?"

"No."

"Not one of them?"

"No."

He stared at me in disbelief. "And there I was going around thinking at least one of us had some luck this year. Then you tell me you didn't either."

I looked at him and smiled, clinked my bottle against his, drank the last drop, opened another.

"Who did you have your eye on?" I said.

"Tone," he said.

That was the girl who had rejected my approach while she was brushing her teeth.

"Yes, she's nice," I said. "I went after her as well, but she wasn't at all interested."

"No, it's not easy," he said. "But I've got a chance. We're going InterRailing together. Well, not just us two, there will be four others, but, Jesus, a month traveling together through Europe, surely there's got to be a chance."

"You're InterRailing?"

He nodded.

"Me too," I said. "Well, it's not InterRailing. I'm going to hitch down through Europe with a friend after the Roskilde Festival."

"Then I'll do my best to avoid you," he said. "I don't want to warm her up just so that you can take over."

"You must have a very high opinion of my qualities as a seducer," I said. "If there's one thing I can't do, it's that."

"My strategy is to be present," he said. "That's the only chance I have. Amble along behind her like a dog, always be there, and then hope she'll cuddle me sooner or later."

I shuddered. "That's a terrifying image."

"You're right, but it's true."

"That's why it's so terrifying. There's a little of the doggie in me as well."

He stuck out his tongue and panted heavily a few times.

"Anyone else you've been trotting along behind this year?" I said.

"Liv," he said, staring straight at me.

"Liv?" I said.

"Yes," he said. "All the girls our own age have left the village. But she's unbelievably pretty. Don't you think?"

"Yes," I said with a smile. "Have you seen her body? Her backside?"

"Oh yes," he said. "She's gorgeous. Camilla isn't bad either."

"No, that's true," I said. "But at least Liv's sixteen. Camilla's only fifteen."

"Who gives that a second thought?" he said.

"You're right there."

We opened another beer. He smiled, his face was bathed in sunlight.

"Her breasts," he said. "Have you seen them?"

"Naturally," I said. "I've hardly looked at anything else in the classes with them."

"She is pretty. But she can't beat Liv."

"No," I said.

I turned and gazed into the distance. A car was coming up the hill from the fish hall, farther along the road a kid was holding a stick and hitting the poles used to demarcate the edge of the road in deep snow. A seagull was sitting on the ridge of our roof surveying the scene.

"And then there's Andrea," I said.

"Yes," he said.

"She's a real beauty too. Have you seen her?"

"Yes."

"Actually, I've thought a lot about her," I said.

"I can imagine," he said.

"What else could we do?" I said. "They were the only ones around!"

We laughed and said *skål*.

"She has such incredible eyes," I said. "And what long legs she has."

"It's true. What about Vivian then?"

"Nothing compared to her sister."

"No, that's true. But she has something. A charm of her own."

"Yes."

"What do you think would happen if anyone heard this conversation?" I said.

He shrugged.

"We'd never get a teaching job again. That's for sure."

He laughed and raised his bottle to me.

"A *skål* for schoolgirls!" he said.

"*Skål!*" I said.

"What about their mothers then?" he said.

"I've never thought about them."

"Haven't you?"

"Have *you?*"

"Oh sure, of course I have."

"I think I might have been a little in love with Andrea," I said.

"I had a soft spot for her too," he said. "But I wasn't in love. Liv, on the other hand. She brightened my days."

"Yes," I said. "But it's good it's all over."

"Yes," he said.

The next day I packed my things, taped up the cardboard boxes again, and carried them to Nils Erik's car. He was going to drive me down to the express boat quay in Finnsnes, where I would have them sent to Bergen. Apart from the new stereo, some records, and quite a few books, my belongings were identical to those that had come up the year before.

Once that was done I fried some sausages and potatoes, which I ate with Nils Erik in the kitchen. This was my last meal in the village. Nils Erik would be staying on for a few more weeks, he was planning to spend the time hiking, and except for my bedroom, which I lightly dusted, he would deal with cleaning the house.

"I'll keep the deposit on the bottles as my reward," he said with a smile. "It'll add up."

"OK," I said. "What do you think, should we get going?"

He nodded, and we got into the car. We slowly drew away, said our goodbyes to east and west, and for every meter we covered, part of the village disappeared for good for me, I didn't look back and I would never, under any circumstances, set foot here again.

The chapel disappeared, the post office disappeared, Andrea's house disappeared, Hege and Vidar's house disappeared, and then the shop was gone, and my old flat, and Sture's house. And there went the community center and the soccer field, and then the school . . .

I leaned back in my seat.

"How absolutely wonderful that it's over," I said as the darkness of the tunnel filled the car. "I'll never take a job again in my life, that's for sure."

"So you *are* a shipowner's son after all?" Nils Erik said.

"Yes," I said.

"Same shipping, new wrapping," he said. "Whack a cassette in, will you?"

After a night in a cheap hotel in Tromsø, I caught a flight for Bergen the next morning, and at three I jumped off the airport bus in Bryggen and headed for the Hotel Orion, where Yngve worked at the receptionist desk. I was wearing black cotton trousers, wide at the thighs, a white shirt, a black suit jacket, black shoes, and a pair of Wayfarer Ray-Bans. Slung over my shoulder was my seaman's kitbag. The sun was shining, the water in Vågen glittered, a gentle wind blew in across the fjord.

I saw myself as a kind of primeval inhabitant going to a city for the first time, because every time a car revved or a bus or a truck thundered past I was jolted, and the sight of all these faces moving back and forth on the sidewalk made me feel insecure. Then I was reminded of something Yngve had once said, that his friend Pål always called them prime evil inhabitants, and once that was in your mind it was impossible to see anything else.

I smiled and gleefully slung the kitbag over my other shoulder.

Yngve was at the reception desk when I entered, wearing the hotel uniform, hunched over a little map on the counter explaining something to an elderly couple in shorts, caps, and fanny packs. He looked up and motioned with his head to the sofa, where I slumped down.

As soon as the Americans had gone, he came over.

"I'll be done in about ten minutes. Then I'll have to get changed and we'll be off. OK?"

"OK," I said.

He had a car now, a little red Japanese number he had leased from the volleyball team he played for, and half an hour later we were heading for his flat in Solheimsviken. It was situated some way up the mountainside, toward the end of a long row of brick-built terraced houses originally designed for shipyard workers.

We sat on the doorstep with cold beers in our hands. From the living room "Teenage Kicks" by the Undertones wafted over, evidently this summer's favorite band.

"So, are you going to Roskilde?" he said.

I nodded. "I think so."

"I might come down there too," he said. "Arvid and Erling are going, and lots of others too, so I'll just have to scrape together some cash . . . the Church are playing, you know?"

"Are they?"

"Yes. I wouldn't want to miss out on the chance to see them."

Cars were parked nose to tail on both sides of the street. People were constantly going in and out of the neighboring houses. The town beneath us was buzzing, an endless stream of cars passing through the streets. In the sky there was the occasional flash of a plane, long white plumes of condensed water hovered in the air long after they had gone. The sun burned in the sky to the west. The roofs down the mountainside shimmered in red and orange, and between them stood trees swaying in the breeze.

After a while we went indoors, Yngve made pasta carbonara for dinner, and then we had another couple of beers on the doorstep. Our conversation flagged, it was as though a little distance had grown between us since we last met, but it didn't matter, it could have been for all sorts of reasons.

In one of the letters he had sent he'd, very discreetly, told me to remember to use a condom. I appreciated his concern, but I had smiled when I saw that, because he would never have been able to say it to my face. It was only possible in a letter, and then en passant. Or if he was drunk.

"Are you still suffering after Kristin?" I said after we had sat down.

"It's one big suffering," he said.

"And you can't get her back? There's no chance of that?"

"Do you think I would be sitting here with you if there were?"

"Maybe not." I smiled.

"It was my fault. I took her for granted. All of a sudden she didn't want to continue, and by then it was too late. Shit, that's the hardest part to deal with, that I *could* have prevented it. But I took it for granted. I didn't value it highly enough."

"But you do now?"

"Now I'm in the privileged position of being able to see what I had, yes."

The sun was no longer shining on the doorstep, and I took off my sunglasses, folded them, and put them in my shirt pocket.

"You shouldn't keep them there," Yngve said. "It doesn't look good."

"You're right," I said, and took them out again.

"And while I'm at it, that studded belt of yours might have had its day."

"It's possible," I said. "But I'll give it a while yet."

There was a silence. We smoked, gazed down at the sunless but warm street.

"Can I ask you something?" I said after a while.

"Of course," he said.

"When did you . . . well, first do it?"

He glanced at me. Then gazed down again.

"When I was eighteen. On the trip to Greece. When I went with Helge, if you remember. On Antiparos Beach. At night. In the moonlight."

"Is that true?"

"Yes, it was late but good. Or, in retrospect, it seems better than it actually was. Why?"

I shrugged.

"Don't tell me you haven't slept with a girl yet? You're not a virgin, are you?"

"No, no, of course not," I said. "You know I'm not."

We fell silent again. The air around us was full of noises. All the windows were open, all the shouting, bikes occasionally whizzing past, cars creeping slowly up the mountainside, the wonderful solid sound of car doors shutting.

It wasn't a lie. Technically speaking, I wasn't a virgin, I had penetrated that girl at the *russ* party – not much, a centimeter or two – but for Christ's sake there had been contact, I had fucked. It wasn't a lie.

"I'll order a taxi," Yngve said, getting up. "We'll swing down to Ola's first. You've really got to meet him."

My possessions arrived a few days later, we picked up the boxes from the *hurtigrute* quay, put them in the cellar, and then I traveled down to Kristiansand, where I mostly stayed in Lars's studio. After Roskilde we were going to hitch down through Europe together, and we planned the journey, first to Brindisi on the southeastern tip of Italy, and then across to Athens, and from there to the Greek Islands. I suggested Antiparos, he agreed. I managed to squeeze in a visit to Grandma and Grandad too, and Gunnar, who'd heard I was in town, invited me to their place on the last evening. I had to meet my cousins, we were a small family, as he put it, it was important to stay in contact. He picked me up from Rundingen, Tove was waiting for us with dinner, we spent the evening talking, his two sons kept crawling all over him, and the fact that they weren't frightened of him – actually they exuded trust, this struck me every time I was there – gladdened my heart. No one said a word about Dad, and that was fine, it seemed to me. I slept in their cellar, and in the morning, after a hurried breakfast, Gunnar drove me to the ferry terminal, where Lars and his girlfriend were waiting for me.

During the crossing to Denmark we were mostly up on deck. The sun was shining, the sea lay like a vast sheet around us, we sat in deck chairs drinking and smoking, got up now and then and drifted around, especially me, I was so restless.

After arriving in Roskilde by train, we lined up, were given our armbands, and went to the campsite. I had borrowed a small, brown, two-man tent from Lars, he would share his girlfriend's.

Once the tents were up, I left Lars and went to look for Bassen. We had arranged to meet at the rendezvous point, we had agreed to check in every hour on the hour, and the first time I went there, he was already waiting.

"Hi," he said, and smiled. "Want to go for a drink?"

He laughed when I told him about Northern Norway. I said nothing about Andrea, I wouldn't ever do that, not to anyone, there was no reason.

We went for a scout around, not many people had come yet, he said he was hungry, I was hungry too, I said, and when we passed the Hells Angels campsite and saw that they were grilling enormous chunks of meat over a fire he stopped and shouted to them.

"Hi! Could we have some of your food? We're starving! A bit of meat for two Norwegians!"

One of them got up and made a move toward us.

"He's going to let us in," Bassen said. "They're much better than their reputation. If you're not aggressive toward them, they aren't aggressive toward you."

"Hi there!" he said when the Hells Angel – who not only had long hair, a hefty handlebar moustache, leather pants, leather jacket, and a bandanna around his forehead but also impenetrable black sunglasses – was only a couple of meters away.

He moved quickly toward us and did not look enormously friendly. But perhaps it was just as Bassen had said, they just *looked* dangerous.

He stopped, then spat at us, turned, and went back.

The glob of phlegm hit Bassen on the chest.

"Jesus Christ," he said as we hurried away, angry and frightened. "He *spat* at us! Why did he do that? All we wanted was something to eat!"

"Oooh, shit," I said. "I think we got off easy there. It seems they *are* dangerous."

Bassen laughed.

"Yes, now we're out in the big wide world, Karl Ove!" he said.

I laughed too. We went for some more to drink and a bite to eat. After an hour I returned to the tent, I had to spend some time with Lars and the others as well, after all I had come with them. They were sitting outside drinking wine with a girl I'd never seen before.

"Say hello to our neighbor," Lars said.

"Hi," she said. "I'm Vilde."

I shook hands. It transpired she came from Kongsvinger and had traveled from Norway to the festival all on her own. Later she was going to visit a friend of hers in Århus, she told me.

She was dark-haired, a bit plump, forward by nature, sometimes obstinate. She was two years older than me, her eyes were brown, not always open, but they revealed sudden flashes of softness.

The bottle of wine made the rounds, when it was empty Vilde went to find another from her tent, knelt down, and opened it. The pressure made her thighs as fat as tree trunks.

"Here," she said, and handed it to me. She smiled.

Half an hour later it too was empty.

Lars and his girlfriend exchanged brief glances.

"Well," Lars said, getting up. "We're going to have a look around."

He grabbed her hand and they were gone.

I trembled, fearing something terrible was about to happen.

What though?

I didn't know, but it ran through my mind that it had been a mistake to come here, I'd had enough and now I couldn't take much more.

"We don't have any more wine," Vilde said. "Feel like coming with me to buy a few more bottles?"

"Sure," I said.

On the way I kept a lookout for Yngve and his friends, but it was hopeless, there were tens of thousands of people here.

"He-llo!" Vilde said. "Contact! Contact!"

"Hm?" I said.

"You're walking with me! Be a little friendly."

"OK," I said. But I couldn't think of a thing to say.

"Are you looking for someone?" she said.

"My brother's here, I think. And his friends."

"Is he as good-looking as you?"

I flushed and looked down at her. She laughed and lightly ran her hand across my shoulder.

"I'm just teasing," she said. "It's so funny to see you go red."

"I didn't go red," I said.

"You definitely aren't as tough as you look!" she said.

We stopped in front of one of the counters, she bought three bottles of wine and then we went back.

Vilde said, "Shall we go to my tent? It's big and we can hang out inside and drink."

"Sure," I said, and a chasm in me opened.

We went into her tent. We sat down, she opened a bottle. We looked at each other. She made a grab for me, I made a grab for her, she lay down, I tore her T-shirt over her head and her breasts flopped out. I undid her trousers and pulled them down over her hips. Oh my God, so much flesh. I bent down and kissed her white thighs, stuck my nose in her black panties and at the same time stretched for her breasts with both hands, and then she said, get your clothes off, come on, hurry, hurry, I want you now, and I jumped up, dragged my T-shirt over my head and pulled down my trousers as I watched her wriggle out of her panties and lie there naked and raise her legs slightly as she parted them, and I could barely breathe, my underpants stuck out like a small tent and I took them off and sank down on her, she put her hand behind my head and I tried to enter her, missed the target, oh no, no, God, please not now, hang on, she said, I'll help you, that's it, yes, oh, there we are, and I was inside her and I managed to thrust twice before everything contracted and I held her tight.

Oh, it was brief, and it was embarrassing.

She stroked my hair a few times.

I lay on my back beside her.

At least it had gone inside.

That was the first time.

I smiled.

"Would you like some wine?"

"Love some," she said.

We each took a swig.

"How many girls have you had?" she said.

I flushed and concealed my embarrassment by raising the bottle to my mouth again.

Then I pretended to count.

"Ten, actually," I said.

"That's a lot," she said.

"And you?" I said.

"Three."

"Three?"

"Yes."

"Am I the third or the fourth?"

"The third. But wouldn't you like to be the fourth too?"

"Yup."

This time it went a little better, perhaps twenty seconds passed before we were lying next to each other again. We drank more wine, I put my arm around her, snuggled up to her well-upholstered body, and that was how we fell asleep. When we woke up it was dark. We did it again, and then again.

We lay talking, laughing, and drinking, and I thought, is it true, is it really true, am I lying beside a naked girl with whom I can do what I want?

We fell asleep, when we woke up we made love again, and then we went for a walk, saw two minutes of a gig, shared a bottle of wine, and then we hurried back to the tent. We stayed there all day. We got drunker and drunker. I couldn't get enough of her ass and her big soft breasts, couldn't fathom what happiness had befallen me. As we kept at it she suddenly lunged to the side and put her hand to her mouth, I knew what was happening and withdrew, she crawled over to the tent opening, pulled down the zip and then, with her backside in and her chest out, she threw up. Groaned and another spasm ran through her, and I saw her big ass before me, suddenly I couldn't resist it, placed my hands on her hams, poked it in, and began to pump away again.

RAINMAKER TRANSLATIONS *supports a series of books meant to encourage a lively reading experience of contemporary world literature drawn from diverse languages and cultures. Publication is assisted by grants from the Black Mountain Institute (blackmountaininstitute.org) at the University of Nevada, Las Vegas, an organization dedicated to promoting literary and cross-cultural dialogue around the world.*